THE GALATHEA CHRONICLES

Shadows of the Void Series

Book One

J.J. Green

INFINITEBOOK

GENERATION

PREQUEL

Sign up to my reader group for a free copy of *Starbound*, the Shadows of the Void prequel that tells the story of what happened to Jas Harrington in Antarctica, and for discounts on new releases, advanced reader opportunities and other interesting stuff:

https://jjgreenauthor.com/free-books/

ONE

Jas Harrington snapped her visor in place and took a deep breath of the purified, cooled air that flowed into her combat suit. For the last fifteen minutes she'd been ignoring the prickles that ran down her spine as she prepared her team for the routine LIV—Locate, Investigate, Vacate. But she couldn't ignore the feeling any longer.

"AX7," she said as she entered the shuttle airlock with the fifteen burly, androgynous defense units under her command. The door to the passenger cabin slid closed behind them, and a hiss permeated the enclosed space as the planet's atmosphere entered through newly opened valves, equalizing the air pressure differential.

"C.S.O. Harrington," the unit replied.

"Station yourself at the rear."

"Affirmative, C.S.O. Harrington."

AX7 had been injured in a skirmish with a hostile species a few planets back, and though the unit had self-repaired as programmed, it wasn't factory-perfect like the others were, and those prickles were telling her to expect an attack.

The part-organic, part-robotic Polestar Corp androids shuffled aside in the narrow airlock to allow AX7 through. Jas's excessively long childhood on Mars had resulted in a height of just over two meters, but at two meters thirty the defense units dwarfed her. As usual at close quarters, she was acutely conscious of the difference. The units resembled linebackers padded up, except they had no padding. Thin armored material that was highly resistant to penetration and extreme temperatures coated their large forms.

If the defense units short-circuited and turned on her, well...Jas pushed memories of incidents involving prototypes to the back of her mind. These were the latest, state-of-the-art models, though she wasn't naive enough to imagine Polestar supplied them to protect the crew. No, in the event of an emergency, she was sure the units' first move would be to save precious resource samples.

AX7's face expressed no emotion as it moved to the back of the group, though it had the intellectual capacity to understand why Jas had put it there. Despite her extensive experience working with the units, she hadn't figured out if they genuinely had no feelings at all, or if they weren't able to express them.

"What's the weather like out there, Lingiari?" she asked the shuttle pilot through her radio.

"A little precipitation. Temperature just below zero."

A spark of nostalgia flickered through Jas's sense of foreboding. "Snow? It's snowing?" She hadn't seen snow since attending training college in Antarctica, the last place on Earth it had snowed in twenty years.

"Sure looks like it," the pilot replied.

Jas's brief moment of pleasure was swamped by the realization that snow meant reduced visibility. The prickles down her spine grew so strong she itched to rub her back, impossible though that was in her suit. "Still no bio readings?"

"Nothing bigger than a rat's dick."

Jas rolled her eyes and thumbed a switch on her weapon, changing the setting to flamethrower. Not many life forms could withstand fire. She didn't instruct her defense units on their weaponry. They would compute the optimum response according to the situation, probably better and faster than her. The smartest command strategy was to leave them the hell alone to do their job, unless she knew something they didn't, but as in most LIV assignments, she was the blind leading the blind.

A light flashed above the airlock's outer door. Ten flashes and it would open. The shuttle computer was simultaneously relaying the countdown to the units electronically, but their eyes were also on the light. Defense unit behavior was disarmingly human at times.

The door opened, and the airlock flooded with light and swirling flakes of snow. Jas's visor instantly dimmed, shadowing her view of the terrain outside. A flat, plain landscape stretched to the horizon, lightly powdered with snow and peppered with tough scrub. Except for the low, dull vegetation, the area seemed empty of life. A dark gray structure made up of overlapping hexagonal boxes two or three meters tall dominated the view, against a pale gray, cloudy sky. It wasn't the most inviting planet Jas had visited.

She gave the order to disembark. Moving as one, the defense units set off down the ramp. She followed and took her place at their side. The one point two Earth gravity made moving a little more effort than usual, but it was manageable. Her boots broke through the thin layer of snow, and the familiar thrill of being the first human being to set foot on a new planet surged through her, despite her trepidation.

"No Class P life forms within one K," came Lingiari's voice through her radio. His close-range scanners were telling him the same as the starship's less sensitive long-distance surveillance equipment had indicated before they set out—nothing to worry about, supposedly. Jas'ss grip tightened on her weapon as she accompanied the units toward the matte gray structure.

"Your scanners are penetrating that rock construction, right?" she asked Lingiari.

"Yeah, as far as I can tell, but they aren't picking up anything.

Seems to be empty. But it isn't rock. It's a crystal-metal amalgam. And another material the scanners can't identify."

"Artificial?"

"I think you might be confusing me with a scientist. I'm forwarding the results to the ship."

"Sorry. Thanks for the info," Jas replied. Of course the pilot didn't have the knowledge or authority to interpret the data. What was she thinking? She deliberately tensed and then relaxed her muscles. An officer aboard the *Galathea* would update her on anything they thought important. At that moment, no one was saying anything.

She'd reached a hole in the wall of the structure. The defense units were waiting in formation. The hole was hexagonal, mirroring the shape of the structure's blocks. Inside, all was dark.

"C.S.O. Harrington, permission to enter and search," AX5 said.

"Permission granted. AX12, you too."

The two units stepped over a low wall at the base of the hole and dipped their heads as they went inside. Motionless, the other units waited, snowflakes settling on their wide shoulders. A few minutes later, AX5's calm voice came through Jas's radio. "All clear."

She released the breath she hadn't realized she'd been holding. "Follow on," she instructed the rest.

As Jas went in, her dimmed visor cleared, and a light beamed out from her helmet, slicing through the darkness. She was in an empty room just large enough to hold her and thirteen units comfortably. AX5 and 12 were investigating a neighboring chamber. The floor was the same crystal-metal amalgam as the walls and ceiling, and it sloped gradually downward toward several hexagonal holes at the far end. A few steps inside, and Jas could raise her head.

AX12 and 5 appeared at a hole—or doorway?—on the far side. The place was still and silent. The scanner reports seemed accurate. It looked empty, totally devoid of life or artifacts. She divided the units into groups and sent them to investigate deeper inside, accompanying one of the groups herself.

The next room looked the same as the first. No sign of life nor signs that anything had ever lived there. The only break in the monotonous walls was more holes, leading to identical rooms and heading downward, underground and deeper into the structure. From Jas's position as she peered through a hole, the rooms seemed endless.

An hour passed, then two. Jas and the units penetrated deep into the labyrinthine construction. She had to activate her suit's pathfinder function to avoid getting lost. By the time she surfaced, she'd found nothing different from the empty room at the entrance.

Jas had conducted LIVs on many planets. According to strict regulations, they had to vacate immediately at the first sign of intelligence. If there was no intelligent life, the planet's resources were up for grabs to the first corporation that claimed them.

In Jas's experience the evidence of high-level, sentient species was usually clear. Whatever the form of intelligence, evolution always seemed to favor certain expressions of it: the use of tools, modifying the natural environment, storage of resources, training of offspring, and the systemization of food gathering or production and distribution. On K.67092d, the evidence was not clear. The regular, straight lines of the structure indicated artificial construction, but there seemed to be no other evidence of intelligence. If sentient life forms had built the place, where were they? Why had they left, leaving nothing behind?

Leaving the structure, Jas scanned the surroundings again. It had stopped snowing. Nothing moved except the spiny, spindly, leafless branches of the low shrubs, bending slightly, creaking in the steady wind.

"Preliminary report, Harrington?" Akabe Loba's voice came over her radio.

Jas stiffened. As always, the master of the *Galathea* was

pushing her, his eye focused solely on his schedule and bonuses. "Initial LIV not complete, sir."

"But no sign of intelligence?"

"It's hard to tell, sir. The structure's—"

"I can see it through your relay, Harrington. Looks geological to me. And there are no artifacts."

Jas's lips drew into a thin line. She knew what was coming. "Sir, it's a little early to conclude—"

"I'm not asking *you* to conclude anything, C.S.O. Harrington. Is the area secure?"

When she didn't answer immediately, Loba repeated his question, louder.

"No hostile life forms encountered, yet," Jas replied through her teeth. *Damn the misborn.* But what could she say? Prickles down her spine didn't count as a reason to delay resource assessment.

Two

Prospecting ships like Polestar Corp's *Galathea* ran to a tight timetable. To provide an acceptable return on the company's investment, the crew had to locate and claim at least ten resource-rich planets uninhabited by intelligent life per mission, on average. After that—or maybe before if they stumbled across a planet loaded with a highly valuable substance such as mythrin, base ingredient of blissful, stupor-inducing mythranil —the crew would start to stack up bonuses. Bonuses were the only thing that made it worth enduring the nearly endless boredom and starvation wages of space prospecting.

The ship's master took the lion's share, of course, and the rest of the crew's dividends were portioned out according to rank. As chief security officer, Jas's rank and dividends were in the middle range. She wouldn't be relaxing in the perfumed seas of Balgamon, as First Mate Haggardy planned to do when that mission was over, but neither would she be handing over every penny she had for the most basic genetic upgrade to her as-yet unconceived child, as one of the maintenance crew had mentioned.

Not that Jas planned on having kids anyway. Her own childhood hadn't exactly endeared her to the concept, and she had an irrational fear that her child might turn out to be someone like

Master Akabe Loba, into whose blood-threaded eyes she was currently staring.

"Enough arguing, Harrington. Twelve sites. Twelve LIVs, and you've found nothing but some kind of bushworm, gliding non-venomous spiders, and an ambulatory slime mold. Twelve LIVs that turned up no hostile life forms or territory, and you're *still* not prepared to give the all-clear?"

Loba was leaning across a horizontal screen that projected a spinning hologram of K. 67092d. They were in the mission room, where Jas had been summoned to 'discuss' her delay in clearing the planet for resource assessment with the master and other high-ranking officers. The master's head was thrust into the moving holographic image, and the miniature topography played across his features, lending him an even more than usually crazed effect. His carefully coiffed, white-dyed curls seemed about to uncoil and stand on end.

Jas knew she was fighting a losing battle, but she was going to fight it anyway. She was head of security. The safety of the entire crew was her responsibility, and if she had a hunch something on a planet was dangerous, she was going to damn well act on it. She'd never been wrong before.

"I've already told you my reasons. It makes no sense that we've found no intelligent life. Those structures were built. They aren't geological. The building material is artificial, manufactured. We've found nothing else on the planet like it. Something sentient made those buildings. That's what Haggardy's report says." She turned to the first mate for back up. He was seated at the far end of the table and picking at his nails.

First Mate Haggardy held up his hands. "Now wait a minute, Harrington. I wouldn't go that far. I only said we can't conclude it's natural *or* artificial. That's all." He glanced at the master, who was glaring at him.

Jas cursed under her breath. That wasn't how his findings read, and he knew it. Was he planning on rewriting his conclusions? She suspected Haggardy was as interested in his bonus as

Loba was, or he was even more of a wimp than she'd taken him for. He was a scientist. He should know better than to risk everyone's lives on a lack of immediate evidence.

She swung back to Loba. "Just because we can't find what built those structures, that doesn't mean they weren't built. The life forms responsible might be hiding. Maybe because they're afraid, or maybe they're waiting to attack. We can't allow Resource Assess on the surface until we know more. We don't have enough defense units to protect them from a full onslaught."

"You seem to be getting confused, Harrington," said Loba quietly, "with your talk of what *we* can and can't do. I shouldn't have to remind you that *I'm* master of this vessel." His facial muscles were rigid. He stood straight and drew himself up to his full height, which was a head shorter than Jas's.

Her stature had always bothered him, she knew, like it seemed to bother many men. But she couldn't help that any more than she could help doing her kratting job.

"The presence of artificial structures does not prohibit a resource claim under deep space property law," the master continued. "Several precedents have been set where such items were found to be relics of extinct species. Maybe the structures are buildings, but if that's the case it's most likely that whatever created them has long since died out—"

"But the fact—"

"THE FACT remains that if there's no sign of intelligent or hostile life after twelve LIVs, the planet's safe enough to assess for resources. Your refusal to give the all clear is a dereliction of duty, and—"

"Sir," exclaimed Navigator Lee, jumping out of her seat like a jack-in-the-box, "if I could—"

"What?" barked Loba, not taking his eyes off Jas, who held his glare and made a special effort to look down at him.

Lee seemed to momentarily regret her decision to come to Jas's aid, but she soldiered on. "C.S.O. Harrington's service has been exemplary throughout the mission," she said quickly, and didn't stop when Loba opened his mouth to speak, but gathered speed. "She saved many lives when we were attacked on K. 87593g." She ran the numbers together: eightsevenfiveninethree. "The defense units were all in the right place at the right time. If it hadn't been for her command of the evacuation, some of us wouldn't be here right now." She looked pointedly at Haggardy, who gazed into space.

"Your point?" asked Loba.

"I just think, if she's worried about the safety of the planet, we should listen."

"Thank you for your input, navigator," said Loba sarcastically, "but if Harrington's prior performance is under scrutiny, your example hardly helps her, does it? After all, if she was any good at her job, the crew would never have been in any danger in the first place."

Jas ground her jaw. She'd warned him. She'd gone to his cabin and warned Loba that there had been an overnight increase in animal tracks around the assessment site, and that she recommended withdrawing the team until she could investigate. It was a warning he'd conveniently forgotten. She wasn't going to let him forget this one.

Her fist thumped the screen and the hologram of the planet wobbled. The officers at the table jumped in their seats. Haggardy got up and backed away.

"I'm chief security officer, and I'm telling you that planet isn't safe. I can't tell you why, and I can't tell you when or where an attack might come from, but I know it *will* come, and I'm *not* giving the all clear. *You* might like to play fast and loose with the lives of two hundred people for the sake of a fat bonus and a regular supply of mythranil, but I sure as hell don't."

As soon as the words were out of her mouth—before, even—she knew she'd gone too far. As she finished, she drew back from the screen. Everyone was still except Lee, who raised a nervous finger to her lips as her gaze flicked between Loba and Jas.

Without taking his eyes from his security officer, Loba

murmured, "Hologram, off." The slowly spinning image disappeared and without its illumination, the room became dim. No one moved a muscle to switch on the lights.

Loba was an addict. The whole crew knew. It was why no one was allowed to disturb him for six hours of the quiet shift, on threat of dismissal. It was why he dyed his hair white, to cover up the tell-tale crimson tinge. It was why he breathed quickly even when not exerting himself. In the silence his quiet panting was plain to hear.

"Your judgment is clearly impaired, C.S.O. Harrington. For your own safety and the safety of this ship's crew, you are confined to your cabin until further notice. Should you leave your cabin without permission, you will be placed in the brig for the remainder of the mission. I'll consider your release if you pass a mental health assessment. Haggardy, accompany her."

The first mate rose to his feet and moved toward the door.

Jas whirled on her heel, her fists clenched at her sides, looking for a single sign of support from the other officers. Officers whose lives she'd protected on every planet they'd visited that mission. None met her gaze but Lee, who only grimaced in sympathy.

Haggardy was at the open door, waiting for her. There was nothing to do but leave. She stomped over and exited without another word to Loba or the rest of them. Haggardy struggled to keep up as she marched through the corridors to her cabin. What did it matter if she couldn't tell them why the planet wasn't safe? Didn't her years of experience count for anything?

But though Jas was furious, a stronger emotion overrode her anger: fear. In her eleven years in the job, she'd never been wrong when it came to sensing danger. And all her alarm bells were ringing.

The first mate was the closest person to take out her frustration on. "Thanks for your support."

"Harrington," replied Haggardy, "your case is weak, and we're on a schedule. And you certainly didn't do yourself any favors back there. You shouldn't have lost your temper like that. Mentioning the master's indulgences? Bad move."

Jas turned to him as they arrived at her cabin. "There's something down there. I know there is," she said quietly.

"Been running the blood yourself?" was his reply as her cabin door closed.

THREE

Carl Lingiari wished for a storm. A super cell or a tornado, like the ones that swept the western New South Wales plains of his boyhood. Storms he'd grown up learning to dodge while crop dusting the family farm. Oh sure, he'd encountered a few. At the last planet but one—he never could remember those strings of Kepler numbers—the place he'd mentally dubbed Arse End of Hell, there'd been a beauty of a buster to dodge. He grinned as he remembered the RA team's cheer when they made it back to the ship. Though the passenger cabin still smelled faintly of vomit, that had been the kind of ride that made piloting worthwhile.

Not this ferry tripping. He took his feet down from his console and scanned the instrument panel. Descent was going smoothly. All readings were normal. They were nearly there. He thumbed the mic on his headset. "Touchdown in five." The 'five' was drawn out as he fought to stifle a yawn. He thumbed his mic off and put up his feet again. The shuttle could just about fly itself. It *did* fly itself most of the time. He was like a parent holding a toddler's reins: only there to stop the kid from doing something stupid.

One day, Carl would pilot a starship. A starship like the

Galathea. Massive starjump engines below, Raptor Xs to the rear, control and living quarters long, sleek and neat along the top. A handful of pulse cannons on the off chance they encountered a hostile space-faring life form. It hadn't happened in the history human space travel, but you never knew. *That* was the kind of bird he'd fly.

Carl wouldn't be copilot, understudy, backup-in-case-of-disaster anymore. He wouldn't be stuck doing the school run in a rustbucket while someone else got to commute in the latest model. He stretched his arms wide, put his hands behind his head, and closed his eyes.

In his imagination, he was sitting at the control panel of the *Galathea*. His Polestar Corp uniform was clean, crease-free, and neatly buttoned to the neck. His pilot's hat was on his head, set at just enough of an angle to make him look sneck. Wearing your hat while aboard ship wasn't strictly required according to regulations, but he had the corporation's image to consider.

Yeah, he would fly that bird through space with style.

A tall, shapely female figure appeared in his daydream. She moved to his side in the pilot's seat on the *Galathea's* bridge. Who was this? Could it be C.S.O. Harrington, in her tight-fitting combat suit? And what was she doing? She leaned down to whisper in his ear. She had to tell him something important and personal, something that couldn't wait. As she leaned toward him, her breasts came so close to his face he could feel their warmth—

"Landing gear lowered." The shuttle's announcement sounded in the cabin, loud and formal. *Krat*. Drawn roughly back to reality, Carl's feet landed on the floor with a thump. He checked the instruments again. No problems. Through the plexiglass window, he saw the planet's surface rising rapidly. To one side, about five K from the landing site, was one of those hexagonal structures. The rest of the view was mostly ocean. The RA was to take place at a shoreline.

The sun was coming up, and the RA team would have about

five and a half hours before it set. The day promised to be uneventful for Carl, who would wait for the team to take their samples before he had to shuttle them back to the *Galathea*. He wasn't allowed to leave the immediate vicinity of the shuttle in case there was an emergency and they had to make a quick getaway, but that wasn't so bad on this planet. He didn't think he'd ever been anywhere so boring. The shuttle touched down and rolled across the stony beach to a stop.

"Prepare to disembark," Carl said into his mic before pressing the switch to open the airlock. He removed his headset, undid his harness, got up, and pulled on a jacket. They were on a warmer landmass compared to some on the planet, but the temperature remained chilly. By the time he opened the cabin door, the RA team had left, and the passenger cabin was empty but for First Mate Haggardy, who was supervisor this trip. The team was sticking to the master's orders to get a move on and gather their samples and data. Carl went between the rows of seats and out the airlock. He jumped off the ramp, landing roughly on loose pebbles. He staggered.

As he straightened up, he saw that one of the RA team was lingering by the shoreline, her back to the others, who were retrieving their equipment from the hold and setting out to get their samples. Her shoulders were shaking.

Carl went over and stood behind the woman, unsure what to do. He glanced back, but no one else seemed to have noticed her. Gently, he laid a hand on her shoulder. The woman jumped a little and turned to him, hastily wiping her eyes.

"You okay?" Carl asked.

"Yeah," the woman replied. She looked at her feet. "It's just...it isn't how I imagined it would be. Space travel, I mean. I thought it would be exciting, adventurous, you know? But instead it's...kinda..."

"Boring, right? Is this your first mission?"

"Yep. I signed up straight out of college. Everyone else on board seems to have friends already. People they know from previous trips." She looked down again. "I don't seem to fit in anywhere."

Now Carl remembered her. He'd seen her sitting by herself at meals. He'd thought that was what she liked to do, or he would have sat with her. Some people were loners. Was her name Pasha or Sasha? He couldn't remember, and it would be embarrassing to ask. He had a feeling she was with geo-phys.

"You fly the shuttle really well," the woman said. "I hardly felt that landing."

"Huh, the shuttle just about flies…I mean, I trained for five years…to fly starships, and…" He faltered. "Looking forward to a good day…taking…rock samples?"

She laughed. "I don't take rock samples. I operate that." She pointed to a large metal instrument another member of geo-phys was pulling out of the cargo hold. It looked like a device for torturing medium-sized, warm-blooded mammals. Like humans.

"Right," replied Carl, nodding, "I see. And that's a…"

"GPR. Ground Penetrating Radar."

"Hmm…" He rubbed his chin. "Thought I recognized it."

The woman laughed again. "You're funny." She paused a moment to look at the ocean, then back at Carl. She pulled on an earlobe. "After we get back, I don't suppose…" She paused and looked away. "Do you want to meet up for dinner?"

His eyes widened. "Sure, that'd be great." But where? The ship's refectory was the last place aboard for a potentially romantic dinner. "I tell you what, meet me in the shuttle bay when you've freshened up, and I'll bring something special to eat."

Carl had been hoarding a care package his mother had sent him for the mission. She did it every time he went away. Now would be a good time to break into the tinned and packaged luxury foods.

"Okay," said the woman, smiling. "See you then."

Carl watched as Pasha or Sasha went to the other side of the shuttle to pick up her torture device. She wasn't Harrington, but she seemed really nice and in need of a friend. Harrington was confined to quarters anyway. Personally, he thought the woman's quick temper was sneck, but Loba didn't agree. But Carl wasn't going to pine over her. It wasn't every day a Pasha or Sasha invited you on a date.

———

The day passed slowly for Carl due to the promise of a pleasant evening with the geo-phys scientist. He spent some of the time watching the RA team surveying and sampling the air, plants, water, rocks, sand, and dirt of the planet. He tried not to be too obvious about paying special attention to Pasha or Sasha, but then she and the rest of geo-phys went away over the sand dunes in the direction of the hexagonal structure. After Haggardy fell asleep in the passenger cabin—he hadn't set foot outside the shuttle the entire time—Carl played the games he'd surreptitiously uploaded to the shuttle's console while he waited for the RA team to return.

As the sun began to set, PashaorSasha came back, walking with the rest of geo-phys as they returned from the alien structure. They'd been gone two or three hours, and Carl wondered what they had all been doing inside the building for so long. The team made their way down the beach dunes, and at the same time other RA members began to straggle back to the shuttle. The sampling session was over. Haggardy sat up and rubbed his eyes, before asking the team members vaguely how the session had gone.

When everyone was aboard, Carl put on his headset and did a final passenger check. He closed the airlock, fastened his harness, and smiled to himself at the promise of an enjoyable dinner ahead.

FOUR

Three days in her cabin hadn't lessened Jas's anger at Loba for putting his bonus before the crew's safety, but it had evened it out somewhat. If she were to see him, she didn't think she would throw him in a garbage airlock and press Purge right away. She might give him time for some last words first.

She turned on the screen angled above her bunk. A menu of entertainment options appeared: vids, games, music, recorded fly-on-the-wall cam footage, and educational programs. You could watch or play almost anything aboard ship that you could on Earth. The crew of the *Galathea* also had access to mail and videos from home on their private comm systems, options that might have made being cooped up more bearable for Jas, but she had nothing in that vein. No family. No ties to Earth or Mars. At first, she'd thought that made her better off than most others aboard the prospecting ships on their long voyages in deep space. No one to miss and no one to miss her. But over the years, she'd realized that it made it worse. Unlike the rest of the crew, she didn't look forward to the end of a mission. After a year or longer away from the closest thing she had to home, stepping off the ship with no one to meet her was hard.

She blinked and shook her head. It was no good allowing depressing thoughts to take hold. That was what she hated most about being confined. It gave her time to brood. She needed to *do* something, anything. Her cabin was already spotless, and she'd arranged and rearranged her scant possessions countless times. Looking up at the screen, she could barely focus on it.

Her door chimed. She raised herself on her elbows. Who was risking Loba's wrath by fraternizing with her? Or was it the master himself? She'd told the few crew members she was friendly with to stay away for their own sakes. "Door, open."

Navigator Lee stood waiting. The petite officer was cringing slightly as she looked in.

Jas turned off her screen and swung her legs off her bunk as she sat up. "Come in."

Lee checked from side to side along the corridor before entering the room. She relaxed a little as the door closed behind her.

"Don't want to be seen visiting me, huh?" said Jas. "Wouldn't do much for your reputation, would it?"

Lee looked taken aback. "Maybe I should go." She half-turned.

"Sorry," Jas said. Why did she always push people away? "Don't go. Come and sit down. I'm just stir crazy."

The navigator relented. She pulled out the chair tucked under Jas's desk and sat down. She opened her mouth to speak, but Jas interrupted.

"I'm glad you came. I wanted to thank you for sticking up for me in the mission room. It was brave of you, and I appreciate it. You were the only one who dared side with me against Loba. That took some guts."

The frown on Lee's forehead faded a little. "Thanks, but I wouldn't put it like that. I didn't mind helping you out and all, but I meant what I said. You did save our lives back on 87593g. I've seen you work. You know what you're doing, and if you say 67092d isn't safe I believe you, even if you can't say why. That's what you're paid for, right? To protect us from all those hostile life forms that're out to get us. I mean, what's your incentive for making shit up? What's in it for you? Nothing, right? So if you're saying we need to steer clear, I'm right there beside you. Don't matter what Loba says. There's more important things than money, you know?

"I've read plenty about what can happen to RA teams," Lee continued, "and seen plenty on the news." She gave a shudder. "It ain't safe down there. One of my cousin's friends…or was it someone at his work?…anyway, he knew someone who was just petting a little alien creature for five minutes, and three days later he was dead. Radiation sickness. Wasn't nothing they could do for him. And in another case I heard about, an animal just brushed up against a researcher and ran off. The woman didn't think much of it, but the fur that touched her hand was coated in a poison that penetrated human skin. She lasted a week, and she contaminated a couple of others in her team before they knew about it."

Jas wondered how many more disaster stories Lee had.

"And there was that attack I heard about a while ago," continued Lee. "The ship's security officer didn't even LIV the site the RA team landed at. I heard no one survived. Did you hear about it too? I think they kept it quiet, you know? Didn't want to scare folks? Now, what was that other one…?"

"Yeah, well, like I said," said Jas, standing. "I appreciate the support. Thanks for stopping by." She was beginning to remember why she'd never been more than acquaintances with Navigator Lee.

The navigator smoothed her cropped blonde hair, appearing not to notice Jas's hint. "How have you been? It's been three days now, right? Have you heard anything from the master? Any idea when he might let you out? I'd go crazy sitting in my cabin day after day with no one to talk to. I mean, what on Earth do you do? Do you have comm to the rest of the ship? Can you talk to people?"

Jas sighed and sat down. "No, no contact with the rest of the ship. And you're my first visitor. Loba said something about a mental health assessment, but I haven't heard anything about that either."

"Well, if there is something terrible on that planet, at least it can't get you while you're up here. We're safe here, right?" Lee's eyebrows rose questioningly. When Jas didn't answer, she said, "That's what I think anyway. That's why I never leave the ship."

"You never leave the ship? You've never been planetside? Ever?"

The navigator pinched her lips together and shook her head. "The only planet surface I've ever been on is good ol' Earth. You wouldn't catch me down there. God only knows what might happen."

Jas took a moment to process this statement. "Then...what are you doing here? Why work on a prospecting ship? Why not stay home and get a nice, safe desk job on Earth?"

Lee gave her a questioning look. "Uh, I'm a navigator? My daddy suggested it when I was choosing my degree, and he was right. It's easy for me, and the pay's good. As long as I never leave the ship, I can pretend to myself I only have to step through an airlock to be home."

Jas put her head in her hands. The only supporter she had among all the senior officers was paranoid. What did that say about her? Was she wrong about K. 67092d? Was she crazy too? After her years of service, was she beginning to crack?

"Anyway, I don't like all this talk of hostile aliens," said Lee. "Let's talk about something else. Have you watched *Their Eyes in the Stars* yet? I loved it. Couldn't stop watching it. Had to watch the whole thing through. Took me eleven hours."

Jas's door chime sounded again, and she exhaled with relief, but as she told the door to open, her relief changed to misery. If there was anyone she wanted to see less than Loba, and now Lee, it was the person waiting.

Standing in her cabin entrance, clutching an interface to his chest and smiling a beatific smile, was Sparks. The medical officer was a renowned brown-noser who had clearly decided which section of the crew he favored and which he did not, based on unspoken and unspeakable factors.

He was there for her mental health assessment. Sparks would be itching to have a hand in that.

Lee jumped to her feet, her features confused. She reddened, no doubt embarrassed to be caught in Jas's cabin, but she also seemed pleased to see Sparks. He was definitely glad to see her, if anything could be gleaned from the radiant expression on his face.

"Navigator Lee, what a pleasure to observe you providing comfort to a friend in her hour of need."

The officer's blush faded as she beamed. "I thought C.S.O. Harrington would be lonely in here all by herself."

Sparks's already round eyes widened, and he nodded. "Of course, of course. That was very considerate of you. Do you mind if I join you both?"

"I'm sure you're here for an official reason, Dr. Sparks, so I'll get out of your way," said Lee.

Jas almost regretted it as the navigator left them alone.

"Do you mind if I sit here?" asked the doctor as the door closed behind Lee. He sat in the chair the navigator had vacated. Putting his device face down on the desk, Sparks turned to Jas, leaned forward, put his elbows on his knees, and steepled his fingers. His features assumed an earnest expression. "How have you been?"

"Fine," replied Jas.

Sparks tilted his head and raised his eyebrows. "Have you been sleeping well? Any headaches? Appetite problems?"

"Look, can we cut straight to the mental health check?"

Sparks straightened up. "Hmpf. I'd prefer to do a preliminary general health assessment. It's helpful in order to make an exact diagnosis."

"Is that what this is really about? You've got machines for the general stuff, haven't you? I'm mentally sound, and I'd rather not sit through a load of BF."

Giving her an 'I'm not angry, just disappointed' look, the medical officer picked up his interface and handed it to Jas. "I think we have rather more to talk about than you imagine, Harrington, but if you're refusing to cooperate..." He sighed. "It looks as though your outburst in the mission room was probably a symptom of a serious issue. But let's see the results of the assessment before jumping to conclusions."

He pointed to the first question on the list. "This one is very important."

Jas read the question and scowled. "It's illegal to ask if someone's natural or modded."

"You're right, and for very good reasons of course. But senior medical personnel can make an exception for clinical reasons. A person's genetic status gives essential information about potential mental health issues and other conditions." He spoke in a low tone. "And you can rest easy. Your answer is completely confidential."

The problem was, Jas didn't know if her genes had been modified. Her parents had died in a colony disaster on Mars when she was a baby, and her records were destroyed at the same time. No one in the orphanage had bothered to have her tested, and as she grew up and witnessed the increasing discrimination against naturals, she'd decided against finding out for herself.

She studied the question and looked up at Sparks, who was gazing at her. She didn't believe a word of what he was saying. She thought he was digging about her genetic status so he could slot her into his 'us' and 'them' boxes, but if she didn't pass as mentally fit, she might never get back on duty and find out what was on that planet—before it harmed the crew.

FIVE

Retiring to his cabin after his duties were complete was almost Master Akabe Loba's favorite time of day, excepting only what came after. He closed his cabin door, set his corridor-side panel to read *Do Not Disturb* and shrugged off his jacket, dropping it on the floor as he went to his closet. From the top shelf he took a cylindrical container. He popped off the lid and slid out a roll of very old paper, though it might have been another material such as parchment or vellum. Loba was no expert on such things. He sometimes wondered if he'd been duped into paying an exorbitant sum by the vendor, but it didn't matter. If the document was fake, it was convincing to him, and he enjoyed the ancient feel and look of the thing. Most importantly, he had found it to be accurate.

His ritual had been the same as far back as he could remember, though if the truth be told, his memory wasn't as good as it had once been. He should cut down on his habit, he knew, but not today. He would start tomorrow, or next week, when they had cataloged this latest planet, and he could relax a little. Damn that Harrington for causing a delay. He found himself beginning to gasp, and he pushed the memory of the defiant security officer from his mind.

Loba undid and dropped his pants. Stepping out of them, he took two paperweights from the table. One was a fist-sized iridescent crystal he'd picked up from the desert floor of a long-forgotten planet in the days when he'd been working his way up the ranks. The other was a long block of polished ebony: wood of a now-extinct Earth tree. Unfurling the document on the floor, he placed the crystal on one end, then unrolled the rest of the scroll to its full extent before securing the other end with the wooden block.

Every day the same.

Traced in faded ink on the sheet was the figure of a naked man. His arms and legs were outstretched, and his blank eyes were open. Wavy hair surrounded his head like a halo. The figure itself was unimportant to Loba; it was the lines that ran through his body, from his head and spine to his fingertips and toes, that were the focus of his interest. They were meridians: energy paths, where the greatest pain—and pleasure—could be felt.

He ran a fingertip down a line that skirted the groin and followed through to the thigh and leg. It was the meridian he had used for yesterday's dose. To achieve the greatest effect from his drug of choice, Loba had to apply the doses at each point along the meridians according to a strict rota. Yesterday's dose had contacted a point at the left-hand side of his groin. Today, he would administer it fifteen centimeters below, in the thigh. Loba relied on memory alone for the order of the dosing points. If any record of his habit were found, it would be professional suicide. This was why he possessed only a physical document to guide him, a document that could be purged into space in less than a minute. Digital information was much more difficult to erase.

Drug abuse had impacted Loba's functional ability in many areas of his life, but in the matter of remembering the dose position order, his recall was excellent.

He pressed an invisible button on the ebony paperweight. As the block of wood popped open, his breathing quickened. In the lead-lined center of the block was a clear glass vial of carmine liquid. Mythranil. Exquisite purveyor of bliss. Lying next to the vial were a set of fine, hollow needles. Loba could hear himself panting.

Soon, soon.

He removed the vial and a needle and went to the sterilization unit in his bathroom, where he placed the needle in the unit and let it sit for thirty seconds. His hand trembled as he retrieved it.

Only a minute to wait.

He sat on his bunk and removed the stopper from the vial. After inserting the needle in the liquid, he gently sucked at the other end, careful not to draw the mythranil into his mouth. Ingestion destroyed the active ingredients of the drug, and each drop was a week's wages. He slipped the needle from his mouth and quickly placed his thumb over the hole to prevent the liquid from dripping out. Loba took a last look at the image of the spread-eagled man, lay down on his bunk and felt down from the sore spot on his groin to a point roughly fifteen centimeters below.

Just a few seconds now.

Joy suffused Loba as he thrust the needle home, grinning through the pain. His aim was true. He'd hit the meridian line spot on, and ecstasy flowed through him. All cares, worries, and concerns of reality melted away, and he sank into a blissful daze.

———

Loba was in nirvana. He had achieved a state of perfection. He floated in infinity, where time and space were without end, and where his spirit poured forth and returned replenished, fulfilled, endless, and enduring in the void. Colors with no names whirled through his perception, and indescribable emotions washed over him in blissful waves, cleansing his soul, bathing his mind, washing his ego free of corrupting impurities. For an eternity, it seemed, he existed, each moment filled with limitless joy.

A great bell sounded from behind him. What was this intrusion? Loba turned and tried to gaze into the abyss, but he couldn't find the source of the sound. Again, it rang in his ears, discordant, breaking the serene flow of the universe. He grew confused. Where was the noise coming from? How had it entered the everlasting cosmos?

A third time the bell rang, and Loba cried out as all creation began to disintegrate around him. The terrible noise of the bell was breaking everything apart. He had to find it. He had to stop its chiming before it was too late. He had to destroy it.

Loba flailed in his bunk so hard he fell out and hit the floor with a thump. The shock and pain of his fall brought him somewhat back to reality, and he realized the sound he'd been hearing, which had intruded into his drug-induced state of euphoria, was his door chime. But it was too soon. Someone had disturbed him before the effects of mythranil had worn off.

As if at the flick of a switch, Loba's mood altered from befuddlement to black rage. He took a moment to figure out where each of his limbs were before rising to a crouch and staggering to his feet. Hands trembling and chest heaving, he snatched the meridian map from the floor and put it in his closet before shutting the door. He put the vial of mythranil and needle into the ebony box and snapped it closed.

He staggered to his cabin door just as the chime sounded for the fourth time. Whoever it was, the idiot still hadn't realized the grave mistake he was making. Loba turned on his video link to the corridor. A woman. A member of an RA team. He couldn't remember her name. "Door, open.

"What the hell do you think you're doing?" he bellowed. "Are you blind or stupid? How dare you disturb me..." Loba tailed off. The woman was speaking at the same time as him, apparently unaffected by his anger.

She repeated herself when he paused. "Master Loba, we found something on the planet surface you need to see urgently."

"What? Now? What the hell's so important...?"

"I can't explain. You must come with me to the planet. You must come with me immediately."

"The hell I'm going to. I'm not going anywhere. Explain yourself. What is this about? What did you find there? Pah, I don't care what it is. File a report like you're supposed to and stop bothering me..." The world spun. He grabbed the door frame.

"It's very important," the woman said. "Very valuable. You must come with me and see for yourself. There's no other way."

What was wrong with her? Why wouldn't she obey him? He was master. Loba clutched his head. Was this even real? Or was he still in a mythranil dream? His initial fury began to melt into bewilderment and confusion. Maybe he should go with the woman. If this was all part of his vision, he might return to bliss by doing what she said.

He peered at her. Why hadn't she reacted to his fury? He felt chilly, and with sudden horror, he realized he was standing there in his underwear. The woman hadn't reacted to that either.

Calm descended on Loba. None of it was real. He was still under the influence of mythranil. But it was strange. He'd never run like this before. Maybe he'd gotten the dosage or position wrong. He would just have to go with the flow, see the vision through, and then perhaps he would return to paradise for some time before he woke up.

"Okay, I'll come with you."

The woman seemed satisfied.

Six

Carl was in the middle of destroying the evil mastermind behind the invasion of Planet Zytron when someone rang his door chime.

"Better hide, mate," he said to a pale brown, furry creature that was clinging to an air vent with his feet and wing hooks. The animal looked like something between a bat and a sugar glider, and it had been Carl's friend since childhood. Ship's pets were strictly prohibited on any Polestar vessel, but Carl had always thought little Flux would never cause any harm, so it was no big deal if he smuggled him aboard.

"Righto," the creature replied, and flew across the room to an open cupboard. He went inside and a wing hook appeared, gripped the door edge, and pulled it nearly closed.

Carl had gone to bed disappointed and hungry after Pashaor-Sasha had failed to show for their date at the shuttle bay. Video games were poor compensation for female company, but he'd concluded that if something seemed too good to be true, it probably was, though he couldn't understand why the woman would go to the trouble of inviting him on a date only to stand him up. Some people were weird.

He frowned and checked the time. Who could it be at this

hour? Had PashaorSasha had second thoughts? Or maybe she'd been delayed and come over to apologize for the no show? A small flame of hope flickered. He leapt up and put on his shirt.

He stepped into his pants and, pulling them up, he hopped to the door. As he opened it, his heart sped up. It *was* the geo-phys scientist. "Hi, great to see you. What happened...?" His face fell. Master Loba was a short distance away in the corridor. "Sir," he said, buttoning up his shirt, but the man didn't reply. He looked out of it.

"You have to take us planetside," said PashaorSasha

"What?" Carl's fingers hesitated. "You want me to fly you down there right now?"

"Yes. Immediately. The master must go to the planet, to the site we were at today. There's something I have to show him."

"But that's, that's..." Carl scratched his scalp. Was it even daylight at that site right now? He didn't know off the top of his head. He looked at the master again. Loba was leaning against the corridor wall, his white curls mussed up, and his eyes didn't seem to be focusing too well. Carl had heard the rumors.

He pushed his shirt into his pants slowly, buying time to think. It was all completely against protocol. *Teams* went down to the planet, not just two people, and it had to be for a legitimate reason. No tourist trips. Polestar didn't fund deep space vacations. If geo-phys had found something, there was a process to follow. But this was Loba's order, and the man was known for his vindictiveness. If Carl disobeyed without good reason, there would be serious consequences.

Stepping into the corridor, he closed his door before going over to Loba. "Sir, is this right? You want me to take you planetside?"

The master seemed to take a moment to realize that the pilot was there. He pushed himself off the wall and wavered as he stood upright. "Take us...me and her..." He pointed at PashaorSasha. "Now. Special assignment."

Carl's frown melted away as everything became clear to him.

PashaorSasha had stood him up because she'd had a better offer. The master of a starship, no less. And now she wanted him to take her and her new boyfriend on a drugged-out trip to an alien planet. *Great.*

"Right. I get it. Fine, just fine." What could he do but agree? He didn't want to kiss his career goodbye. If he refused, it would mean no flying starships through deep space. No sneck uniform. No female crew members to impress.

"Come on then," he called over his shoulder as he strode away toward the shuttle deck. He knew he shouldn't talk to the master like that, but the fool was too off his face to notice, probably.

PashaorSasha and the master didn't act like a couple who were hot for each other, Carl noticed as the two came with him and finally sat down in the shuttle's passenger cabin, but maybe that was their kink. Maybe they were role-playing. His heart sank lower at the thought that *he* could have been the one pretending to be on 'official business' with PashaorSasha.

Taking his pilot seat, he contacted the bridge. His request for clearance to fly was met with predictable confusion. Of course, the lust-sick master hadn't informed them of his plans. Carl switched his mic to broadcast in the passenger cabin. "Sir, bridge requires your personal order. You'll need to step into my cabin."

A few moments later, after fumbling with the door, Loba appeared, looking a little more alert and focused. Taking the spare headset Carl handed him, he spoke into the mic. "This is Master Loba. I...er...I authorize this trip, for...er...scientific reasons." He blinked and looked at Carl as if he were recognizing him for the first time.

After a small delay, the 'clear' signal flashed on Carl's controls as he heard the spoken confirmation. Loba's verbal order must have passed the security check. Myth clearly didn't impact the voice much.

The master's hand was resting on the back of Carl's flight seat. The man hesitated, as if he were about to speak, but he retreated to the passenger cabin.

With more force than necessary, Carl flipped the take-off switches and input the previous day's coordinates into the flight plan. Would it be night or day at the site by the time they touched down? He didn't have any idea. Would it matter for what PashaorSasha and the master had planned?

Carl thrust the clips of his harness home.

———

Loba's head was clearing. Something was very, very wrong. The mythranil was wearing off. His run was coming to an end, and he hadn't returned to bliss by following the woman. Her interruption of his vision, his requesting the copilot fly them to the surface, and their boarding the shuttle—none of it had been the effects of the drug. It had all been real.

The shuttle had landed. Loba unfastened his belt and got up unsteadily before following the geo-phys scientist to the open air lock. An icy breeze hit him as he stood on the shuttle's ramp in the pre-dawn light. He shivered. He wasn't dressed for such weather. He was wearing only the uniform that he wore aboard ship. What the hell was he doing here? He hadn't set foot on an alien planet in years.

The woman was already walking away into the gloom. She was determined to show him something, but what? What could possibly be so important, so valuable, to drag your master from his bed and all the way to the mission planet?

His first impulse was to order the scientist back, return to the warmth of the shuttle's passenger cabin, and direct the copilot to fly them back to the ship, but he considered that might not be the best path of action. The trip was already unorthodox, outside of company regulations. He would face additional scrutiny from his officers if he aborted the expedition as soon as he arrived. They would be too cautious to say anything outright, but his behavior would be rich fodder for anyone who wanted to accuse him of incompetency.

Secondly, his curiosity was piqued. Had the woman found something truly remarkable; something that really did deserve his scrutiny, and his scrutiny alone? Perhaps it was a find that would make him so rich he could buy enough mythranil to last a lifetime.

He started after the scientist. She was heading over the dunes in the direction of one of those structures Harrington had been investigating. Those places she had been getting her panties in a twist over. *Misborn.* Her excessive caution had been a thorn in his side this whole mission. He wouldn't hire her again, and he'd write an unfavorable reference if anyone asked. He hoped she'd failed the mental health assessment he'd ordered the doctor to give her. The report was due in the morning. If she passed, maybe he could persuade Sparks to tweak the results. The man was usually quick to pick up on hints.

Loba caught up with the geo-phys woman. She didn't speak as he fell into step beside her, seemingly intent on reaching the structure as quickly as possible.

"What is it you're going to show me?" he asked. "Is it a new mineral? Or something very rare? What's important enough to bring me here?"

When she didn't answer, Loba's temper rose. As always, coming down from mythranil left him fragile and moody. "I command you to tell me immediately." He grabbed the woman's shoulder and spun her round. She slipped on the sand and fell to her knees. Her expression unchanging, she rose to her feet.

"You have to come with me," she said, and went on. It was all she would say, no matter how much Loba quizzed her.

They reached the structure. The pre-dawn glow faintly gilded the edges of the hexagonal blocks but didn't penetrate the dark interior.

The woman went inside, turning on a flashlight she had brought with her. Exasperated beyond words, Loba followed, brushing the wall with his fingertips as he entered. The material was glassy, smooth, and cold. The master shivered and hoped it was warmer inside.

Within the room they'd entered was another opening. The woman immediately passed through it, and Loba followed. The next room was identical to the last, except the floor sloped downward. The woman quickly took the nearest doorway again, and again, and again. Loba could barely keep up as she led him deeper and deeper within the structure. Soon, he was completely lost. Sometimes only the beams from her flashlight told him where the woman had gone. He called out to her as they went, telling her to slow down, asking where they were going, how much farther they had to go, what they were going to see, but she never answered. He ordered her to stop, on pain of dismissal, but it was as if she didn't hear him for all the notice she took.

Did the scientist know where she was going? The structure seemed larger than it had looked on the outside. But maybe they were now underground. Loba was very tired. Mythranil sped up the metabolism and sapped the user's energy levels, and he hadn't eaten his usual post-run high calorie breakfast. The cold seemed to bite his very bones. He begged the woman to stop so that he could rest. He staggered on through another few rooms. Then, before he knew it, she was gone. He was in complete darkness. He shouted for the woman. There was no answer. He was deep within the structure. He was exhausted, hypothermic, thirsty, and hungry, and he didn't know the way out.

Loba collapsed onto his hands and knees. For a moment, the ache of his muscles distracted him from a strange tingling in his palms, but the sensation grew stronger and more unpleasant. He gasped in pain and tried to lift his hands from the floor, but he couldn't move them. It was as if they were stuck with a strong adhesive. He pulled harder. It felt like he was pulling off his skin. He cried out in agony. His hands had somehow become melded with the floor. Loba whimpered and wept. He shouted for the woman to return to help him, for anyone to help him. His hands were on fire.

Even the edges of his sleeves were stuck to the floor. They were sinking in. His hands were sinking in, too. The floor was absorbing his hands.

"Nooooo," screamed Loba. "Nooooo, help me, please. I'll do anything. I'll give you everything I have. Pleeeeeease."

As his wrists and arms began to disappear, he fought and flailed, flinging his body backward and forward in an effort to free himself. He would have broken his bones, torn his own skin off, to free himself, but he could not. His writhings brought his cheek in contact with the alien surface. Immediately, his face was stuck. It also began to sink in. Jaw, then cheek disappeared. The edge of his lips reached the floor. Loba shrieked incoherently until his mouth and nose were absorbed. After that, only the muffled noise made by his slowly disappearing vocal chords could be heard.

SEVEN

Lying on her back in her bunk, her arm over her face, Jas groaned quietly to herself. The mental health assessment hadn't gone well. In fact, it'd gone very badly. She could have sworn that Sparks had been deliberately, subtly antagonizing, but also, just maybe, she'd let her emotions get the better of her.

Her memory of the encounter was painfully clear.

He didn't believe her. Despite all her explanations about how the records of her conception were lost, how she'd spent her first few years in a government institution on Mars, how she'd never wanted to have herself tested, she could tell from his expression that he thought she was a natural, and she was lying to cover up the fact.

He gave her a patronizing look, rested a hand on her knee, and said, "You don't need to say any more. I understand your caution, but it isn't as if you can help it, is it? We can't choose our parents, after all, nor their economic situation. Don't worry. As I said, the answers you give are completely confidential." He leaned closer. "I won't tell a soul."

The force with which Jas knocked his hand away was a little too strong, because Sparks fell forward and toppled to the floor. As he got to his feet, his practiced mask of serene benevolence broke for a moment. He scowled before regaining his composure. He straight-

ened his tunic and resumed his seat. Raising a hand, he said, "I understand this is a difficult subject for you. No need to apologize."

Jas hadn't been about to apologize. "I've told you as much as I know about my genetic status, okay? I'll answer the rest of the questions." She pressed the fingerprint scanner on the interface screen. Her name flashed up as the device registered her identity. She skimmed the questions. Did she ever wish to harm herself or others? She threw a hooded glance at Sparks as she pressed no. Did she ever feel restless, agitated, tense, or frantic? Only when confined to her cabin for three days. No.

It was standard, obvious stuff. Anyone with half a brain could fake their answers to make it appear they were functioning normally. Jas answered as she thought someone who wasn't mentally ill would answer, with one or two slightly questionable responses just in case the test was set up to identify fakers. Most of her answers were true anyway.

She handed the interface back to Sparks. "Don't you have a brain scan for this kind of thing these days?"

"Not yet, though I believe they're working on it. But we do have a physical assessment. The physician interprets the results."

"What?" Jas scooted back a little on her bunk. Sparks was going to examine her? And it was up to him to say if she passed? It was game over. The man couldn't tell the difference between the thermatic plague of K.76309c and the common cold, and even if he were competent, there was no way he would clear her as mentally fit now that he thought she was a natural.

"Can I refuse?"

Sparks smiled. "Who in their right mind would refuse?"

Jas grimaced and turned onto her side as she recalled what happened next. Sparks had shone a small flashlight in her eyes and tracked her eye movement. He'd tested her reflexes and made her go through a set of physical exercises. She'd grown gradually angrier. What he was asking her to do was ridiculous. She'd suspected he was making it all up. Playing with her. Finally, she'd lost her temper.

"I'm not taking any more of this. Get out."

The doctor was in the middle of keying his findings into his interface. He looked up. "What?"

"You aren't going to pass me no matter what I do, are you? Get out of my cabin."

Sparks looked amused. "I appear to have upset you." He brought his hands together as if in prayer. "I'm so sorry." A slight smirk appeared on his lips.

The smirk had been the final straw. She'd grabbed him, opened her door and pushed him into the corridor.

Jas shook her head. She was an idiot. If she'd just played ball, if she'd just lied and said she was modded, she might have been back on duty the next day. Finding out what it was on that planet should have been her focus. She shouldn't have let that obsequious, two-faced bigot get to her.

She sighed and her arm fell to her side. Opening her eyes, she gazed, unseeing, at the low ceiling. How was she going to protect the crew? She had to do something, but what? She had to get out of her cabin, for a start. She couldn't do anything trapped in there.

She turned on her bunk screen to check the time. It was the quiet shift. Most of the crew would be asleep. She might be able to get around the ship without being seen if she were careful. But where to go? The answer was obvious. The danger was on the planet. If she could get down there and continue her investigations, she might find something concrete she could show the master; if she displayed the evidence in front of the other officers —something he couldn't ignore—he would be forced to act.

There was only one way to get planetside. She removed her comm button, which contained a tracer, and placed it on her bunk.

———

A short detour to collect one of the defense units was worth the additional risk of being seen, Jas decided. If she encountered something dangerous, she would need all the help she could get.

No one crossed her path in the ship's corridors on her way to the unit storage room. The defense units were all exactly as she'd left them, facing each other in two rows on either side of the room in the dark, as they always were when not in use. She'd often wondered if they ever spoke to each other while they were alone.

"AX10, come with me."

One of the figures turned and moved toward her.

"Close the door," she said over her shoulder as she left. The unit's footfalls were heavy as it followed her to the shuttle bay.

She was in luck. The door to the hold on the shuttle had been left open. She climbed into the dark, bare, metallic interior and directed AX10 to do the same. Stowing away in the passenger or pilot areas was out of the question. There was nowhere large enough for her to hide, and definitely nowhere the defense unit would fit. But tucked in a corner of the equipment hold they wouldn't be easily seen. The RA teams wouldn't check the interior before throwing in their equipment.

She'd brought along her combat suit. As soon as she heard the crew arrive for the next assessment trip in the morning, she would suit up. Though the hold offered some protection from the extremes of space, she stood a good chance of dying if she wasn't wearing a suit, and though the planet's atmosphere had been cleared fit to breathe, she might need the suit's protection.

She lay down and rested her head on the unit's thigh while she waited. Its large, firm muscles didn't make much of a pillow, but it was better than nothing. In a way, being uncomfortable was a benefit. She couldn't risk falling asleep.

"Hey, AX10."

"Yes, C.S.O. Harrington?"

"Do you units talk to each other when you're alone?"

"We do not."

"Why not?" Long experience of working with defense units

had taught Jas she was on shaky ground asking one of them a 'why' question, but she needed to stay awake.

"We have nothing to say, C.S.O. Harrington."

Jas was about to ask another question, but she snapped her mouth closed. Footsteps. Someone was entering the shuttle bay. More than one person. It sounded like two or three. She sat up. What was going on? It was much too early for an assessment trip. The starship was on down-time, geostationary above the side of the planet currently facing away from the sun so the scanners could take night-state readings.

Whoever was in the shuttle bay, they weren't talking. The footsteps were headed toward the shuttle. Surely they weren't going to board and fly out?

She couldn't take any chances. Jas grabbed her suit and hastily began to put it on. She thrust her legs and arms into the holes and sealed the front. She froze. Someone was walking toward the hold. She couldn't see the door from her position, but she heard it swing down and clunk closed. She was in pitch darkness before her helmet light blinked on. The floor began to vibrate as the engines started up. The shuttle lifted, and she was tossed onto her side. She clipped her helmet in place and pulled down the visor just in time as they entered space.

Eight

Deep within the alien structure, a bulge appeared in the wall of a chamber. The bulge swelled and rippled. It took shape. The shape of a human head. Colored the matte gray of the surrounding wall, the head turned from side to side, and its as-yet unseeing eyes opened, also a uniform gray. The mouth gaped in a silent scream. A neck, shoulders, and a torso emerged. Arms broke free. Below the torso a gray knee appeared, followed by a thigh and foot. A leg took a step out of the wall, the foot gripping the floor for traction, and dragged the rest of the body out after it.

The figure stood, unsteady, as color bled across its surface and the facial features refined. Hair grew from the head, swirling into white curls. Cloth rose from the skin and separated from it, forming clothes. The creature breathed in for the first time, and needles of fiery pain spread from its opening lungs.

Ah, an atmosphere-breathing organism with a nervous system. Exquisite agony. To breathe, to feel again, after eons of confinement.

Nerves spasmed into life, sending signals from the being's periphery, information about ambient temperature and the movement of air. The sensations were unpleasant. The environment was too cold for this organism. The material that covered the creature also stimulated its nerve endings, though the sensation was more satisfying. The cloth captured the animal's heat and protected it from the cold.

The heart beat once, twice, and settled into a steady rhythm. Newly formed blood moved sluggishly then faster through opening veins and arteries. The visual organs, the eyes, remained unstimulated. The creature speculated that light must be required for them to operate. Outside, they should work more effectively.

Two limbs...legs...adjoined the lower half of the body, and two more sprang from the upper half. Arms. The being moved its legs and toppled to the ground. More pain. It lifted itself up and balanced again. The legs appeared to be the only method of locomotion. It tried again and fell once more.

A short time later, the creature took a few staggering steps. Once it had succeeded in this task, its learning was exponential. Within a few minutes, it began to walk confidently. After encountering a wall and experiencing pain, it used its arms to supplement the poor quality of information coming from its visual organs. The arms had many nerves at their far ends, in the hands and fingers, and the creature navigated its way in the darkness, using them to locate obstructions.

The sensation of being separate was strange, and it took some time for the creature to reconcile the information it received from its nerves with its previous experience of being at one with the structure and the void beyond it, and the others of its kind. But in time it perceived the building as a discrete entity, and that it was located inside. At this realization, it ceased wandering randomly and began to work its way to the surface.

As the being went, it grew accustomed to its new mind, and millions of pieces of information began to manifest, drawn from the alien life form the structure had absorbed. Memories, knowledge, language. Certain vocalizations were very important. The creature opened its mouth, moved its lips and tongue. Brand-new vocal cords, moist and fresh, vibrated.

"Ah-kah-be-lo-ba."

A name. A sound signifying a thing. It was the name of the absorbed creature. But the sound was not quite right. "Akabe." Pause. "Loba." That was correct.

Visual signals from the eyes were strengthening. The light around the creature was growing brighter. It was nearing the exterior. In its mind, neurons fired, channels of information flew open, and new torrents of information poured forth. The animal called its species *human*. The species was dimorphous. The absorbed creature had been of the type called male, or man. It had been the most important man on a vessel that traveled between the stars. An autonomous reaction from the nervous system fired, and pleasure flooded the creature.

The light intensity grew bright as the creature neared the structure's exit. Its eyes didn't adjust quickly enough, and pain registered. It closed its eyelids halfway. Waiting at the exit was one of the others from which it had separated, and this one had also transformed into a human. It was a female of the species, and it had brought Master Akabe Loba to the structure to be replicated.

As the creature joined the female, the pair did not speak. They had no need, for their minds were one. Only their newly adopted physical forms were separate—a temporary, necessary inconvenience. First, they must bring more humans from the orbiting starship to the structures for absorption. If most of the humans were not consumed and copied, their entity would face dangerous hostilities. They also needed many more copies of humans and other alien species on the physical plain to achieve their final goal.

Outside, the movement of the cold air was brisk and uncomfortable. The creature began to shiver. The other led the way to the vessel that would take them to the starship. The shuttlecraft was small, but it looked well made. An attractive item of technology and likely to be only one of many more the humans had created. A vista of replication, domination, acquisition, and, ultimately, complete control of this physical expanse opened in the creatures' shared mind.

It was time for generation to begin.

NINE

Jas waited, squatting on her heels. When the shuttle had landed, and she'd heard the ramp descend and two sets of footsteps walk down it, then silence. She racked her brains as to what was going on, but none of it made any sense. Two people weren't enough for an RA team, and the teams weren't due out until morning anyway. An RA team also wouldn't go on a trip without equipment. She wondered if Lingiari had taken the shuttle on a whim and flown down with a friend. But he would never have gotten clearance from the bridge, and even Lingiari wasn't stupid enough to fly without clearance. He'd be sacked and blacklisted in the industry forever.

Who had the authority to order an unscheduled visit to the planet? Only Loba. But why on Earth would he do it? His was the archetypal hands-off, don't-bother-me approach.

The circle of light from Jas's headlamp wobbled on the bare, metallic equipment hold floor as her head shook slightly in perplexity. AX10 remained motionless behind her. With no room to stand up, she crawled toward the door. She swept her headlamp's rays across the door's seams. As she expected, there was no way to open it from the inside.

She sat back. She'd come here for a reason. Could she continue as planned, despite the odd circumstances?

"AX10, can you connect to the shuttle's computer system?"

"Affirmative, C.S.O. Harrington."

"Tell it to open the hold. You can do that, right?" She didn't know if the two who had descended the ramp were still around. They'd had enough time to leave the area. If they were still near the shuttle, they might interpret the hold door opening to be a glitch. It was a chance she was prepared to take.

"I can," said the unit. "Do you want me to do that?"

"Ye—wait." Jas had worked with defense units long enough to get to know their ways. They were intelligent, but they lacked empathy and theory of mind. It might be necessary for them to kill intelligent, sentient species, and the ability to imagine how another creature was feeling and thinking would make them inefficient. But the units' mental foibles also meant they struggled to imagine how information available to them might be useful to someone else. Jas had learned that, as a result, they had a kind of fail-safe. They would check an order if they knew something that they suspected might jeopardize the maneuver. "What might I need to know, AX10?"

"We are not traveling in the passenger cabin; therefore, I believe we are hiding. I do not know if the pilot should be aware of our location. If I tell the shuttle's computer to open the door, it will communicate the action to him."

"You mean it'll announce, *AX10 is opening the hold door?*"

"Affirmative, C.S.O. Harrington."

Krat. Assuming it was Lingiari who'd flown the shuttle—she didn't think the main pilot, Grantwise, would agree to such an unorthodox trip—he might still be aboard. She didn't want to get Lingiari in trouble, but on the other hand, if she couldn't get out and look around, the safety of the entire crew might be at stake. Also, once Lingiari knew he had a defense unit on board, he might guess she was accompanying it and not come into the hold with weapons blazing.

"Okay, AX10, go for it. Tell the shuttle to open the hold door."

A moment later, with a clunk and a judder, the door swung up. Gray light filled the hold. An ocean moved outside, waves sweeping the shore. Jas opened her visor to make it easier for Lingiari to recognize her. A tangy odor accompanied the chill breeze from the water. Pale stars winked in the pre-dawn light.

Slow, heavy footsteps came down the ramp. He was taking his time. Jas rolled her eyes. If Lingiari's hold were filled with murderous aliens, they would have killed him three minutes ago. She would have to upgrade the crew's combat training. A man's lanky figure came into view, silhouetted against the sky, his hand gripping a small weapon.

"Lingiari," Jas whispered, just loud enough to be heard above the ocean, "it's me."

"Harrington?" The pilot's broad, honest features became visible and brightened as he stepped closer. "What the hell?"

She climbed out and jumped down from the hold. "Shhh...is anyone else around?"

"No. Loba and the geo-phys woman left ten minutes ago."

"So it is Loba. And he's with Margret?"

"No, Pasha, or Sasha. I can't remember her name."

"There's only one woman with geo-phys, and her name's Margret Stratton."

"Oh, in that case, yeah, Margret. They're tagging up over there somewhere." He waved toward the dunes, a disappointed look on his face.

"Loba and Margret? BF."

"Yeah, they are. Why else would Loba make me fly them down?"

"Lingiari, were you born on Balgamon? Loba probably hasn't raised the flag in years. That's the first thing to go when you're running the blood."

The pilot's eyes widened. "Glad I never tried it." He looked at her intently. "No myth's affected my ability. Everything's working fine down there."

Jas frowned. Why was he telling her that? He had a weird look on his face.

Lingiari continued, "So Loba let you out your cabin?"

"Not exactly. I snuck out and stowed away so I could check out the planet some more. There's something not right here. I have to find out what it is."

Lingiari rubbed his head. "You mean you're still confined to quarters?"

"Yeah. You won't say anything, will you?"

The pilot hesitated, then said, "No, 'course not. I won't dob on you. I've always liked you, Harrington."

There was that weird look again.

"Err...thanks, Lingiari. You said they went over there?"

"Yeah. They didn't say when they'd be back, but I hope it's soon. I need to get back to the ship and pick up the RA team. It'll be daylight in a couple of hours."

"I'm going to see what I can find. Don't take off without me, okay? Can you scan the hold for life forms?" The copilot nodded. "Good. Check we're on board before you take off. I'll try to get back before Loba and Margret."

Telling AX10 to follow, Jas set off at a lope toward the dunes. Following the direction Lingiari had indicated, Jas scrambled upward, slipping on the stones and sand. As her head crowned the rise she was greeted by the sight she'd feared. About a kilometer away was one of the hexagonal structures. It was no surprise. They were dotted across all the planet's landmasses. The ship's scanners had even detected a few on the ocean floor. She was sure it was in the structures that the danger lay, whatever it was.

Loba and Margret were nowhere to be seen, which meant they must have gone inside. She couldn't follow them into the building. If Loba saw her, it would all be over.

She debated returning to the shuttle and waiting for Loba and

Margret to return, but there was no rush. She would have plenty of time to get back as soon as she spotted them. She decided to observe the landscape while she was there. After pulling down her visor, she activated its zoom and checked her surroundings in detail.

Lingiari was walking up and down the shoreline, his hands in his pockets, kicking the sand. Beyond him, a group of small creatures briefly lifted out of the ocean waves. Nearby, slime molds inched along among the rough dune plants. AX10 was squatting, still and silent, awaiting his next order.

After more than an hour's observation, Jas concluded there seemed nothing threatening outside the artificial structure. Her bored gaze returned to it. Why had Margret taken Loba there? Had she discovered the threat and wanted to show him personally?

The approaching sun gilded the horizon. Movement at an opening in the building made her freeze. The swiftly rising sun's beams illuminated two figures emerging. Loba and Margret. They'd done whatever they'd come to do and were returning to the shuttle.

Jas watched them approach. Lingiari's theory that the two were tagging up was ridiculous. And they certainly didn't behave like a couple in love, or lust. They were walking a short distance apart and not even looking at each other. They also didn't appear to be talking.

Something was weird about their gait. It was familiar, but it didn't look right. For a moment, Jas couldn't figure out what it was, then it came to her. They were walking like defense units. Their steps were almost mechanical, and they were facing consistently forward with no interest in what was around them. She watched them as they covered nearly the whole distance to the dunes, but their behavior didn't change.

Frowning, Jas took one last look before slipping back to the shuttle.

TEN

Navigator Sayen Lee straightened her pillow and smoothed the covers on her bunk until they were free of folds and creases. She felt a little queasy. Was she coming down with a stomach virus? Or was it food poisoning? She'd had the Asiatic option for breakfast: congee, pickled vegetables, steamed bun and soy milk. The pickled cabbage had tasted a little strange. She wouldn't be surprised if the chief steward cut corners when it came to food hygiene, under pressure from the master to save money.

Sitting down at her desk, Sayen said, "Open interface," and the entire desk surface became a screen filled with numbers and mathematical characters. Sayen was about halfway through the calculations for the next starjump on the *Galathea's* schedule. She didn't actually need to do the calculation herself. The ship's computer would do it, but she figured it out herself every time anyway, for relaxation. Her result always matched the computer's.

Her math professor at college had seen her doing a starjump calculation one day, and after looking over her shoulder for a few minutes had asked her what it was. When Sayen explained, the woman laughed and told her not to be ridiculous; that the computation was beyond the ability of a single human being and it would take years to work it out.

Sayen had shrugged and said she'd figured out a few short cuts. The professor had smiled condescendingly and replied, "Yes, of course you have," before walking away, shaking her head and laughing.

It hadn't mattered to Sayen then that her professor didn't believe her, and it didn't matter now. On the rare occasions she'd been the center of attention, she'd felt uncomfortable. She had no incentive in broadcasting her abilities; she was content to use them as necessary to secure a high-paying job, but no more.

Sayen studied the calculation and worked on it for some time before she realized that she was due on the bridge soon. Closing the screen, she stood and faced a wall of her cabin. "Mirror." The wall became reflective and displayed an image of a petite woman with short, blonde, razor-cut hair, wearing an immaculate Polestar uniform. She checked her clothes for spots and lint, turning and looking over her shoulder to see the reflection of her back.

Sayen's stomach churned a little, and she put a hand to it. She would have to pay Dr. Sparks a short visit before her shift started. She still had time if she hurried. She had one last thing to do before leaving her cabin, however: the final stage of her morning routine.

She went into her shower room to wash her hands, but as she passed through the door, she remembered she'd run out of hand sanitizer. Her face fell. What was she going to do? She always washed her hands before going to work. Always. But the last time she'd asked the chief steward for an extra bottle of sanitizer he'd told her that was the last one she was allowed.

There was nothing else she could do, she would just have to skip visiting the doctor and go see the chief steward instead. He had to give her some more sanitizer. He had to.

She stepped out of her cabin in a hurry and walked straight into Lingiari, the copilot. The two collided. Lingiari was barely affected by the impact, but Sayen bounced off the rangy man and nearly fell down. At the same time, Lingiari gave a great sneeze, showering Sayen in a spittle spray.

"Oughh," she exclaimed, wrinkling her nose. "That's disgusting." She wiped her face with her hands and looked down at her uniform.

"Sorry," said the copilot. "I wasn't expecting you to pop out like that."

Sayen backed away, wiping her hair and each hand in turn. "Do you have a cold? Don't tell me you have a cold."

"I don't think so, I just...got a bit..." He gestured behind him in the direction of the shuttle bay. He appeared to be about to say something, then changed his mind. "I don't think I've got a cold."

"Oughh." Sayen gave a slight shudder and went around Lingiari, giving him a very wide berth.

The chief steward's office was on the other side of the ship. She would have to hurry if she wasn't going to be late for her shift. She quickly turned a corner, but stopped. Harrington was coming toward her. C.S.O. Harrington, who was supposed to be confined to her cabin. The security officer was racing down the corridor.

"What are you—" asked Sayen.

"Shhh," hissed Harrington as she passed by, "don't tell anyone. Please don't, and I promise if you ever need protecting from aliens, I'll be right there."

"Oh, I...okay," she said to the security officer's retreating figure.

Today was turning out to be odd. But she didn't have time to figure out what was going on. She had to get to the chief steward. Fifteen minutes later, panting, she pressed his door chime.

"Who is it?" came the man's voice over the intercom.

"Sayen Lee."

There was a sigh of exasperation. "What is it this time? Disinfectant? Polish? Sanitizer?"

"That's it. I need some more sanitizer. I know you—"

"No. I've already told you. No more. Use the UV box like

everyone else. Sanitizer is redundant and outdated. That's why we—"

"But I really need it. If no one else—"

"No."

"But—"

"No."

The light on the intercom went out. The chief steward had turned it off.

Panic rose in Sayen's throat. She had to wash her hands. A disaster would happen if she didn't. What kind of disaster, she didn't know, but it would be something really bad.

Sayen went back the way she'd come. Where could she get some hand sanitizer? The communal restrooms didn't have any. They only had UV boxes. And what good were they? On one level she knew they were the most efficient way of killing germs, but she didn't feel right using them; she didn't feel hygienic. She needed that reassurance of spreading sanitizer all over her hands and the tingle of it evaporating.

The corridors were filling with crew members on their way to their workstations. Maybe one of them could help? There had to be someone else on board who still liked to use hand sanitizer. She stopped and scanned the faces as they passed. At last, she saw someone who might be able to help—Sayen had introduced herself only the day before as the woman had seemed lonely—though now she didn't seem to have noticed her.

"Hi. It's Margret, right?" asked Sayen as the geo-phys scientist had almost passed by. When she didn't stop, Sayen grabbed her arm. Margret turned slowly, as if she were in a trance or deep in thought.

"Margret, I'm Sayen, remember?" she said when the woman still didn't seem to recognize her. "I was wondering if you have any hand sanitizer?"

"Hand sanitizer," echoed Margret.

"Yes, do you have any?"

"No, I don't have hand sanitizer."

Sayen peered into Margret's face. Her expression was blank. "Are you feeling okay?"

Margret didn't reply, but began to walk away. Sayen followed her. "Are you sure you don't have any? Could you check? Hey, I think your cabin's this way," she said as Margret took a wrong turn into the storage section. Something was definitely wrong with her. She would have to tell Dr. Sparks. After grabbing the woman's hand, she led her the right way.

They arrived at Margret's cabin. As soon as they were through the door, Sayen went into the shower room. Her heart leapt. There it was, on the side of the basin: a nearly full bottle.

Eleven

Jas's cabin walls seemed to close around her after she returned from stowing away on the shuttle. The few hours' freedom had been a welcome break from confinement, despite the deeply worrying revelation that the master of the *Galathea* was now compromised.

Both Loba and Margret had been acting as if they were in a kind of trance. There was no doubt in Jas's mind that something was within the artificial structures on K. 67092d, something neither she nor the defense units had spotted in all the LIVs they'd conducted. What they'd missed was still a mystery, but as far as she was concerned, her initial suspicions had been vindicated. The problem was, she was the only person aboard who understood that at least two crew members had been infected by an alien organism, and that the rest of them were in danger. Though Lingiari had acknowledged something wasn't right, he hadn't been convinced the threat was serious enough to raise an alarm.

How could she convince anyone to listen to her? Her reputation was at an all-time low. None of the officers would believe what she had to say. And if she told anyone she'd been planetside, she'd be put in the brig and dismissed, or even prosecuted and fined when they returned to Earth, assuming they made it that far.

Her only hope was Lingiari. She'd asked him to come to her cabin when his shift was over. She was sure he'd show. He'd seemed enthusiastic about the idea. She had to talk him into trying to alert the others that something was wrong with Loba and Margret. If Sparks examined them, surely some medical evidence would show up.

In the meantime, she had several hours to kill. Jas lay on her bunk and turned on her screen to access the ship's massive database. She stroked the image displayed, scrolling through the long list of options, until she found the section she was looking for: Hostile Extraterrestrial Life Forms.

Each species was cataloged under its Earth name in phonetic script. She'd logged a few of these dangerous aliens herself. Though humans had never encountered a species that posed a threat outside its own planet, there seemed to be plenty of nasties lying in wait for unsuspecting prospectors on new worlds. Many of the more recent additions were unfamiliar to Jas. She clicked on a promising link on surprise attacks. It was a passage on long, lithe, ground-dwelling organisms that burrowed up from the dirt and into the feet of animals walking overhead. The creatures quickly tunneled through flesh and bones and into the main body, drawn to the central nervous system, which they then devoured.

Jas recalled the news of the life form's discovery. It couldn't penetrate combat suits, and neither the C.S.O. leading the LIV nor his defense units had felt or taken note of the small thumps against the soles of their boots. The C.S.O. had given the planet the all-clear. The organisms had quickly massacred the first RA team to land. Had the team been wearing combat suits, they would have been fine, but, despite their own massive salaries, Polestar Corp's executive board had judged the provision of combat suits for RA teams to be too expensive.

Jas scrolled on. Previously unknown intelligent life—or, more correctly, life that Polestar acknowledged as intelligent, despite the obvious disincentive— was rare, but hostile life was common. The role of chief security officer was nigh on impossible to perform well. What new horrors a planet might hold were highly unpredictable, yet after a few short LIVs, security officers were expected to clear the areas as safe for resource assessment. Though their contracts stated that they carried no personal liability if they made a mistake, the emotional toll of seeing friends and colleagues die because they made a bad call could be devastating.

Jas counted herself lucky that, so far, no one had died on her watch, though she'd had some close calls. She couldn't do her job properly with Loba tying her hands. It was poetic justice that it looked like the master himself had fallen victim to his own lax expediency.

She filtered the information in the database for parasites, body possession, mind control, and influence on human behavior. The results dwindled to a handful. The only case she could find that sounded similar to what was happening on K. 67092d was an incident involving a gas in a planet's atmosphere that scanners had failed to detect. The security officer in that case couldn't be blamed for what had happened. Wearing his combat suit, he hadn't breathed the local air. It wasn't part of the job. Scientists were the testers. Security officers weren't canaries in coalmines, and defense units don't breath. When the RA team had arrived, the gas had entered their bloodstreams and crossed the blood-brain barrier. It'd destroyed their higher brain functions, and the team had been reduced to living, breathing vegetables within minutes.

She closed the database screen, and rested her arm over her eyes. Despite these terrible accidents, people continued to sign up for work aboard the prospecting ships. Life on Earth grew harder every year, and the chances of achieving a financially comfortable, long life and peaceful retirement grew slimmer. Jas understood only too well why companies like Polestar had an endless queue of applicants. The get-rich-quick prospect was tantalizing to many, and employers downplayed the risks. How long would her lucky streak of protecting these crews last? Maybe it was time for her to consider another career.

Her interface chirruped. She had a message from Sparks. Reading it, she groaned. She'd failed the mental health assessment. Of course. The doctor prescribed a muscle relaxant, an anti-psychotic, and an anti-anxiety medication. He was going to dope her up as revenge for her forceful eviction of him from her cabin. She thumped the wall with her fist so hard she hurt her hand. *Damn the misborn.* But she couldn't refuse treatment. Loba—or whatever was now controlling him—could have her put in the brig, where there would be no way to sneak out. If she was restrained indefinitely, for the rest of the mission, who would protect the crew? She grimaced. She hadn't been doing that great a job of protecting them herself.

She turned on her side. She had to think of a plan, but nothing would come. After some time, mental exhaustion forced her eyes closed, and she slept.

She was back in Antarctica. It was summer, and the ice was melting. The ground was slick and treacherous. Soon, there would be no ice left, they said. Great sheets had broken off over the previous few decades, floating away to slowly melt into the ocean. Billions of tons of fresh water ice, gone forever.

Jas was looking out over the ocean. At first, she couldn't remember why she was there, then it came to her. She was looking for something. She'd lost something in the water, and she had to find it.

She rolled up her pants legs and took off her boots and socks. The first touch of the icy water on her toes made her suck in a breath. She waded deeper, and the waves soon soaked her pants up to her thighs and numbed her feet and calves. What was she looking for? She couldn't remember, except that it was something important. A sense of urgency rose up in her. She went deeper in, up to her waist. She had to find it quickly, or it would be too late. A wave took her full in the face, and she choked on seawater.

Something heavy bumped against her thigh. Was this it? She

grabbed blindly in the water. Her fingers met cloth. She took hold of it and pulled. This was it. Finally, she'd found it.

A face rose up: skin deathly pale, eyes open and still, mouth spilling water, black hair trailing. Jas tried to scream, but another wave took her, ripping the man from her grasp. It lifted her from her feet, and crushed her under its weight. She couldn't breathe. She fought to reach the surface, but she was trapped in the rolling water. She was going to drown, she was—gasping, awakening.

Jas sat upright in her bunk. It took her a few moments to realize where she was, that she wasn't back at training college in Antarctica, and that it had all been a dream. The same nightmare as always.

She lay down and, after some time, she slept.

———

Her door chime woke her. Groggy with sleep, for a tense moment Jas thought Loba or Margret had come to take her to the planet so she could be possessed by an alien. She sat up, trying to figure out who was at the door. Was it a drone with Spark's prescription? No, the pills had been put through her door slot. Her memory fully returned. She'd asked Lingiari to come over. "Door, open."

The rangy copilot stood in the entrance, clutching a box and looking pleased, for some reason. Maybe he'd figured out what they should do.

"Come in," said Jas. "What's been happening? How are Margret and Loba acting? Has anyone else been affected?"

"Woah, slow down," said Lingiari. "Have you eaten? Are you hungry?" He sat down and put the box on her desk. He began to open it.

"No, I'm not," replied Jas, though her stomach rumbled as she spoke. *What was the man doing? Didn't he understand the situation?* The copilot was peeling the lid off a foil pack. A rich, fishy scent escaped, and Jas's mouth watered. "Tell me what happened on the RA trip today. What did you see?"

"Eat up, and I'll tell you all about it." He held out the package and a fork. "It's smoked oysters."

"Lingiari, I don't know what the hell you're doing, but, please, cut it out and answer me."

The man seemed to deflate. He took back the oysters, sighed, and started to eat them himself. "What do you want to know?" He spoke from the corner of his mouth as he chewed. "I took a team down for an RA and brought them back when they'd finished. That's it."

"Where did they go? Did they enter one of the structures? Were they acting strangely like Loba and Margret when they came back?"

Lingiari swallowed and licked his fork before plunging it into the oysters again. "They weren't near any buildings this time. It was a volcanic zone. Pretty active. Had to get out when the ship's scanners detected that a potential earthquake was building."

"That's a relief. It sounds like the RA team was safe this time, but we've got to do something, Lingiari. If we don't, the whole crew's in danger."

The copilot's attention was on a large forkful of pale brown oysters on its way to his mouth, dripping oil. "Yeah, but…" he popped the oysters in and looked thoughtful as his mouth worked, "what?"

"We need to convince the other officers that Loba isn't to be trusted, and they'll declare him incompetent and take over the running of the ship. They'll get us away from this planet. Sparks can try to find out what's happened to the master and Margret. I might be able to convince them if you back me up. They must have noticed that Loba's acting oddly by now."

"Take over the running of the *Galathea*?" Carl put down his fork. "Isn't that mutiny?"

"Not if the master's incapacitated, it isn't. It's the only sensible thing the officers can do. I just need to persuade them. You'll support me, right?"

"I'm right by your side, Jas. Can I call you Jas, Harrington? I'm with you. In everything." He gazed into her eyes.

"Great," replied Jas, wondering briefly if Lingiari had been infected too. But he wasn't acting vacant like Loba and Margret. Just...peculiar. "In that case, you can come with me."

"What? Where are you going?"

"Where do you think I'm going? The bridge. And you're coming with me." She jumped up and strode past Lingiari. The copilot hastily pushed his fork into the tin of oysters, but it slipped out and fell to the floor with a clatter.

"Don't you think you're being a bit quick off the mark?" he asked. But Jas was already on her way out.

TWELVE

Her mind was made up, and Jas acted. She sped through the *Galathea* toward the bridge, where Loba and other high-ranking staff could be found when they were on shift. From behind her came the sound of Lingiari'ss footsteps, half-running to keep up.

"Harrington, hey, slow down."

A crew member gaped as he recognized her. The news that she'd been confined to her cabin must have been hot gossip around the ship. She brushed past him, nearly knocking the man from his feet.

"Wait a minute, Harrington," the copilot called.

"We don't have time for any more talking, Lingiari," she said over her shoulder. "Every RA team that goes down to the planet is vulnerable. We know Margret and Loba have been infected. How many more are there? We have to convince the officers about what's happening and get them to call a halt to the assessment trips."

Lingiari caught up with her and grabbed her arm. "You know, on second thoughts, I don't think this is such a good idea."

Jas stopped and faced him. "Do you have a better one?" They were in a high-traffic corridor. *Galathea* crew members passed on either side, giving the pair looks. One woman paused at the sight of them and moved a short distance away before speaking into her comm button. When Lingiari didn't answer her question, Jas said, "I have to get to the bridge, now. Before it's too late."

She strode away without checking if Lingiari was following. If he wasn't going to support her, she would just have to try her best by herself. A moment later, she burst into the flight control room. All eyes turned to her as she stood at the door.

Jas rarely went to the bridge, but the oval area was just as she remembered it. Displayed on the walls around the room were images of the star systems and planets scheduled for investigation and assessment that mission. Below the planets that they had already assessed was a set of figures estimating their resource availability and potential revenue. The figures were red. When the *Galathea* claimed sufficient resources to bring in bonuses, the numbers below the planets would be green. The display had been Loba's idea, to keep everyone's mind on the money. It was a constant reminder to the officers to work faster and harder.

The master was in his usual spot, seated on an elevated plinth toward the back of the room. First Mate Haggardy was to one side, reading an interface. The second mate's seat on the other side of Loba was empty, but the rest of them—the chief engineer, third mate, pilot, quartermaster, RA team leader and a handful of cadets—were at their stations. Navigator Lee was looking at her with her mouth open.

For a moment, no one spoke. Now that she was there, Jas wasn't sure what to say; how could she convince them that their master was compromised, with Loba sitting right there looking exactly the same as always? But couldn't they see there was something wrong? He should have reacted strongly to her presence. He should have commanded her removal. But he only stared like the rest of them. Couldn't they tell, or were they too afraid of being the first to say something?

Haggardy was the first to act. He pressed the comm link on his desk. "Security to the bridge." His eyes narrowed at her.

"You're disobeying orders, Harrington. You heard what the master said. If you leave your cabin, you're to be sent to the brig."

"Wait, listen to me. Loba went planetside with Margret Stratton. You know that. They've been taken over by something on the planet. I don't know what it is, but you have to halt the RA trips before we have more victims. The master isn't fit to serve and should be removed from duty."

"Dr. Sparks forwarded your report," said Haggardy. "You're suffering from a mental illness. These thoughts you're having are just one of your symptoms."

"I'm not sick," Jas exclaimed. She pointed at Loba. "Haven't you noticed he's been acting strangely?"

Haggardy turned to Loba, who only returned the gaze and shook his head slightly. "Stop right there, Harrington," Haggardy said. "I don't care how ill you are. I won't have you accusing the master of this vessel of incompetency."

"What about that trip he took, Haggardy? Any of you?" She scanned their faces. From their expressions, she wasn't convincing anyone. She clenched her fists. "When has he ever done anything like that? Look at him. He's been acting weird since, hasn't he?" No one would meet her eyes. Lingiari had come in with her, but he was hanging in the background, looking non-committal. "Lingiari agrees with me," she blurted.

"That's enough," said Haggardy. "Don't start dragging other crew members into your fantasy."

The bridge door opened, and Jas turned to see two on-ship security officers enter. *Her* officers. They looked embarrassed and a little afraid.

"Take her to the brig," commanded Haggardy.

Jas swung back to face him. "I'm not going anywhere until you listen to me. You cannot leave that man in charge of the ship. You have to stop the crew from going down to the planet."

Haggardy motioned with his head to the security detail behind her. Hands gripped her arms. The situation was getting annoying. She back-fisted one man, breaking his nose, and drove her elbow into the solar plexus of the other. As the men staggered back, she turned and kicked the head of the man holding his stomach. He fell down senseless. The one whose nose she'd broken drew his weapon. Blood dripped from his chin, and his eyes watered.

Jas put her hands on her hips. "Frank, really?"

Frank quailed under her stare, and in his momentary distraction, Jas kicked the weapon from his hand and moved in for a headlock. "Sorry," she said, as she knocked his skull just hard enough against a rail that he dropped, unconscious, to the floor. She would have to improve training for on-ship security. That was much too easy. They'd gotten slack. Jas scooped up the fallen weapon and took the other man's from its holster. "Thanks, Haggardy. Now you have to listen to me." She swept the room with the weapons. Lingiari had backed into a corner. "Just go," Jas told him.

As the copilot left, Jas began to outline to the flight control room what they had to do. Loba, Margret, and everyone else who had been to the planet without the protection of a combat suit—there had to be a reason she was unaffected, despite entering the structures—was under suspicion and had to be relieved of duty while they were tested. All RA trips had to be cancelled, and the *Galathea* would have to return to Earth and enter quarantine while the xenobiologists figured out what to do.

While she was speaking the assembled officers and cadets remained silent. She stopped. There was an uncomfortable pause. To her surprise, Haggardy said, "Maybe you have a point there, Harrington. Tell us some more." He glanced at the door. He must have called another security detail while she was distracted with dealing with the first one. *Damn the misborn.* She'd have to fight these officers too. It didn't matter. She could take down any of her on-ship guards. Being better than them was part of her job. Eventually, Haggardy and the others would have to listen to her.

The two men she'd knocked out were coming around. She trained her weapons on their figures. Behind them, the bridge door opened, and Jas's jaw dropped. *Krat.* Haggardy hadn't called on-ship security, he'd summoned two of her defense units. AX7 and AX10 lumbered onto the deck. There would be no defeating these two. No intimidation nor recourse to personal history. Defense units obeyed the highest-ranking officer's commands unquestioningly and unrelentingly. Taking her to the brig was just another task for them.

At least they hadn't activated their weapons yet.

Her only chance was to disable them quickly. At close range, she might manage it. She knew where they were most vulnerable. Jas lifted her laser guns and took aim, but her fingers wouldn't press the triggers. She couldn't fire on them, even though she knew they would eventually self-repair. She couldn't bring herself to damage these part-organic machines. Whatever injuries she inflicted, the units would do whatever Haggardy commanded with no regard for their own safety.

They came toward her. She held her weapons steady. She had to shoot. She had to put them out of action, but still her fingers froze. It wasn't the expense that bothered her, nor the fact that they were two amazingly intricate, complex items of equipment. It was her long experience of working with them. She'd gotten to know every facet of their behavior, including all the little quirks and individualities they weren't supposed to have.

The idea of harming either of the units turned her stomach. She threw down the weapons.

"Fine," she exclaimed, turning back to Haggardy. "Put me in the brig. And when you see I was right, that he's possessed," she stabbed a finger at Loba, "come and get me to help you sort out this mess."

AX10 and AX7 took her by the arms and pulled her toward the door.

"The rest of you: do not go down to the planet. Do you hear me? There's something in those structures. Don't set a foot down on the planet. And watch anyone who does."

Thirteen

Sayen Lee was sleeping restlessly when stomach pangs brought her to full consciousness. She needed a physician. Though it was the quiet shift, she didn't think Dr. Sparks would mind seeing her. He was always so obliging. In a short time, she was at his desk.

"Navigator Lee, how pleasant to see you again. Please take a seat." Sparks smiled widely and gestured to the chair opposite him.

Just seeing the man made Sayen feel better. She loved the way he'd set up his consulting room like the physicians' offices of the twenty-first century. There were none of the bulky scanners and equipment that now filled health clinics to the brim: machines to analyze the breath, upright full-body scanners, equipment to extract and test blood. He had these devices and more, but he hid them away in the back, out of sight. She'd even heard there was now a machine to perform gynaecological exams. She gave a slight shudder.

Sparks put his elbows on his desk, steepled his fingers, and gazed into Sayen's eyes. "And what can I do for you today?"

This was what she liked most. Sparks made an effort to talk to his patients. She put a hand on her stomach. "I've been feeling queasy ever since breakfast yesterday, Doctor. I think I might be coming down with something. Or maybe it was something I ate."

"Hmmm, I see." He turned to a screen and typed into a keyboard. "Any other symptoms? Changes to your bowel habits? Have you vomited at all?"

"No, that's it. But I did feel worse after that incident with Harrington on the bridge. So maybe it's something to do with my nerves?"

"That was very unfortunate. Very sad." Sparks shook his head. "If only she'd taken the medication I prescribed." He stopped typing and leaned toward the navigator. "I probably shouldn't say anything," he said, lowering his voice, "but she's a natural, you know. Means she's a little unstable." He tapped the side of his head.

Sayen's eyes grew wide. "Is that right? I didn't know. That naturals have worse mental health, I mean."

"That's only the start of it. They're more vulnerable to most medical conditions, which is why it's helpful for me to know who's who among the crew, if you know what I mean. But the powers that be have tied my hands in that regard, I'm sorry to say." He paused. "But that isn't you're problem, is it, Navigator?"

Sayen gave a short laugh. "No, my parents paid for the works for me and my brother." She frowned. "And yet, I seem to get sick all the time. Why is that, I wonder?"

"Hmmm, well..." Sparks scanned his screen. "As I've said before, your profile indicates a strong immune response to viruses, so you can thank your modding for that. I suppose it's possible that when you come into contact with a virus, your immune system's reaction is excessive. Many symptoms of infection are in fact due to the chemicals the body produces as a response to pathogens. When someone with a weaker response fights off a virus, they might not notice, but *your* body's mounting a full-out attack, and you're feeling it."

"Uh-huh. That makes sense."

"But let's be thorough about this, hm? Hop up on the couch, and I'll examine you."

A pleasant warmth suffused Sayen. Dr. Sparks always took her concerns seriously. She climbed onto his examining table and pulled up her tunic, exposing her midriff. The doctor rubbed his hands together as he approached the table. "Wouldn't want to shock you with my cold hands." He placed his open palms on her bare skin and gently pushed, palpating her internal organs. Sayen's tummy gurgled, and she giggled.

"Nothing to be embarrassed about. It's a good sign, in fact," said the doctor. "Indicates everything's working normally."

"Thanks, Doctor. I already feel a little better."

"Good, good," said Sparks. "You can get up now." He returned to his desk. Typing on his keyboard as Sayen got down from the table, he added, "I can't find anything abnormal. I think it's just a case of a little anxiety, especially as you say the problem got worse after witnessing our chief security officer's outburst today. I'm going to prescribe a medication that will calm your stomach."

"Thank you, Doctor." Her comm button chirruped. "Excuse me." She clicked on the Polestar symbol fixed to her chest and lifted it up to read the message. It was from Loba. *Navigator Lee, report to the shuttle bay.* Sayen froze.

"Is something the matter?" asked Sparks.

"I think…I think…Master Loba wants me to go down to the planet." There was no other reason she could think of that would require her presence in the shuttle bay in the middle of the quiet shift. Harrington's warnings echoed in her head. Her mind whirled.

"That'll be a nice trip for you. I often wish I had more of an opportunity for exploring new planets, but my duties nearly always confine me to the ship."

"I always stay aboard the ship. Always," Sayen blurted.

"Now's your chance then. I envy you." Sparks pressed a final key on his keyboard and turned to her, smiling. "I'll have a drone drop your medication at your cabin. It'll be there in ten or fifteen minutes."

Her consultation was over, but Sayen didn't want to leave. "Dr. Sparks...Harrington, before she was taken to the brig, she said that the master had been infected by an alien, and she warned us not to go to the planet, and now..."

The doctor smiled. "C.S.O. Harrington is suffering from a mental illness. You shouldn't take any notice of what she said. I'm sure there's nothing to fear."

"But it's strange Loba would command that, right after Harrington said—"

"Navigator Lee, I'm surprised. I never thought you would be the type to question the master's orders. Perhaps you've been spending a little too much time around C.S.O Harrington."

Sparks's smile was gone. He was watching her. She had no choice but to leave. All concerns about her minor stomach complaint were gone from her mind. She did not want to go planetside, whether Harrington was right or not. She had to think of a way to avoid the order.

First, she headed in the direction of her cabin, but it occurred to her that Loba would send someone to look for her if she didn't show up at the shuttle bay, and then she would have no choice but to obey the order. Her heart raced. She needed to stop panicking and think. Turning on her heel, she headed toward a different part of the ship. She would have to find somewhere to hide. Her comm chirruped. Another message. *Navigator Lee, you are expected at the shuttle bay. Please report immediately.*

Her throat was tight. *Don't set a foot down there,* Harrington had said. Had Loba been taken over by an alien? Was he trying to get her infected too? It made sense. The navigator was essential to the ship's operation. Programming starjumps incorrectly could be disastrous. If the aliens wanted the *Galathea* under their control, they needed her.

She imagined another creature possessing her, and her skin crawled. She began to run. She had to find somewhere to get away from Loba...and Margret! Her odd behavior suddenly made sense. The geo-phys scientist had been taken over too, just as Harrington had said.

Sayen tried to think of a good hiding place. Where would no one think to look? She jogged along the corridors, attracting glances from the few crew members she passed. Her comm chirruped again. She didn't answer the call. Remembering the button held a tracker, she pulled it off and tossed it to the floor. That would delay them a bit.

Her pulse was racing. Flashbacks from her childhood ran through her mind. Memories of playing hide-and-seek in her large family home. Driven indoors by midday temperatures, she and her brother had been forced to play quietly to avoid bothering their parents, who both worked from home.

Three years older, her brother had always been better at hiding than her. She would spend hours wandering the house in frustrated searches. At the time, he'd been careful to never give away his secrets. It had taken years before he'd admitted he'd been hiding above doorways, perched with one foot on the open door and the other on the doorframe. He'd also hidden spread-eagled under covers to make the bed look empty.

She was panting now. Once her comm button was found, they would know she was on the run. Then they would put out a ship wide—

"Navigator Lee, report to the shuttle bay immediately, on pain of disciplinary action," came the ship's synthesized voice over the corridor intercom. "All crew members, please conduct a search for Navigator Lee and report her whereabouts to Master Loba directly."

Krat.

She was in a residential section of the ship. The corridor was empty for now, but her luck wouldn't hold for long. She had another childhood flashback. Her brother's best strategy, his last confession when their hide-and-seek days were long over, was that he'd never stayed in one place. He would move into areas she'd already searched, and the first hiding place he'd used was her own room.

Margret's cabin! Margret had been possessed. She would be out searching for her. Her cabin would be the last place she'd look.

FOURTEEN

Disabling Margret's door lock took a matter of moments. Polestar's on-ship security systems were cheap and easily circumvented by someone who, as a child, had delighted in taking apart any computer that strayed under her fingers. The door slid open, and Sayen went inside. Silently, the door closed behind her. Looking around the familiar room, Sayen thought of Margret, and wondered what the alien had done to her. Was she conscious of being possessed, but unable to do anything about it? She suddenly felt chilled.

It looked like Harrington wasn't mentally ill. She'd been right all along. Sayen wished she'd done more to support the security chief, but the woman had acted so angry and wild. If she'd stayed calm and explained properly, Sayen would have listened. Now that she'd gotten herself locked up in the brig, who was going to save them?

She sat on Margret's bunk and popped her knuckles as she considered what to do. Darn but that woman was messy. The bunk was unmade. She stood up and paced the cabin. It was only a matter of time before she was found. She had to do something to stop the possessed Loba, but did she have to act alone? Sayen recalled that the copilot, Lingiari, had come onto the bridge with

Harrington. He must have known what was going on, too. She had to find him, but she couldn't use the comm system. Her messages could be picked up and traced. What to do? She paced some more. She couldn't figure out how to find Lingiari without getting caught. Maybe Loba was already forcing him to fly to the planet.

There was a soft knock at the door. Her heart stopped. Had she been found, or was someone looking for Margret? But who would knock instead of using the door chime? She went to the viewer, and her stomach dropped when she saw who it was. The copilot. What the hell was he doing there? She thumbed the intercom. "Lingiari?" she whispered.

"Lee, open up."

She did as he asked, and, glancing from side to side, the copilot slipped into the room.

"What the hell are you doing here?" asked Sayen. "How did you find me?"

Lingiari reached up to the wall vent and pulled off the cover. A winged creature climbed out and walked up his arm and onto his shoulder, where it sat like a pirate captain's parrot. "This is my mate, Flux. I asked him to look for officers who had disobeyed Loba's order and were hiding out. He flies around the aeration system for exercise. Knows the ship like the back of his wing."

"But...you can't have an animal aboard ship," spluttered Sayen. "Especially not an alien animal. It's against regulations."

"Yeah, but it's no big deal, right? And, believe me, if it weren't for Flux here, the cockroach problem would be a lot worse. Isn't that right, mate?"

Flux waggled his ears in reply.

Sayen was flummoxed and a little alarmed by the presence of the alien, but they didn't have time to waste in further discussion about it. "What's happening, Lingiari? Loba was ordering me to go to the shuttle bay. Is he going planetside, and how come you aren't taking him?"

"I was supposed to be taking him. Him and everyone who was

ordered to the shuttle bay. We all got comm'd about the same time. It was me and the senior officers. Some of them went, but the rest had seen or heard about what Harrington'd said, and they wouldn't go. They were standing around outside their cabins in the officers' section, trying to figure out what to do. Where were you?"

"I got the same comm, but I was on the other side of the ship seeing Dr. Sparks."

"Lucky for you. Loba called in the defense units, or whatever's possessing him did. He must've figured it out after he saw Haggardy order them to take Harrington to the brig."

"He used defense units to round the officers up?"

"Pretty much. Nothing they could do. No one was armed. Caught them by surprise. I only got away because I had a bit of a head start, thanks to Harrington. I was out of sight of the rest when I heard the units running up and the officers shouting."

"This is a disaster," said Sayen. "Did anyone try to stop Loba?"

"As far as I could tell, he left it all to the units. He wasn't there, and anyway, it all happened too fast. You've seen them fellas. No one's going to try tackling a defense unit. It would only have taken a few of them to do the job."

"Where are the rest, do you think?"

"Waiting for Loba's orders, probably."

Sayen sat on Margret's bunk. She had a sudden, insane urge to tidy the cabin up and clean every inch of it. She put her head in her hands. This wasn't supposed to be happening. If she'd wanted a dangerous job, she would have joined the military. "What now?"

"Dunno, but I'm guessing the units got most of the senior officers to the shuttle bay, and since Loba doesn't know where I am, he's going to make Grantwise fly them planetside."

Resting her forehead on her fingertips, Sayen frowned. She looked up at the copilot. "What if we tell the rest of the crew what's happened? We could get control of the *Galathea* while Loba's planetside with the officers."

"It'll be hard. The officers got taken fast, when most of the crew was asleep. I don't know if anyone saw anything. We'd be asking them to commit mutiny just because of something we told them. Why should they believe us? No one's going to bang on Loba's door in the middle of the quiet shift to check he's there." The copilot sat next to Sayen. His pet was still sitting on his shoulder. Flux leaned across to Sayen's head and began to delicately inspect her hair, pulling it apart with his wing hooks.

The navigator twisted her head away from the animal's reach, grimacing. "Lingiari, tell your animal to leave me alone."

"Sorry," said Flux, "I was just checking for parasites."

"It can talk? Ough, I hate these modded animals." She scooted to the far end of the bunk. "And I *don't* have parasites."

"I'm not modded, and I'd appreciate it if you didn't talk about me like I'm not here." Flux climbed down from Lingiari's shoulder and slipped into a gap in his shirt, in an apparent sulk.

"Never mind, mate," the copilot murmured in the direction of his chest. "I know you mean well."

"Mutiny," Sayen said, as if it were the first time she'd heard the word. What a pair of mutineers they made. She, small and bookish; he, a lanky second-best pilot. But they were all they had. Or were they? "Hey, we're forgetting something. Loba's trip in the shuttle will give us some time. Maybe enough time to spring Harrington from the brig."

Lingiari's face brightened, but then he said, "How're we gonna do that? Security's tighter than a gnat's arse over there."

"You're forgetting some things. One, I'm an expert on the ship's computer."

"And what's the other thing?"

"Not thing, things."

FIFTEEN

Carl couldn't believe what he was about to do. It seemed impossible, but Lee had seemed convinced it would work, and it made sense, yet... He surveyed the defense units that remained on the ship, standing in a row in their storage room in the half-light. What if they ignored his command? Or worse, what if they attacked him? He was conscious of the soft warmth of Flux's body against his chest. He'd tried to persuade the animal to return to his cabin for safety, but he'd refused. There was no reasoning with him when he was in a sulk.

Carl took a breath. He could do this. "Defense units..." His voice petered out as the huge, identical heads turned to him with blank stares. The androids had always given him the willies. The only thing human about them, in his experience, was the way they looked. He'd always tried to avoid them as much as he could. "Defense units, arm yourselves...?" It was a simple request. A test to see if Lee was— He exhaled as the units' thick forearms opened and weapons slid into their hands. The navigator was right. They really would obey him in the absence of orders from a higher-ranking officer.

In a stronger tone, he continued, "Follow me to the brig." He waited, but the units didn't move. *Krat.* Had he said it wrong?

"Defense units, follow me to the brig." Still no reaction. Then he realized what was wrong. He was an idiot. He'd told them to follow him, but he wasn't going anywhere. They were waiting for him to leave. Carl went into the ship's corridor, watching the units as he walked. They immediately left the room and came up behind him.

He led the way, and the units followed in single file, exactly equidistant from each other, weapons held at an identical angle. After a short while, Carl grew bolder. "Units, double-time to the brig," he barked. He was forced to leap out of the way as they ran toward him, threatening to run him down. He sped after them as they drew away. So his *follow me* order had been superseded by the next order. Commanding the massive androids wasn't straightforward.

At the brig, the guards didn't seem to have noticed that Lee had remotely inactivated the locks when Carl and the defense units arrived. They must have been alerted by the thumps of the units' feet, however, for the two of them had run forward and were gripping their weapons and looking nervous as the units turned into the corridor. Carl stayed well back. He'd given the defense units their orders and was going to let them do their job without interference.

The guards' eyes widened and their mouths grew to Os at the sight of the towering androids bearing down on them. One froze entirely. The other snapped out of his trance long enough to lower his weapon, take aim, and fire at a unit. He hit it dead center, and the unit fell back, smoking from a hole in its chest. Carl winced. Harrington wasn't going to like that. Everyone knew how protective she was of them.

One shot was all the guard had time for before the rest were upon him and his partner. True to Carl's instructions, they were careful not to hurt them. Their weapons were for intimidation only. The units didn't even stun the guards, only disarmed and restrained them.

"Lingiari," said a guard as Carl approached. "What the hell are you doing?" A defense unit stood behind him, holding him in a bear hug. The guard's face was pink with exertion as he struggled to free himself.

"Sorry, but I've gotta get Harrington out," replied Carl. "An alien's controlling Loba, and it's trying to take over the ship. He's ordered the officers onto the shuttle and taken them planetside. We're going to stop them from docking when they get back, or something, I don't know. But we need Harrington."

"Krat," said the guard, ceasing his struggles. "That's news to me. I tell you what, order this misborn to let me go, and I'll help you."

"I don't know about that."

"Come on, man. Seriously, I thought there was something up. Harrington's been telling us all about it. She wouldn't stop going on about how Loba wasn't to be trusted. I didn't believe her. Sounded like BF, but if you're saying it too, I'm right with you. Come on. You're going to need all the crew you can get."

"Hmmm...okay," Carl said. He looked at the unit holding the guard. "Let him go." When the android didn't respond, he reframed his command. "AX..." he peered at the unit's breast-plate, "...5, let go of the man you're holding."

The minute he was free, the guard stooped to pick up his weapon and lifted the barrel to aim it at Carl. A blow from the fist of the unit who had been holding him struck the side of his head, and he fell to the floor unconscious.

"Err...thanks," said Carl. "AX5, could you—"

"Affirmative. I will restrain him, copilot Lingiari."

Carl left behind the units and guards at the brig entrance and slid the unlocked door into the wall. It was reinforced plexisteel, but useless against Navigator Lee's infiltration into the ship's control center. The copilot wondered where she'd gone to gain access to the computer. Inside the brig were four cells, two on either side of the corridor, large enough to hold twenty or so people. The walls between the cells and the corridor were checkerboards of opaque and transparent cubes. All the cells were empty but one.

Jas Harrington's face was pressed against a transparent cube, which distorted her nose somewhat. Carl thought she still looked great.

"Lingiari?"

"Call me Carl, hey?" he said in a rush of excitement and pride. This must be how it felt to be a hero. "Come out, Jas. It's open. Your door's unlocked. Lee's deactivated every lock in the place."

Harrington pushed the door and looked at it wonderingly as it opened. "I didn't hear a thing. How...?"

"Dunno. I'm just doing the grunt work. We had to get you out. Loba's got most of the officers on the shuttle, and he's taken them planetside."

The chief security officer's expression was grim as she stepped into the corridor and moved toward him. Carl half-lifted his arms toward her. Jas gave him a puzzled glance as she passed him on her way to the exit, saying, "What happened to the guards? And what's that lump in your shirt?"

Carl's arms dropped to his sides, disappointedly. He followed her. "Your defense units took the guards out."

Harrington spun to face him. "What? How come? What did you do?"

"Lee said they're programmed to obey the orders of the highest ranking officer. So I went and...what?" Harrington's expression was unnerving him.

"You commanded my units?"

"You say that like it's a bad thing. What did you want me to do? We had to get you out somehow."

"Did any of them get hurt?"

"One of them got...one of them got a bit singed."

Harrington ran the rest of the way to the entrance of the brig, where the defense units were still restraining the guards. The guard who had been knocked out was coming around. The unit was holding him upright. His head was slumped forward, but it lifted as Harrington approached. His eyes immediately sought his weapon, but it had been kicked well out of his reach.

"You'll regret this, Harrington," he said. "You never were mentally ill, were you? I know what this is. It's mutiny. But you won't get away with it. We'll hunt you down, and when we get back to Earth you're going to jail."

Ignoring the guard, Harrington went straight to the defense unit who had been hit. Carl followed her. The unit had retreated down the corridor and around a corner, and it was standing motionless, a wisp of smoke eddying up from its chest wound.

"Why are you always the one that gets hit? AX7, damage report."

"Grade 5 internal damage affecting temperature regulation, gross motor control, and energy distribution, C.S.O. Harrington. Injury repair initiated."

"Can you make it back to storage by yourself?"

"Affirmative, C.S.O. Harrington."

"Return and repair."

The defense unit obeyed. Harrington went back to the guards. "You're lucky I don't know which one of you shot my unit." She sighed and passed a hand over her eyes. "I know how this looks, but believe me, there's something on that planet that's got control of Loba. He isn't himself. I'm going to find out what it is and destroy it, and then we're getting out of here. If you've got any sense, you would avoid the master and the officers as best you can. And, whatever you do, don't go down to the planet, even if it means disobeying a direct order."

She addressed the units holding the guards. "AX5 and AX10, put these men in the brig, secure the doors, and return to storage. All other defense units, return to storage now. Let's go," she said to Lingiari.

After they were out of hearing range of the guards, she asked, "What are we going to do?"

"Me and Lee kinda hoped you would know," Carl replied.

Sixteen

First Mate Jack Haggardy rubbed his graying stubble. Around him, in the passenger cabin of the shuttle, sat most of the *Galathea's* officers. Eight defense units stood at the edges of the cabin, as many as the space accommodated. The rest of them had been left behind on the ship. The units were unseated, and their weapons were fixed on the officers. No one was speaking.

Haggardy certainly wasn't going to attract any attention. Not rocking the boat had been his MO for his entire career aboard prospecting ships, and it had served him well. Always following orders to the letter, no matter what, never gainsaying superior officers in public or private, never back-stabbing, being constantly congenial and easy to work with, and so on. He was no one's enemy, and everyone thought him their friend. Over time, Haggardy had risen steadily through the ranks.

It didn't bother him that he'd never made master. A master's bonuses were attractive but not worth the additional responsibility. First mate was as high as you could go while still being able to pass the buck when a mission was unsuccessful, or people died, or if there was a governmental inquiry into claiming a planet inhabited by an intelligent species. Making first mate but not master was, in Haggardy's opinion, a great success. The current mission was supposed to have been the final one before his retirement.

But this latest turn of events had put everything in jeopardy.

Judging from the looks on the other officers' faces, they were shocked and scared, but none of them seemed to be up to saying or doing anything. Haggardy was not going to be the first to resist. He'd seen people ruin their careers or even die that way. Let others take the risk. He had too much to lose.

Stealing a glance at Loba from the corners of his eyes, he noted that the man's face was expressionless. The geo-phys woman sitting next to the master looked the same. Though he hated to admit it, there was clearly more than a little truth to what Harrington had been harping on about. Physically, the master was unchanged, as far as Haggardy could tell, but his behavior was unfathomable. He'd offered no explanation for the trip to the planet, and his use of the defense units to force the officers to comply was barbaric.

So, Loba and the scientist were possessed by aliens. Haggardy had heard of stranger things in his long career. Reluctant though he was to act, if he didn't do something to save himself, he would end up the same.

If only he'd paid heed to Harrington's warning not to go to the planet. He'd been taken by surprise as he was relaxing in his cabin, and before he knew it, he was forced into the shuttle. But maybe the security officer had said something else that would help him. He frowned as he tried to remember her rant, which he hadn't paid much attention to at the time. She'd mentioned something about the structures on the surface. They had something to do with it. He had to try to avoid going into them.

"Haggardy," murmured Javek, the resource assessment chief, in the next seat. Haggardy could barely hear her. Her voice was so low, in fact, that he felt confident in ignoring her as if he hadn't heard her speak. But he couldn't possibly ignore the elbow Javek thrust in his side a few moments later. He stifled a grunt. Loba glanced in his direction, but he failed to locate the source of the noise. The master returned to staring ahead.

"This is madness," continued Javek. "What are you going to do?"

"I don't know what you mean."

"Don't be ridiculous. Loba's been infested by something, just like Harrington said. You have to do something about it. You're first mate, next in command. It's your responsibility."

"We must follow the master's orders. Failure to do so is cause for dismissal and—" He sucked in a breath as Loba turned and stared directly at him. Haggardy clamped his lips together.

He didn't speak again for the rest of the trip. His thoughts were focused on how to avoid entering the structures on the planet when they landed. Perhaps he could get away somehow while the others were forced in, but he couldn't think up a plan.

Touchdown was heavy. The shuttle bounced when it hit the ground, eliciting gasps and a few small screams from the terrified passengers. The ship's pilot, Grantwise, was clearly out of practice with small ships.

Loba commanded the officers to leave the vessel, and under the threatening weapons of the defense units, they silently obeyed. The scene was dreamlike. The officers knew they were going to a terrible fate, yet none of them seemed able to do anything to prevent it. Haggardy was reminded of a herd of cattle walking obediently to the slaughterhouse.

A keen, cold wind swept his long hair into his eyes as he reached the bottom of the shuttle's ramp. He brushed the hair away and saw that among the uneven scrub of the planet surface, one of the structures sat ominously near. If he was going to do something, it had to be soon.

It was another officer who broke first. Javek.

"Sir," she exclaimed, her cheeks flaming red. The master stopped. He was at the front of the line that had been threading its way slowly toward the structure. The defense units brought up the rear. For a moment, only Loba's back registered that he had heard. He turned, his expression inhuman. The master stared and did not speak.

Javek continued, "I must protest, sir. Bringing us all down to the planet in this manner is unacceptable. Why are we here? You must allow us to return to the ship immediately. If any harm comes to the *Galathea's* crew, the armed forces of Earth will respond. What...what are you?" She swallowed. "Your kind, whatever you are, whoever you are inhabiting our master and Stratton, you will not survive."

It was an empty threat, and Haggardy knew it. The officers looked fearful. Some were openly weeping. They were a long, long way from home, and the Global Government had little interest in the fates of prospecting crews. The employees took their chances and reaped their rewards or suffered the consequences of their deep space voyages.

Loba made no sound. He pulled a hand laser from his jacket. Javek backed away. The officers barely had time to scatter before he fired the weapon. Screaming, Javek fell. She crumpled to the ground and continued to cry out and writhe. Loba approached her. Was he going to finish her off? Haggardy was horrified and fascinated. But the master only inspected the injured officer. He spoke to a defense unit. "AX9, bring her."

The unit lifted the groaning Javek and put her over its shoulder. Loba's shot had scored a blackened line across the woman's right hip. Enough to incapacitate but not kill her. Haggardy guessed that Loba must want them alive.

His mind was working furiously. He had to think of an escape. He wondered if there was any residue of the master's original personality left behind. Could he appeal to the inner Loba? If he tried, maybe he would meet the same fate as Javek, who was being carried, sobbing, at the back of the line. In a few moments they would be at the structure.

Haggardy dropped back to the end of the line with Javek, acutely conscious of the weapons held by the units behind him.

He could do nothing now, but perhaps, once they were inside, his options might open up.

He'd read Harrington's reports thoroughly. As they entered the structure, the plain gray walls and lightless rooms were no surprise. No alien life or artifacts. Nothing. He wondered how the mechanism for alien infection worked. Were they already being taken over?

"Press your hands to the walls," Loba said.

Cowering before the defense units, which had followed them, most of the officers obeyed immediately. The unit carrying Javek lifted her hands and pushed them against the wall. Haggardy hesitated, but Loba pointed the laser gun at his temple. He had no choice but to touch the cool metal/crystal amalgam with his open, bare palms.

As Loba turned to check on the other officers, a young cadet swung violently around and knocked the master to the floor. His weapon fell from his hand. Another officer immediately pounced on it and fired at a defense unit. Another officer tackled Margret, but she brought a weapon up to his throat.

"Units, wound, don't kill," shouted Loba from his prone position. The cadet disappeared out of the door. Simultaneously, a unit fired on the officer who had picked up the master's weapon. The man shrieked as the laser beam severed his arm. Smoke and the scent of burnt flesh filled the enclosed space, and one or two officers gagged. Though the beam had partially cauterized the injured officer's wound, it steadily dripped blood. The man sank, gasping, to his knees. Loba plucked his weapon from the frozen fingers of the amputated limb.

Haggardy was loitering near the exit. He could see the cadet running back toward the shuttle, flinging dust from his heels. He would never make it. The defense units were too fast and accurate. Haggardy hesitated, then pointed at the young man. "Master," he said, "someone's getting away." His comment drew curses and exclamations of disbelief from the other officers.

Loba was out of the entrance in a trice. He instructed a

defense unit to disable the cadet. The unit fired, hitting his shoulder. The man fell, but was quickly up and running again, though more slowly.

"AX15, retrieve that human," Loba said.

The named unit set off after the cadet, and Haggardy and the officers watched. AX15 was closing the distance to the racing man easily, despite being twice his bulk. But the cadet had a good lead. If he made it to the shuttle and locked himself in before being caught…if he knew how to fly the shuttle back to the ship…Haggardy began to sweat. The news of what he'd done might be passed on to the wrong people. His fingernails bit into his palms as he willed the unit to run faster.

"Come on, Arkady," murmured a voice. Other officers echoed the words. At the range and from their viewpoint, it was difficult to tell how far apart the unit and cadet were, but it looked like the man might make it. "Come on, hurry, please," whispered a voice nearby.

The unit stopped. Haggardy held his breath. Had it given up? Had it received a counter-command radioed from the *Galathea*? It was drawing its weapon. It fired, and the beam hit Cadet Arkady square in his back. The officers cried out.

AX15 stumped over to the fallen cadet and lifted him up. The officers watched silently as the unit returned with the young man, cradling him in his arms like an oversized doll. When the unit was in hearing range, it said, "Minor order deviation, Master Loba. I stunned Cadet Arkady in order to retrieve him."

SEVENTEEN

Loba herded the officers into the next room and turned on a flashlight. He ordered the units to remain at the entrance. Two officers were told to drag the limp Arkady between them. The man was beginning to come around. Haggardy had no choice but to comply and go with the rest of them, but he'd made his switch of allegiance clear, and he hoped it would count for something. As Loba directed the officers through the next opening, and the next, Haggardy dropped back a little, slowing his pace until he was just in front of the master, who brought up the rear. Margret was leading the group.

"Sir," he said. Loba didn't acknowledge his words. "Is that what I should call you, sir?" When his question met no response, Haggardy decided to forge ahead, regardless of the dark glances the officers were throwing at him over their shoulders.

"As I understand it, you're taking us to be possessed by others of your kind. Am I correct? I wanted to tell you that for me, there's no need. I'm willing to come over to your side, as I showed you just now. I'm with you. And I can be useful. You'll need someone who understands how humans think and act. I can be your intermediary."

"Shut up, Haggardy," shouted a man. "Misborn coward."

The first mate made a mental note of the officer's name. He wouldn't forget it if they got out of this predicament unharmed.

"Sir," he continued, "I can give you information...data that doesn't exist in the ship's computer. Knowledge you can use. I..." Haggardy half-turned to look at Loba. The man's face was eerily underlit by the flashlight's glow. He wasn't even looking at him. He didn't seem to have heard a word Haggardy had said.

The first mate's hands began to tremble. Droplets of sweat appeared on his forehead, despite the freezer-like chill inside the structure. There was no point in appealing to whatever it was that possessed Loba. Haggardy's betrayal of the young cadet had been in vain. He silently cursed. After many successful years of appeasing those in authority, his methods were failing him.

Loba forced the officers deeper into the structure. Haggardy wondered if he was taking them to a special, central area that Harrington had failed to discover: a secret area, closed off from the rest. What might happen there, he did not want to dwell on. But now it was only Loba and Margret, and they had only two weapons. If Haggardy kept his wits about him, he might still survive.

The officers were becoming very cold. Javek was limping, and a man had her arm over his shoulders. The officer whose arm had been severed was staggering, dazed with pain. Haggardy diverted his mind from the others. He needed to concentrate. He was keeping a careful mental note of the turns they took and the number of rooms they passed through.

Haggardy had been born blind. He was a natural, and his blindness was just one of the many conditions modding would have prevented at conception, except that for his parents' generation, the process had been new and prohibitively expensive. So the young Haggardy had waited ten years for his parents to save up the money for the treatment to fix his sight problems. But the best cure available at the time couldn't undo all the effects of sightlessness during crucial stages of vision development. Haggardy had worn contacts all his life, something he never revealed to even his closest friends. At last, his childhood years of ridicule and shame might pay off. Though the memory of his blindness had lost its edge, he retained a measure of an ability to move around sightlessly.

They must have been a mile or more underground by then. Haggardy had figured out a pattern to the path they were taking. It was complex, comprised of fourteen steps, but the pattern had repeated three times, and he was sure he had it. If he could remember it, he might be able to make his way out in the dark and avoid the fate that Loba had in store for them.

"Stop," ordered the master. The officers must have worked something out in low whispers during their journey, for five or six of them turned and lunged at Loba. The ones at the front threw themselves on Margret. Haggardy stepped to one side, out of danger's way. Loba managed to kill three officers, but the flashlight fell to the floor, and from then onward, Haggardy saw nothing but dark, struggling shapes in the fight between Loba and Margret and the attacking officers. Everyone but the first mate joined in, adding new forms to the dark, writhing mass.

"Argh, my hand," shouted a voice. "I'm stuck to the floor." "I'm stuck too," called another. "I can't move." "Help," said a third. Officers were grunting in pain. "I can't let go of you." "Where's Arkady?" "I...argh...don't touch anyone. We're sticking to each other."

Shouts were turning to screams and shrieks. The beam from the flashlight shifted and rose. Loba had picked it up and turned it on the struggling officers.

"You...you monster. You freaks. What are you doing to us?" wailed a woman.

Loba played the flashlight around the room.

———

An hour or so later, Loba and the officers emerged from the entrance to the structure, where the defense units awaited them.

In single file, they marched to the shuttle. Haggardy was at the back of the line. After they had climbed up the ramp and into the passenger cabin, something that resembled the pilot, Grantwise, took the pilot's seat. The officers sat down and buckled their safety belts. The defense units surrounded them, but Loba didn't order them to train their weapons on the officers. Like the others, Haggardy sat looking forward, not speaking, his expression impassive.

Eighteen

Lee came jogging toward Jas and Lingiari as they left the area of the brig and headed for the bridge.

"Nice one, Navigator," said Lingiari as she approached.

"Stop," said Jas. "Wait a minute." She ran back to where the defense units were restraining the guards. She picked up the guards' weapons. "I think we'll be needing these." Returning to Lingiari and Lee, she held out one of the weapons for one of them to take while putting the other over her shoulder. They had no time to pay the armory a visit. Lee lifted her hands and eyebrows in alarm at the sight of the laser gun. Lingiari took it and peered at it. "I dunno how to—"

"Never mind," called Jas, running on. "Just point it like you mean it. I'll teach you later if I have to. I hope I don't. Come on."

"Shouldn't we bring the units with us?" asked Lee as she ran to catch up.

"Can't risk it," Jas answered. "If we meet a possessed officer who ranks higher than me, the units will follow their orders. They'll turn on us."

The bridge was on the other side of the ship. They would have to cross the entire thin upper deck that lay above the *Galathea's* massive engines. Though it would have been possible to house the crew cabins, the hold, sample storage areas, auditorium, mission room, cafeteria, bridge, and so on all in one area, such as at the front or back of the ship, Polestar Corp preferred spreading out the occupied areas in order to provide healthy exercise for the crew. Their shipbuilding budget didn't stretch to a gym. Jas could easily have done without the exercise right that minute.

"I don't get what we're supposed to do when we get there," panted Lee.

"When that shuttle returns," replied Jas, "it's most likely going to be full of officers possessed by aliens. If we let them aboard the ship, we're sunk. The crew won't be able to tell them apart from unaffected officers like us, and most of them probably aren't even aware of what's happened. I don't know what the aliens have in mind, but whatever it is, we aren't going to be able to stop them once they're aboard. The crew will do whatever they say."

"So, what are we going to do?" asked Lee.

"If we get onto the bridge, we can put out a ship-wide alert. We can explain what's happening. If we try to talk to the crew one by one, no one will believe us, so we'll download the security camera vids of the defense units forcing the officers onto the shuttle, and show them on all channels. The crew will be warned. And we can stop the shuttle from docking."

"How are we going to do that?" Lingiari asked. "Close the shuttle bay doors?"

"Yes. And if they start to breach them, we can use the *Galathea's* plasma cannons."

"What?" Lee stopped dead. Lingiari also drew to a halt.

"You're saying we should fire on the shuttle?" asked Lingiari.

"But twenty or more officers are aboard," said Lee. "They might be infected by aliens, but they're human, Harrington. They're our friends and co-workers. We can't just kill them."

Jas faced the two across the corridor. "I understand how you feel, and I don't like it any more than you do, but what's the alternative? If they get aboard ship, we can't capture and confine them. They have units with them, units I can't command with Loba there. It would be impossible, and we'd all end up dead."

When neither Lee nor Lingiari answered, she continued running toward the bridge. The navigator and pilot soon began to catch up to her. She wondered if they would stick with her to the finish, no matter what. Could they fire on their shipmates and friends?

"Wait a minute," exclaimed Lingiari, "why don't we starjump? The shuttle won't be able to reach the ship then."

"Of course," said Jas, slowing down. "If we leave now, when they get back, all they'll find is empty space. We can alert Polestar and explain to the crew what's happened in the safety of another star system. Great idea. You sure you can do it?"

"I'm a pilot, aren't I?"

It would take about half an hour to jog from the brig to the bridge, but there was plenty of time. Lingiari and Lee had broken her out of the brig around the time the shuttle had left. The round trip to the planet took hours, and Loba and the officers would be within the structure a long time too, according to Jas's observation of Loba's entrapment by Margret. As soon as Lingiari was in the pilot's seat, he could start prepping the starjump engine. Lee could find the nearest safe star system and input the coordinates. They could jump in two hours or less.

Jas's conscience was eased. They wouldn't be forced to sacrifice the officers in order to save the rest of the crew. Maybe there would be a way of rescuing the possessed men and women at some point, too.

At last, the three officers drew to a halt at the bridge door. Lee gripped her sides and drew in lungfuls of air as Jas outlined her plan. She would enter first and fire off stun shots to quickly subdue whoever Loba had left in charge. Lingiari would back her up. Jas showed him how to fire his weapon and set it to stun. She wasn't sure what opposition they would encounter once they were inside, but their chances were good.

"Let's go," she said, slapping her palm to the security scanner. It flashed red and an alarm sounded. *Krat.* Loba had primed the security system. On-ship guards would already be on their way.

"Let me try," said Lee, but the door didn't open, and the alarm continued to sound. Lingiari's palm brought the same response. The noise was deafening. "We've triggered a shut down," shouted Lee.

"Krat, krat, krat," exclaimed Jas. She'd been focusing on what to do once they were on the bridge, not on how to get through the door. The escape for them and the remaining crew was on the other side, but it might as well have been light years away. Unless…? "Step back," Jas yelled. She aimed her weapon at the control panel.

"No," exclaimed Lee, as Jas blasted it apart. The door remained closed. "You've sealed it."

"I didn't know," said Jas. "Well, how about…" She lifted the gun again and fired it square at the door. Paint blistered and oozed down, and the corridor filled with smoke. Lee and Lingiari stepped back. Soon, all three were coughing, and their eyes were watering. The metal beneath the paint turned black but was otherwise unaffected.

"Stop it," shouted Lee above the hum of the gun. "You're not gonna get through it that way, either."

"Why didn't you say something?" yelled Jas.

"I just did." She screamed and ducked as Jas swung her weapon toward her. The security officer fired off two shots, and cries of pain echoed from behind Lee. Two guards had appeared in the corridor, and Jas had shot them, leaving them unconscious.

"Watch out. More guards," said Lingiari. He was looking over Jas's shoulder. She turned and fired, blasting their weapons out of their hands.

"It's no good," said Lee. "We can't get in. We've got to leave."

Jas was forced to agree. "Where to?"

"This way," shouted the navigator, jumping over the unconscious guards.

"Where are we going?" asked Lingiari.

"The only place they'll never find us," replied Lee.

NINETEEN

"Isn't this kinda dangerous?" asked Carl as he, Harrington, and Lee climbed down a narrow ladder that led down into the bowels of the *Galathea* and its engine maintenance tunnels.

"Yes, it is," Lee replied. "If the ship starjumps while we're down here, we're fried."

The copilot paused mid-step. Flux must have also heard the navigator's words, because he squirmed against Carl's chest.

Lee was above him on the ladder and didn't notice he'd stopped. She stepped on his head with her booted foot. "Hey, people coming through here. You can't just stop. Get a move on."

Carl looked down at the ladder. It stretched below them until it disappeared into the gloom. He looked up toward the closed service hatch they'd left behind some time ago. The tunnel they were descending through would have held four or five Carls cross-ways, but it didn't feel nearly large enough. "I don't think this is such a good idea."

"Keep going, Lingiari," called Harrington from her position on the rungs above Lee. "We've got to get out of sight before the shuttle returns. If Loba or one of the possessed officers finds us, they'll blast us off the wall."

"But—"

"Move it," commanded Harrington.

Carl's jaw tensed as he put a foot and a hand down onto the next rungs, and the next, and the next. The chief of security was losing all her former allure. He wondered why he'd ever been attracted to her.

"Of course it's dangerous," continued Lee. "Starship engines aren't designed to provide living conditions for humans. But this is the only place we have a chance of hiding out. The service tunnels are like a labyrinth. They could search for days and never find us, especially if we split up and keep moving."

"But what if they jump while we're in here?" Carl asked.

"My guess is that Loba wants to get all the crew down to the planet and infected before he goes anywhere," said Harrington. "That's going to take a couple of days."

"Your *guess*?" asked Carl.

"I think she's right," said Lee. "Let's get going. I don't like it anymore than you do. These rungs are disgusting, but we're better off saving our breath for getting down this ladder."

Carl continued grimly climbing down the ladder. His muscles were aching with the exertion, but he forced them to move. Wet with sweat, his palms were in danger of slipping on the rungs. A chain of lights that were embedded in the walls blinked on as they went. When they had climbed down about another fifty meters, Lee told him to look for tunnels branching off to the sides.

He'd been keeping his gaze fixed firmly on the wall fifteen centimeters from his nose. Grimacing, he looked down to find the tunnels. The view swam before his eyes, and he gripped the rungs tighter. It was crazy. He was a pilot who was afraid of heights. He spotted the tunnels Lee had predicted, their dark entrances leading away from the main wall next to the ladder. "I can see them. We should've brought flashlights."

"No need," answered Lee. "The side tunnels are lined with the same motion-activated lights as this one, for the engineers.

Just don't take the first one you get to. Don't be obvious. Pick one farther down, and we'll go from there."

Carl did as Lee suggested and swung off the ladder into the fifth tunnel he saw. Bending his head to avoid hitting the tunnel roof, he moved in to make room for Lee and Harrington. He realized why starship engineers were always short. Carl shifted the weapon he'd been carrying across his back to the front. Flux seemed to have fallen asleep, creating a soft bulge where the copilot's shirt met his pants. Lee maneuvered herself off of the ladder, and a moment later, Harrington joined the two of them.

The tunnel walls were made of metal gridwork, unadorned. A simple panel at the entrance bore the number 8.7.1.

"We made it," said Carl.

Harrington sat beside him and immediately cursed. "I'm an idiot," she added. "What am I thinking? I've got to go back."

"What? No," said Lee. "Loba and the others will be back soon. You can't risk it. If they find you, you won't stand a chance."

"But the defense units," said Harrington.

Lee groaned and leaned on the tunnel wall. "You're right. Why didn't I think of it? We're dead."

"What's wrong?" asked Carl, though he had a pretty good idea. He just wanted to be wrong.

"All Loba has to do is send the defense units down here to find us," said Harrington, destroying Carl's false hope. "Fifteen relentless, unstoppable androids. They'll keep looking until they locate us, and we can't destroy them. If we manage to hit them, they'll just retreat until they've healed enough to carry on."

"Would they really hurt you, Harrington?" asked Carl. "After you've commanded them for so long?"

"They're just machines," replied the security officer, "or as good as. They don't care about me. They'll follow Loba's orders. No one outranks him. And he doesn't even need to be with them. He can command them through the ship's comm system."

"No, wait," said Lee, "that's not true. Not if I can get to them first."

Harrington shook her head. "You can't override the command hierarchy protocol. If you try to tamper with it, they'll shut down. But then, that might not be so bad. No one'll be able to command them then."

"I won't need to override the hierarchy protocol if I can disable their comm links."

Harrington's eyes widened. "So they'll only respond to voice control?"

"Voice control only. Wait, no, forget it. They'll self-repair, right? Then we'll be back to square one."

"They will self-repair, but not immediately. We should have a window of a few hours at least. Let's do it." Harrington began to walk, stooping, to the abyss at the end of the tunnel and grabbed the ladder rungs. Lee followed her.

"Hold up," said Carl. "I'm coming too." He put a hand down his shirt and pulled out Flux, who blinked sleepily.

"What the...?" said Harrington, looking back at him. "I wondered what it was you had down there."

"I'll introduce you later," Carl said. He spoke to Flux. "Gotta leave you here for a while, little fella. Wait for me, but if I don't come back, well, you know what to do." He put the creature down. Flux folded his wings and turned his back on the copilot in reply.

Carl's muscles ached just at the thought of climbing all the way back up into the ship, but he swung the strap of his weapon out of the way over his shoulder. "Right behind you."

―――――

By the time he emerged through the service hatch and into the bright light of the corridor, some time later, his muscles were screaming at him. It took a lot more effort to climb up the ladder than down it, as it turned out.

Even Harrington seemed to be feeling the strain. Sweat had soaked through her uniform in dark patches, and she was looking pale and drawn. And Lee was in worse shape. The navigator looked as though she could barely stand.

"This way," said Harrington, setting off at a lope. Lee staggered after her. Carl pulled his weapon around and pointed it forward. News of their exploits had probably gotten out, and the crew would be on the lookout for them. He followed the two women. The engine access point was in an unfamiliar part of the ship, and Carl hoped the defense unit storage wasn't too far away. He also hoped they had a long time before Loba returned.

Their luck was holding. The crew members they encountered backed away and ran at the sight of long-limbed Harrington bearing down on them, weapon at the ready. And it seemed that no one had thought of activating the defense units to capture them. Carl couldn't imagine Loba, even a possessed Loba, making such a mistake. He must have left behind only a few cadets on the bridge: terrified adolescents who were wondering what was going on.

When they reached the storage room, the defense units stood creepily in the half-light as they had when Carl had first commanded them. The scent of melted plastic from the unit the brig guard had shot tainted the air.

"All of them," exclaimed Harrington, turning on the light. "All fifteen are here. That means the shuttle must be back. We don't have much time before Loba figures out he can send them after us. All units, allow access to your CPUs. Lee, do your best."

A wide slot in the units' midriffs opened, but otherwise they didn't move. Lee was already at the nearest one, looking inside.

"How do you know how to do that?" Carl asked her, peering over her shoulder.

"I don't."

"What? Then how are you...?"

"We had android servants at home. I used to open them up and mess with them. Taught one of them to tap dance. I'm guessing defense unit CPUs are pretty much the same. I just need to find the receiving antenna and disable it. You keep watch with Harrington."

They'd left the door only slightly ajar. Harrington was peering out. Carl peeked over her shoulder, trying to get a view of the corridor.

Lee began humming last year's smash hit. It was the only noise for several minutes, except for Carl's heartbeat thumping in his ears. After what felt like a very long time, but was probably only a few moments, the navigator muttered a soft *Got it.*

"Give me your earring, Lingiari," said the navigator.

"Huh?" His hand went to the elongated platinum leaf he wore in his right ear.

"I need something sharp. Quick."

Carl pulled the jewelry free and passed it to Lee. He had a feeling it would be returned the worse for wear. Lee reached into the unit's midriff. A short screech of metal on metal made Carl wince. Lee moved to the next unit. A second later, there was another screech.

Then came the sound of approaching footsteps.

Twenty

"Hurry up, Lee," said Jas quietly. Officers had appeared at the far end of the corridor. They had the same gait and fixed look that she'd seen with Loba and Margret. She closed the unit storage room door to a slim crack.

"Two down. Thirteen to go," said the navigator.

Jas's finger hovered over the trigger of her weapon as the officers approached. Were they looking for her, or the other two? Had they only come to retrieve the defense units? Loba would probably want to use them to force some more reluctant crew members onto the shuttle. Or were the officers on their way somewhere else?

"Eight to go," said Lee.

Jas's breathing quickened. The officers weren't going to pass by. They were looking at the door, looking directly at her, if they'd known it. At the last possible second, she switched her weapon to stun and slipped the barrel through the door crack. She fired. The leading officer collapsed. The rest reacted, but slowly, too slowly. She had time to stun another two before the rest fled. These aliens were still getting used to operating in human bodies.

Jas turned to see what was happening inside the room. Lee moved to another unit and put her hand in its chest, holding something silver in her fingers. Now that the infected officers knew they were in the defense unit storage room, it would only be moments until one of them comm'ed Loba. As soon as he got the message, he would—

"Last one," said Lee, stepping to the final unit. Simultaneously, it lifted an arm. Lee shrieked and backed up. She didn't move fast enough. The unit grabbed her throat and lifted her up. Her hand was in its chest. She choked and turned imploring eyes to Jas. The unit would snap the navigator's neck like a twig before she had time to swing her gun around, Jas realized.

A beam pulsed from Lingiari's weapon, hitting first one of the unit's arms then the other. Plastic and flesh burned, filling the room with smoke. Lee was turning purple. Her toes barely touched the floor.

"AX3, release Navigator Lee," commanded Jas.

Its fingers opened marginally. Lee had disabled the unit's CPU so that it no longer received Loba's commands, and it was trying to obey Jas, but Lingiari's close-range shot had disabled it. The slight movement of the unit's fingers was enough for Lee to pull herself free of its grip. She slipped out and down until her feet were flat on the floor. She rubbed her throat. "I did them all," she croaked.

A shot hit the door. It swung open. The officers had returned.

"All units, defend us from the adversaries in the corridor," shouted Jas, and stepped out of the way as the fifteen androids pushed past her, their weapons sliding into their hands. "Stun only," she added.

The fighting automatons did their job with practiced ease. The alien-infected officers barely got a shot in before the defense units laid them low. One at the back stopped trying to fight and turned to run. A stun beam caught him, and he fell. In less than a minute, the fight was over.

Jas counted the unconscious bodies. Twelve officers. At least twelve members of the ship's command had been possessed by an alien force. There had to be more. Loba would have kept some with him on the bridge.

But she couldn't worry about that now. They had only a short time before the master knew the defense units weren't responding to his commands through the comm system. "We need to get out of here with these units, before Loba turns up to counter-command me."

Lee was still rubbing her throat. She shook her head. "I've had it, Harrington. I can't go much further, and I certainly can't climb down into the engine again. You two go without me. I'll only slow you down." Her eyes were bloodshot from being choked, and exhaustion lined her face. Lingiari didn't say anything, but he looked as if he was at the end of his strength too.

Come to think of it, Jas realized, she was exhausted herself. Yet they had a hard run ahead of them before they were safe. The sight of the waiting units gave her the answer. Something she'd been tempted to do for fun, but had never dared to do for fear of losing all dignity. "Can you hold on to something? Grip on tight?" she asked Lee. "Do you have strength for that?"

"Hold on to what?" asked the navigator.

Jas motioned to a defense unit with her eyes.

"You mean...? No. No way."

"Come with me," said Jas, taking Lee by the hand and dragging her over to AX12. "Climb aboard." She grabbed the woman under the armpits—now wasn't the time for decorum—and told her to jump. As she hoisted the petite woman onto the back of the unit, Lingiari got the idea. He went over to AX6 and motioned Jas away as she approached. He clambered up by himself. Jas leaped onto AX10's back and commanded the units to return with them to the engine access point.

The fifteen units lumbered off, the corridor vibrating with their movement. "All units, anyone you see, except me, Lee or Lingiari, stun them." Jas's voice wobbled from the motion of AX10.

If they could get away fast, and if no one saw where they

went, they had a chance, though she didn't know what their next step should be. They had to prevent Loba from taking the rest of the crew down to the planet somehow— "Wait, shuttle bay. All defense units to the shuttle bay."

With an abruptness that almost made her lose her grip, AX10 and the other units changed course.

"What are you doing, Harrington?" called Lee. "We can't go to the planet. We can't survive down there."

"We aren't going to the planet."

"What then?" asked the navigator, then her eyes widened. "Oh, I get it. Good idea."

"What?" Lingiari asked. "What are we going to do? Shouldn't we get back to the engine before Loba catches up with us?"

"We have to prevent him from getting the rest of the crew infected," said Jas.

"But how can we stop him?" asked Lingiari. "He only has to take them down to the surface, and he has his officer mates to help him now...Oh, no. Wait. No, no, no. We can't do that."

"We have to," replied Jas.

"There's gotta be another way."

"Sorry, Lingiari."

It was risky. It was crazily risky. But if they didn't act now, they would give Loba time to think it all out and get one step ahead of them. They had to do their worst while the ship was in disorder and the possessed officers were finding their feet.

The defense units could run faster than the fastest man. They brought the three humans to the shuttle bay within five minutes, encountering only a few crew members on the way. Most seemed to have fled the public areas.

Lingiari had gone very quiet during the journey, and Jas thought she saw tears in his eyes as they arrived at the shuttle bay. The bay was empty. They'd caught Loba out again. The copilot whimpered as Jas gave the order. "All defense units, fire on the shuttle, maximum power."

Blinding white light arched from the defense units' weapons.

Their arms were more powerful than the weapons available to the crew. They were charged by the units' inner power core. The shuttle hull glowed scarlet, then white. The metal popped, fizzed, then began to melt as the units' beams breached the outer hull and penetrated the interior. Jas had to duck below AX10's back to shield herself from the heat of the destruction.

"Units, cease fire," she shouted and looked out. Through the smoke, the shuttle was little more than a white-hot ruin. Loba wouldn't be flying anyone anywhere in that ever again.

"Defense units, kill your passengers," came a voice from behind them.

Jas whipped around. A group of alien-infested officers had come up while they were destroying the shuttle. She recognized the fourth engineer, chief steward, and two or three uncertificated mates.

"Units, stun the approaching officers," she said, and held her breath. The units turned and aimed their weapons, and she exhaled. The officer who had commanded them was lower ranking than her. The fight was brief and decisive, and Jas commanded the units to return to their previous course.

As they passed through the group of fallen officers, Jas gasped. The last of the bunch was Haggardy. So the first mate had been infected too. He could have countermanded her and prevented himself and the others from being stunned. He could have stopped their destruction of the shuttle. Didn't the alien infecting him understand the ranking protocols? Or was it still getting used to Haggardy's body? Why hadn't it spoken?

Twenty-One

The creature that looked like Loba reached out with its mind as it strode through the ship in the direction of the shuttle bay. It had arrived at the defense unit storage room too late. The human called Harrington and the ones who had disobeyed its order to go to the shuttle bay, Lingiari and Lee, they had taken the units. The creature could no longer communicate with them through the ship's system—a serious impediment to its plan. The defense equipment items were far superior in skill and strength than their human controllers. They had proven extremely useful, and the creature had anticipated using them for several more tasks in the suppression and replication of the remaining humans. But though the alien had made a grievous miscalculation in not accompanying the others to retrieve the units, the insurgent humans had made a worse one.

They had only made unconscious the others of its kind it had sent. They had not taken the opportunity to destroy them. Why this was so, the creature was not certain, but possibly the humans did not understand that they were only copies of the ones they had absorbed. Perhaps they imagined the dead humans lived on somewhere within the bodies they saw, and they had an attachment to them that prevented them from causing harm. If they were reluctant to damage the forms that the creature and the others had assumed, this would prove of great benefit.

The Loba creature was becoming aware of the minds of those it had left behind at the defense unit storage room. They were regaining consciousness. But it could detect nothing from the remaining ones that should be at the shuttle bay. It walked faster. It ran. The sensation of speed on the physical plane was dizzying and confused its senses. It reached out with its mind. Still nothing from the shuttle bay. Were those others unconscious? That could only mean one thing.

It had to protect the shuttle. The small ship was a precious item, and they needed it for transportation to the planet. Their numbers were not enough. They had to absorb and replicate more.

Signals from its olfactory organ. Knowledge from the copied Loba mind told the creature the signals indicated smoke. The smell of destruction. It was too late. It had failed again.

A second loss. Emotions flooded the creature. Anger. Fear. The humans who had destroyed the shuttle had guessed its intentions and subverted them. They knew what it wanted. It must locate the three humans responsible, and it must do so before they communicated their knowledge to the rest. It must end their lives as soon as possible. It would not wait to submit them to absorption and replication. They were too dangerous.

The odor of smoke grew stronger. In the corridor before the alien were the others it had sent to the shuttle bay, lying unconscious. It stepped through the bodies and made its way into the bay. The wreck of the shuttle sat at the center, its metal glowing, twisted, melted, scarred, scorched.

A beautiful artifact, destroyed beyond recognition. The Loba creature closed its eyes to shut out the sight of the ruin. The legs of the creature weakened. It found itself lying down. Their transportation to the planet was lost, but it was more than that. The shuttle was gone. Sorrow overwhelmed it. How could they do it? Humans were an evil species.

What should it do now? It had failed, failed, failed. It cast its mind wide, trying to contact and connect with the others of its kind, preparing itself for their censure. Separation was hard to bear.

Twenty-Two

Jas surveyed her two human companions and fifteen defense units, deep within the labyrinthine maintenance tunnels of the *Galathea's* engine, taking stock of the situation. Lee and Lingiari were slumped on the metal gridwork, while the defense units sat on their haunches, too tall to stand.

Of the three officers, she was the only one trained in combat, but they had the units, and they were fully armed. They also apparently had some kind of weird alien creature that Lingiari had smuggled aboard. Trust him. The animal—what did he call it? Flux?—was hanging upside down from the tunnel roof, the claws of its feet clinging to the metalwork, its wings folded over its head. Beneath the transparent wings, its eyes and little sharp-toothed mouth were closed.

"I can't believe we did it," said Lee.

"Me neither," said Lingiari, holding a fist for Lee to bump. He next moved his fist to Jas, but she looked away. They didn't have time for this.

"You were awesome," said Lee to the copilot. "If you hadn't shot that unit, I'd be dead."

"Thanks. You weren't so bad yourself."

"How did you get to be such a good shot? I thought pilots

only did basic combat training."

"Huh, it was pretty close range. Anyone could have done it, but I got a lot of practice when I was a kid growing up on the family farm. We had a rumpabug plague pretty bad. Used to take them out with a rifle while I was crop dusting, flying my dad's twin engine."

"What's a rumpabug?" asked Lee.

"You never heard of rumpabug? They were only the third worst alien infestation ever. We were overrun. You seriously never heard of them?"

"I was kind of sheltered as a child. All my parents cared about was—"

"How many officers went down to the planet with Loba?" Jas asked Lingiari.

"Err...nineteen or twenty."

"Is that counting Margret?"

"No," said the copilot.

That made at least twenty-two compromised crew members, including Loba and the geo-phys scientist, and about a hundred and eighty who couldn't be expected to do more than follow Loba's orders. While Jas, Lee, and Lingiari had two weapons, and the defense units with their inbuilt armory, the other side had the entire ship's arsenal. It was going to be a tough fight. Very tough. What was worse, they would be fighting their shipmates, their friends.

They had to act soon. It would be hard for Loba to find them now that they'd taken his best tools, but they couldn't last down there forever without water or food. They would be forced to steal supplies, and to do that they'd have to go out into the ship. The crew still didn't know exactly what was going on, and Loba would have them search the ship from top to bottom. Eventually, someone would figure out where they were hiding, and then Loba only had to post guards at each entrance hatch to the engine. Thirst and hunger would eventually force them out. Jas's eyes closed as she thought of a worse possibility.

"Geez, I'm bushed," said Lingiari. "I'm going to take a nap." He slid down the wall he was propped against and stretched out his lanky limbs.

"No, you can't," said Jas. "No time."

"Aw come on, Harrington. We've got to rest," said the copilot.

"Yes," said Lee. "If those units hadn't carried us down the ladders, I don't think I could have made it. We need to recuperate. I'm exhausted."

Jas tutted internally. This was why she preferred working with defense units. They never complained, and they never questioned orders. "Look," she said, an edge to her voice, "Loba probably has the entire crew looking for us right now. How long do you think it's going to take for them to realize where we must be? And what do you think he'll do when he knows we're here?"

A silence. Lee blanched. "Start the engines and starjump?"

"He might," replied Jas. "I'm not sure that he would, but it's a possibility. I think he's going to want to get the rest of the crew infected, which means sticking around this planet. But he could starjump and come right back. He has the math for at least the next two jumps in the computer, right?"

Lee nodded glumly.

"As long as the infected crew are a minority, he knows he's at risk of us convincing the rest about what's happened," continued Jas. "He knows we could gather the crew for a mutiny. The safest thing for him to do is to get everyone possessed as quickly as he can."

"But he can't now that we've destroyed the shuttle," said Lee.

"He can. The shuttle wasn't the only way of getting down to the planet."

"Of course," Lee said. "He could fly the ship down."

"Woah," said Lingiari. "Fly the *Galathea* through a planetary atmosphere? Deal with planetary gravity? Starships aren't made for it. RaptorX engines are only intended for orbit adjustment and interplanetary travel. Grantwise'll never do it."

"He'll try, that's my best guess," continued Jas. "But if he does that, we won't be in immediate danger. He'll just be burning rocket fuel, not starting the starjump engine. And the RaptorX engines are way astern of us. Loba'll have to force us out another way. He might turn off the lights."

"Can the defense units navigate in the dark?" asked Lee.

"Yes, it won't matter to them, but we're handicapped without light, and we need supplies. We can't stay here indefinitely. We have to do something, and it has to be soon, before Loba knows where we are."

"Okay," said Lingiari, sitting up. "What do we do?"

Jas bit her lip and looked from the navigator to the copilot. "We can't risk trying to talk to the crew to convince them about what's going on. Loba will have spun them a story to explain what's happened and pin the blame on us, and they're more likely to believe the master than someone who's been locked up in the brig, or either of you. Loba and the others don't look any different, after all. As soon as we go near any of the crew they're going to jump on us and ask questions later, or not at all. There's no other option. We have to take control of the ship."

"By ourselves?" Lee asked. "How the hell are we going to do that?"

That was the hard part. "To be honest, I don't know," replied Jas. "Look, I can't figure this out by myself. I need you two to help me. Lee, you knew about this place. Do you know the rest of the ship's layout as well?"

"I think so. Most of it."

"Is there an interface with the ship's system down here? Can you deactivate the bridge door from here, for instance?"

"There have to be system access points around here for the engineers, but they won't be any help. Loba ordered a security update, remember? We're all locked out of the system now."

"Krat, you're right. Well, we've just got to get onto the bridge and stop Loba from taking the ship down to the planet. The sooner the better. If he manages to get more of the crew infected, it's over. And we have to take out the rest of the officers."

"Wait a minute," said Lee. "What do you mean by 'take out'? You don't mean we're going to kill them?" She and Lingiari exchanged a look.

"I'm sorry, but if it comes to that, yes, we'll have to kill them." Not this again. Jas raised her voice over Lee and Lingiari's protests. "I made a mistake back there when we were retrieving the units. Stunning only lasts five minutes, and there are more than twenty of them. If we don't take them out permanently we'll never defeat them."

"Gee, Harrington," said Lingiari, shaking his head, "I don't know about that. I don't think I could—"

"They're possessed by aliens, and if we don't do something they're going to get the rest of the crew infected, and then they could return the ship to Earth so the aliens can overrun the whole planet, or spread across the entire galaxy."

Lee was frowning, and Lingiari still looked doubtful. "Couldn't we round them up? Put them in the brig?" suggested Lee. "Maybe Dr. Sparks has some idea how to—"

"Sparks is a useless gasbag," said Jas. "Do you think Loba's going to just stun us?" She closed her eyes and pressed her lips together. She tried taking a deep breath, but it was no good. She couldn't believe Lee and Lingiari were being so obtuse. Couldn't they see the danger everyone on the *Galathea* was in?

"We don't have time for this," she exclaimed before continuing, between her teeth, "We just don't have time. We need to mount a coordinated attack on Loba and the infected officers, now. Both of you have to lead a team of units. We have to move fast. Lee, where are all the exits from the service tunnels?"

The navigator stuttered a reply, adding, "There's no call for losing your temper, Harrington."

Maybe she was a little testy, but she couldn't help that. She couldn't afford to take people's feelings into account when it came to saving the crew. Why couldn't Lee or Lingiari see that?

Twenty-Three

Sayen's heart felt like it was going to jump right out of her chest. She gripped the ladder rungs tightly as she fought to control her rising fear. At least she didn't have to carry a gun. At least she wouldn't be forced to kill one of her shipmates —maybe someone she'd eaten dinner with, or sat next to on the bridge, or laughed at holos with on entertainment nights. But the six defense units clinging to the ladder above her, the ones she was supposed to command...Harrington had told her to instruct them to use lethal force if necessary. She wouldn't be killing anyone, but the units she was commanding might. She wasn't sure if that was different.

When she'd helped to break the security officer out of the brig, and when they'd taken the units, they had been acting fast, thinking only a step ahead. Standing on the ladder, waiting for the moment she was supposed to follow the units out into the ship, she had time to think about what might happen, and none of the possible scenarios gave her comfort.

Someone might end up dead. Maybe her. Or Loba might force her to be infected by an alien. She shuddered so hard she nearly lost her grip. Her sweaty palms made holding on difficult.

She dared not look down to the gloomy depths of the tunnel below her.

What wouldn't she give to be in her neat, clean cabin right then. She was filthy, and her skin crawled at the thought of all the germs that must be on her skin.

It couldn't be much longer until the time they'd agreed they would exit the tunnels. Were they doing the right thing? She wished she'd had time to think it through, to talk it out with both of the others, but the security officer had been insistent that this was the only way. Harrington was scary when she was angry, and Sayen didn't have the guts to stand up to her. Neither did Lingiari.

That was the worst of it. What if there was a better way? What if there was a way they could avoid killing the infected officers, but she just hadn't had time to think of it? If only she could talk to Lingiari. They could team up and persuade Harrington to call the attack off, to reconsider. But she had removed her comm hours—seemingly days—ago, and the copilot had done the same.

Her muscles were so sore, and she was thirsty and hungry. She wondered—

The lights went out. Sayen froze. The crew must have searched the ship. Loba must have guessed where they were. A clang came from above, and a square of light appeared in the darkness. This was it. The defense units had been told that if the lights went out, they were to begin the attack immediately. A defense unit above passed through the hatch it had opened, momentarily plunging them back into darkness.

Sayen had no choice but to follow.

She emerged from the hatch. The units were moving fast, and she struggled to keep up as they pounded away from her. The sound of firing came from in front. Loba must have sent guards to intercept them.

How were Harrington and Lingiari faring? Had they even made it out?

The shooting stopped. Sayen raced to catch up to the units. She had to be near them so they could hear her orders. The heels of the last unit were disappearing around a corner. As Sayen turned the same corners she halted abruptly. Two shipmates lay on their backs in the corridor. One was missing the top of her head. The other had a gaping hole in his chest. She recognized them both. They were infected officers, not crew, but still she felt like she was going to vomit.

The pounding of the defense units' feet broke her distraction. They were getting away. She began to sprint. The sounds of more firing came from ahead.

Harrington had given her the easiest of the three attack routes, in view of the fact that she had no weapon to defend herself with. The security officer had speculated that Loba and his officers would either congregate on the bridge, the mission room, or the auditorium, where he could address the crew. They were to attack all three.

She'd been allocated the task of assaulting the mission room, where Loba could access all the files on planets on their schedule and auxiliary files about Earth. Not only was the mission room the attack site closest to the engine access hatch, it was also the smallest of the three rooms and likely to contain the fewest hostile crew members.

Aside from the two infected officers the defense units had killed, the corridors were empty. Either Loba had gathered the crew in the auditorium, or they'd been ordered to stay in their cabins. Sayen was grateful for it.

She was running as fast as she could, but hadn't had enough time to rest and recover. She was much too slow, and the defense units had drawn far away from her. Out of sight. She should have asked one of them to carry her, but she couldn't help that now. She rounded another corner. There it was: the mission room. But there was no sight nor sound of the units. The door was open, but from the angle of her approach, she couldn't see inside. Was it possible the units had gone the wrong way? No, that was ridiculous. Had Loba left the room unguarded? Had she lucked out and there was no one inside?

She drew to a stop just outside, where she had a slim view of the interior. The view told her nothing. Only the walls were visible to her. It was no good. She was going to have to put her head around the door.

She was gasping loudly in the silence. If anyone was in there, they were sure to hear her, to know someone was there. They must have heard her running up, too.

Holding her breath, Sayen shot her head forward. At an equal speed, she drew it back, just in time. A laser bolt came through the door exactly where her head had been and burned the wall on the opposite side of the corridor. The sound of more firing burst from the room, accompanied by screams and cries. Sayen stood with her back to the wall, splayed against it. More cries, shots, thumps of bodies hitting the floor. She thought she recognized some of the voices. One was the third mate, she was sure of it.

Silence. An awful stink came from the room, which Sayen suspected was the smell of burned human flesh. She was sickened. Footsteps. Someone was walking to the door. She should run. She had to run, or they would kill her. But her legs wouldn't move. She mentally screamed at her limbs, but it was as if they belonged to another body. There was nothing she could do. She was going to die.

Sayen closed her eyes as the footsteps reached the door. She didn't want to see which of her former colleagues was going to kill her.

But the fatal shot didn't come.

"Navigator Lee, the room is secure."

Sayen opened her eyes. A defense unit was standing before her, its large form blocking out the overhead lights. She peeled herself from the wall and peeked into the room.

Four officers lay dead. One defense unit was down, its silicon/organic brain exposed in its helmet. Four units had their weapons trained on the third mate, who was on his knees with his hands in the air.

"Shoot her, kill her," exclaimed the man. When the units didn't respond, he said, "Defense units, kill Navigator Lee."

"We are unable to comply," said a unit. "Navigator and third mate rank equally. We must follow Regulation 723g of Defense Unit Lethal Behavior Protocols: *When an officer threatens the life of an officer of equal rank, the officer whose life is threatened assumes supersedence.* When you observed Navigator Lee at the door and tried to shoot her, her command immediately superseded your own. Navigator Lee's order was to secure this room with the use of lethal force if necessary."

The four units that were pointing their weapons at the third mate raised them to fire.

"Units, no. Don't shoot," said Sayen. "Don't shoot him."

The third mate's gaze rested on the navigator. Something was wrong about the way he looked at her. There was nothing behind his eyes. Nothing at all. The hairs along her spine rose.

The sound of running footsteps came from the corridor. Sayen tensed. Harrington? But why would she come here? They were supposed to rendezvous at Margret's cabin. Could it be Lingiari?

It was neither. Master Akabe Loba appeared in the doorway, panting. He pointed a trembling finger at Sayen. "Units, kill that officer."

Twenty-Four

Carl wondered how he'd gotten into his current position, staring into the massive soles of a defense unit on the ladder above him. Harrington's order to kill the infested humans if necessary didn't seem right. And who was she to boss them around? His opinion of the security officer had changed. He'd always found her quick temper kind of exciting, but it wasn't so attractive when it was directed at him.

He would have been better off with Margret. Poor Margret. What if she attacked him? He didn't think he could kill her. Or any of the others for that matter. Even Loba, though—

Flux wriggled against his chest, adjusting his position in Carl's shirt. The animal had insisted that he came along too. His fur tickled, but apart from that the copilot was glad to have him. He'd adopted the little fella—or rather he'd chosen to come live with Carl, as he put it—when Carl was a kid. Flux had flown into his open cockpit while he was out dusting crops one day, giving him quite a fright. The animal had never said where he was from, only that he was taking a long holiday on Earth while 'things cooled down' on his home planet. When he arrived in Carl's cockpit his accent had been British, so he must have spent some time with the Poms, but over the years Flux had acquired Carl's Strine.

"You sure about this, mate?" Carl asked the lump in his shirt.

"Yeah, you're not leaving me behind this time, you dumb..." Flux swore. He could swear like a space marine and wasn't slow to share his opinion. Luckily, he was also prone to long sulks, when he refused to speak. Something that came in handy if Carl had a new girlfriend around.

The lights went out, which meant Loba knew where they were. From above came the sound of a hatch clanging open. The defense units began to make their way out.

Carl swiftly climbed the ladder on the tail of the units, hoping Harrington had reached her exit before Loba cut the lights. The engine maintenance hatch she was taking was right on the other side of the ship, near the bridge. He didn't know what her plan was to get onto the deck, considering they'd failed at that before. His target was the auditorium, where Loba or another officer might have gathered the crew.

In a few moments, Carl was through the hatch, out into the corridor, and hard on the heels of the units. The units had shot two crew members. *Krat.* They weren't even infected officers. Loba had already drafted some of the crew into his schemes. Carl's fingers tightened on his weapon as he sprinted after the units. He saw no one as he ran. He hoped the rest of the crew would act smart and stay the hell out of the way.

Flux was climbing out of his shirt, and Carl winced as the creature's claws tugged his chest hair.

"What are you doing?" he asked.

"I'm gonna help, aren't I?" replied Flux. He scrambled onto Carl's shoulder and leaped off, taking to the air. The animal could fly faster than Carl or even the units could run, and he soon disappeared from view.

Carl sprinted to keep up with the pounding pace of the units, adrenaline cutting through his exhaustion. The auditorium was near. He turned a corner. The units had disappeared from view. They were in the auditorium. Carl heard screams and shouts and the sound of many people moving around. Harrington had guessed right. The crew was in there. Flux came flying out of the room and straight at Carl.

"Run," he shouted as he passed overhead. "You got first prize. Loba's in there."

Carl didn't need telling twice. He skidded to a halt and reversed direction before belting away. Harrington had been crystal clear: if they encountered Loba, they had to get out of there fast. Loba would turn the defense units from their best allies to their worst enemies. The voice of the master came from behind, shouting, "Units, kill Lingiari." Loba must have stepped out of the auditorium in time to catch a glimpse of Carl running away.

But the copilot was gone, racing down the corridor. He didn't stand a chance against seven defense units. He could never outrun them, and as soon as they got a visual on him, he'd be dead. He had to find somewhere to hide.

Where? The doors to either side of the corridor were closed and he couldn't waste even a split second trying to open any of them. He wanted to call out to Flux, to see if the animal had a suggestion, but he had no breath to spare, and his little mate was out of sight. Probably just as well. It looked like it was game over for Carl. The adrenaline that had lent him speed couldn't push his exhausted muscles much farther.

A pale brown shape fluttered briefly into view from a side corridor before disappearing again, leaving the words, "This way, mate," hanging in the air. *You beaut.* Carl squeezed one last effort from his painful legs and put on an extra spurt, slipping down the corridor just as he heard the units enter the one he'd left.

To his right was an open door and a beckoning hand. It shot out and grabbed his arm, and Carl stumbled into the room. The door clicked closed as pounding feet approached in the main corridor. The copilot had collapsed on the floor. A man helped him sit up. He held his knees and sat gasping, unable to speak for several moments. Finally, he managed, "Thanks...?"

"Alef, geo-phys," said the waiting man. He held out his hand

and pulled Carl to his feet. "I've been watching out for you guys, hoping I could help. I was going into the main corridor to bring you here when your little friend happened to fly by. He told me to stay where I was and that he'd get you."

Carl clasped Alef's hand once more. "Lucky you did. Much too dangerous for you out there. Thanks, you old… " He swore.

Alef's eyebrows rose.

"Sorry, I was talking to Flux." The animal was hanging from the ceiling and grooming his belly fur. Carl added, "You said you're geo-phys, like Margret?"

"That's right. I'd been hoping someone would…"

Carl held up a finger to silence him. The sound of the units' footsteps had faded, which meant Carl might have a chance at a bigger prize. He went to the door and opened it the slimmest crack. He put his eye to the opening. It was not long before he saw Loba stride past in the main corridor following in the path of the defense units, probably trying to catch up to them so that he could control them with voice commands. Carl mouthed the master's name to Alef, opened the door wide and motioned for him to come closer.

The geo-phys scientist nodded his understanding. As one, the men ran out and after the master. They tackled him from behind. Alef grabbed him round his thighs, sending him toppling to the floor. Carl landed with his knees on the man's back, forcing the air from his lungs. Alef reached for the weapon the master had strapped to his hips, pulled it out and flung it down the corridor.

Carl wasn't a trained fighter, but he'd seen enough hand-to-hand combat in video games to last him a lifetime. He got Loba in a chokehold to stop him from speaking. If he called back the defense units, it would be all over for them. Together, they dragged the struggling man into Alef's room.

When Alef let go of Loba's legs to close the door, the master took his chance and kicked him in the head, sending him crashing into the wall. With a great wrench, Loba broke free. He ran to the door and bellowed, "Defense units, return to—" His words were cut short as Carl rammed into him, sending him through the door and into the corridor wall. The master's head made contact face first with a crack, and blood streamed from his mouth and nose as he staggered to his feet.

Loba turned and sucked in a breath to shout again, but Carl punched him in the jaw. He reeled back.

A shout came from the end of the corridor. The second mate had followed Loba. He was pointing a gun at Carl, who immediately grabbed Loba and shielded himself with the master's body.

The second mate advanced, and Carl backed up, dragging the struggling Loba with him, one hand clamped like a vice over his mouth. If only he had a weapon...but of course, he did have one. All this time, he'd been carrying the weapon Harrington had taken from the guard at the brig. He'd strapped it across his back. But if he wanted to grab it, he would have to loosen his grip on the master.

The two parties moved slowly down the corridor, the second mate advancing on the pilot and master. The officer passed Alef's room, and the geo-phys scientist crept out and picked up the gun he'd taken from Loba. He lifted and aimed it at the second mate. "Drop it."

Spinning to face the threat behind him, the second mate fired. At almost the same moment, Alef returned fire. Both Alef and the second mate fell, and the moment's distraction this caused Carl was all it took for Loba to free himself. He didn't waste time by fighting the copilot, but took off down the corridor, shouting for the defense units.

Carl cursed and ran to Alef. The second mate had winged him, but he was still alive. The officer who had shot him hadn't fared so well.

"I'm all right. Go after Loba," said Alef.

There was nothing Carl could do but follow the master and try to capture or kill him. He just hoped the defense units' great speed had taken them far beyond the reach of his voice. If no one had ordered them to do anything different, they would still be searching for Carl. He pulled forward the weapon that hung across his back and set off.

He didn't have to go far to catch up to Loba. Only a couple of corridors away was the mission room. Loba was standing at the entrance. He was pointing inside. As the words, "Units, kill that officer," left his lips, Carl shot him.

Twenty-Five

The lights went out. *Krat.* "Defense units, go, go, go," shouted Jas, even as the unit at the top of the ladder opened the hatch and vaulted into the corridor. Above her, the rest of the units poured through the hatch in turn. She raced up the ladder. Laser fire from above told her that guards had been posted.

Jas leaped out and barreled down the corridor. It was a ten-minute walk to the bridge. The units would be there in two. A door opened to her right. The medical center. Sparks looked out.

"Get inside and barricade yourself in," called Jas over her shoulder as she flew past. She wondered what the doctor thought of her mental state now. The units were getting away. She sprinted, her weapon flying behind her on its strap.

Her only hope was that the high-power lasers of the defense units would burn through the reinforced bridge door. If they got through and onto the deck, she stood a good chance of gaining control of the ship. If they couldn't get access to the flight controls, it wouldn't matter if they took out Loba and every other infected officer.

The sound of weapon fire came from up ahead. The units must have reached their destination or encountered resistance on the way. Jas tried to ignore the guilt that arose at the thought that the units might be killing shipmates. None of this was the crew's fault. But if she was going to save the rest of them, it had to be done.

Something hard and heavy struck the back of her head. The floor of the corridor rose up toward her face, and the next thing she knew, she was on her front, nose pressed to tile. Someone was holding her wrists. She forced her arms apart and tried to get up. The strap of her weapon caught on her neck as someone removed it.

"She's coming round," said a voice.

Jas struggled to turn onto her back, but a knee was thrust into the space between her shoulder blades, and an adult's full weight pressed down on her. She could barely breathe.

"Let me go," she gasped.

Strong hands grabbed her wrists once more.

"Keep still, or I'll melt your brains," said another voice. It was the man kneeling on her back. She could see the feet and lower legs of other crew members standing around. From down the corridor came the sound of more firing. The defense units were in a pitched battle, and she wasn't there to command them. Without her order to withdraw, they would fight to gain access to the bridge until they were put out of action, maybe permanently.

"He was right, wasn't he?" said a voice to her right. "He said she might come down this way. Smart guy, that Loba."

"Let me up, you idiots," croaked Jas. "It isn't the master who told you to capture me. He's been taken over by an alien. Most of the senior officers are possessed."

"Bf. You're the one who's been possessed," said the man holding her down. "And he didn't tell us to capture you. He said to shoot you on sight. Only some of us were a bit queasy about that, so it's thanks to our kind hearts you're still alive. But you keep struggling and that can soon change."

"Krat." For a moment, Jas relaxed her muscles. The man's

knee ground harder. If he didn't get off her soon she would pass out. "Okay," she gasped. "I won't struggle."

"What's that she's saying?" asked her captor.

"I dunno." Someone's head lowered near hers.

The world was turning black. "I give up," whispered Jas.

"Says she gives up," repeated a voice.

"That's more like it," said the man. Mercifully, the pressure on Jas's chest lifted.

"Is it okay if I get up?" she asked when she could speak again. Anger at her captors had begun to boil inside her. Just a short distance away, her defense units were engaged in battle, and they didn't have her guidance.

"All right. Just move slowly."

Jas turned over, and soon she was sitting with her legs drawn up, facing the crew who had ambushed her. There were four of them. Two male, two female. All had weapons. One was also holding hers. They were looking pleased with themselves, especially the one who'd been kneeling on her back. He had a particularly annoying grin on his face. He was the biggest and strongest of the four. Slowly, she got to her feet.

"You're not in the brig yet," the man said. "You better watch your moves. If you try anything, I might decide to follow Loba's order to the letter."

"I don't know what the master's told you," said Jas, "but, really, it isn't me who's been taken over by something, it's him."

"Well you would say that, wouldn't you?" said the man.

"I know I can't prove it to you, but...do you know he took the senior officers down to the planet? Have you ever heard of that happening before? I don't know how long you've been working aboard prospecting ships, but that literally never happens. If something were to go wrong and all the officers were planetside, can you imagine the danger we might all be in? It's totally against regulations."

"We destroyed the shuttle to stop Loba from taking the rest of you down and getting you infected by aliens too. We were trying to save you." An edge had crept in Jas's voice. If these fools didn't let her go soon, her only chance to get onto the bridge would be gone.

"Ha, that's where you're wrong," said the man. "It was Loba who destroyed the shuttle, to stop *you* from taking us down there."

"Wait a minute, Karrev," said the other man. "He only told us that. It could have been them, like she says. He seemed pretty mad about it. How do we know who did it? No one saw. And I heard a rumor that the officers were away during the quiet shift."

"No, he's the master," countered Karrev. "How would he get infected by an alien? He'd never be so stupid as to put himself in danger. She's the one whose job it is to go down there. She's the one at risk from aliens."

Jas's fury boiled over. "Don't be so stupid. Of course Loba could've put himself in danger. The man's a myth addict. Everyone knows it. He's unstable, unpredictable, and incompetent. He did go down. He was persuaded to, and now he's possessed. You have to let me go so I can save your sorry asses."

The man's brow furrowed "Maybe you're right and you haven't been infected by an alien. Maybe you just want command of the ship, and all this talk about the master being possessed is a trick to get us to commit mutiny." He pointed the gun between her eyes. "The brig, now, or say goodbye. You choose."

Jas's shoulders sagged, and she took a step toward the man. Interpreting her movement as acquiescence, his eyes flicked triumphantly to his friends. At that instant, Jas lunged forward and under his weapon, forcing him against the wall. The laser gun fired and scorched a line across the ceiling. The man's companions stepped back in alarm. Jas grabbed his arm and wrist and twisted them so his weapon was pointing at his face. Her forearm was across his throat, and she held him immobile, his gun centimeters from his nose.

The man gave a cry and thrashed his legs, kicking Jas's shins. She didn't blink. With her full weight and strength on him, he was helpless. After a few moment's struggle, while his shipmates stood frozen in indecision, the man released his weapon. It slipped from his fingers, and Jas grabbed it as it fell. She stepped back and fixed the barrel on the man. "Go," she shouted to the crew. "Drop your guns, and go. That way. Run, or I'll blow his kratting head off."

With only a second's hesitation, the remaining man and both women took off in the direction Jas had indicated.

"Don't...don't," said the man, his gaze on the barrel's end in his face.

"Of course I'm not going to hurt you. If you'd just listened to me, it wouldn't have come to this." The sounds of the battle for the bridge had ended several moments before. Jas had to find out what had happened. She scooped up her weapon from the floor, set the man's gun to stun, shot him, and was on her way before his body hit the floor.

Twenty-Six

A familiar smell assaulted Jas's nostrils and alerted her to the outcome of the battle for the bridge before she reached her destination. Laser fire on defense units fried their organic, plastic, silicon, and metal parts, creating a unique odor: part refuse dump fire, part barbecue. As always, it made Jas nauseous.

Swallowing the increased saliva in her mouth, she stopped. Judging by the reek drifting down the corridor, and the fact that none of the units had come to find her and give a combat report, she concluded that they'd failed to gain access to the bridge. Loba must have concentrated his defenses there, protecting the *Galathea's* flight controls and Grantwise. If that was the case, her guess that he would try to land the *Galathea* on K. 67092d was probably correct. The aliens could then take over the rest of the crew, but if Lingiari was right and landing a starship on a planet was nearly impossible, they were going to crash and everyone, infected and uninfected, would die.

She crept forward, a gun in each hand. All was silent. At each corner, she stopped and peered cautiously around. A short distance from her goal, she spotted an infected officer. She was armed

Jas withdrew quietly. She could shoot and kill or stun the officer easily, but what would be the point? If the defense units couldn't get onto the bridge, she didn't stand a chance by herself. It was no good. Time to retreat and regroup. Turning, she ran softly away and figured out the fastest route to the planned rendezvous point, hoping that, even though she had failed, Lee and Lingiari might have succeeded, hoping they were still alive.

What she found at Margret's cabin surpassed her expectations. On the floor was a bound and gagged Loba. The copilot was sitting on him.

"We ordered our defense units to return to the maintenance tunnels," said Lee, "in case he got free."

"Good thinking," said Jas. She squatted down next to the prone Loba. His eyes were bloodshot. He looked furious, but the gag kept his thoughts silent. With him as a hostage, maybe their prospects weren't so bleak after all. "What about the crew?"

"They scattered like gene dealers in a raid," said Lingiari.

The copilot and navigator briefly told her what had happened. "I nearly died," said Lee. "I had everything under control, then Loba turned up. He told the defense units to kill me. I thought I'd had it, but they didn't obey. I don't know why. Then Lingiari shot him."

The master didn't seem injured. "You stunned him?" Jas asked the copilot.

"Yeah, I know what you said," replied Lingiari, "about how stunning them wasn't enough, but..." He shrugged.

"It's okay," said Jas. "I get it. And it might have worked in our favor this time."

"How come the units didn't follow his order to shoot me?" asked Lee.

"Did he preface his command?" Jas asked in return. "Remember what I said? If you don't address them first, they won't do as you say. I can't imagine the kind of trouble we'd be in if they did whatever someone around them said."

"Yeah," said the copilot, "like, bugger me sideways."

The two women looked at him.

"It's just a joke."

"This isn't the time for joking, Lingiari," said Jas.

"I'm pretty sure he did address them first," said Lee, "but he said, *kill that officer*. They probably didn't know who he meant. The third mate was there, too. So they didn't fire. Lucky me. But what are we going to do with him? Take him into the engine with us? I don't know how we'll get him down a ladder tied up like this."

Loba gave a great wrench and tried to squirm out from under the copilot. Lingiari grabbed the man's white curls and pushed his face into the floor. "Better cut that out, mate."

"We can't take him down into the engine service tunnels," said Jas. "We can't let him anywhere near the defense units, and we don't have time for a long-term strategy. I couldn't get onto the bridge, but we have to, and soon. We have to get Grantwise away from those controls."

"Is there an autopilot?" asked Lee. "Could he activate it and lock it even if we get onto the bridge?"

"Yeah, there's an autopilot, but you can't lock it in to land on a planet. That's the last thing you'd want to do in an emergency," Lingiari replied. "That's not the problem. Look, to pass pilot training you've gotta land the simulator ship as if you were landing on Earth, just once, using the RaptorX engines. Took me twelve tries, and I was one of the better ones. That planet below us isn't Earth, and while Grantwise might stand a chance of landing on it without crashing on a good day, I can't speak for that thing inhabiting him."

"That decides it," said Jas, standing up. "Come on. Bring Loba. We're going to the bridge."

"What's the plan?" asked Lee as they pulled the master to his feet.

Lingiari grabbed one of Loba's arms and pointed the muzzle of his weapon at his head. Jas held her weapon to the other side as she also grabbed an arm. "Simple," said the security officer. "If they don't let us onto the bridge, we kill him." Loba struggled as they half-pushed, half-dragged him out of the cabin.

"But what if they don't care?" asked Lee.

"You think they won't care if we kill him?" asked Jas. "But he's their..." Her words dried as she realized what the navigator meant.

"Loba's our master, doesn't mean he's theirs," said Lee. "We don't know what status the creature inside him has. He might be a nothing. Or they might not pay individuals any mind. The aliens could be a community species, and he's only one unimportant individual."

"Krat," said Jas. "For someone who's terrified of aliens, you sure know a lot about them."

"That's *because* I'm terrified of them. Know your enemy."

Lee had made a good point. Jas was assuming the aliens would act like humans. Mistake number one in the starship security officer manual. How could she have been so dumb? Maybe it was because she was used to aliens that looked like aliens. "Do you have a better plan?"

"No, I was just pointing out the problem," said the navigator.

"Gee, thanks."

Loba was struggling like a wildcat as they dragged him along. He tripped and fell, landing on his knees. Jas found grappling him to his feet while holding onto her weapon to be a struggle. Lingiari was doing his best to help, but he was also holding a weapon in one of his hands. Before she knew it, the master had slipped from their grasp and managed a few steps. It was several moments before Jas and the copilot could get him under control again. The thing inhabiting Loba certainly seemed to fear what would happen when they got to the bridge. Maybe Lee was right and the rest of them would let her fry his head. If that happened, she, Lee, and Lingiari were toast too.

Jas took comfort in the cool, smooth feel of the weapon in her hand. If the worst came to the worst, she would get as many of them as she could before she went down.

They were nearly at the bridge. "Hey," she shouted. "Hey, whatever you are, we've got Loba, our master, so we've got whichever one of you that's inside him. And we'll kill him if you fire."

"Maybe," Lee piped up, "maybe I should stay back? In case...you know?" The navigator suddenly looked very small to Jas, and more than a little frightened.

"She's right," said Lingiari, "in case we don't get out of this, and even if we do, one of us should stay out of it. Someone has to send a packet to Earth to tell them what's happening. We have to try to break through the security."

It was another thing Jas hadn't thought of. Everything was piling up on her. "Yeah. Lee, go and try to get into the comm system. We can buy you some time to get around Loba's security blackout. If you can, send a packet to Polestar and tell them everything that's happened. What am I talking about? Tell the Global Government. They have to know, or else the *Galathea* could turn up and infect the whole planet."

"Right," said Lee with undisguised relief. "Good luck," she called over her shoulder as she moved in the direction they'd come from.

"And hide," shouted Jas, after a moment's thought. "Pretend you're a techie...or something." But the navigator was gone. She didn't know if Lee had heard her.

TWENTY-SEVEN

Hauling the struggling Loba to the bridge was hard, even with Harrington's help. Carl had always admired her strength and fitness, and now he appreciated them even more. The master was heavier than he looked, and fought to free himself so strongly that Carl suspected he knew the other aliens wouldn't do a thing to save him. The master was also shouting, but his gag muffled the words.

As they got close to the bridge, they passed signs of a viciously fought battle. The walls, ceiling and floor were melted, pitted and scarred, and the infrastructure of the ship showed through. A horrible stench hung in the air.

"Ready?" asked Harrington, her expression pained.

"As I'll ever be," Carl replied. He grunted as they dragged the master over the holes and beams that were all that remained of the corridor floor. His feet trailed, bumping against metal ridges. They were nearly there. Had the infected officers heard Harrington's warning? Would they pay any attention? If he and the security officer were going to die, it was now.

Five possessed officers were blocking the corridor. They eyed the two of them and the bound and gagged Loba.

"Stand up," said Harrington, pushing the muzzle of her

weapon roughly into the master's temple. His eyes hooded, the man grudgingly supported his own weight and stood. He averted his head from the watching officers.

"We know he's one of you," said Harrington. When none of the officers answered, she added, "And if we kill him, the one of you that's inside him will die."

Still the master and officers were silent. "You're thinking we won't kill him because he's the ship's master, right?" Carl asked. "You're wrong. The man's an arsehole, and we don't give a shit." He pointed his gun at Loba's foot and fired. The man screamed and fell to his knees, grabbing his wounded foot. Blood seeped through his fingers.

"Gee, Lingiari," whispered Harrington.

"Start talking," said Carl, "or I'll shoot higher."

"What do you want?" asked an officer. The words sounded a little strange, poorly formed, as if the man wasn't used to speaking.

"Let us on the bridge, now, or he dies." Harrington grabbed Loba's arm and hauled him, whimpering, to his feet. The master favored his uninjured foot and leaned against Carl.

The officers didn't reply or move. Carl wondered if they were speaking telepathically. Loba hung his head and closed his eyes. Was he begging for his life?

Carl sneaked a glance at Harrington. Her profile was set, fearless. He suddenly wished he'd had a chance to get to know her better. There had to be another side to this tough, cranky woman. He hoped they would get through this.

Still no one said anything. What if the stalemate continued? They didn't have a plan for this scenario. Harrington shot him a look, but he couldn't read her expression.

At last, the officers broke. "Give him to us," one said, "and we will allow you to enter the bridge."

These aliens had a low opinion of human intelligence. "We're not stupid," said Carl, and he aimed his gun at the master's other foot. Loba tried to move it out of Carl's sight, but this meant he had to put his weight onto his injured foot, and he partially collapsed.

"Time's up," said Harrington, and moved her finger to her weapon's trigger. Loba's eyes became wide. He yelled through his gag and wriggled violently. Carl had to dig his fingers into the man's bicep to maintain his grip.

"We will allow you onto the bridge," said the officer. "You do not need to give us your master." The other officers stepped away, clearing the path along the corridor. Their weapons dropped to their sides.

"Stay back," said Harrington. She pulled Loba forward, and Carl helped her drag the man through the waiting officers. He turned and pointed his weapon behind them as they passed, while Harrington kept hers trained on Loba's head.

"Think they'll let us in?" Carl asked the security officer softly.

"We'll soon find out."

The aliens must have been communicating telepathically, because the bridge door opened as they approached. The large room was empty but for one man. Grantwise, or rather, alien-infested Grantwise, sat at the ship's controls. The visual screen was up, and the planet surface was zooming up, the horizon flattening even as they watched. He was already taking the ship down.

"Krat." Dropping Loba, Carl ran to the intercom and thumped the button with the flat of his hand. An alarm blared out, and the ship's lights began to flash. "Crew to crash seats, now," he shouted into the intercom. "This isn't a drill. This is not a drill. Crash seats immediately. Everyone."

Harrington had dragged Loba to the flight controls. She was trying to pull the pilot out of his seat while not losing her grip on the master. She couldn't do it. Loba wrenched himself out of her grasp and tried to escape, but as soon as he put his weight on his injured foot, he collapsed. He got to his feet, but Carl ran at him. He threw his shoulder into Loba, sending the master flying. Carl was on him. The two men grappled.

Infested officers poured into the room. Carl tried to bring his weapon round to fire at them, but Loba punched him in the head, and his shots went wide. The master landed another punch, spinning Carl around and knocking him nearly senseless. Everything seemed to slow down. As he turned, he saw Harrington struggling with Grantwise. She lifted her gun to his head. She was going to kill him. *Krat.* Then there wouldn't be anyone at the controls. What was she thinking?

Carl felt like he was floating. That was some punch Loba packed. Then Carl realized he really *was* floating. He was hanging in midair, halfway to the ceiling. Everyone was floating. The officers were spinning lazily, their hair trailing. Even Grantwise was lifting out of his seat. Harrington's expression was so surprised, Carl almost laughed.

What must have happened came to Carl in a flash. Confused by the increasing pull of the planet's gravity, the *Galathea's* gravity drive had cut out. But the ship was falling so fast their descent was matching the attraction of the planet's mass, canceling out the force's effect. Falling. They were dropping like a stone. The ship wasn't flying through the atmosphere, cruising to land. Whatever the hell Grantwise had done, the ship was out of control and they were going to crash.

Harrington hooked her feet under the flight control desk. She grabbed the pilot by the scruff of his neck, pulled him out of his seat and pushed him away.

Carl tried to move toward the controls, but ended up swimming comically in the air, not making any progress. He needed something to push against. Craning behind him, he saw Loba, who was grabbing for a weapon that was floating just out of his reach. Droplets of blood were gliding from his foot wound.

Two birds with one stone. Carl gave the master a mighty shove with his feet, sending the man spiralling out of the vicinity of the gun and himself closer to the flight controls. Harrington gripped the control desk with both hands and swung her body round so that her feet were toward him. No need for an explanation. He reached for her ankle and hauled himself hand over hand along her body until he was in reach of the desk.

A deep, searing pain ran up his leg. A shot had grazed his thigh. *Drongos.* If they didn't let him try to land the ship, they would all die. A series of hums sounded beside him as Harrington returned fire. He folded himself into the seat and slotted his legs under the desk. After putting his arms through the harness, he snapped the buckles closed. He was still floating a few centimeters above his seat, but he could concentrate on his task.

The horizon was a flat line. The next minute would be a killer.

Twenty-Eight

Jas had one job: protect Lingiari. The loss of gravity had taken everyone by surprise, but now Loba and the officers were becoming accustomed to the weightlessness. Though she'd shoved him away as hard as she could, Grantwise was still the nearest of them. He floated only a couple of meters away from the flight control desk. Jas pointed her weapon at him. The man stopped reaching to get a grip on something, but from the corner of her eye she saw the other officers were taking advantage of her focus on the pilot. They were edging closer. She swung her weapon round.

One of her feet was hooked through the back of the pilot's seat, where Lingiari floated against the straps of his safety harness. He was furiously swiping the pilot's interface, bringing up fast-flowing figures. He began keying in numbers and dragging his fingers across the screen, altering levels. The visual on the planet surface told her there was only the remotest chance they would make it.

A shadow to her left. Grantwise had managed to lock a finger on the pilot's seat. Without even thinking about it, she fired at the hand, severing it at the wrist. The pilot floated away, blood flowing from his stump, a look of disbelief on his face. His hand remained hooked by its pinky finger on the seat. The pilot's blood had sprayed the back of Lingiari's neck, but he didn't seem to notice.

"Come on," he muttered, glancing at the visual. "Come on, girl."

Jas swept the remaining officers with her gun. Grantwise's experience had dampened their enthusiasm about attacking. Or maybe they'd realized that the copilot was their only chance of survival. Everyone needed him to succeed now. The officers hung in the air, watching.

"What's happening, Lingiari?"

"Working on it."

"Have we had it?"

The copilot didn't answer. They were going to die. There was no way Lingiari could pull the starship out of its dive. It was impossible. This was it.

Jas gazed at the alien-infested officers. She wondered what they were saying to each other in their heads. Were they wishing they'd done things differently? Did they regret inhabiting the foreign species that had come to their planet?

Did she have any regrets? She'd always thought things might end something like this, given the nature of her job. At least the loss of her life wouldn't break anyone's heart. She had no parents or siblings who would never see her again, no child who would lose its mother. Was there anything she would have done differently? She recalled Lee's comment about her temper. Maybe the woman had a point. Maybe if she hadn't gotten angry that day in the mission room, if she'd taken the time to talk to the other officers privately and gotten their support, none of this would have happened. If she'd done things differently, Margret, Loba, and the rest of the officers might not have got possessed. Or Haggardy. What had happened to him? She hadn't figured that out.

Maybe this was all her fault.

A hand gripped her calf. Reflexively, she pointed her gun down, only to realize the hand belonged to Lingiari.

"I've done all I can." He was shouting, though the bridge of the *Galathea* was eerily quiet. It was strange how they could be traveling so fast yet so silently.

"We're gonna crash," Lingiari said. He was pulling her down into the copilot's seat. In the visual ahead, the scrubby landscape of K. 67092d flew up dizzyingly fast.

"I've leveled her off the best I can. Full reverse thrust." Lingiari was still shouting for some reason.

Jas was fumbling with the buckles of her harness. "Can starships—" she said as they hit.

Twenty-Nine

Carl could never remember much of what happened when the *Galathea* crashed on K. 67092d. The hull of the deep space vessel protected those inside from the sound of it sweeping through kilometers of soil, rocks, and vegetation, cutting a swathe along the planet's surface. He vaguely recalled the flight control visual showing the landscape flowing past like a runaway express train before the connection was destroyed and the screen went blank. After that, there was only the terrible juddering that made him feel as though his teeth were being shaken out of his head and his bones shattered.

With more than a hundred meters of engine lying between them and the ground, Carl dreaded to think what the juddering meant in terms of the prospect of the engines ever working again and allowing them to leave the planet.

Grantwise, Loba, and the other infected officers had dropped to the floor like stones when the *Galathea* had hit, and the one point two Earth gravity of the planet had become suddenly and terribly present. Carl kept his gaze averted from them while the ship was grinding to a halt. There was nothing he could do anyway.

After what seemed like forever, the shaking stopped. Carl realized his eyes were closed. He opened them. The main lights were out. Emergency lighting had come on, making the bridge look like something from a low-grade horror movie. Only the monsters looked human, and they were lying in contorted positions around the deck, not moving.

He hardly dared to look toward the copilot's seat, but after a moment's hesitation, he stole a glance. He exhaled. Harrington was alive, though her expression was drawn and, if it weren't for the dull red lighting, he was sure she would be as white as a ghost. She returned his look and seemed glad that he'd made it too. She gave him a weak smile. In his memory, it was the first time he'd ever seen her do that. He liked the effect.

"Good job, Lingiari," the security officer said.

"How're you doing? Break anything?"

Harrington unclipped her harness and moved her arm and legs, rotating her wrists and ankles. "I think I'm okay. How about you?"

"Still alive, so no complaints." He risked another look at the bodies around them. "Can't say the same for those poor buggers."

Grantwise must have been head down when the *Galathea* had impacted the planet surface. Blood mixed with brain matter oozed from his shattered skull. Loba was on his back, his eyes open and blank, his mouth gaping and bloody. Half a severed tongue lay next to him. The rest of the officers were also visibly, graphically dead.

Vomit forced its way into Carl's mouth, and he turned his head to let it out. When his stomach was finally empty and he could retch no more, he collapsed back into his seat and closed his eyes. The rustle of clothing to his side told him Harrington was getting up. He should, too. They had to check on the crew and find out who needed their help. He unclipped his harness and pulled himself to his feet. He took another look at Grantwise. He'd always envied the man. His job, his status, his distinction, and popularity were all that Carl had wanted. It was funny that now that *he* was the pilot, the only pilot on board, he found he didn't care anymore. And he was sure Grantwise would have given it all up to be able to live.

The shuttle was gone and the *Galathea* was unlikely to fly again. Now, their lives would be a matter of survival until they could be rescued. Status, distinction and popularity—none of them would count for anything.

Harrington was already at the ship's comm center. Carl joined her. She was pressing the panel, but it stayed dark. She spoke into the mic. "Ship's crew, ship's crew?" No sound of her words came from the corridor outside. The comm system was down. "Looks like we're operating on face-to-face comm," she said.

"Figures," said Carl. "That was some crash landing. We'll have to see what else it took out. Let's have a look around."

They went first to the medical center. There would be injuries, no doubt, and they needed to know how well Sparks was set up to deal with them, assuming he'd survived.

The door was closed but not locked. They slid it open, pushing it into its recess. Dr. Sparks had obeyed Carl's instruction to get into his crash seat, and he hadn't left it. The man was trembling, and the whites of his eyes showed. It was only after repeated assurances that he was safe that he undid his harness and rose from the seat. Harrington told him to check his equipment and find out what was still working. She also told him to ready his first aid supplies, because they would no doubt be sending him some casualties soon.

The man said barely a word in reply. As they left him, he was counting the same bandages over and over again.

A few people wandered the corridors, dazed. The crew members were beginning to venture from their cabins. Sounds of groaning and crying were coming from some rooms. Carl and Harrington located the injured personnel to see what they could do to help. Most of the traumas the crew had suffered weren't severe. The copilot and security officer matched up healthy crew with those in need of medical treatment, and instructed them to take the injured along to Sparks and give him what support they could. Some of the crew were on this already.

They came across several dead infected officers, including Margret and the second mate, whom Alef had shot. They were in the personal cabin area, checking each room. Carl was pondering how they were going to get down the side of the ship to the planet surface, and if they even *wanted* to get to the planet surface, when a thought struck him with horror. He hadn't seen Flux. He didn't know if the little fella had survived the crash.

He dashed into a cabin. It was empty. Leaping onto a chair, he pulled the covering off an air vent and shouted his friend's name into the aperture.

"I forgot about your pet," said Harrington.

"He's not a pet," replied Carl before shouting the name again. He waited. No familiar rustling of wings was coming from the shaft. He waited some more. Carl stepped down from the chair and ran a hand through his hair. Where might Flux have gone? Had he heard Carl's warning? Had he been able to get somewhere safe before the ship had crashed?

"Try not to worry," said Harrington. "He seemed pretty tough to me. Come on. I'll help you find him."

"Thanks, but I dunno where to look. He can fit in places people can't. He could be anywhere."

"Well, where's his favorite place? Maybe he went there."

Carl frowned, then his face brightened. "I know." He ran from the cabin, and arrived at his own room in record time. Though it was his own, it looked unfamiliar. He could hardly believe he'd last been in it less than a day ago. "Flux?" he called into empty air. There was no answer. *Krat.* He noticed the covers on his bunk were lumpy. One of the lumps was Flux-sized. Could it be him? Under Carl's covers was the animal's favorite place to sleep. If it was him, why wasn't he answering?

"Could you..." he said to Harrington, pointing at the bunk, "could you check there for me?"

The security officer went over and gently lifted the Polestar blanket. The pale brown creature was lying in the middle of the bunk, wrapped in his wings, taking up the best spot, as was his habit. His eyes were closed. A wave of despair welled up in Carl's chest. He put a hand over his face and turned away.

"Hold on, I think he's asleep," said Harrington. "Look, he's breathing."

Carl leapt to the bunk and gently picked up the animal. His wings unfolded, and his eyes opened. He gave a great yawn. "Flux, you..." Carl cursed at his buddy.

"Woah, calm down you...," Flux swore at Carl in return. "I was only taking a nap." He climbed onto Carl's shoulder and began grooming himself.

Harrington also swore. "Lingiari, there's someone else we're forgetting. Where's Lee?"

Carl's eyes widened. "You're right. Where would she be? Where haven't we looked?"

"I told her to send Earth a packet. She could do that from any comm access point, but she would have been trying to hide from the infected officers. I don't think she would have gone to her own cabin."

"I know. Maybe she went back to our rendezvous point," said Carl.

The two of them ran to Margret's cabin. Carl's guess had been correct. The navigator was there. But she was on the floor by Margret's bunk. In her concern to send a message packet to Earth, she hadn't sat in the cabin's crash seat in time. She was on her back. Her eyes were closed, and her face was peaceful. She looked as though she were sleeping, but when Harrington listened to her chest, she couldn't hear a heartbeat.

Thirty

The ship was falling. Things were going badly wrong. It was ever thus on the physical plain. The same problem plagued them once they left the void. Now that they were inhabiting individual bodies, they could no longer meld and flow into and through each other, and they began to differ.

The alien had not been identified by the humans, and it needed to remain hidden. Soon, it might be the only one of its kind left aboard the starship. The one who had replaced the commander of the space vessel had failed. It had made errors of judgment, underestimating the resourcefulness of the humans called Harrington, Lingiari, and Lee, and allowing them to take control of the equipment items used for attack and defense. It was also due to the failed one's incompetency that the humans had destroyed the shuttlecraft, the best method of transportation to the planetary traps.

Error upon error compiled. The commander replacement deserved to die, yet it had begged for its life. Foolish. Already, it had lost its understanding that they were all one. Its ending did not matter if they succeeded in their aim. One life signified nothing. And the others...the others had agreed to save it! They had identified their own individuality within the threatened one. They had empathized. Madness.

Its arguments had gone unheard. The others had decided to risk everything to save one, an insignificance, as they all were when compared to the whole.

Before they left the void, the steps were laid out clearly: replication, generation, domination. Nothing else mattered. Its kind were not like the species of the physical realm. It pitied their separation. It did not wish to become like them. The others had adopted this insanity, but it would not. It would hold true to the plan.

Its advantage was that it had not acted with the others. The humans did not know it for what it was. For the time being, it could safely move among them, unrecognized. If the others did not succeed—and according to the thoughts it could read as they fought the humans at the ship's controls, it looked as though they would not—it could continue to work toward its goal, undiscovered.

If the others were destroyed, it would survive as the last replicant. Only one was needed to move onto the next step. Let the humans kill its fellows. Seduced by the egoism of individuality, they were useless already. They did not deserve to return to the void and reunite. They would bring only contamination and perversion.

Only let it survive this terrible fall to the entrapment planet, and it would hold true to the goal of its kind. They would dominate this solid world. They would control all its inhabitants and bend them to their will. They would have everything they wanted. All they needed was another world on which to open their traps. These humans were wise to their ways, but on a new planet, they would find fresh bodies to absorb and replicate.

It must stay silent and safe, and all would be well in time.

A voice came over the intercom: "Crew to crash seats, now. This isn't a drill. This is not a drill. Crash seats immediately. Everyone."

It slipped into a seat in the cabin and fastened its safety belt.

THIRTY-ONE

"Grab her legs," said Jas, lifting the navigator's shoulders.

"But, I thought she's..." said Lingiari.

"She's not dead," shouted Jas. "She's not dead until she's warm and dead. Let's see if that misborn doctor can do his job."

The copilot's features clouded. "I get what you mean, but do really think she'd want that? Here? When there's no hope...?"

"I'm not asking you, Lingiari. It's an order. Help me carry her or damn me but I'll drag her there by myself."

The copilot lifted the limp Lee's legs, and the two of them ran with her, carrying the navigator between them like a hunting kill.

At the medical center, Sparks was surrounded by injured crew and uninjured crew members who were trying to help him. The place was in chaos. It was a chaos that Jas cleared with a bellowed order for everyone to get out of their way. The crowd cleaved, creating a path to the beleaguered doctor, who was talking to a patient with a bloody, gashed knee who was sitting on his examining couch. The patient hobbled out of the way at the sight of Jas and Lingiari carrying the fatally hurt navigator. They laid her down gently.

The doctor stiffened at the sight of Jas, and quickly hunched over Lee. He held a stethoscope to her heart, shone a torch into her eyes, and rubbed his knuckles against her chest. Jas watched like a hawk. When his brief examination was complete, Sparks looked at the floor and shook his head.

"No. We can put her in stasis," said Jas.

"I'm afraid it's too late for that," replied the doctor. "She's been oxygen-deprived for too long. I could operate, but her brain has been irreparably damaged."

"No, it isn't too late. People who have been dead longer than her have been brought back. Put her on life support, now, and we'll start up the stasis bank."

"But—"

Jas leaned toward the doctor until their noses almost touched. "Life support. Now," she breathed.

As if touched by a cattle prod, Sparks leapt into action, calling for help to move Lee.

The security officer and Lingiari went next door to the stasis room. Like the rest of the ship, only emergency lighting illuminated it. Jas went immediately to one of four small, square doors set in the metal wall and pressed the screen next to it. It remained black.

"Harrington," said Lingiari. Jas ignored him and tried another panel, which also failed to light up. "Harrington." She tried a third panel with the same result. "H—"

"WHAT?" Jas turned on the copilot, rage threatening to overwhelm her.

The man shook his head. "Never mind."

Jas breathed deeply in and out. "Sorry. I'm sorry I shouted. I overreacted. I'm trying to get a handle on that. What did you want to say?"

"The stasis containers aren't working because we're on emergency power. Preserving what's left of the dead isn't a priority on a stricken ship. I'm sorry, Harrington, but Lee's had it."

Jas gazed into the man's eyes as she tried to comprehend what he was saying. He was right, but his words didn't fit with what she wanted to hear, with what she needed to hear. Though the last twenty-four hours had been harrowing, she felt like she'd developed a bond with this man and with the woman lying all but dead in the medical center, a bond that was closer than she'd ever been to another human being but one.

For a moment, for a split second, Jas nearly let down the adamantine facade she'd built up to protect herself from the vulnerability of human companionship. She nearly fell into Lingiari's arms and sobbed. Then the moment was gone. She wasn't prepared to lose anyone ever again. She would not let that happen. "The units," she exclaimed. "The defense units. We can use their power to keep Lee in stasis."

The copilot's eyes widened. "Do you think?"

"We have to try, Lingiari. Come on."

———

Locating the defense units took longer than Jas liked, and several of them—the ones who had tried to force entry to the bridge— were still too damaged to be of any use, but eventually they had four of the remaining ones jerry-rigged up to the stasis unit.

Jas and Lingiari watched as Sparks placed Lee in the stasis container. A couple of hours on life support had lent the navigator a deceptively healthy color, and it was difficult to believe, watching her chest rise and fall as the machine breathed for her, that she was essentially dead. Jas's hope was that enough of her mind had survived, and that, when they finally made it back to Earth, even if the rest of her brain was useless, the cloners could grow her another body in which to transfer the personality, experiences, and memories that comprised Navigator Lee.

There might have been some murmurs of resentment among the crew that the defense units, their most valuable assets, were being devoted to the probably hopeless endeavor to preserve the mind of a single crew member, but Jas chose not to hear them. And so far, no one had stepped forward to question her authority.

Several hours later, a thorough survey of the ship had revealed many facts. Fresh water still flowed through the pipes, though no one knew for how long, and there was no air movement from the vents, not even a breath. This meant that the ship's air wasn't being recycled, filtered, or replenished with oxygen. Though it would take weeks for the loss to be noticeable, if they couldn't fix the system, they would eventually have to open up the ship to allow the planet's atmosphere inside. Without air being warmed, the temperatures aboard ship would align with the local levels, which were uncomfortably low. They lacked waste recycling, too, and without that they would be relying on the finite supply of food in the hold. There'd been no indication there was anything fit for human consumption on the planet.

In short, they couldn't survive being stranded there forever.

———

Jas was lying on her bunk in her cabin, beyond exhausted and trying to sleep, when there was a knock at the door. She wearily got to her feet and pushed it open. What she saw snapped her awake. Two of the crew had brought Haggardy to her. First Mate Haggardy, technically now the master of the ship.

"Bring him in," she said, returning to her bunk.

She'd almost forgotten about the man. Nearly every crew member of the *Galathea* had been accounted for. The infected officers they knew of were all dead, though there was a question over exactly who else might have been infected. The rest of the crew had survived without life-threatening casualties.

And then there was Haggardy.

"I know what you're thinking," said the first mate.

"You do, do you?" Jas leaned back on her arms. "What's that?"

"It's no secret I went down to the planet. I was forced to, like the others, but I wasn't affected like the rest. I was never possessed by aliens. I outwitted Loba, and pretended to be one of them. I had nothing to do with what they did. I didn't hurt anybody."

Jas recalled that Haggardy had been there when they destroyed the shuttle, and that he hadn't countermanded her when he'd had the opportunity, but she wasn't going to help him out with that tidbit.

"I don't know, Haggardy. Why should I believe you? I have no way of telling who you are. The simplest solution would be to force you off the ship."

"Don't do that," he blurted, glancing behind him at the two crew members who hovered in Jas's doorway. "I tell you what, I promise I'll defer to your command. Now that Loba's dead, I'm next in rank, and I should assume leadership. But I won't. I'll stand aside, and I'll tell the crew that. You can be master of the ship."

"Me? Master?" Jas hadn't thought about who should lead them now. "But shouldn't it be...?" She paused and tried to remember who was above her in the chain of command.

"They're all dead, Harrington. Second and third mate, chief engineer, purser, and I hear you've put Lee in stasis. Below me, there's no one left until we get to you."

The enormity of what the man was suggesting grew in Jas's mind. She'd felt like her job was done. Together, she, Lingiari and Lee had defeated the aliens in their attempt to take over the ship.

But now someone had to coordinate the survival effort, lead the crew, and keep them safe from the aliens that still threatened them. While they waited for rescue, someone had to maintain morale. Could she do it?

She regarded the first mate. One thing was for sure—she couldn't trust this man.

"Take him to the brig."

As Haggardy was led away, Jas lay down. She was exhausted. Tomorrow, she would think about what to do next, but for now, she would sleep.

STRANDED

ONE

J as Harrington was watching Haggardy in his cell, looking for signs of alien possession. The man was eating his rations, hunched over a plate as he sat on his bunk, and Jas was looking through one of the clear cubes in the wall, set to observation mode so that he wouldn't know she was there. The former first mate had been in the brig a couple of days, but Jas was no closer to figuring out whether he was infected with an alien, or if he was just the same play-it-safe Haggardy she'd always known and not particularly liked.

When the rest of the *Galathea's* officers had been infected on K. 67092d, Haggardy had been with them, there was no doubt about that. He'd admitted as much himself, but he maintained that he'd managed to avoid the other officers' fate. All that he would say about what had happened was that it had been too dark to see much, and he'd escaped as soon as he could. After that, he'd fooled their dead master, Loba, and the rest of the infected officers by copying whatever they did.

The problem was, Jas wasn't sure what she was looking for. Possessed individuals looked and behaved nearly the same as usual. Most of the *Galathea's* crew members had been duped by the infected officers, and they'd nearly taken over the ship. Jas had been one of the few to notice a slight change, a certain distant, cold taint to a victim's manner and an emptiness behind the eyes. Her perception was due to her years of working with the part-human, part-synthetic defense units, which had made her sensitive to that touch of inhumanity.

Doctor Sparks had run every test he knew of on the disgraced Haggardy. As far as he could tell, there was no sign of alien infection. The former first mate's DNA, retinal scans, and fingerprints matched those on Haggardy's file. But Jas guessed that the other infected officers would have also passed the tests.

She couldn't understand it. Haggardy's behavior had seemed entirely human ever since he'd been arrested. Before that, he'd gone along with the possessed Loba's plans. Only one thing counted in his favor: when Jas had commanded the defense units to destroy the ship's shuttle so that Loba couldn't take any more of the crew to the planet surface, Haggardy hadn't taken control of the units himself. As the higher-ranking officer, he could have, yet he hadn't. It wasn't enough.

Carl Lingiari appeared at the door to the brig, and Jas's mood lifted at the sight of him. As well as saving all their lives by turning the crash of the *Galathea* into a crash-landing, the lanky pilot had been a helpful support and ally as Jas had organized the crew afterward.

He gestured to her to step outside. "Let's take a walk," he said as they left the brig.

"What do you think about Haggardy?" Carl asked. "Made your mind up yet?"

"I can't make him out," replied Jas. "Whatever he is, he's staying in the brig. He didn't lift a finger to stop Loba and the others. I don't trust him. He's a traitor."

"I hope Polestar agrees. We better have a pretty good excuse for locking up the first mate."

"When they see the security vids, it should be obvious. Whatever. There's not a lot I can do about it."

They toured the ship's corridors, passing small groups of crew members who were making the best repairs they could to damage caused by weapon fire and during the crash. Jas had assigned everyone tasks to keep them occupied and not dwelling on what would happen now that they were stranded on K. 67092d, which was inhabited by hostile aliens.

It was a few moments before either of them spoke, and then they both spoke at once.

"You go first," said Lingiari.

"Have you been on the bridge? Has anything arrived at the comm desk?"

"I've been there all morning. Nothing's come in from Polestar or anyone else. How long has it been?"

"The fight with the officers was three days ago." replied Jas. "If Lee sent a message packet to Earth like I asked her to, I think a reply should've come by now. Do you know how long a response should take to reach us?"

Lingiari grimaced. "If they replied right away, we should have their answer by now. I checked. A couple of days is plenty of time."

"I know the comm desk isn't displaying sent messages, but will it show if we receive a reply?"

"If nothing's broken, I think it should."

"And if something's broken, would we be able to tell?"

"I suppose we might not."

Jas cursed. "So we can't get a message out, and we don't know if Lee sent one because she's in stasis. We might have received a reply, but the comm desk might not be showing us. Or Polestar might not have replied yet."

"You think the company wouldn't reply right away?"

"I don't know, Lingiari. Maybe they would. Or maybe they're still figuring out what to do about us."

The pilot stopped and turned to Jas. "You mean they might not send a rescue ship?"

A group of men and women working on replacing a section of wall nearby paused at Lingiari's words and turned to hear more. Jas grabbed the pilot's arm and pulled him along the corridor to a deserted area, where they couldn't be overheard. "For krat's sake, be careful what you say around the crew. The last thing we want is people thinking we might not be rescued.

"Look, Polestar doesn't exactly have a good track record when it comes to employee welfare, does it? There's a reason we sign away our compensation rights before embarking on a mission. *We* take the risks, Polestar takes most of the profits, and that's just the way they like it.

"We might not have received a reply because they're still weighing up the costs of a rescue against the potential benefits. We're about halfway through the mission, and we're only at break-even point. We've sent them the information on the planets surveyed up till now. Are we worth the cost of diverting a ship to come and pick us up? Or would it be more profitable to send one to cover the planets we didn't reach?"

"But," said Lingiari, frowning, "even if Polestar decides we're expendable, the *Galathea's* worth billions. They aren't going to give up on her that easily."

"We have to think about the information Lee sent, too," said Jas, "assuming she sent it before we crashed. She didn't know we would be stranded. She didn't send a Mayday. She would have told them about the hostile aliens, infected officers, and the threat to the ship. With no more information, as far as Polestar knows they could be sending another ship and its crew into a deadly conflict. Even if Lee sent a packet to them, they haven't heard anything since. They don't know why we've gone silent."

"They might not want to risk another ship," said Lingiari.

"Exactly. Polestar isn't a military setup. That's the responsibility of the Global Government, and in a century of deep space exploration, they've never had to deal with hostile intelligent aliens. If Polestar's told them about us, there's no knowing what they'll do. Whatever it is, rescuing us mightn't be the first item on their agenda."

Some moments passed. "So what do we do?" asked Lingiari.

"I don't think we should be relying on anyone to rescue us. The more I think about it, the less likely it seems that's going to happen. If we're going to get off this planet, we're going to have to do it by ourselves."

"I dunno how," said Lingiari. "I won't be able to lift her into orbit, let alone star jump. Both the starjump and RaptorX engines must be gone after that crash-landing, and we're not gonna find any spare parts around here."

"I've told someone to have a look at the engines. Her name's Toirien MacAdam. She's only an engineer-in-training, but I remember the chief engineer saying he was really impressed with her. Said she was a natural with a wrench."

"Yeah, I know her," said Lingiari. "She did some great work with the shuttle."

"I'm hoping she can do something, enough to get us off this planet anyway." Jas frowned and looked down. "She's all we've got. The rest of them, the chief, first, second, and third engineers, they're all gone."

Lingiari put a hand on Jas's shoulder. "It's not your fault."

She shook her head. "It was my job to protect them. All of them." The pilot went to speak, but Jas cut him off. "I don't know how MacAdam's going to repair the engines, but we've got to help her try. And we can't forget about the threat on board. We don't know if all the infected officers died. You weren't sure exactly how many Loba took with him to the planet. Possessed personnel could be walking among us right now.

"What's more, Haggardy's sitting in the brig, maybe infected by an alien and maybe not, but he's another threat either way. It wouldn't surprise me if some of the crew think *he* should be leading them, not me."

"I'm waiting for the good news."

"Keep waiting."

Two

Toirien MacAdam rested her brow against the hatch on the *Galathea's* outer shell. The cool metal soothed her hangover a little, but the effect was quickly lost when she lifted her head to resume her work releasing the bolts. She would've asked Dr. Sparks for a painkiller, but the fussy man would want to know why she needed it, and he would soon see through her lies. Alcohol and all other drugs were strictly forbidden. He would test her blood and report her. Though in their current predicament, Toirien wasn't sure what difference that would make.

Right then, she had enough to contend with. She didn't need to confirm the doctor's prejudice against naturals and add his disapproval to her list of things she already held against herself. She tried releasing the door's fixings with an electric spanner, but when she pressed the trigger, the machine whirred uselessly. Like all the others, the access hatch had been damaged when the *Galathea* had crashed, and wouldn't open. Toirien replaced the electric spanner with a wrench, and hit the handle of the wrench with a mallet until the fixing released a little. Then the spanner did the work of removing it.

Getting drunk had seemed Toirien's best reaction to being

stranded on K. 67092d, though long experience had told her that alcoholic oblivion was only a temporary solution. As was her habit, the previous night's Toirien had chosen to ignore the fact, leaving that day's Toirien to suffer the consequences.

Two more fixings to remove, then she might be able to open the hatch. Why the higher-ups wanted to open the *Galathea* to the outside, she didn't know. K. 67092d harbored dangerous aliens, aliens that had infested the rest of the engineers, leaving her the only one with knowledge of the ship's engines. No pressure, though.

Toirien imagined how drunk she would get that night.

Alcohol—easily made aboard ship—wasn't the only substance she could turn to for a little temporary oblivion. Pills to energize, or soothe the emotions, get you all loved up, or expand the consciousness, were also available, if you knew who to ask. Illegal, of course, on Earth as well as the *Galathea,* and the crew had to pass a drug test to be hired.

There were ways around the test, such as by giving the tester a hefty bribe, but Toirien had been clean when she came aboard. She'd stayed clean, too, but since the crash she'd lapsed, given in to temptation, and leapt off the wagon.

Emitting a grunt, she swung the mallet at the wrench handle. The final fixing loosened, and the wrench swung round before falling with a clatter to the floor. Toirien wiped her forehead with the back of her arm. Though her head still ached, the pain seemed to be lessening. It was the manual labor that did it. She'd always enjoyed the simple, honest, plain work of fixing things, tinkering with engines, taking devices apart, and putting them together again to figure out how they worked. Computer systems with their chips and impossibly fine wires puzzled her, but she understood mechanical devices, and there was a satisfaction to working with them that she'd experienced with nothing else in her life so far. In all other things, she freely admitted to herself, she was a screw-up.

That was it. The final fixing was out, and it was time to test whether the hatch would open. But Harrington, the chief security officer, who seemed to be the one in charge for the moment, had told her not to attempt opening it alone. She'd been instructed to inform the woman when she was ready, and with the comm system out, that meant going to the bridge.

Toirien dragged her bag of tools to one side and set off across the ship.

The beating the *Galathea* had taken as she'd slid across the rocky, barren surface of K. 67092d showed its effects in the walls, floors and ceilings of the ship's corridors. Surfaces were warped, and in some areas they'd split open, revealing the ship's thick metal beams.

The effects on the crew were more subtle, but now that the initial shock of the crash was wearing off, they were beginning to show. Toirien had seen many of her shipmates weeping uncontrollably, while some stared endlessly into space, apparently immobilized by the situation. Others shouted angrily to whoever would listen about the incompetency of the officers who had led them into the crisis.

She arrived at the bridge. A piece of metal had been forced into the door to hold it open. Inside, the red emergency lighting revealed two figures: the chief security officer and the pilot. They were talking, and Toirien hesitated at the door. Authority figures made her freeze up. Too many bad memories. The pilot, Lingiari, spotted her and waved her in.

Toirien hadn't had much to do with either of these individuals previously. Her job had been mostly below decks, servicing and testing the starjump and RaptorX engines. But she knew Harrington by sight. She was a giant of a woman, and with her deep olive skin and striking, dark reddish-brown hair and eyes, she was difficult to miss. The pilot wasn't much shorter than the security officer, and he was well known and liked for his easy smile and his stowaway pet, who had made most of the crew's acquaintance even though he wasn't supposed to exist.

"You've found a hatch you think will open?" asked Harrington. She and the pilot were sitting at the flight controls. The screens were dark.

"I did. I released everything that's securing it to the ship," Toirien replied. "I left it closed, like you said, but it should open with a bit of work, one way or another. That area of the ship doesn't seem too badly damaged, and I don't think there's much force holding it in place. But once it's open, we won't be able to shut it again in a hurry. I'd have to reseal it bolt by bolt."

"Okay, I understand," said Harrington. "What else can you tell us? Have you completed a full inspection of the engines?"

Toirien's brows knitted together. Who did this woman think she was talking to? She was only an engineer-in-training, barely a step above a mechanic. She ran a hand through her ginger curls. "I spent most of today working on the hatch after I got your order. I haven't had time to...I mean, with the crash and everything..."

Harrington didn't try to disguise her look of disappointment. She stood. "MacAdam, you're the best we've got. We're relying on you for our chance of getting off this planet. You understand that, right?"

Toirien shrugged. "I suppose." Seeing Harrington's dark eyes narrow, she added, "I understand."

"Good." The security officer turned to Lingiari. "Shall we get it over with?"

"We're ready as we'll ever be."

"Come with us, MacAdam. We're going to open that hatch."

Toirien wasn't sure she wanted to find out what was outside the *Galathea*. She'd heard the various rumors and the official version given out by Harrington, that the aliens were living inside strange structures on the planet. But what if some of them had scaled the ship and were waiting for them to stick their heads out?

She followed Harrington and Lingiari as they went to retrieve four defense units from storage. At first she thought they wanted the units to help open the door. She didn't think they would be necessary, but she didn't have the confidence to tell Harrington that.

Where they went next, however, made her realize why they needed the units. In an emptied-out cabin was a stack of long, plastic, body-shaped sacks. It was impossible not to understand what was inside. It was the dead bodies of the officers who had been infected by aliens. Somewhere in that pile were men and women she'd worked with, eaten with, joked with.

"What're you going to do with them?" Toirien asked as the defense units shouldered two bodies each.

"We have to put them out through the hatch," Harrington replied.

"You're going to just throw them off the ship?" Toirien blurted.

The security officer's expression was stony. "We don't have a choice. As far as we know, the aliens that infested them are still inside. They could be alive, despite their hosts dying. Even if we had the facilities and energy for storing them, they could infect more crew members. We have to get rid of the bodies, and we don't have any other way of disposing of them. No furnaces or disintegration units on the ship are big enough."

"So you're going to dump them outside, without a ceremony, with no one saying a word over them?"

Lingiari said, "She's right, Harrington. Someone should say something."

"I can't risk anyone getting close to them. It's risky enough for us to do this. The crew can say something later if they want. I don't want anyone hanging around that hatch."

It took the defense units three trips to carry all the bodies to the access hatch. When they'd brought the last one, Harrington asked the defense units to scan the exterior for life forms. They found nothing, so Toirien started work on the final stage of opening the hatch. She gave Harrington and Lingiari crowbars, and together they worked at the hatch, gradually loosening it until it swung to one side, hitting the wall with a resounding bang. After days of emergency lighting, the daylight that flooded in was painfully bright, and it was some time before, blinking in the bitterly cold air, Toirien could focus on the terrain outside.

Harrington had commanded the defense units to be ready with their weapons, but nothing was waiting to attack or force its way aboard. The view of the barren scrubland looked depressingly similar to Toirien's native Ireland. The only relief in the monotonous landscape was a building of dark gray, hexagonal blocks on the horizon.

Lifting and dropping the bodies like sacks of rice, the defense units did their job. The distance from the hatch to the planet surface was so great, there was no sound of them hitting the ground. Toirien didn't know which of the sacks contained the chief, second and third engineer, and she didn't want to know.

When all the bodies had been disposed of, a unit climbed down the side of the ship. After it had reached the bottom, the bright glow of its flamethrower could be seen as it gave the dead officers an informal cremation. No one spoke. Toirien replaced the hatch's fixings after the unit returned, and the security officer and pilot left.

That night, someone among the crew conducted a quickly put-together ceremony in the canteen to commemorate the lives of those who had died. Toirien didn't remember too clearly who it was that spoke. By the time the ceremony had started, she was already drunk.

THREE

Pausing on the ladder down to the maintenance tunnels of the *Galathea's* engine, Toirien adjusted her equipment bag over her shoulder. She was going to test the functioning of each section of both engines. The ship's computer was giving confusing readings, so she had to test the sections individually. The process would take her at least her entire shift.

Not that the crew worked in shifts any more. Everyone had been allotted tasks, and they were expected to do them whenever they weren't sleeping or eating. They had to assist with health care, repair, and distributing supplies. It had given them all something to do, but it didn't prevent discussion on how long they would be there, what was going to happen to them, and if they could expect a rescue ship. No one was answering their questions, and the uncertainty bothered a lot of people. It worried Toirien. She knew of crew members who would take advantage of the general feeling of dissatisfaction and despair.

Still, she didn't know what she could do about any of it. She continued down the ladder, the rhythm of her hands and feet matching the pounding in her head from the previous night's binge. Starting at the lowest level, she would work her way up, checking each section methodically for damage. She recalled the violent juddering of the crash. When she thought of what she might find down there, she was overcome with dread. She realized it was that dread and fear that had put her off going into the engines all that time. If they were trashed, and if no rescue was coming from Earth…she swallowed.

Toirien looked up to see how far she'd come. Looking down made her dizzy. The engine access point was a small square high above, brighter than the surrounding lights. She must be nearly at the bottom. As she risked a peek downward, she drew in a breath. The engine floor was directly below, and it was severely warped. The *Galathea* might no longer be airtight, let alone contain working engines. With RaptorXs running, they might have limped to a planet capable of supporting human life, if one were close by. But from the look of the damage, it would be a miracle if anything was working. The engines would need extensive repair and replacement parts. Parts they didn't have.

After a long moment surveying the wrecked floor, Toirien climbed down the final meters of ladder. She stepped into a service tunnel and went to the end, where an instrument panel was embedded in the wall. She had many hours of testing ahead.

———

A long while later, halfway through her engine check, Toirien took a rest. The testing wasn't going well. Not every panel was giving results. The crash-landing had damaged them, and because they weren't working, she had no way of telling if that section was functioning as it should, except for opening it up and taking a look. Only Toirien didn't know what she was looking for. She hadn't got that far in her training.

She sat on the metal mesh floor and took her lunch out of her bag. She needed a drink, but she'd mustered the self-control to not pack any alcohol. She needed to keep her wits about her if she was going to complete a report for Harrington. It was going to be a short one: without help from Polestar or someone else, they were screwed. She only had to figure out the details of how and why and to what extent they were screwed.

In Toirien's lunch pack, along with her food and water, was something she probably shouldn't have brought with her. She pulled out her personal interface, which contained all the vids, mails, images, and other digitized content dear to her. In the silence and solitude of the tunnel, and after her hours of disappointing work, she couldn't help but open the device, knowing full well that it was a bad idea.

Two faces looked up at her from the screensaver she'd had for years. The sight of the faces tore at the deeply scarred wound she bore inside. They were the faces of two little girls hugging, their curly ginger heads pressed tightly together. They were laughing excitedly. Toirien's thumb swiped them away, only to reveal a more deadly weapon—a list of mails from the girls, which she'd received in the early years when they'd been learning to write, and their memories of her were fresh in their minds.

Mammy, we dont like it here. we mis you. Wen are you comming back? We want to com home. Grace is sad. Pleez com and tak us with you.

I luv you

Joan

Toirien was helpless under the spell of the simple messages. She read each mail, though she'd read them so many times they were etched on her mind. When she'd finished the mails, she watched the few vids she'd made of the girls when they were babies. In some of the vids the camera shook, as if she'd been under the influence of something as she made them. It had taken her a long time to admit it to herself, but she probably had.

She drank in each feature of her daughters' faces. They both closely resembled her. Their ginger hair and brown eyes were the same, and they would probably develop her boxy figure. Some features differed—the looks they'd inherited from their fathers, whoever they might be. Toirien knew it was one of two men who had fathered Joan, but for Grace she had no idea. That period in her life was hazy to her now.

Tears dropped onto the screen, distorting the small, moving images of Grace and Joan playing at a beach somewhere. She wanted to reach through the screen and touch them, grab them, pull them to her, and hold them close, smell their hair, and feel their soft skin.

The device slipped from Toirien's fingers and onto the gridwork floor. She rubbed the heels of her hands into her eyes and smeared her tears over her face. It was her own fault. She'd done it to herself, and to them. She had no one else to blame. The authorities had been right to take Joan and Grace away. Naturally conceived and born to a drug-addicted mother, their future would have been grim if they'd stayed with her. The agency had promised she could have her children back if she cleaned herself up. If she could stay sober and pass all the tests, they could be a family again.

But it had been so hard. Without her children near her, and suffering the shame of being an unfit mother, and the worse criticism she heaped on herself, she'd found everything harder to resist, not easier. She'd needed to escape then more than ever.

Toirien wondered what Grace and Joan looked like now. Did they even remember her? She rose to her feet, grabbed her bag of equipment from the floor, and threw it against the wall. The tools and instruments spilled out, and the tunnel echoed with their clatter.

Her job, this training, had been the first steady work she'd had in years. It was supposed to have been the start of a new future. A future where she would stay off the booze and drugs, where she would earn enough to rent a small home and prove that she was reliable and fit to be a parent. It was how she would finally get her kids back. But the ship had crashed, and it looked like even if she were as clean as a whistle and the perfect citizen, she would never see her daughters again. They would never know how hard she'd tried, or how sorry she was for what she'd done, or how much she loved them.

Four

Opening the doors to the dead officers' cabins was easy. Karrev couldn't understand why more of the crew weren't doing the same and taking whatever was up for grabs. He'd discovered plenty: jewelry, rare perfumes, luxury foods, drink, and other goods from Earth, and expensive alien artifacts. He'd often wondered what it would be like to live on an officer's pay, what they spent their bonuses on, and his curiosity had been more than satisfied with the many items he'd discreetly removed. It wasn't as if the dead officers would be needing them after all, so he didn't see how he was doing anyone any harm. He was just using his smarts. But he'd been stupid, too. He'd been slow to go for the top prize: Loba's quarters.

Karrev pushed open the door, revealing a room that was surprisingly lacking in expensive items, which made the man pause. Had someone got there before him? But the room didn't look as though it had been ransacked.

As master of the *Galathea*, Loba should have had an excess of products to indulge himself with during the long mission. Karrev had never been in a master's cabin before, and he hadn't been sure what to expect, but it wasn't this.

After a few puzzled moments, Karrev shrugged and turned to

leave, but something drew him back. The look of the room was oddly familiar. It wasn't austere so much as poor, as if Loba had sold off everything he'd had. As if he'd been short of money, which was crazy, unless...Karrev's eyes widened.

A thrill passed through the man, straightening his stooped posture and brightening his features. He scanned the place, taking in every object, every detail, every potential hiding place. If his guess was correct, he would have to search very, very thoroughly, but it would be worth it. A prize like that would be worth pulling the place to shreds.

Karrev went to Loba's bunk and lifted the mattress. He ran his fingers under the frame. Nothing. Of course not. That was a hiding place for amateurs. It was where the elderly hid their worthless paper money. Neither Loba nor anyone else who could afford his habit was an amateur.

Most addicts needed only a few drops per day. A supply to last a year or longer could be hidden inside a small object.

His pulse racing, Karrev took another look around the room. He would have to be methodical about his search. He would start in one place and work his way out, leaving nothing overlooked. He decided to begin in the deceased master's closet. As he opened the door, his gaze alighted first on a large piece of paper on the floor. Karrev hadn't seen paper for years. He wasn't one to visit art galleries or museums, but he recognized it.

Holding up the sheet, he saw the spread-out figure of a naked man. Lines intersected by points ran from the head and spine to the tips of the fingers and toes. A slow, triumphant smile advanced across Karrev's face. If he'd wanted or needed proof of his suspicion, this drawing was it. He threw the paper down. It was worth a fair bit, but what he was looking for was worth a lot more.

More than two hours later, Karrev sat on the floor in the center of the master's cabin, his brow deeply creased. Around him, the room was in complete disarray. He'd pulled apart and discarded every one of Loba's few possessions. The closet shelves, desk drawers and bunk were empty, and the floor was covered in detritus. Karrev had even dismantled the comm system. Its innards were spread out, smashed in a moment of frustration.

It had to be there somewhere. He reminded himself that he needed to stay calm. He needed to focus on the task. Loba hadn't been stupid. He wouldn't have risked hiding it anywhere else aboard the ship. His cabin was the only place he could have guaranteed his privacy. Up until his untimely death, of course.

Karrev rubbed his forehead. How would the master have gotten the substance aboard? He could have bribed the inspectors of course, but the price would have been extremely high, and addicts avoided paying for anything other than their addiction, hence the bare room.

If Loba hadn't paid a bribe, he would have hidden a bottle and needles in something made of a dense material that would fool the scanners.

Karrev's gaze travelled the room once more. Peeking out from under some crumpled bedclothes was the edge of a black box. He'd already inspected the box closely for an opening, but he'd found nothing, and he'd tossed it to the floor in favor of more promising objects. It was so plain, so simple...so easily overlooked.

Reaching over, he pulled the box from under the sheets. Squinting in the low light, Karrev examined it again. This was definitely it. It had to be. There was nowhere left to search. But how did it open? Beginning at one edge, Karrev pressed the box's surface, painstakingly working his way across it, leaving no part unexplored. He was over halfway through his experiment before he was finally rewarded. He applied pressure in an area that looked no different from the rest, and like fruit cleaving under a knife, the box opened.

Karrev's hand trembled. He had to grab the box with his other hand to prevent himself from dropping the precious find. Within the box's center, alongside a set of hollow silver needles, was a bottle of vivid crimson liquid.

Karrev had never set eyes on mythranil before. His upbringing had barely afforded him the cheapest of drugs. But he'd heard all about it. The name everyone used for it—myth—suited it well. The drug was legendary in its reputation. A single drop of myth, it was said, gave you a run so good you'd kill your own mother for another. And here he was with a whole bottle of it right there in his hand, worth enough for a deposit on a starship.

The door to the cabin began to slide open. Karrev snapped the box shut and shoved it under the bed sheets. Micah, a fellow lab tech, looked in. He jumped a little when he saw Karrev. The man grinned sheepishly. "You had the same idea as me, then."

"Dunno what you mean," replied Karrev, trying to sound casual as he got to his feet.

Micah stepped into the room and surveyed the results of Karrev's search. "Come on, you've obviously torn this place apart. Find anything good?" He looked Karrev up and down, his gaze dwelling on the flat pockets of the man's uniform. His left eyebrow lifted quizzically.

Karrev gave a small chuckle. "Ah, you got me." He slapped Micah on the back. "Why shouldn't we help ourselves, though? If it wasn't us doing it, it would be someone else, right? Who knows how long it's going to take Polestar to rescue us? We've got to look after ourselves."

Micah also laughed. "That's right. Nothing wrong with looking out for number one. It isn't like the owners are coming back, is it?" His smile faded, and he looked Karrev in the eye. "So, what did you find?"

Spreading his hands wide, Karrev replied, "Not a thing. Searched everywhere, as you can see. You'd think, with him being a master, there'd be plenty, but...nothing. I can't figure it out. Maybe someone thought of it sooner."

Micah held Karrev's gaze a few moments before frowning at the trashed cabin. "I might have a look myself."

"Go ahead," said Karrev. "Let me know if you find anything. I'd be interested. But I've had enough of this. I'm going to check out Lee's cabin. Her family were loaded, I heard."

"But she isn't dead."

"Dead, in stasis, it's all the same, isn't it? And if they do bring her back, I don't think she's going to be asking about her genuine wool bedspread or whatever, is she?" He went to the door. "Good luck. Like I said, let me know what you find."

Micah hesitated. "No, wait, I'm coming with you. Looks like you did a thorough job on this place. You're right. Lee's cabin's a better prospect."

"Now hold on a minute. That was my idea. I didn't say I was going to share her stuff. I wish I hadn't mentioned it now."

"Fair's fair, Karrev, what's in her cabin isn't any more yours than mine. Look, I promise I won't tell another soul, and we'll split it all fifty—fifty."

Karrev's eyebrows rose.

"Sixty—forty then."

Karrev's eyebrows rose higher.

"All right, all right. Seventy—thirty."

Shaking his head, Karrev said, "I've always been too soft. Come on." As Micah left the room, Karrev took a last look, his gaze resting momentarily on the bump beneath the sheets. What wouldn't he give to retrieve that box right now. After all the effort he'd put into finding it, the myth was his and his alone. But he couldn't risk Micah knowing about it. He would have to be patient.

When he could slip away unnoticed, he would come back and get it, and then...The possibilities rose before him like angels ascending to heaven. What or who was there aboard that he couldn't buy for a drop of myth? Who was there that he couldn't compel to do his bidding?

All his life Karrev had been last in line, bottom of the pile, looked down upon, forgotten, taken for granted, taken advantage of. Now, through his smarts and hard work, he'd finally turned the tables. Now, it was going to be his turn.

FIVE

s Jas shut down the interface screen and stood up, she
concluded that going over the supply list had been even
more tedious than she'd imagined it would be. The
numbers didn't mean anything to her by themselves anyway. She
needed to know what they meant. Jas set off to the storeroom to
speak to the second steward. The chief steward had been infected
and had died during the crash-landing, but his subordinate
seemed organized and dependable.

She found the man snapping open the locks on the lid of a
box. He looked up as she entered.

"I thought you might be over," he said. "You got the report I
sent?"

"I've just finished reading it. Things don't seem too bad,
providing the crew love freeze-dried sweet potato powder."

The second steward smiled. "I believe it was one of the
master's favorites. We seem to have a lot of it."

"I've come to ask you, what does it all mean in terms of day-
to-day supplies? How long do we have before we run out of
food?"

"I've been working it out. I calculate that, at the current rate of consumption, we have about two months. But the ship's cooling. I've already had to put on extra clothes to stay warm. When the temperature has equalized with what it is outdoors, people will need to eat more. So if we don't get the heating going, you can take a week or two off that estimate. That's without cutting down on calories, though. If we put the crew on starvation rations today—"

Jas raised a hand. She didn't even want to think about that. Two months. It didn't seem a very long time, but it was long enough to find out if they could fix the engines; it was long enough for a rescue ship, if one was coming.

"If we could get the waste treatment system working again," continued the steward, "we could last longer—much longer. No one likes eating the nutrient bricks, but they do supply the necessary calories. And we could convert many inedible items to nutrients. Anything that was once organic. If we could power up the waste treatment...?" He looked hopefully at Jas.

She sighed. Power. It always came down to the same thing. Power for heat, water, lighting, food, repairs, comm, everything. Up until then, they'd been running on emergency power. She didn't know if they could reinstate the power supply from the engines. That was another job for MacAdam. If they couldn't, it looked like they had two months before things got bad.

Then again, if the engines couldn't supply power, it would mean they were beyond repair, and it would just be a matter of surviving as long as they could.

She realized the second steward was watching her. "Sorry. Thanks for figuring all that out."

The man shrugged. "It's my job, whether the ship's flying or not."

"How are you getting the food out to the crew?"

"I've allotted a daily ration to each person. They've formed themselves into groups, and usually one person comes and collects that day's ration for their group."

"And do you think they're sharing out the food fairly?"

"I think so. No one seems worried about food supplies yet. I haven't heard any complaints. People understand it's an emergency situation. I don't know how long that'll last, though.

"I use the chief steward's office to dispense the food. I didn't think it would be wise for them to see the amount of supplies we have, especially if stocks begin to run low."

"I agree," said Jas, "but I don't like this idea of one person receiving the food for their group. It's too open to exploitation. What if someone decides someone else doesn't deserve their food, or demands favors before they hand it out? No. Let's make it so that each person collects their own food. I know it'll take longer to give it out, but—"

"No, you're right. I'll say it's up to everyone to get their own. I'll make them show their ID and check them off when they collect their rations." The second steward paused and surveyed the storeroom. "I sleep in here, you know. Just in case. I can't lock the door anymore, you see. If the crew starts worrying about the food supply...I'm not sure what I could do if a gang came to help themselves, or to take over the stores and kick me out."

"There's nothing you can do to secure the door?" asked Jas.

"I've tried all kinds of things, but without power..."

They were back to power again.

"I could barricade it, I suppose," continued the second steward. "But then I'd have to take the barricade down every morning and put it up every night. And anyone who was determined enough could break it down."

Jas sighed. "How about if you had a defense unit outside the door round the clock?" She had a limited supply of units and defense concerns of her own. She had them stationed at the ship's exit hatches, where they should be—protecting the crew from outsiders. The second steward's worries weren't a surprise to her, but devoting a unit to protect food supplies seemed a waste. The crew shouldn't need protecting from themselves. But the man had a point. If someone got control of the supplies, they would have control of the entire ship.

"A defense unit outside the room would certainly keep people away," said the steward, "but it might also increase fears about the supplies running out. I'll take up your offer, but I'll keep the unit in here, somewhere out of sight, in case of an emergency."

"Whatever you think best. I'll send one over."

Leaving the second steward to his inventory, she went to find MacAdam. The woman was supposed to have brought her a report on the state of the engines, but she hadn't shown up. It was strange. She had to have finished by now, but she hadn't come to the bridge as ordered. Jas would have to go and find her. She needed to know if there was any hope of them leaving the planet by themselves.

MacAdam wasn't in the canteen, nor any of the communal areas. Jas asked around, and eventually other crew members directed her to the engineer's cabin, though they had odd expressions on their faces that Jas couldn't understand. When she pushed open the door to the room, the reason for their expressions was soon apparent. The place stank of alcohol. Ship-distilled gut rot.

It was a narrow, mean room, containing little more than four bunks and accompanying interfaces and cupboards. MacAdam was the cabin's only occupant. The woman was on one of the top bunks, flat on her back and snoring, an arm and leg hanging lazily down.

A slow rage began to build in Jas. Here she was with the responsibility of nearly two hundred lives on her shoulders, two hundred people who she might have to watch die because she couldn't help them, and this woman, this woman who was supposed to be such a brilliant mechanic, who had just one job… She strode over to MacAdam, grabbed the front of the engineer's uniform and, with some effort, shook her awake.

MacAdam's eyes opened halfway, then went wider as she caught sight of Jas's angry face. Her mouth worked as if she were about to speak, but instead of words coming out, she coughed and retched. Jas wasn't able to get out of the way before sour-smelling vomit poured from the engineer's mouth and down the front of Jas's uniform.

Uttering an exclamation of disgust, the security officer stepped back hastily as MacAdam hung over her bunk and threw up again, the thin liquid splashing to the floor. Jas raised the back of her wrist to her mouth and wrinkled her nose. "For krat's sake," she spat. "What the hell do you think you're doing, woman?"

MacAdam clung to the side of her bunk, as if worried she would fall. "Sorry," she mumbled. "I fell asleep, and—"

"BF. You didn't fall asleep. You passed out. How much have you drunk, and where did you get it from?"

"I know, I know...sorry...I was just, looking at my, my...and it makes me sad...y'know. Not their fault. S'mine...and—"

"What are you talking about? Did you check the engines? Did you write your report before you decided to get off your legs?"

"I didn't...no point...we've had it. I'll ne'er see them again. Ne'er see them." She flopped back and began weeping.

Jas's anger boiled over. "You're right," she yelled. "No one's going to see anyone again unless we get those engines working. We're relying on you, MacAdam. You're the last engineer on the ship. We need you. We need you sober and working, or we're all dead. Do you understand me? Do you get it?"

Jas continued with her tirade, but the woman's eyes were closing.

The sound of the cabin door opening drew Jas's attention. It was Lingiari.

"I've been looking for you," he said. "I asked around and got sent in this direction. Then I just followed the sound of your voice."

"Look at her," exclaimed Jas. "Our last kratting hope. Off her legs."

"Yeah, well, I don't think she can hear you anymore, even if the rest of the ship can, so maybe you should rein it in?"

Jas took a deep breath and closed her eyes. She opened them again and said, "What did you want to see me about?"

"You know how we were wondering if Lee had managed to send a packet to Earth? Sparks says we can ask her ourselves."

Six

Karrev tried to time his return to Loba's cabin to the quiet shift, but the shift system was breaking down, and random patterns of work, sleep, and eating had developed. He picked the time when fewest people seemed to be up and around, and set off, weighing up his chances of being observed against those of someone else discovering Loba's secret stash of bliss before he could collect his find.

As he pushed open the cabin door, he thought something looked different about the room, but he couldn't figure out what. It was just as messy as when he'd left it, so it was difficult to tell if anything had been moved or disturbed. But it didn't matter, even if Micah or someone else had been searching. Karrev had spotted the edge of Loba's strange black box sticking out from under the pile of sheets.

He stooped and picked it up. He'd memorized exactly where to press the box to make it open. His heart thudded as the lid lifted. The bottle of mythranil lay, deep crimson, in the center. He basked in the glory of his treasure for a moment before the closet door flew open and a figure sprang out and crashed into him, propelling the box from his hands. Karrev let out a scream of rage that was cut off as he hit the floor. His assailant—Micah

—dove on top of him. The black box landed upside down, and Karrev's fingers scrabbled for it, fighting the weight on his chest.

"I knew it," came Micah's voice in his ear. "I knew there was something in here you were hiding. So what is it?"

Karrev was freed as the other man dashed for the box. Micah gasped as he picked it up and saw what lay on the floor beneath it: scattered silver needles and the bottle of myth, miraculously unharmed.

Micah's voice was reverent. "Is that—"

Karrev rose in a rage and flew at Micah as he reached for the myth. He knocked the man violently against the wall. The box fell from his grasp. Pressing him against the wall, Karrev fastened his hands around Micah's throat, but he had a bull's neck, and he tensed his muscles, fighting Karrev's chokehold as he pulled on his arms. The two men struggled, Karrev trying to choke Micah, Micah fighting to free himself from Karrev's grasp. Micah's eyes were wide and staring, and the veins stood out on his forehead. The men struggled silently.

Micah drove his knee between Karrev's legs, and pain exploded from the man's groin to his stomach. Karrev collapsed, gripping his genitals, immobilized with agony.

Rubbing his throat, Micah coughed harshly. He scanned the floor until he spied the bottle of mythranil. He picked it up with a gentleness that contrasted his large frame. Seemingly mesmerized, he held the bottle up to the meager light and gazed at the contents.

"Never seen it before," he said, as if to himself. "Heard plenty, but never seen it. I wonder if it's as good as they say."

Water pouring from his eyes and nose, Karrev was regaining some control. He pulled his knees beneath himself so that he was kneeling, one hand resting on the floor, the other gently nursing his groin. He squinted up at Micah. "I'll go fifty—fifty with you," he growled.

"Ha, you're not in much of a position to be bargaining."

"I found it. I pulled this place apart. I figured out where it was. I got the box open. It should be mine, by rights."

"Not from where I'm standing." Micah pulled open the front of his uniform as if looking for somewhere safe to stow the bottle.

"Sixty—forty, then," said Karrev, his breathing easing as the waves of pain from his stomach subsided a little.

Micah looked down his nose at the crouching man. "Why should I give you anything?"

"Thirty—seventy."

Micah snorted a laugh and took a step toward the door. Karrev stood up. The heavy black box was in his fist. Micah paused. He took another step to the door.

"Give it to me," said Karrev, holding the box like a weapon. He held out his other hand, palm upward.

Eyelids hooded, Micah edged farther away.

"Give it me," said Karrev, "or so help me, I'll—"

Micah held the bottle out at arm's length. "If you hit me, I'll drop it. From this height, it'll smash. Is that what you want?"

"If I can't have it," roared Karrev, "neither of us can." He flew at Micah. The man raised his arm but couldn't move fast enough to ward off the blow. The box struck his head with a hollow thunk, and the bottle of mythranil fell. Karrev dove and caught it before it hit the floor. Micah staggered, blood leaking from his wound.

Karrev carefully placed the bottle at the edge of the room, out of danger, before returning to the stricken Micah. He hit him again with the box, sending him to the floor. Karrev hit him again and again, spattering the man's blood over himself. Micah's skull shattered. It wasn't until Karrev glimpsed the man's brain that he paused, panting, his arm aching.

He drew himself upright and wiped a sleeve across his face, smearing the blood and mixing it with his sweat. He listened for sounds from outside for a moment, but none came. Apparently, no one had heard the fight. The ache from his genitals began to register once more. He limped over to the bottle of myth, picked it up, and put it in his pocket. Then he gathered Loba's sheet and used it to wipe off Micah's blood from his skin and clothes as best he could.

As he tossed the sheet down, he took another brief survey of the room. He scooped up the scattered needles, tore off a piece of cloth and wrapped them with it before putting them in another pocket.

Micah's body gave a convulsive twitch, and he released a long breath. Then he was utterly still. Karrev scowled at the man's ruined face. "Thirty—seventy, pah." He spat on Micah's upturned eyes.

Seven

Lee looked almost alive in the coffin-like stasis container. The injury that had as good as killed her was a trauma to the back of her skull. Her brain had swollen, and her heart and breathing had stopped, Sparks explained to Jas. The internal pressure from the swelling and the lack of oxygen had severely damaged Lee's brain. Stasis kept her bodily functions going artificially, albeit at an extremely slow rate, so that what remained of the brain tissue wouldn't deteriorate further. Her skin retained its plumpness, though it was pale, and if Jas ignored the fact that she wasn't breathing, Lee looked like she was in a very deep sleep.

It was as though Jas could reach out a hand and wake her up.

The doctor was fitting electrodes to Lee's skull, pushing aside her cropped blonde hair, and fixing tiny circles of thin plastic to her scalp.

"It looks so twenty-first century," said Lingiari. "You sure it'll work?"

"If there's anything left of her mind, we should get some kind of response," replied Sparks, "though what exactly, I don't know. I've never done this before. It was only a small part of my training, because there's little use for this on Earth, of course. There, we would immediately read and store whatever was left of the patient's mind, to be ready for uploading to a clone, if the family could pay. But here, with no cloning facilities, we have to retain as much of Lee as we can for as long as we can. I don't know exactly what's there. My scanner isn't sensitive enough to read low-level brain activity, hence the electrodes."

He placed the final one, "There," he said and stepped back. He turned to a control panel. "Now, let's see—"

"Wait a minute," said Jas, placing a hand on the man's arm as he reached to press the screen. "What are we actually doing here? I mean, are we just listening in?" If they couldn't talk to Lee, it might take hours to hear the answers to their questions. Meanwhile, they would hear what was going on in her brain, things she might prefer that they didn't know.

"It really depends on what's left," replied Sparks. "Lee's mind was exceptional—highly modded, highly developed, which increases the chances of some parts of it surviving. Like spilling water from a container, to put it crudely. Most of us carry a couple of cups of water. A severe injury like this would mean both cups are empty. But Lee's mind was like a bowl. She had water to spare." He reached for the panel. "The electrodes will both stimulate her brain and read the activity in whatever remains of her mind."

A knot formed in Jas's stomach. Lingiari was standing on the other side of the receptacle where Lee was lying. The pilot's features were clouded. He and Lee had grown close in their fight for control of the ship.

"But, what I want to know is," insisted Jas, "will we be able to talk to her? And if we can, how will she understand? Will she know where she is? Will we have to tell her what's happened?"

Sparks shook his head. "I just can't tell you for sure. I really have very little experience with this. I'd forgotten that accessing the mind of the person in stasis was a possibility. It was only when I saw that Pilot Lingiari had come to visit and talk to her that I was reminded. So I checked, and the equipment is here. If Lee's auditory nerves are functioning, she will hear us, and she may respond. If not, we may only be able to listen to her thoughts. Of course, the worst case scenario is that we hear nothing."

Lingiari had been visiting Lee? Jas's insides twisted up some more. Yeah, they'd gotten close, but she should have visited her too. She'd been so busy...

Sparks was watching her, waiting for her.

"Go ahead," she said.

The doctor pressed the screen. He, Jas, and Lingiari waited, watching the still figure and listening. Jas wondered what they were listening for. What did an active mind sound like? Sparks had said they might hear silence. Did the silence mean there was nothing there? Was her mind destroyed? The doctor cleared his throat and nodded at her. He wanted her to speak.

Jas swallowed. "Lee? Can you hear me?"

Nothing.

Lingiari leaned over the prone figure. "Sayen, it's Carl Lingiari." He reached out and gripped her small, perfectly manicured hand. "Don't be scared, okay? You're all right."

A voice came from the speaker. "Carl?" All present except for Lee breathed out, and the collective sigh was audible. But the voice wasn't Lee's voice. It was the digitally generated sound of a random, female voice. It sounded human, but not anything like how Lee had spoken. The hair on the back of Jas's neck stood up. It was like talking to the dead, as if the barrier that divided life from death had distorted Lee's personality, and turned her into something else.

"Yeah, it's Carl. Harrington's here, too, and Dr. Sparks."

"Am I in the medical center? How come I can't see you? Have I gone blind? What happened to me?" Despite the panicked words, Lee's face and body were utterly motionless. The voice was flat and conveyed no emotion.

"Navigator Lee," said Sparks, "I'm sorry to inform you that the *Galathea* crash-landed on the surface of the planet we were surveying. During that crash, you sustained considerable injuries."

"What kind of injuries? What's happened to me?"

Jas waited as the doctor explained to Lee what her injuries were. She was almost grateful that the machine-generated voice didn't express the emotions that impacted Lee one after another as Sparks told her, essentially, that she had died, and that the chances of recovering her personality and memories—of recovering everything that had made her who she was—hung by the finest thread.

Jas found it difficult to look at the dead woman's immobile face as she listened to her talk to the doctor. Her gaze roamed the room, not settling anywhere, especially not meeting Lingiari's eyes. She thought if she looked into the sadness that hung there, she might break.

The doctor finished his explanation, and Lee was quiet.

After a moment's silence, Jas said, "I'm so sorry."

"You don't have anything to apologize for, Harrington," came the electronic voice. "You must have defeated the infected officers if you're here talking to me. You did well. You and Carl saved us."

That wasn't how Jas saw it, but she wasn't about to argue.

"Where have you got me?" Lee asked. "If my injuries are so bad, how come I can talk to you? I feel weird."

"You're in the stasis room," replied Lingiari. "We're keeping you alive, and we're going to take you back to Earth, where they can help you. We'll fix the engines, or we'll get rescued. We're not—"

"Is it clean?"

"What?" asked Jas.

"I must be in a stasis container. There isn't any dust or anything, is there? I can't stand dirt. I don't want to be lying in some dirty box."

Jas laughed. "Yeah, it's pretty clean."

"Pretty clean isn't good enough. Can you get someone to wipe it out for me? I've got some sanitized wipes in my cabin."

Lingiari was laughing now, too.

"I'm glad y'all find it so funny. Hey, what I can't figure out is, why did you wake me up? Must be pretty creepy talking to a body.”

“You’re right. We did wake you up for a reason,” said Jas. “We need to know something. That packet I asked you to send to Earth, telling them what was happening. Did you manage to send it?”

“I sure did. Got it off right before we crashed. I included everything. About Loba, Margret, and the officers, and K. 67092d. I told them everything. It took me a while, and I didn’t have time to get to my crash seat before we hit.”

Jas and Lingiari locked eyes. If Lee had sent the packet, that meant Earth had had plenty of time to reply. But no message had come as far as they knew.

“Is there anything else you want to know?” asked Lee.

“Not right now,” replied Jas, “but we might need your help. Is it okay to wake you up to talk to you like this? Or would you prefer to sleep until we get you back to Earth?”

“I’d like you to wake me up and speak to me whenever you can, even if you don’t have anything to ask me. It’s kinda lonely here.”

Jas recalled how the navigator had been the only one to come to her room when Loba had confined her to her cabin, and how chatty she’d been. “I’ll come talk to you whenever I can.”

“So will I,” said Lingiari.

Sparks left them alone as they spent the next half hour bringing the navigator up to speed on everything that had happened since the crash-landing. When no one had anything else to say, Jas asked her if she wanted them to turn off the electrodes until next time.

“No, leave them on,” replied Lee. “I’d like to think a while.

EIGHT

J as awaited MacAdam's arrival at the mission room, which remained a meeting and planning place during the emergency situation. It was the only part of the ship apart from the bridge where the emergency power extended to computer access.

Jas had asked the engineer to meet with her to give a full verbal report on the state of the engines, but she had another reason for requesting a one-to-one with the engineer. She hadn't yet gotten over her shock at finding the woman drunk. Jas wasn't naive. Though she didn't take part in the alcohol and drug abuse that everyone knew went on aboard the ship—a minor part of her job was to try to keep it under control, in fact—she couldn't comprehend what had gotten into the engineer's head that she'd thought it was an acceptable alternative to reporting on the state of the engines. It was beyond her comprehension that someone who had everyone relying on her would mess up so badly.

But Jas also knew she hadn't handled the situation well, and she needed to put that right. Losing her cool like that hadn't been the reaction of a good master. What was more, MacAdam was possibly *the* most important person aboard the *Galathea*. Her judgment and capabilities had to be unimpaired, and that meant

Jas had to treat her with kid gloves. She had to make the woman understand how important she was, but not put so much pressure on her that she needed to escape.

While waiting for the engineer to arrive, Jas switched on the hologram of K. 67092d. She recalled the last view she'd had of the image, when Loba had been quizzing her as to why she wouldn't give the all-clear to Resource Assess the surface. That moment seemed like a long time ago.

A cough caught her attention. MacAdam had arrived and was waiting in the doorway. Jas had a feeling it was the second time she'd coughed.

"Thanks for coming. Sit down."

The woman took a seat on the other side of the horizontal screen that displayed the spinning globe. Jas switched it off and took another seat. Everyone looked ill in the ghostly emergency light, but the engineer looked particularly bad. Her cheeks and eyes were hollow and shadowed. Jas could almost make out the shape of her bony skull beneath her ginger curls. An acne spot flared almost comically at the end of her snub nose.

Jas had expected MacAdam to offer an apology for her behavior, but none seemed forthcoming. The engineer didn't meet her eyes. An angry rebuke rose to Jas's lips, but she bit her tongue. "What can you tell me about the engines? Did you complete a full survey?"

"I did. I tested each part. The upper levels have normal function according to the readouts, but I didn't get much information about the lower halves of the engines. It's to be expected. Judging by what the impact did to the engine housing, both the starjump and RaptorX engines are damaged, as far as I can tell."

"So, do you know what's broken, and the minimum we need to fix to get them working again? Can we cannibalize the upper levels for replacement parts?"

MacAdam shrugged. "I only know how to do diagnostic checks and some servicing and maintenance. I don't have a good idea of how each part functions. Engineers train for six years, and this was my first year." The woman glanced up. "Is there any news on a rescue?"

Jas rubbed between her eyebrows. "Please don't say anything to the rest of the crew, but we can't rely on being rescued. We might have to make it out of here ourselves, and we need more information on the engines than the function readouts."

MacAdam studied the backs of her hands. "I understand, but what can I do?"

You could start by not getting off your legs. "I was disappointed to find you drunk in your cabin yesterday. You understand that alcohol and all other drugs are banned aboard ship? You know that, right?"

The engineer was silent.

Jas wished the woman would meet her halfway at least, not this silence. What did it mean? She couldn't figure her out. She wished she was back with her defense units, who were much easier to understand than people. "MacAdam, I know there's a lot of pressure on you right now. When you signed up, you didn't know we would crash or that you would be the last engineer on board, with all of us depending on you. But I can't help that. No one can. It's just how it is. But I can try to help. If it ever feels too much...if you ever feel the need for someone to talk to...Dr. Sparks can offer counseling." Jas's stomach turned at the thought of sending the woman to the bigoted quack, but she had to admit he did have people skills.

The engineer's head was still down, and she was slowly shaking it. Tears splashed on her hands, which lay folded in her lap. Jas felt for her, but she didn't know what she could do to help the woman's situation. MacAdam was saying something.

"What?" asked Jas.

"I said, I'll do my best."

"Thanks, MacAdam. I appreciate it. We all do. You can access the ship's databanks in this room. They contain the engine schematics. Feel free to come here whenever you want, and whatever help you need, just let me know, okay?"

The engineer nodded but didn't raise her head. The woman seemed so crushed, so sad. Jas got the feeling there was more to her problems than the pressure she was under to fix the engines. "MacAdam, is there anything else I should know?"

"No...I, I'll study the schematics."

"And if you need a defense unit for some heavy lifting, I've got one or two to spare."

"It's okay. We—I—have my own equipment for that."

"Right, come over here, then." Jas took her across to an interface where she could access the database. After she'd shown the engineer how to retrieve the information, she returned to the hologram screen and switched on the image of K. 67092d. She wondered how much danger they were in from the planet's inhabitants. They'd crashed near one of the planet's poles, in an area that hadn't been close-scanned or RA'd. Not that it would have made much difference. They hadn't found anything that had seemed dangerous before, yet look at them now.

Jas's mind returned to the structure she'd seen when they'd disposed of the officers' bodies. It had seemed identical to all the others. Something in those structures infected people with an alien life form that took possession of them. But the answer as to what those things were, and how they operated, eluded her. Were they going to come out and attack their sitting-duck ship? If possessed officers remained on board—maybe someone like Haggardy—would they try to retrieve them?

Leaning over her data screen, MacAdam gave a satisfied *hmpf*.

"Have you found something?" asked Jas.

"No, but I've found out how I might be able to find something."

"Huh?"

"I just noticed the ship's scanners are still operating. They weren't affected by the crash-landing, though the computer isn't logging the information. I think I can turn them a little closer to home and get a detailed scan of the engines. Maybe I can see what's happened down there. If I can find out what's broken, I might be able to figure out how to repair or replace the parts to get the engines working again."

Jas turned to the image of K. 67092d. "What about the rest of the planet? Can you scan the area around us?" The ship's scanners were long-range. Now that they were on the planet surface, maybe they could penetrate deep underground and see what she and the defense units had missed inside the structures.

"I'll try to...doing it," said MacAdam. Jas waited in silence while the scanners did their work. After a few minutes, MacAdam said, "Sending the data over to you."

The hologram of K. 67092d disappeared and was replaced by an image of the planet surface and what lay beneath. The representation was a confused jumble of lines and textures that Jas couldn't interpret at first. The image scrolled slowly across, too large for the screen to display all at once. She plunged her hand into the picture to stop it. She had spotted the *Galathea.*

Everything around them seemed to be innocuous except for the regularly shaped hexagonal blocks, which lay on the surface but also extended far underground. Jas moved her hand to the spot and widened her fingers to expand the area.

MacAdam joined her at the screen. As the hologram zoomed in, something came into view that they both spotted simultaneously. "What's that?" asked MacAdam. Near the base of the artificial structure was a dark blob. Jas closed in on the blob. It looked nothing like the geology surrounding it. Black, vaguely rectangular, and large compared to the nearest block, the image gave no clue as to what it might be.

Jas shrank the hologram until they could see the *Galathea,* the hexagonal structures, and the button-sized blob beneath it. According to the hologram readout, the structure was about twenty kilometers away, and the blob was a hundred meters below the surface.

With a handful of defense units, Jas could get to it and find out what it was.

NINE

Outside the *Galathea's* access hatch, the sky was lightening with the approaching sun. Jas looked down the side of the ship. It was a long, long drop to the ground, where she could make out the remains of the body bags they'd thrown out a few days earlier. Strapped to the back of a defense unit, she should be safe enough on the trip to the surface. The units could climb up or down anything, gripping with specially textured hands and boots.

If only Lingiari weren't being so difficult about it. The expedition made perfect sense to her, but he wouldn't stop glaring, and with that animal sitting on his shoulder, she was having difficulty taking his objections seriously.

"What if you don't make it back, huh?" asked the pilot. "What happens then? You're in charge of the ship." His pet, Flux, was preening his bat-like, transparent wings, messing up the man's hair.

"Lingiari, it isn't like this is my first time. I know what I'm doing. If anyone should go and investigate that structure, and maybe find the aliens that infected those officers, it should be me. If I don't come back—which is very, very unlikely—someone else will have to take over. Whoever's next in command." Jas looked upward as she took a moment to figure out who that was. "Which is you."

The pilot had his hands on his jutting hipbones, where his uniform trousers clung to his rangy frame. An earring curved from one ear, and his sugar glider/bat alien pet was inadvertently pulling his hair over his face. Maybe the man had a point about the next in command. But that couldn't be helped. As long as they were stranded on the planet, they were vulnerable to the alien presence, which had demonstrated its hostility. Knowing *what* they were up against was the best defense they had.

"What makes you think you're going to find what you missed last time?" asked Lingiari.

A pang ran through Jas's conscience. "I've got something to look for now. A target. That thing under the structure has to be important. It's like nothing else I saw in them. Maybe there was another one under the structure where Margret and the others were infected, but the shuttle scanners didn't pick it up."

MacAdam stood by, ready to bolt closed the access hatch as soon as Jas left. The engineer stood silently waiting. The steady, chill wind that seemed to blow everywhere on K. 67092d was making her blink.

Lingiari sighed. "Just promise me you won't do anything different from what you did before. Wear your combat suit, send the defense units ahead—"

"I'm not an idiot, Lingiari."

"Try to stay in contact."

"I'll try. But I'll be okay. I'm sure. I just hope I see something worth the trip."

The pilot seemed to have run out of objections and reminders. After a last check outside at the barren, empty landscape, and the structure in the distance, Jas climbed into the harness she'd fixed to AX7, and fastened herself in. Feeling like a very large baby in its mother's sling, she commanded the unit to climb out of the access hatch and down to the ground. She had a backpack of supplies in case she had to spend the night on the surface, but she hoped to be back before dark.

The unit maneuvered through the hatch, carrying her on its back. Jas commanded AX12 to follow.

"Good luck," said Flux.

Though Jas had encountered aliens who could communicate in English, she couldn't get used to the creature's Australian accent. "Err...thanks."

"Lee says good luck, too," said Lingiari.

AX7 began to work its way down the metal skin of the starship.

"You've been talking to her?" There was that strange feeling twisting in her stomach again.

Lingiari leaned out of the hatch and looked down at her. "She likes the company."

Jas had meant to go and spend some time with Lee, too, but she'd had so much to do. "Great. Say hi for me." She had an afterthought. "And ask her if she can think of anything, any ideas that might help us."

"Yeah, she's already working on it." The pilot's head and shoulders were silhouetted against the brightening morning sky.

AX7 developed a steady rhythm as it climbed down the ship's side, its movements sure and steady. Jas rested her forehead against the android's broad back. Its skin and combat suit were one and the same thing, which meant that, though the androids were part-organic, no warmth radiated from them. Nonetheless, Jas found the smooth surface oddly soothing. She closed her eyes and waited for AX7 to reach the ground.

After a short while, she looked up toward the access hatch. Lingiari had gone, and the hatch was closed. Jas was uneasy at leaving the crew alone, even with defense units to protect them, but she'd decided that not knowing what faced them was a greater threat.

The planet's sun rose as Jas and the units descended. When she finally reached the surface, Jas did her best to ignore the blackened remains of the officers' bodies. Though in one sense, she was relieved that they were still there. She'd feared that, zombie-like, they might rise from the dead, the aliens that had inhabited them somehow re-animating the burnt corpses.

The two defense units set off. As they ran, Jas wondered what the creatures that had possessed the officers looked like. If they could inhabit another species, were they some kind of liquid that could enter and take up residence in the brain and nervous system? Or were they a powder that the officers had unknowingly breathed in? Her experiences with the alien life forms she'd encountered so far had taught her that, no matter what her expectations were, reality would exceed them.

By the time she and the units had arrived at the structure, Jas was sore from AX7's jarring gait. She gratefully unclipped herself and slid to the ground. After taking a moment to stretch and return the sensation to her numb extremities, she lowered the visor on her helmet and instructed the defense units to ready their weapons and enter, assess, and survey. They went in. When they gave the all-clear, Jas followed.

She went after them as they cleared each empty room in turn and progressed deeper into the structure. Lacking the units' tracking function, she realized that any humans who traveled through the many rooms within the building would become seriously lost. But none of the RA teams were supposed to have done more than check out the exteriors. That had been her recommendation. Unless Loba had ignored even that?

Her headlight had switched itself on, and along with the defense units,' it swept the bare, dark gray walls. Her auditory system was picking up no noise other than the tramp of their boots. She brought up the ship's scanner image on the interior of her visor, showing the path to where the dark blob lay beneath them. It grew larger and drifted in and out of view as they worked their way toward it.

It wasn't until they were quite close that she realized *how* much larger it was than the rooms they were passing through. The dark blob loomed massively on her screen. It was only a representation of the recording, so the details didn't become more refined the closer they got.

Finally, she understood that the blob must lie in the next room. Her muscles tensed.

She waited, listening. No sound or light came through the entrance. She told the defense units to ready their weapons. AX7 went in, followed by AX12.

"All clear, C.S.O Harrington."

Jas stepped through.

The thing that lay before her was only partially exposed. One side of it protruded from broken rock. They had reached the very bottom of the structure, and the gray walls had finally disappeared. They were in some kind of cavern.

She went over to the thing she'd been seeking. It looked so out of place in that underground environment that it took her some time to recognize it for what it was. She ran a gloved hand over the surface. It was ridged and metallic, and at one time it had probably been very strong. The species that had created it must have been visual, she realized, as there were many reinforced windows giving tantalizing glimpses of the interior.

" AX7," said Jas, "can you comm a unit aboard the Galathea?"

"No, C.S.O. Harrington. We are down too deep. I have not been able to contact defense units aboard the *Galathea* for some time."

Jas would have to wait until she returned to the surface to tell the others that she'd found what looked like the remains of an alien starship.

Ten

Karrev had stolen a fancy, pure silk bag in which to carry the bottle of mythranil, but that was the least of his work since securing the drug as his, and his alone. He'd made sure that Micah had an unfortunate accident in the engine. Dr. Sparks's tests on what remained of the body had found alcohol in his blood, so it wasn't difficult to conclude that the man had climbed into an engine access hatch while intoxicated, and slipped and fallen.

Karrev had also bribed two guards with a couple of drops of the precious myth for access to the small armory. He'd passed two of the weapons he purloined to a couple of burly friends and promised them a once-a-month run in return for their services. The rest of the weapons were to be distributed to those who would go along with his plan.

Now, he had to get the support of a sizeable proportion of the crew. Most of them were like him—only basically modded, or even naturals. Shut out of the circles in which society's elites moved, their hard lives were made more bearable by regularly resorting to narcotics. They would be familiar with the rumors about myth, though few would have had the money or opportunity to try it. He could offer them the prospect of hours of bliss in return for simply switching allegiance from their current masters to him.

And now that Harrington was off the ship, it should be simple to take control.

He'd put out the word: anyone who was unhappy with the current situation was to meet in the auditorium at a certain hour. Karrev hadn't been surprised when he saw the large turnout. Morale was low. There'd been no mention of getting off the planet, or a rescue ship. All they'd heard from the higher-ups was work, work, work; do this, do that. Meanwhile, it was getting colder, and everyone knew the food wouldn't last forever.

When it looked like no one else was coming, Karrev stepped up to the podium and ordered that the doors be shut. The room buzzed. He held up a hand for silence. He would let his greatest asset do the talking for him. He pulled apart the strings of his bag, reached in, and took out the bottle. As he held it up, the assembled crew members exhaled as one. But Karrev didn't achieve the shock factor he was hoping for. Word had gotten out. "He really does have myth," said a voice. "I never believed it till now."

"You'd better believe it," said Karrev. "I found it in Loba's cabin, locked away in a safe that only I could figure out the combination to." It was simpler than explaining about the box, and Karrev had kept it to store the myth in while he slept.

"*Found*," someone said. "That's a good way of putting it."

Karrev smiled. "It was there for the taking. Finders keepers, as they say. But it can be yours, too, if you follow me."

The shipmates Karrev had persuaded to be his bodyguards stood on either side of him, gripping their weapons.

"I don't know," said an older woman. "Even if it is myth, that doesn't mean we should do what you say."

"Haven't you heard what this stuff does?" a member of the audience retorted. "A few tiny drops is worth a mission bonus to the likes of us. What must the run be like? Use your imagination."

"Yeah, I'm too old for all that. Keep your drugs. I'm going to bed." The woman walked off, and the rest of the audience shifted restlessly.

A hand rose. It was the hand of a short, round man, who was a sanitation worker. "I used to deal in such things. I've sold myth in my time, though I've never seen so much all at once. Could I have a look?"

Karrev hesitated. He'd assumed the stuff was myth, or else why would Loba have hidden it so well? But he didn't know for sure. If he didn't let the man look at it, however, he would lose all credibility.

"'Course. Come up here. Help yourself," he said expansively.

The crowd opened to let the man through. Reluctance gripping him, Karrev handed over the bottle. The man held it up to the light before turning it on its side and watching the liquid as it flowed. Lastly, he opened the bottle and held it under his nose. Closing his eyes, he sniffed deeply. Immediately, he staggered, and Karrev snatched the bottle from him. He firmly screwed the lid on and frowned.

The man's eyes glazed over. They rolled back in his head, and he collapsed gracefully, his knees leading the way, followed by his tubby body and limp arms. A few hands half-heartedly caught him and broke his fall.

Karrev said nothing, allowing the spectacle of the chubby man to speak for him. He raised the myth in his right hand, and the crowd cheered. As the shouts and whoops died away, he cut through the fading noise. "If you want a taste of this, you do what I say, right?"

The audience gave their assent loudly.

"First," said Karrev, "we take the ship!"

ELEVEN

Sayen looked identical to how she'd been when Carl had last left her. Cushioned on a water-filled base in her stasis container, which undulated gently to help prevent pressure sores, she lay under a sheet. Beneath the sheet, tubes had been inserted into her body to maintain its temperature and systems at a level that kept her just alive. Her arms were above the sheet, with her palms face down, and her head was resting to one side. Her mouth was slightly open, and a thin line of drool ran from the corner.

Carl pulled his sleeve over his hand and wiped the spittle away. Sayen's hair was growing out of its short-cropped style. He felt like he'd got to know the woman better in the last few days than he had in all the previous months aboard ship. Her exclusive modding, private schooling, and privileged upbringing in her family's large home in the southern United States among nannies and servants could not have contrasted more with his rough-and-tumble childhood in rural New South Wales, Australia.

Sayen had told the pilot many stories, such as tales of dinner parties her parents had held, where they'd served strange, imported, alien foods to impress their wealthy guests. Sayen had been expected to try each of them without making a face, probably to demonstrate to her parents' friends how sophisticated she was, when really her favorite thing to eat was a PBJ sandwich. Other stories recalled the amazing trips she'd taken, like the time she'd flown in her parents' private jet to the beach just for the day, only to be told she couldn't play in the sand in case she got dirty or hurt herself.

In turn, Carl had related his childhood tales—how his first memory was of flying, strapped into his dad's twin-engine. He could remember his dad's head outlined against a brilliant blue sky, the roar of the engine, and the wind taking his breath from him. His second memory was of sitting on a horse's back, gripping its mane in chubby fingers, while his mum walked it on a lead around the paddock. All his childhood, he seemed to have been moving in one way or another. Telling Sayen about it all had brought back the memories vividly. He'd felt a sudden urge to see his parents' sunburned, wrinkled faces again and feel the hot Australian sun on his back.

"Are you still there, Carl?" came the electronic voice that conveyed Sayen's thoughts.

"Yeah, sorry, I drifted off for a bit. How are you doing?"

"I've been thinking about Harrington's trip to the alien structure and the infection mechanism. You know, I think she'll be okay."

"What makes you think that?" asked Carl.

"Well, we can guess the defense units didn't get infected because they aren't human, but the only difference between the LIVs she conducted and Margret and Loba's encounter with the structures, as far as we know, is that she was wearing a combat suit. Margret and the rest of the RA teams wore Polestar uniforms, which means their skin was exposed. I'm wondering if it's something to do with physical contact with one of the alien buildings. If someone touches a structure, maybe it triggers a reaction, reads their DNA, which results in the infection. If I'm right, providing she stays suited up, she should be safe."

"That makes sense. I'll comm her to tell her. Do you think I can speak to her through one of the defense units in here powering your stasis?"

"I reckon so."

Carl went to the nearest unit to read its designation. "AX1, can you comm one of the units out with Harrington?"

"Pilot Lingiari, do you mean can I communicate with AX7 or AX12?"

"Yeah. Could you tell them to pass her a message?"

"I can. Would you like me to comm AX7 or AX12?"

"AX7'll do. Tell it to tell Harrington not to take off her combat suit. She shouldn't touch the walls with her bare skin. Can you ask it to tell her that?"

"Do not take off your combat suit. Do not touch walls with your bare skin. Is that the message?"

"Yep, that's it."

Flux swept into the room. "Lingiari, you better get out. There's trouble on the way, mate."

Shouts and laughter came from the corridor.

"Urgent report, Pilot Lingiari," said AX1.

"What's going on?" asked Sayen.

"What's happening, AX1?" Carl asked.

"Weapons have been discharged in the storeroom, on the bridge, and in the living quarters. Units are awaiting instructions."

"What?" *Krat.* "AX1, tell the units to go to the conflict areas and...I don't know, stun the fighters. Anyone holding a weapon. Except each other."

"Affirmative, Pilot Lingiari." The unit lifted its hands to the cable running from its chest to the stasis unit. The three other units powering the stasis system did the same.

"Whoa, hold on. All units in here, what are you doing?"

"AX1 has relayed your message to all units, and we are going to the nearest conflict area," all four responded at once.

"No, not you guys. Don't disconnect, we need you to power

the stasis. All defense units in this room, disregard my previous order."

The units unplugged their cables.

"Wait, what the hell are you doing?" exclaimed Carl.

"Pilot Lingiari, you commanded that we disregard your previous order," said the units. "Your previous order was not to disconnect ourselves, so we have ignored that order."

"Arghhh…NO. All defense units in this room, reconnect your power supply to the stasis system." They did as they were instructed, and Carl closed his eyes in relief. "All units in this room, do not disconnect yourselves, I repeat, DO NOT disconnect yourselves from the stasis system unless it's at my order. Is that clear?"

"Affirmative, Pilot Lingiari," they said. "We will not disconnect ourselves from the stasis system unless we receive a command from an officer ranking higher than pilot."

"Good." It would have to do, and he was the highest ranking officer aboard, wasn't he? Harrington had said so.

Twelve

Karrev hadn't included the defense units in his plan, and he regretted it bitterly. His instructions to his followers had been simple: secure the supplies and order anyone who wasn't already his supporter to declare their allegiance to him. If they refused, they were to be brought to him there, in the auditorium, stunned if necessary. He'd planned on taking great pleasure in forcing them to accept him as their new master.

But those great, hulking beasts, more robot than human, couldn't be coerced. The minute that news of his takeover had gotten out, someone had ordered them to squash his rebellion, and they were doing it in their usual efficient style. How could he have been so stupid? Listening to the sounds of weapon fire in the corridors, Karrev took out the bottle of myth and gazed at it. What wouldn't he give to inject just a drop or two and escape this mess he'd created. This wasn't how it was supposed to be.

But myth offered only a temporary answer to his problems. He put the bottle away again in its silk bag. If he wanted to be master of the ship, he needed to think of a way to get control of those units for himself. Then, once they'd gotten the *Galathea* working again, he and his crew could roam the galaxy, discovering new planets, hijacking ships, and taking whatever they wanted. Once he had control of the defense units.

The security officer, Harrington, the one who'd put herself in charge, had gone somewhere, so it wasn't her controlling them. Who else could it be?

Everyone knew that her and the pilot had gotten close. It was they who'd spread the rumor about Loba and the rest of the officers being possessed by aliens. He hadn't believed it for a second. It was too much of a coincidence that most of the officers had been killed when the ship had crashed. It was more likely Harrington and Lingiari had executed them. No one had seen the bodies before they threw them off the ship.

The more he thought about it, the more Karrev realized that his plan to commit mutiny had been nothing of the kind. He was fighting *against* mutineers. He was dispensing justice against Harrington and Lingiari.

He stood up and slung the silk bag around his neck. With newfound enthusiasm, Karrev resolved to continue to fight for control the ship. He would be a hero.

The pilot, Lingiari—that was the one who Harrington must have left in charge. It had to be. If he could find him and kill him, it would be no more than the man deserved, and no one else would command the defense units. No, that was wrong. *He* would command them.

"Hey," he called to one of his bodyguards, who was standing sentry at the auditorium door. "Everyone has to put down their weapons. Spread the word. They have to stop fighting the defense units. I'll send another order later." The units were only attacking those who put up a fight against them.

After thrusting a weapon into his belt, Karrev left to find Lingiari, taking a couple of bodyguards with him.

His first stop was the mission room. Telling a guard to go first, they went inside. There was no sign of Lingiari. The engineer was the only occupant. She watched him carefully but said nothing. Karrev gave her a curt nod. She would be useful later.

Next, he tried the pilot's sleeping quarters. The room was empty but for that stupid pet of his. Karrev took a shot at it, but it disappeared into a vent. He'd get it next time. He hadn't eaten fresh meat in months. He looked briefly into the shuttle bay, but all that was in there were the melted remains of the shuttle. Where was the man?

"I think I know where he might be," said one of his bodyguards. "The medical center. I heard he goes to visit the dead navigator."

"He does, does he?" replied Karrev. "Must be into corpses. Thanks for the tip."

His guards flanking him, Karrev crept up to the stasis room door, which was slightly open. He could just make out the figure of the pilot. He had his back toward him, and it looked like he was leaning over a long container that had been pulled out from the wall. That had to be where the navigator's body was lying. The man was talking, but he couldn't make out exactly what he was saying. Something about 'worry' and 'ready.'

There didn't seem to be anyone else in the small room. He pulled out his weapon. The glimpse he had of the pilot was too narrow to shoot at accurately, and he might only get one shot. He was about to stride in, flanked by his guards, when a memory, sparked by the bright lights of the room, made him pause.

Soon after the crash, when everything in the ship had been in chaos, he'd heard complaints about the navigator's medical treatment. People had complained that they were using four defense units to power the stasis room, even though the ship needed all the power it could get—even though the navigator was a gonner.

Defense units in the room. *Krat.*

Karrev slid his weapon in his belt. He couldn't kill the pilot until he'd gotten control of the defense units, and he couldn't get control of the defense units until he killed the pilot. He would have to go back to the mission room and try to figure it out.

He hadn't gone far when heavy boots tramped the corridor ahead of him. It was the kind of sound only defense units made, and they were heading his way. Karrev turned and walked quickly in the opposite direction. Could they be after him? Had someone talked? Or had the pilot figured out what he would do? "Come on," he shouted to his guards, and he began to run. Then came the sound of units in front of him. He slowed. He had nowhere to go.

"Shipmate Karrev," came the cool, modulated voice of a unit behind him, "you are under arrest. Stop, or we will shoot you."

He wasn't going to go without a fight. He spun round and aimed, but didn't get a shot out before something exploded against his stomach, and the floor of the corridor came up to meet his face.

When Karrev came around, he was being carried like a sack of meat over a defense unit's shoulder. His nose ached, and blood was dripping from it. He tensed his neck to prevent his nose from banging—he was sure not for the first time—against the unit's back. He lifted his head, but saw nothing but retreating corridor, though he could hear the thump of feet ahead. His guards must have also been stunned, and they were also being carried by units.

Karrev recognized the area of the ship they were in. They were nearly at the brig. Once inside, that would be it for him. Mutiny carried a death penalty. If he was lucky, they would keep him alive until they got back to Earth, but he couldn't afford any fancy attorneys who would tell the true story about what Harrington and Lingiari had done. If he wasn't lucky, well, as soon as Harrington was back that hard bitch probably wouldn't think twice about throwing him off the ship like she had the dead officers.

He wasn't going to give up. There had to be something he could do. He racked his brains, but as he got closer and closer to the brig, no escape plan emerged in his mind.

The bag containing the myth was still hanging from his neck. The stupid unit hadn't even thought to take it off him. Ah well, at least he could spend the time he had left in bliss.

"Karrev?" asked a voice. The unit stopped, and the brig guard walked around it to look at the suspended man. For a moment, Karrev was mildly surprised. He'd forgotten the brig was already guarded; that there were already prisoners in there. Then he remembered who was imprisoned, and his heart stopped.

"What's this?" asked the guard, taking the bag from his neck. The man gasped as he looked inside, and his eyes popped. "I'd heard the rumor, but I didn't believe it." He drew out the bottle and held it up reverently. "AX9, take your prisoner inside," he said without taking his eyes from the crimson liquid.

As the unit carried him and his guards into the four-celled prison, Karrev sought out the prisoner—his method of escape, his Get-Out-of-Jail-Free card. He didn't want to give up control of the ship, but anything was better than this. His gaze alighted on a figure slumped on a bunk.

"Sir," he shouted. "First Mate Haggardy, wake up."

The first mate's eyes opened blearily.

"Sir, quick," continued Karrev, "these units are yours to command. Order them to get you out."

Haggardy's eyes snapped wide. He leapt to his feet as the unit carrying Karrev opened the door to a cell.

"Units, kill the brig guards immediately," Haggardy said. "Unlock my cell. Release me."

Karrev's unit dropped him like a stone, and his skull banged against the floor, momentarily stunning him.

A short time later, when the sparks had stopped firing in his vision and his thoughts cleared, he realized he was still inside his cell, and the door was closed.

He staggered up and went to look into the corridor. The two brig guards were lying facedown, and the smell of burnt flesh hung in the air. Pools of blood were slowly forming beneath them. Haggardy was walking away.

On the guards' table was the bottle of myth, ignored.

Thirteen

Toirien had tried. For a little while, she'd been inspired by Harrington. The woman had really seemed to believe she could do it. But she'd given it her best shot, and it wasn't good enough.

Sitting at the screen in the mission room, she sank her head into her hands. She just didn't have the knowledge, nor, she guessed, the intelligence, to understand the engine schematics. She had a basic idea of how the RaptorX engines worked, but while she'd been amazed and impressed at the invention of star-jump technology more than twenty years ago, like most people, she'd never really followed the lay explanations the media had published.

It wasn't like she hadn't received basic modding at conception. Her parents hadn't been entirely irresponsible. No, she wasn't dumb, but neither was she bright enough to wrap her head around this technology, at least not without having it taught to her. She realized she'd probably only gotten her job because Polestar had been desperate for recruits.

Her head ached from going over the engine plans and reading the manuals. She thought she understood better now, but without the chief engineer or someone else to ask, how was she supposed to know if she was right? She couldn't risk starting up the engines. She worried that she could blow up the ship and kill everyone.

So that was it. No one was going home, and it was her fault. She would never see her girls again.

Toirien got up and wandered out of the room. She needed a drink or something stronger, and she needed it fast. She went to her usual supplier, but the man was nowhere to be found. In fact, it occurred to Toirien, the ship seemed strangely empty. She'd heard some kind of commotion earlier, and that goon, Karrev, had broken her concentration when he'd come into the mission room looking for someone. Had she missed something important? Maybe Harrington had come back, and she had some news.

Speeding up her pace, Toirien went to the bridge. It was empty. The canteen was the same. It was dinnertime, and though everyone was making do with rations, most people still congregated in the canteen out of habit. Where had everyone gone?

Eventually, she heard some noises and headed toward the sound. It was coming from the auditorium. There were angry shouts and loud disputes.

Arriving at the scene, she found sixty to seventy crew members in jumbled groups, some lying, some sitting on the floor, some getting physical with each other in minor skirmishes. Ten or fifteen were crowded in a corner. Toirien began to push through them to find out what was so interesting.

"Don't give out so much. There's only a little left. I want my share," came complaints from the group. "It's a waste of time. It's not the real thing. It's a fake. I don't feel anything. Not a thing," others shouted from around the room.

Toirien elbowed more shipmates out of the way, and came upon a couple crouching over a bottle of something. They had tiny droppers, and they were dispensing the bottle's contents into thimble-sized plastic cups. It took Toirien a moment to realize what it was, and the reason for the crew's dissatisfaction. A man received his thimbleful, and tossed it back like a shot.

Misborn. What a waste.

In her long acquaintance with substances that provided an escape from reality, she'd had the privilege of using myth once, just once, but that was enough. The drug had haunted her dreams night and day for months, if not years, after. These idiots didn't understand it had to be injected, not taken by mouth, and it had to be injected at certain points for the full effect.

Myth. A whole bottle. Where had they gotten it from? Who'd managed to smuggle a bottle of myth aboard, and how could they have afforded it? The bottle was nearly empty, but, from the amount of people in the room who seemed to have had some, it must have been full. Someone who lived frugally could retire for life on the cost of that much myth. But, as Toirien knew too well, if you had that much, you were an addict and never thought further than the next run.

She had to have some. Just one more moment of diversion from her misery before a sad, lingering death trapped on that barren planet.

A hand was at the neck of her uniform, dragging her back. She turned and smashed the owner of the hand in her face. The two shipmates in charge of dispensing the myth looked fearful at her violent reaction, and silently handed her a few precious drops.

Holding the cup as steady as if her life depended on it, Toirien went in search of a hypodermic needle and syringe.

———

Carl hated arguing with Sayen, and it felt weird to debate with her blank face and unmoving lips, but he stuck to his guns.

"It's for your own safety," he told her.

"I don't want to be safe. I want to know what's going on. If I'm hooked up, I can hear at least."

"If you're hooked up to electrodes, your container has to be out in the room. Anyone who comes in here can see you. And I can't stay here to protect you. You were right that the ringleader of the mutiny would come here to find me, but it was dangerous. I can't risk leaving you out here alone."

"But why would anyone want to hurt me? I haven't done anyone any harm."

"Sayen, you heard what happened. Things are getting wild out here. I have to put you away." He didn't want to tell her about the resentment the diversion of the defense units' power to the stasis system had caused among the crew.

"Carl, I'm worried that if you disconnect me, that'll be it. No one will wake me up again."

He exhaled. "I know. I get that's what this is about. But I promise, I *promise* I'll wake you up again, and it'll be like you never went to sleep."

No answer came from the stasis' voice. Carl reached over and gently pulled the electrodes from the woman's scalp. Just before he detached the final one, he heard a quiet, "Goodnight, Carl."

He pushed Sayen's container into its slot. As he turned, he saw a figure passing by along the corridor.

"MacAdam," he called. He hadn't seen the engineer all day. He wanted to know if she'd made any progress with the engines.

He waited a few moments, but she didn't return. He went to find her. The door to the medical center was closed, but Carl had a feeling that was where she'd gone. He opened the door and encountered MacAdam making her way out. Her eyes were wide with panic.

"What's wrong? Do you need to see the doctor?" he asked. Recalling that Harrington had found the woman drunk, his first thought was that she might have been trying to find drugs, but they were all well secured, and she hadn't had time to break open the store.

"No," replied MacAdam. "I mean, yes, I was wondering if he was here. I had a terrible headache. But I'm okay now. It seems to be getting better. I'll just go and lie down."

"How did you get on today? Any news on the engines?"

The woman's gaze dropped. "No, I'm sorry. No news yet.

They're rather complicated, you see, and I'm not sure yet what's wrong."

"I wanted to say, if you need any help...I sometimes tweaked the shuttle engines. I could lend a hand, if you tell me what to do."

MacAdam didn't seem to be paying much attention. She shifted her weight from foot to foot. "Thanks. So, I'll be getting along."

"Wait," said Carl, "don't you have to open the access hatch soon? Harrington said she'd be back around sunset. It must be getting on for that now."

"Oh yeah. Yeah. I just need to go get my tools."

"Right. I'll see you there."

Fourteen

Carl checked the time. He wanted to meet Harrington at the access hatch before taking her to speak to the mutineers in the brig, but he also wanted to check on Flux. He hadn't seen the little fella since he'd flown into the stasis room to warn him about the mutiny attempt. If he was quick, he could take a short diversion to his cabin.

Flux's favorite place in the world was Carl's bunk, where he would sleep under the covers with Carl, the sharp little talons at the ends of his wings scratching Carl and waking him. He sometimes wished Flux would sleep hanging upside down like the bats he resembled, but on the other hand, the fur on his belly was very soft and warm.

Carl pushed open his cabin door. There was no sign of Flux. His bedcovers had no familiar bump. Carl checked under them to make sure. The creature wasn't there. He opened his top cupboards nearest the air vent, but they contained no talking alien animals. He stood on a chair and stuck his head into the vent. He called his friend's name and waited.

The vents led throughout the ship and were very good echo chambers. Flux also had excellent hearing, far more sensitive than that of any human. If he was somewhere in the system and *wanted* to go to Carl—he had been known to sulk and refuse to come out on occasion—he would get to him within around five minutes. Carl waited a while and called again. Flux didn't appear.

He began to get worried. He couldn't find his friend, and he needed to get to the access hatch, right then. Why would Flux hide from him? He had nothing to sulk about, Carl didn't think. Had he been harmed during the attempted mutiny? He had to find the animal, but he didn't know where to look. Flux could be anywhere on the *Galathea*, including many places humans couldn't go.

Leaving his cabin, Carl wondered if he should ask if anyone had seen the animal. Flux wasn't supposed to be aboard ship, but since the crash, the rules and protocols seemed to be sliding. He could think of worse things than confessing he was harboring a stowaway, things such as never seeing his childhood friend again.

A woman approached, returning to her quarters with her food ration.

"Hey, I don't suppose you've seen a little flying creature around?" asked Carl. "He's about—" Carl was going to demonstrate Flux's size, when the woman interrupted.

"Your pet, you mean?"

Wide-eyed, Carl replied, "Well, he's not exactly a pet."

"No, sorry. I haven't seen him since yesterday. He's gone missing?"

"That's right."

"I'll ask around. Good luck finding him. Wouldn't like to lose the little scamp. He's a bit of a ship's mascot."

Carl watched the woman as she walked away. *A bit of a ship's mascot?* It seemed that Flux had been getting around. So much for all his efforts to keep him a secret.

Word that Flux was missing spread quickly. The next two people Carl saw commiserated with him and said they would join in the search soon, and that there were others already searching. Though Carl was relieved that half the crew, it seemed, were looking for his lost friend, his anxiety continued to mount.

"Lingiari," a voice called.

Carl turned. One of the crew was some way behind him, beckoning.

When Carl hesitated, the man said, "We've found your pet. Come with me. I'll take you to him."

Carl jogged over and followed the man as he set off. "Where is he?"

"Flight deck."

"What's he doing there? Is he okay?"

"Yeah, yeah. He's fine."

Carl's pace slowed. If Flux was fine, why was he going to him, instead of the other way round? "How come he's on the bridge?"

The man glanced over his shoulder at the pilot. "He's, er, he's hurt himself. Just a little. Didn't want to worry you too much."

Slowing his run to a walk, Carl asked, "How'd he hurt himself?"

"It's his, er, wing. He flew into something."

Carl stopped. Flux had never flown into anything in his life. Except that one time he'd drunk a bit too much of Carl's beer. Something wasn't right.

Noticing Carl had stopped, the man called out, but not to Carl. "The pilot's here. This way."

It was a trap.

Carl started running in the opposite direction, but he wasn't quick enough.

Two explosions against his back were all he remembered before waking up. He was on the bridge. Haggardy's face was the first thing that swam into focus. How had he got out of the brig? The next thing he noticed was the trussed up form of his little friend. They really did have him. That part about getting Carl to go to the bridge had been true. Easier than searching the ship for him and running him down, he supposed. He wondered why Haggardy hadn't killed him. Yet, he mentally added.

"Pilot Lingiari, so glad to see you're awake. That was quite the massacre of the officers, wasn't it? You and Harrington should be congratulated."

Harrington. Was she aboard ship yet? Did Haggardy know when she was coming back?

"We didn't kill anyone," Carl said. "They died when the ship crashed. And it crashed because the master who you brown-nosed ordered Grantwise to land on the planet."

"Hmpf. Let's just say it was very convenient for you. I'll let Polestar and the Global Government decide the truth. For now, my confinement to the brig was unjustified, and it's fortunate for you that I was somewhat inadvertently released. As first mate, I am next in command, therefore the running of the *Galathea* is now down to me.

"However, I'm quite sure C.S.O. Harrington will hold a different opinion, and that's where you come in. It's clear you and she are close, and I'm sure it would pain her deeply to see you harmed. You, my lovely Australian flyboy, are my collateral. You'd better hope she accepts me as the rightful master of the ship. If she refuses, either you or your little friend here will persuade her with your suffering."

He turned to regard the strung up Flux.

"I don't mind which of you it is. I'll let you decide."

Flux cursed loud and long.

Haggardy's eyebrows rose. "Well, I've never heard such language from an alien before." He turned to the man who had tricked Carl into following him. "Put a gag on that filthy-mouthed beast, will you?"

FIFTEEN

Jas didn't know how long the starship had lain there, or how it had arrived in its position deep underground. Built to withstand the rigors of space travel, something had worn it to pieces.

Weapon at the ready, she easily found access through its crumbling walls. Her mind whirled over the possibilities. Did the starship belong to the aliens who had infected the officers of the *Galathea*? Was it somewhere like this that Margret and the others had been when they'd become possessed?

It seemed unlikely. This place was rotten with decay. It reminded her of an ancient wasps' nest, the occupants long gone, and the narrow passages crumbling. She stepped over holes in the floor, placing her hands carefully against the soft walls for balance. She imagined the air smelled musty and close.

How could a starship end up so far underground? If it had crashed or flown directly into the planet's surface, Jas didn't think it would have gone so deep without entirely disintegrating, and there would be an impact crater. Or was it some kind of tunneling machine that had been abandoned there?

She went deeper into the ship, following the path secured by AX7 and AX12. They led her to a cylindrical room that had a ring of holes at eye level in the wall encircling it. Shining her head-light into a hole, the beams glinted on a material like glass at the end of a short tunnel. Beyond the glass was rock. She was looking out of one of the same kind of windows she'd seen from the outside. It definitely seemed like the ship had been intended originally for travelling through space. Or could it be a deep-water vessel? The planetary survey had revealed three deep oceans, but they were all far from where the *Galathea* had crashed.

Drawing back from the hole, she turned, and stopped. Her headlight had swept the center of the room and glanced upon something she hadn't noticed before—something different from the rest of the place. Something alive. Jas lowered her head to focus the light on the object.

Fleshy lumps were spread over the floor of the chamber, about as high as Jas's waist. They weren't old and decaying like the rest of the ship. They looked like some kind of fungus or inverted living bags.

Jas took a step toward the lumps. Immediately, joy overwhelmed her. She fell to her knees. Her heart lifted. She wept.

Through the excess of emotion, she tried to understand where the feeling was coming from, but mostly, she didn't care. She remained kneeling, unable to do anything within the grip of her feelings.

AX7 and AX12 remained motionless, awaiting her instruction, for a long time. Every so often, Jas would sob or gasp.

Some time later, the waves of raw feeling subsided a little, and Jas broke away from their hold on her. She got up, finally registering the pain in her knees, and turned, puzzled, trying to understand what it was she was experiencing. What had happened immediately prior to the explosion of emotion? She had stepped toward the fleshy objects in the room's center. She swung around to them once more, lighting their smooth, satiny surfaces with her flashlight. Another surge of ecstatic happiness arose, and Jas fought to prevent herself from being overwhelmed by it.

It was those things. It had to be. Somehow, they were

affecting her emotionally. Were they projecting their own feelings into her? If they had been alone down here while the ship had been decaying, it would be natural that they would feel joy at being finally found.

She turned on her mic to broadcast outside her helmet. "Hello?" she said. She took a step toward the lumps, but hesitated. Were these the aliens that had infected the crew? She knew she should get out of there, but she found she didn't want to. Something was telling her the aliens weren't harmful. She had to approach them, and it wasn't that she couldn't fight the compulsion, but that she didn't *want* to fight it.

Ripples of happiness coursed through her. In spite of herself, she grinned. The aliens seemed very pleased to have her attention, whatever they were. She gently prodded one with a gloved hand. A brief moment of fear sparked inside her, then pleasure.

In all her years in space, Jas had never encountered an alien so weird. How on Earth did they survive down there?

"What are you? How are you making me feel like this?" Jas didn't often pay much attention to her emotions. In fact, she would have described herself as pretty emotionless. These creatures were making her uncomfortable.

"AX7," she asked the unit, "do you notice anything different in your systems?" The defense units were intelligent in a sense, but they weren't supposed to feel any emotion, though she had never quite believed that.

"I notice no change in my systems, C.S.O. Harrington."

Jas was relieved. At least the defense units weren't vulnerable to these aliens.

She didn't know what to do next. She'd come here to find the aliens who had infected the crew, but instead she seemed to have found something entirely different. Were these fungi left behind by whatever had flown this starship? What should she do about them?

And should she continue the search for the hostile aliens? She'd been through the entire alien structure and found nothing.

Nothing had approached her or tried to infect her, to her knowledge. She was none the wiser for her trip.

The joy the fungal bodies had somehow transmitted when they realized they'd been found indicated that they wanted to be rescued. Looking around her, it wasn't difficult to see why. If they remained there, the starship would eventually collapse and crush them. Also, these strange organisms might have benefits to offer. They'd survived all this time within the trap of the hostile aliens.

She couldn't decide what to do. To give herself time to think, she left the chamber to continue her search of the ship. In response to the sensations of despair that threatened to take over her, she turned to the creatures, and said, "I'll be back. I promise."

Commanding AX7 and AX12 to go first, she hadn't taken more than a few steps when the floor collapsed, already weakened by the heavy tread of the units. Jas tumbled down, hitting and then breaking through three floors in succession, until she struck hard metal. The surface was uneven, and her combat suit didn't completely protect her from the knobs and spikes that thrust into her back and thighs.

She was lying on top of a huge, complex machine. It looked like the starship's engine. She quickly checked her helmet display. No radiation. Unlike the rest of the ship, the engine looked comparatively untouched. Could MacAdam possibly use parts from this machine to fix their own engine? It seemed unlikely that the technology of different galactic species would be similar enough for that to work, but it was worth investigating.

It was time to get back to the *Galathea*. She had one, possibly two, important discoveries to report, and Lingiari had made her promise she would be back before sunset. She had been in the bowels of the alien structure too long.

By the time Jas had worked her way out of the starship and then up through the structure to the surface, she was bone weary. She gratefully strapped herself to the back of AX7 and told it to return to the ship. It was already dark, and brilliant stars were piercing the deep black sky. As AX7 jogged across the plain, she wondered what had been going on aboard ship while she'd been gone. She hoped MacAdam had made some headway with the engine schematics.

The access hatch was a dark hole in the side of the downed ship. MacAdam had opened it as instructed, and Lingiari must have kept it open, despite her lateness. She looked forward to seeing the pilot again. She would also go straight to see Lee. She'd been neglecting the navigator.

AX7 methodically climbed the side of the ship and swung up and through the hatch. As it entered the corridor, Jas unhitched herself from it and slid to the floor.

When she looked up, she found that her welcoming committee was somewhat different from what she'd anticipated. MacAdam was there, but there was no sign of Lingiari. In his place was the last person she'd expected—Haggardy, out of the brig.

Haggardy, free as a bird, standing right in front of her, an oily grin on his face.

"C.S.O. Harrington. How nice to see you again."

Sixteen

Jas was trapped. Sitting across from Haggardy in the mission room, next to MacAdam, she might as well have been as tied up as Lingiari. Haggardy not only had the pilot as hostage, but he could also command the defense units, and that meant he could do just about whatever he wanted. Maybe he already knew he didn't need Lingiari, and he was just having fun. Or maybe he knew that if it weren't for the fact that he might harm the pilot, she would be far more reckless about risking her life to go against him.

"So, Harrington, what's your assessment? You say there's a starship beneath the structure you visited, and that it's of alien make. Is it native to the planet?"

"I don't know. You tell me. Did you see anything like upturned bags when you supposedly managed to escape the alien infection that took the others?"

Haggardy's eyes narrowed. "I didn't."

"The creatures I found seem to be kind of telepathic, only with emotions, not thoughts. When I found them, they communicated that they were overjoyed, as if they'd been alone a very long time, or in fear of something, or both."

"A telepathic species?" He rubbed his chin. "Polestar might be very interested in those. Could be worth more than a penny. Did they seem dangerous?"

"Not at all. I touched one. It didn't respond, except emotionally."

Haggardy put his hands together, overlapping his fingers. "First things first, we need to get this ship spaceborne. You've heard nothing from Earth?"

"No," replied Jas, "though we don't know whether it's because they haven't sent anything, or the comm hasn't picked up the packet."

"How far have you got with repairing the engines?" he asked MacAdam.

"Not far," the engineer replied. "I don't think I can fix them."

"Hmpf," said Haggardy. "Nothing from Earth, and we can't repair our engines. It looks as though this alien craft might be our best avenue for exploration at the moment. And I'm very curious about those creatures.

"Right. At first light, you and you," he pointed at Jas and MacAdam, "go back to that ship and see what you can find. Take portable scanners. And bring back those creatures. All of them if you can." He stood. "Meanwhile, I'm going to keep all my eggs in one basket. All three of you can spend the night here. The brig's occupied at the moment, with my rescuers." He gave a small smile, and after ordering defense units to bind Jas and MacAdam, he left.

———

The following day, Jas insisted that MacAdam cover herself up entirely before entering the alien structure with her. Lingiari had explained Lee's theory to them overnight, about how the structures might require a sample of their DNA to begin the infection process. Jas wished she'd had a combat suit to lend the engineer that would fit her stocky frame.

The woman had been mostly silent as they'd journeyed across

the plain, and she remained taciturn as they made their way into the structure. Jas wasn't one for talking much, either, but she sensed there was more to MacAdam's behavior than her laconic personality.

"What do you think your chances are of finding something to fix the engines?" she asked her.

MacAdam snorted. "Honestly? Next to zero."

"Is that because it's alien technology? I suppose the two wouldn't marry well."

"It's not that," said MacAdam. "I looked at those engine plans all day yesterday. I read the manuals till my eyes were sore, but I'm not confident that I understand them. I'm sorry. I'm just not cut out for the job. I should never have taken it. It was just..." Her words faltered to silence.

"What?" Jas asked.

"Never mind."

"You need a good reason to work aboard a prospecting ship," said Jas. "Me, I had nothing to keep me on Earth. All the family I had, as far as I know, died on Mars. The colony domes exploded when I was a baby. My parents had just enough time to put me into a safety capsule. I was nearly dead when the rescuers found me. I don't even know who my parents were. The records were destroyed in the explosion. I could be one of several couples' child. No one knows."

"I'm sorry."

Jas shrugged. "I don't dwell on it. How about you? Why did you sign up?"

The engineer didn't answer for a moment, then she said, "If I tell you, do you promise not to laugh?"

"I promise."

"I...er...I signed up to get away from drink and drugs."

It was a struggle, but Jas managed to keep a straight face. "You thought you'd get away from addictive substances aboard a prospector?"

"I know," said MacAdam, shaking her head, "what was I

thinking? Months of travel, confined to a starship with nothing to do but the same boring tasks over and over again. Not likely to find much drug abuse there."

Both women laughed. As their laughs faded, MacAdam said, more quietly, "I wanted to get my kids back. They got taken off me, you see, years ago."

"Now it's my turn to be sorry."

"No, don't feel sorry for me. I deserved it. They deserved better than me, rather. They deserved a chance at a good life. But I thought, I hoped, if I could get my life straight, maybe we could be a family again. But when I think about it, it's probably for the best that they don't see me. They'll be settled with new parents now, and they'll have forgotten about me. If I turn up to claim them, it'll only upset everyone. I should leave them be."

Jas wasn't sure that MacAdam was right. If the children were naturals, there were unlikely to be many couples interested in them. Nowadays, even couples who produced no sperm or eggs could have their own children and shape them to their desires. There were very few people who were altruistic enough to take on someone else's natural offspring, the result of a random genetic lottery with who knew what physical or mental problems waiting to emerge.

The two women followed the defense units down to the base of the structure. Jas led MacAdam into the cavern.

"Is that it?" asked the engineer as the side of the alien ship came into view.

"That's it. We can get in over there. But I warn you, when we approach the creatures I was telling you about, you'll probably feel overwhelmed with happiness for a while, until they get used to us and calm down a bit."

"Overwhelmed with happiness? I can deal with that. I haven't felt that way for a long time."

SEVENTEEN

A block. It was a single, simple hexagonal block Toirien and Harrington had found next to the *Galathea* when they'd returned to the ship. No entrance or other break showed in its smooth gray surface. Harrington had paled at the sight of it, but she'd offered no comment. There seemed to be nothing for either of them to say. Whatever was living on the planet that had infected the officers, it seemed like they knew the ship was there, and they had plans for it. On the backs of the defense units, Toirien and Harrington had gone quickly into the ship and left it to the units to bring up the telepathic aliens. Toirien had secured the hatch tightly once everyone was inside.

Her experience of the telepathically relayed emotions of the aliens, which Harrington had unofficially named Paths, was such that it was like a run, and though the run was indeed high, coming down brought her lower than she'd ever been. She realized that the happiness they filled her with was almost entirely unfamiliar. Only dim, drug-hazed memories of the time she'd had her children with her came close, and since that time, her only moments of pleasure had been when she'd been able to escape the hard reality that was her lot in life.

After passing through the chamber that held the creatures,

she'd descended with Harrington into the ship's engine. But the machinery made no sense to her, based on her understanding of the *Galathea's* engines. She couldn't find any similarities, nor recognize any parts, nor understand how the thing moved the ship through space.

After long hours of exploration and study, she'd silently shaken her head at Harrington. It was no use. Maybe if the chief engineer had survived, he might have made something of it, but understanding the technology was beyond her.

All that had been left for them to do was to transport the fleshy lumps back to the ship. They'd lifted from the floor like fungi pulled from soil, radiating waves of joy. It was impossible to explain why, but both she and Harrington had no doubt that these strange creatures were completely harmless, and they were ecstatic to be taken from the starship. They'd packed them onto trailers and the defense units had hauled them across the plain.

Back aboard the *Galathea*, after placing the aliens in quarantine, Toirien had persuaded First Mate Haggardy to allow her to return to her cabin. The man acquiesced, perhaps realizing she didn't pose him any threat. She had no interest in the running of the ship nor anything else.

Throughout the day, Toirien had been hoping for and anticipating the moment when she could get back to her cabin. When she arrived, it was with great relief that she saw no one had discovered the few drops of myth she'd secreted away along with the hypodermic needle and syringe she'd pilfered from the medical center.

The room was empty. Her bunkmates were away in the canteen eating their evening rations. She needed to start her run immediately, before any of them came back.

She lay on her bunk and pulled down her pants. She tried to recall the place her supplier had shown her to inject the drug all those years ago. He'd told her the myth would work wherever it was injected, but for the maximum effect, you had to hit one of a few perfect spots. She craned her neck to look along the length of her bare midriff and thighs. It had been somewhere between her hip and pubic bone, she seemed to remember.

It was ironic, Toirien thought, that when she was at her lowest, she had the very thing that would take her the farthest she could get from her utter misery. She wondered whether, if it weren't for the promise of the ecstasy of myth, she wouldn't have unclipped herself from the unit that had carried her up the ship to ensure a quick, painless death on the ground below. Maybe, once this run was over, that would be an idea she would carry out. It would be quick at least. She didn't want to be around when whatever was in those blocks decided to come out and get them.

Holding the skin taut between the fingers of her left hand, she guided the needle home and depressed the plunger on the syringe. The second the myth hit her system, she was gone. The syringe slipped from her hand, the needle still in her flesh, and hung to one side. Toirien's respiration sped up, her mouth gaped, and her eyes were open but unseeing.

Eighteen

Jas was in the middle of a standoff with Haggardy on the bridge.

"What do you think we're going to do?" she exclaimed. "Leave the ship? You've got the defense units under your control. Do you think we'll round up the crew and persuade them to commit mutiny? They've already seen what happened to Karrev. It isn't like they're going to want to follow in his footsteps. And if *we* start anything, the units will put a stop to it easily enough. You let MacAdam go. Why not us?"

Haggardy regarded her from beneath his brows as she sat at his feet, her ankles bound and her hands tied behind her back. Jas still hadn't figured out if he'd been infected or not. She'd missed that first phase, when the victims showed that touch of inhumanity. Now, he seemed normal. If Haggardy was infected, she supposed he would have been leading them all into the nearest structure so they could be possessed too. He would be forcing them into that structure that had appeared beside the ship, yet he hadn't. That didn't make sense if he had been taken over by an alien, unless there was something preventing him from doing that, something she wasn't aware of, or that didn't fit in with his plans right then. Maybe the man in front of her really was all Haggardy and nothing else.

He leaned forward. "You never liked me, did you, Harrington? Well, I've got news for you. I never liked you either. Always doing everything by the book, getting in the way of common sense and everyone's chance at a bonus. Ms. High and Mighty, weren't you? You know, it wasn't just me, either. No one liked you."

"Oh, grow up, Haggardy. Doing your job isn't about being liked. Face it—you need us. You need Lingiari to fly the ship, and you need me to keep you safe and everyone else under control." Jas wasn't convinced about that last part herself, but she hoped she sounded convincing to him. She didn't relish the idea of another night on the hard floor of the bridge. The ship's temperature had equalized with the outside, and a chill had seeped into her bones.

"And keeping that animal tied up is totally ridiculous," Jas added. Flux's bindings and gag had been on him for more than twenty-four hours, and the creature looked ill.

Haggardy snorted and stood, but he was knocked to the floor. The ship rocked violently, as if there was an earthquake. The floor shook and seemed to drop several centimeters. Haggardy had lost his smug, haughty look, and he gripped the floor, terrified. Jas stared at Lingiari as she tried to figure out what was going on.

The movement stopped, and Jas went to speak, but before the words left her mouth the vibration started again. They weren't only shaking from side to side, they were lifting and then dropping to a lower level. They were sinking into the planet surface.

Her heart froze as she realized what it meant. That was what had happened to the starship at the base of the structure. It had once been on the surface, but the ground had opened up and it had been drawn gradually deeper and deeper down into the soil and rock.

If they didn't get off the planet soon, the same thing would happen to them.

NINETEEN

A vision played in Toirien's mind. She was traveling head first down a tunnel, carried on a breath of warm air toward a welcoming glow. She knew that everyone she'd ever loved, everything she'd ever wanted in life, lay at the end of that tunnel, bathed in the gentle light. Tears ran from her eyes and down her face, and they dripped from her chin before the balmy breeze lifted them and bore them away. She reached out with her arms, eagerly speeding herself on, anticipating the moment of arrival. The limbs she saw before her weren't her own. Her muscled, freckled forearms had been replaced with long, lithe, tapered specimens, just like the arms of someone modded for physical perfection.

She burst from the tunnel into the light, which was as warm and comforting as a mother's embrace. Joy suffused her being, and she floated, twisting and turning gently in the pure love that seemed to envelop her. Toirien spread herself wide, and her physical body and her mind melded with the glow, suffusing it so that neither were separate from the other.

As a part of this ethereal entity, she oozed herself wide, feeling with her senses the edges of her domain. But she was limitless. She encountered beings similar to herself. Others who were part of the one, unknowable, nameless whole. Toirien reached into the souls of these other beings and became one with them, perfectly harmonious and entire.

Immersed in the completeness, she became aware of others different from the rest. Snatches of thought and glimpses of shadows flitted through her perception, too fleeting to understand or behold. These beings left behind them jarring vibrations that upset the harmonious unity. As these shadows faded, other beings appeared at the edge of her consciousness—beings who seemed to see into the depths of her consciousness, and to the great, weeping wound at her core.

These beings approached and lifted her up, pulling the tendrils of her disintegrated self from the ether, and carried her away. Toirien fought. She rolled and jackknifed and tried to prevent herself from being taken from her bliss. She tried to scream, but she had no mouth and no vocal chords. She tried to hold onto something, but she had no hands and there was nothing to hold on to in that intangible, sublime place.

She struggled until she saw them. She knew who they were immediately. Their small, stocky figures, their bouncing ginger curls, their bright smiles. But as she drew nearer to her children, she realized this couldn't be them. They were too young. They would have grown in the intervening years since she'd last seen them. They couldn't be real, and yet they seemed more real than anything she'd ever known.

The glow faded. Her feet—all of a sudden she had feet—hit pavement, and she was running, running into the arms of her darlings. Wrapped around each other, Toirien couldn't breathe in enough of her children's sweet scent, feel enough of their enveloping arms, bury enough of her face in their soft hair.

"Mammy, Mammy, you came back. We knew you would come back one day. And you're here. We missed you so much. Now you'll never, ever leave us again, Mammy, will you? We love you, Mammy, we love you."

Toirien wanted to say, no, that she would never, ever leave

them again, but somehow she knew the words were wrong. Her children were wrong. Something stopped her from giving into the vision that was playing out before her.

"I can't," she said. "I can't. I can't come back to you. I'm too far away. There's too much space between us, and too much time has passed."

"Yes, you can, Mammy. You can come back. There's nothing wrong. Nothing wrong at all. Silly Mammy. All this time you've been worrying—worrying about nothing. Things aren't as bad as you think. You only need to try."

Toirien's heart raced. She stared into the face of little Grace, trying to reconcile her childish features with the words that were coming out of her mouth.

"Silly Mammy," echoed Joan. "Come back to us. We've been waiting for you a very long time. Don't make us wait any longer."

The little girls broke their embrace with her and held hands with each other. "Bye-bye for now, Mammy. See you soon." They skipped away.

The image of her children was replaced by the view of her bunk screen and the ceiling of her cabin. Toirien's run had ended, and she was suddenly completely sober. A soreness emanated from her hip. She looked down to see the hypodermic needle hanging from her skin. Wincing, she drew it out. A drop of blood welled up.

Her cabin mates hadn't returned, which meant she'd only been gone a short while. The run should have lasted hours. She couldn't understand it. Toirien pulled up her pants and fastened them. Her heart was racing, and she breathed heavily, though she didn't know if these were the effects of the myth or her strange vision.

She could hardly believe what her children had said in her dream. It was all impossible. Yet what they'd said was true. She hadn't believed the evidence of her eyes. She'd always thought she would mess up again, and that she would let everyone down. She'd never believed the fix could be such a simple, easy thing. She hadn't trusted in herself, but had always focused on the worst possible outcome.

Maybe her dream was just the meanderings of her drugged imagination, but even if there was the slightest chance they weren't, if she'd been taken to a place where she could connect with her children and the truth of what they'd said, it was worth telling the others. It was worth trying. What did she have left to lose?

She had a weird feeling that she'd been strongly shaken while she was out. As she swung her legs over her bunk and jumped down, another vibration started up.

Twenty

Toirien pushed open the door to the bridge and staggered as she burst into the room. The ship was shaking again.

"I thought of something," she shouted over the grinding noise. Haggardy, Harrington and Lingiari were all staring at her after her sudden entrance. "I should have said it before, but...I...I couldn't find any damage to the engines when I scanned them. I thought I just didn't understand what I was looking at. But I've just realized...we haven't even tried to start the engines since we crashed. What if they aren't that badly damaged? What if they just shut down because of the crash-landing? We could try to start them up and see what happens."

"Is this correct?" Haggardy asked Jas and Lingiari, raising his voice. "You didn't even *try* to lift off the planet?"

The vibrations stopped. Jas and Lingiari were staring at each other.

"I never thought..." said Lingiari. "The crash was so bad, I just assumed..."

"Me too," said Jas. "We never thought to even try it. To think we might have been sitting here all this time when we didn't need to..."

"Let me try," said the pilot, trying to get to his feet. "Untie me, Haggardy."

The first mate considered a moment, then instructed a defense unit to release Lingiari from his bonds. He slid into the pilot's seat, brushed the screen in front of him with his fingertips, and flipped some switches, but the screen remained dark. He turned to MacAdam. "It was worth a try, but she's dead. Not a squeak from her."

"The systems are dead," said Jas. "Doesn't mean the engines are."

"Same thing," replied Lingiari. "It's not like I can crank her to start her up. Sorry, it's a waste of time." He unclipped his harness and stood up.

"We've got to try again," said Jas. "This vibrating—I think it's the planet drawing us in, like it did with the other starship. Maybe it does that with every ship that lands on it."

"Krat," said Lingiari. "That makes sense."

Haggardy collapsed into the master's seat and ran a hand over his face.

"Wait. Maybe it's just a power thing," said Toirien. "The ship's been on emergency power since we crashed. Maybe there isn't enough power to get the system working."

Haggardy looked up. "It's worth a try." He spoke to Toirien. "You, connect all the defense units to the ship's system and direct all their power to the pilot controls."

"No," said Jas. "Not all the units. We need some to keep Lee in stasis."

"Hmpf," said Haggardy, "I saw you've been using defense unit power to maintain our dearly departed navigator. Well, her prolonged departure has finished. *All* available power, do you understand?" he said to MacAdam. "Can you do that?"

The engineer hesitated.

"No," exclaimed Jas and Lingiari. The pilot flew at Haggardy, but he fell before taking more than a few steps, stunned by a defense unit.

"You can't kill her," shouted Jas, her hands clenched into fists. "She...she's your best asset. I've never known anyone so smart. What if your plan doesn't work and the engines won't start? What are you going to do then? We're going to be dragged down into the planet, and Lee might be the only one who can figure out what to do. You *need* her."

The terrible grinding vibration started up again. The unconscious Lingiari flopped to and fro. Haggardy and MacAdam grabbed whatever they could to stay on their feet.

Haggardy said to the engineer," All the units except those powering the stasis room." He added, looking at Jas, "For now." MacAdam left the room, taking Haggardy's defense unit guards with her. But the man also had a gun, which he trained on Jas.

She nearly wept with relief at saving Lee. She also despaired. She'd never realized how dumb and ruthless Haggardy was. He really would have killed Lee. With him running the show, they'd all be lucky to survive.

After a short time, MacAdam returned. Lingiari turned, groaning, onto his back as she entered the bridge. "I've attached all the units to the pilot control system, except the ones powering the stasis room. We can try again."

Rubbing his chest where the stun beam had struck, Lingiari returned to the pilot seat. He tried the controls once more. The others watched and waited. He shook his head. "Nothing. She's dead."

"Perhaps we need a little more power," said Haggardy. "I appreciate your attachment to your shipmate, Harrington and Lingiari, but honestly, she's dead meat. It's time for a noble sacrifice to save the crew. *You'll* appreciate the sentiment, Harrington, I'm sure."

"You misborn fool," said Jas, pushing herself awkwardly to her feet. She teetered, her ankles bound, her feet pressed together. "I keep telling you that woman is the best asset this ship has. If you turn off her stasis, we're *all* dead meat."

"Hmpf. Well, let's see if you're right, shall we?" He instructed

MacAdam to untie Jas's bonds. "Let's go and speak to Navigator Lee. We can explain the situation, and let her plead for her life."

Blood slowly returning to her feet, Jas wobbled as she followed the first mate to the stasis room. Lingiari and MacAdam came along with them. On the way, the ship experienced another bout of violent vibration. Jas wondered how far they'd sunk into the ground. If the engines really had been undamaged before, were they the same now?

Lee seemed unchanged when they pulled her container out from the wall. Sparks fastened the electrodes to her scalp. Jas's heart was in her throat. It would be unspeakably cruel to wake the navigator up only for her to find out she might be about to die, along with the rest of them.

"Who's there?" Lee asked.

"It's me, Sayen," said Lingiari. "Harrington's here, too, and the engineer, MacAdam—"

"And I," said Haggardy. "How nice to speak to you again, Navigator Lee."

"Haggardy?"

"That's Acting Master Haggardy to you."

Lingiari said, "Sayen, we need your help." He explained MacAdam's theory about the engines, and the fact that maybe they couldn't start them because the ship was on emergency power.

"Wait a minute," said Lee, "the ship's systems would have shut down during the crash. Didn't you try to reboot?"

"We didn't," exclaimed Jas. "We didn't even try to restart them. I don't believe it."

"That's what happens when you have a security officer and a pilot in charge of a starship," said Haggardy, acidly. " Well done, Navigator Lee. You may have just saved your life."

———

Carl had warned the crew. Everyone was in their crash seats. Haggardy had taken the master's chair, and even Flux had been unbound and was sitting in a bag that Carl had strapped into a seat on the bridge. The little fella's head peeked out, and his long, black-tufted ears were switching to and fro. He seemed to have got a lot better as soon as he was released.

Haggardy had insisted that Harrington stay within his sight. She was sitting at the comm control.

Carl's pilot's screen was live, the measurements and graphs glowing as bright as they ever had, which was a welcome sight after days of darkness. Lee's advice had been spot on. The ship's systems had rebooted like a dream. The interior lights had come on, the air circulation system had whirred to life—everything had started up as if it had never stopped. Cheers from the crew had echoed down the corridors.

Haggardy's patience had been tested by MacAdam's insistence that she check and doubly secure the hatch she'd opened. She'd also made the access hatches to the engine airtight. Though the engine could operate perfectly within the vacuum of space, the crew could not, and she didn't know if the hull had been breached during the crash-landing.

Now, the most important thing was to get off the planet.

"All clear," Carl said into his mic. "Lift off in one minute." He would use the RaptorXs to fly them into orbit. It would take a huge amount of fuel to push the massive starship into space, but they had no choice.

A ping sounded from the comm desk.

"It's a packet," exclaimed Harrington. "Polestar's sent a reply to Lee's message."

"Read it out," said Haggardy.

"Packet from Navigator Lee aboard the *Galathea* acknowledged. Please proceed to K. 23198f, otherwise called Dawn, where you will receive further instructions from the resident authorities."

"They don't want us to return to Earth?" asked Carl.

"Doesn't look like it," replied Harrington. "I guess they don't know whether or not we're carrying infected crew."

"So what're they going to do with us at the new planet?" asked Carl.

"We will comply with the directive from Polestar," said Haggardy.

Carl's screen was flashing. "Prepare for lift-off."

The RaptorX engines fired, and Carl's chest constricted. In front of him, the visual of the planet shook before dropping slowly down. Whoops and hollers could be heard from the rest of the ship.

"You beaut," exclaimed Carl. Exhilaration flooded him as the *Galathea* lifted from the frigid, barren plain below and moved slowly toward the horizon, which began to bend into a curve as they flew higher. He'd completed this maneuver once before, just once, and that had been in a simulator.

Both the ship and his nerve were holding up, however. Carl lifted the ship steadily through the atmosphere as it gradually thinned and the sky darkened. Acceleration pressure pushed him into his seat. The first stars became visible, twinkling in the thin gas of the upper atmosphere.

After what seemed like a long time, they achieved orbit, and Carl cut the Raptors. He floated briefly against his seat harness until the *Galathea's* artificial gravity kicked in.

He'd done it. He'd lifted a starship off from a planet, and maybe it had been the first time anyone had done it. He'd never heard of another pilot landing—okay, crashing—a starship onto a planet and taking off again. He might be the first.

"Lingiari," said Harrington, "I've sent over the coordinates in that packet. Do you want to input them? We're going to try to starjump, right?"

Oh yeah. He'd forgotten about that for a moment. Carl shelved his satisfaction for later contemplation.

He had a ship to fly.

DAWN

ONE

Arriving from a starjump was like swimming up from deep water, emerging into the air, and rising to the upper stratosphere. Carl had starjumped more times than he could remember, but he didn't think he'd ever get used to it. Intense pressure on his body and, it seemed, his mind, gave way to a sense of infinite space and incredible lightness. Like the rest of the crew on the bridge of the *Galathea*, he grabbed the nearest fixed object as if to steady himself, even though he was well-secured in his pilot's harness.

The first thing he did was check on Harrington, who was sitting bound to a seat at the comm console. She was looking a little green, but she seemed okay. That misborn Haggardy was taking his revenge too far. Harrington had done the right thing when she'd put him in the brig. What else was the chief security officer supposed to do if she suspected he'd been infected by a hostile alien? As far as Carl was concerned, Haggardy was still under suspicion.

Turning his gaze to the former First Mate Haggardy, now acting master of the *Galathea*, he had an urge to punch the older man in his smug, self-satisfied face. What had he done to protect the crew from the aliens on K. 67092d? Nothing. It had been up to Harrington, Navigator Sayen Lee, and himself to save the ship and their shipmates. Now, the *Galathea* had lost nearly twenty officers, and their prospecting mission for their employer, Polestar, was over. No one would receive any bonuses. The crew was on the verge of mutiny, and it was possible one of them could be possessed by an alien.

"Not bad, Lingiari," said Haggardy, releasing his safety harness, standing, and stretching. "Grantwise couldn't have done better himself."

Carl grimaced. As far as he was concerned, if it weren't for Haggardy's spinelessness, Pilot Grantwise might still be alive. Carl had always longed to pilot a starship, but not like this.

The comm console bleeped. It hadn't taken the governorship of Dawn—the planet they were now orbiting—long to get in touch. Haggardy went over to the panel and swiped and pressed the screen. After briefly scanning the message, he commanded the two defense units who stood guarding the door, and who accompanied him everywhere round the clock, to follow him as he left the bridge.

Carl unclipped his harness and went to Harrington. He unknotted the binding around her ankles and wrists.

"Thanks," she said, "but are you sure you should do this? He could be back any minute."

"Krat him. What's he going to do? Tie you up again?"

"He could put me in the brig, or worse."

"If he puts you in the brig, at least you'll get to lie down. And as for doing anything worse, that'd take guts. Does that sound like Haggardy to you?"

"You've got a point." Harrington rose to her feet and twisted her ankles and wrists in circles. She was half a head taller than Carl, but that had never bothered him. He'd always liked her statuesque frame.

Harrington returned to the comm seat and scanned the screen. "He's taking the call from Dawn in his cabin. I wonder what they're talking about."

"I'm wondering how he's going to spin what happened on K. 67092d to make himself come out smelling sweet," said Carl. "That'll be a job and a half."

"What's he going to tell them about you and me, and Lee?" Harrington shook her head. "It's going to be hard to explain ourselves to Polestar and maybe the Global Government when we don't know the story he's told them."

"No point in worrying about it now." Carl perched on the comm console. "So, what's the plan?"

"I'm waiting to hear what the governor of Dawn has to say. Why did Polestar tell us to come here and not return to Earth for quarantine? We have to be sure none of the remaining crew are infected before we go planetside anywhere in the galaxy. We can't risk those aliens spreading." She thumbed an icon on the comm screen, but it had no effect. "I can't access external comms. I bet we're both locked out of all but the most basic systems. If we get the chance, we have to warn the governor about Haggardy. If only I could contact Dawn directly myself, or even Earth."

The door to the bridge opened, and Haggardy returned. "I don't recall telling you to untie our security officer, Lingiari."

"I don't remember you having any reason to tie her up."

Haggardy's eyebrows rose. "You must have a short memory, then. But never mind. Luckily for you, you've pre-empted my order. I was about to set you free myself, Harrington."

"Came to your senses, finally?" the security officer asked. "Or maybe that alien you're carrying around messed with your brain?"

The acting master's expression hardened. "That's a serious accusation to be throwing around. I'd be careful about repeating it to the governor when you arrive on Dawn. Or you might find yourself under suspicion."

"You're sending her to Dawn?" asked Carl.

"I'm sending both of you. Or rather, the governor has requested that you pay her a visit."

Carl and Harrington's gazes met.

"She would have liked to speak to Navigator Lee, too, but that would be difficult to arrange with the navigator in stasis. The governor's an understanding woman, and she agreed to leave her out of investigations for the time being, until the ship is declared free of infection and safe for her to board."

"But Lingiari and I could be infected," Harrington said. "How does she know we won't spread the infection to Dawn?"

"Dawn is a quarantine and vetting station for ships that might be harboring this infection," replied Haggardy. "The governor explained that it isn't the first time this hostile species has been encountered. Polestar recognized the pattern of events we experienced, and that's why it sent us here. You'll both be tested. If you pass, you'll wait planetside until the whole ship's crew has been examined and cleared. Then, we can return to Earth."

Carl couldn't see how it would be possible to test for something so difficult to detect. He wondered how many false positives they'd found. "And if we don't pass?"

"I've sent a team of defense units to clear the shuttle wreckage from the shuttle bay," said Haggardy. "A transport from Dawn will be arriving soon. You can go there to wait for it. Don't even think about trying anything, Harrington. I can countermand the defense units in a moment, and even if you were to get back control of the ship, where do you think you would go?"

Haggardy obviously wasn't going to tell them what would happen if they weren't cleared of carrying the alien infection. And what did he mean when he said the species had already been encountered? Was it already spreading across the galaxy?

The ship's corridors were quiet as they went to the shuttle bay. The crew were always subdued after arriving from a starjump, and Carl imagined that many were confused and worried by the events leading up to their arrival on Dawn. Like him, they'd probably anticipated a return to Earth, not this detour.

At the bay, the sight of the remains of the small ship he'd flown on countless trips to and from the *Galathea* tore at Carl's heart. The moment that he'd participated in its destruction had been a sad one.

Defense units were busy pulling apart the wreckage and taking it away. Where parts of the shuttle had melted to the floor, they were using their weapons to sever them.

Harrington leaned against the shuttle bay wall, her arms folded.

"We're just going to do what he says?" Carl asked.

"I don't see what choice we have. He's right. We can't do anything while he has the defense units under his control. If we run and hide, they'll find us in the end, and we'd only be putting off the inevitable. Besides, we aren't infected, so we'll pass the tests, and then maybe we'll get a chance to tell our side of the story. And if Haggardy's possessed, they'll find out."

"I'm wondering what else the governor said that he didn't tell us," said Carl.

"Yeah, I'm wondering that too. Hey, Is Flux going to be okay while we're gone?"

Carl had been concerned about his small alien friend, too. "Yeah, he'll be fine. The little fella's got plenty of friends to look after him." Carl smiled at the memory of finding out that Flux hadn't been as much of a secret aboard ship as he'd thought he had.

An alarm sounded, and the shuttle bay lights flashed. A synthetic voice came over the intercom, warning them to evacuate as a transport was approaching. Carl and Harrington waited outside the bay while the transport docked. When they returned, a small, neat, kite-shaped shuttle awaited them. An MT11. It was an old model, but Carl had always appreciated the economy and simplicity of its design.

As they boarded, he noticed a modification: a plexiglass screen separated the passengers from the pilot. A precautionary measure, Carl guessed, to protect the pilot from infection.

They strapped themselves in, and Carl tried to recall what he knew of the place they were going. All he could remember about Dawn was that it was a frontier colony: a resource-rich but undeveloped world that the Global Government had purchased for a fortune from Polestar's rival prospecting company. The Government had strongly encouraged a disaffected group who were generating political tensions to settle there. What had they been called? He couldn't remember.

Dawn was also the only planet where humans had settled alongside a secondary colonizing alien species, the Haidiren.

"What do you think's going to happen if we don't pass the test?" he asked Harrington.

"Why wouldn't we pass?" But from the way she didn't look him in the eye, Carl guessed she was thinking the same thing as him—what if the whole thing was a set up to get them off the ship quickly and quietly? What if there was no test? What might really be awaiting them on Dawn?

Two

The shuttle doors opened, and Jas Harrington unexpectedly got her first close-up glimpse of Dawn. She'd thought there would be some kind of sealed tunnel leading them from the shuttle to the testing center, something to keep them separate to prevent the spread of any infection they might be carrying. What she saw instead, beyond the shuttle runway and perimeter fence, were undulating hills of some kind of mossy material the color of copper. It was a warm, fresh hue, and the air that swept into the shuttle was fresher still, fresh and humid, and had a light scent unlike anything Jas had encountered.

Armed guards appeared at the bottom of the shuttle ramp, and Jas and Lingiari followed them down the runway to a low, white building that looked like it'd been built from a kit, as it probably had. No other shuttlecraft could be seen, though there was a small hangar.

If the governor of Dawn was planning on bringing the crew down for testing two by two, Jas and Lingiari would be there for quite some time.

Inside the white building, they were separated into different rooms. A man in medic's clothes greeted Jas and asked her to lie down on a bed that slid inside a whole body scanner. The man then took urine, blood, saliva, and hair samples from her. Finally, he clipped a device to her finger and asked her a long battery of questions about her childhood, home life, relationships, career, and other life experiences, all the while watching a screen she couldn't see. At some of Jas's answers, such as how she'd grown up in a government institution, how she didn't have any close friends, and how her idea of a relaxing day off was target practice, the man raised his eyebrows.

After several hours, her tests were over. He handed her a few pieces of some kind of printed paper. The Dawn settlement certainly was basic. "You're fine. You gave some surprising answers, but you're human."

Muscles that Jas didn't know she'd been tensing relaxed. She got up, and the man directed her to another room, where she found an older woman sitting at a desk. Jas wondered what had happened to Lingiari.

"Welcome to Dawn," the woman said and gestured to Jas to sit. "You must be C.S.O. Harrington. Your acting master informed me about you."

"Where's the man I came with? Pilot Lingiari?" Jas remained standing.

"I understand your caution, but please don't be concerned. Your colleague also isn't a Shadow. He passed all the tests quickly. He's already gone into town. I wanted to speak to you both about the infection process and to reassure you."

"A Shadow? Is that what you call people possessed by the aliens? You know what the infection is?"

"Yes, we have some ideas. I'm Governor Siam, but you can call me Sashquita."

"You're the governor?" exclaimed Jas. She'd thought this woman was some kind of doctor.

"That's right. You were probably expecting someone a little more formal, right?" She smiled. "Please sit down, and I'll explain." When Jas complied, she continued, "Dawn's just an end-of-the-galaxy colony planet. We're pretty laid back around here. Most of us are working hard just to survive. We don't have much time or patience for formalities.

"It seems like this is the first you've heard of Shadows? That's not surprising. The Global Government isn't exactly broadcasting the news. Aliens who look identical to the people they've killed?" She shook her head. "You can't really blame them for wanting to keep it quiet. Who's to know if a friend or relative is really who you think they are, or if they're an alien? By the way, you'll be required to sign a non-disclosure agreement before you return to—"

"Wait," said Jas. "What do you mean? I thought the aliens infected people...got inside them somehow and took over their minds. You're telling me they clone their victims and then kill them?"

"That's right. It's easy to misunderstand. For a long time, the Global Government also thought the aliens were only possessing their victims. But no, the alien only *looks like* the person they killed. That's why they're called Shadows. They're like dark copies of the original. The aliens seem to read the DNA of anyone who gets caught in one of their traps, then they destroy the subject and appear as his or her copy, housing all the original memories and knowledge. But the personality is that of the alien."

Jas sat back in her chair. It was a lot to take in. "These Shadows, they look and sound the same as their victims. Is the DNA the same? If so, how can you tell them apart from the original?"

"I'd rather not tell you that right now," said the governor. "I hope you understand."

"Can you tell me why Lingiari finished earlier than me?"

Governor Siam paused a moment before answering, "The main difficulty we have with testing is, from what we've seen, that the mind copying they do means a lot of the original personality is there. It can take a while to sort out the human from the Shadow's traits. Some scientists think the Shadow itself can get confused as to who it really is after spending a long time living as a clone.

"But don't be alarmed. You've already passed." She paused and looked down at her hands for a moment before continuing. "Your acting master informed me of what happened aboard your ship. What I told your shipmate, and what I wanted to tell you, is that you can rest assured that our testing is effective. I know you harbor suspicions toward Acting Master Haggardy. But for the sake of harmony and—if I might say—your own career, you would be wise to drop them." She stood.

"I wish you an enjoyable stay on Dawn, C.S.O. Harrington. Now, if you follow the guard, he'll take you to your transportation."

"Wait. What about the Shadows you identify? What happens to them?"

But the governor only pursed her lips and shook her head slightly.

As Jas was shown to the exit, she recalled the number of alien structures she'd visited on K. 67092d. Shadow traps. She'd been inside twelve while securing the resource assessment sites, and another when the *Galathea* had crash-landed on the planet. Thirteen. Thirteen opportunities to leave her DNA. Was she in fact a Shadow and she'd forgotten it? Was Lingiari?

At the outer door, a guard told her, "You've got ID, some money, and an accommodation chit. If you follow the road, around the bend you'll find transportation. It's pre-programmed to take you into town. Just one road, and just one town. It's impossible to get lost around here."

"Where do I go to sleep?"

"There just one—"

"Place to stay. I get it." Her visit to Dawn didn't look like it was going to be very interesting.

Jas quickly found the single-seater vehicles. Small and boxy, they had space for luggage at the back. She tried a door, and when it opened she got inside. The vehicles were similar to all-terrain buggies she'd driven when she'd been at training college in Antarctica. They were wide-wheeled and high-carriaged, as if designed for off-road driving. But the controls on this vehicle were set with only two destinations: Dawntown/Shuttle Base. She pressed Dawntown. *Dawntown?* The settlers of new worlds were always so unimaginative. The machine started up and moved off without any further operation.

It wasn't far to the capital of Dawn. About twenty kilometers away, it was hidden among low, rolling hills. Like the shuttle base, some of the buildings were low, pre-fabricated structures. Others were made of some kind of dried mud or rammed earth, and these were a range of dun colors.

Jas passed the simple houses. There didn't seem to be any shops, and if there were any factories they were undistinguishable. Only one building was three-story. It was on the edge of town, but must have been visible from everywhere due to its height. Jas was surprised how undeveloped the place was. She was sure this colony was at least a couple of decades old. Had they really only managed to build one town on an entire planet?

She attracted the attention of everyone she passed, and small children ran after the slow-moving, one-person car. It pulled into a bay next to some others and stopped. Jas got out. Lingiari was nowhere to be seen. Feeling disappointed that the pilot hadn't waited for her, she set off down a street that had some kind of marketplace at the end of it. She hoped someone would be there who could tell her where she was supposed to sleep.

When Jas was about halfway down the street, a teenage boy appeared at the end, running in her direction. He was longhaired, scruffy, and had the beginnings of a mustache and beard shadowing his lips. As he got closer, two men appeared behind him, running after him. She recognized their uniforms. They belonged to the army of the Global Government. Jas didn't want to get involved in Dawn's affairs, so she stepped to one side to give all three of them plenty of room to pass, but the kid had spotted her. He changed course. He was heading straight for her.

He was about seventeen, she guessed. His hair was wavy and brown, and he was dressed in simple clothes made of coarse-woven, natural materials. That was all she had time to notice before he reached her.

Grabbing both of her arms, the kid exclaimed, "Take me away with you on your ship. I'll do anything you want. Please."

THREE

A second later, the men who were chasing the kid caught up and pulled him away from Jas. They were a lieutenant and a private. The soldiers wrestled with the kid, who fought their attempts to restrain him. "Hey," exclaimed Jas as he went sprawling. The private hauled him roughly to his feet.

The kid continued to struggle. "Let me go. I don't want to go back there. I'm not going home, and you can't make me."

"Huh, we'll see about that," said the private. He pushed the kid against the wall and pulled his hands behind his back. He gasped in pain.

"Take it easy, Trip," said the lieutenant to the private. He went over to the struggling boy. "Look, Makey, don't make it harder on yourself. We have to take you back home. *You* know it. We know it. There's nothing anyone can do about it. If you fight, the only person who's going to get hurt is you."

Makey's arms went limp. The soldier holding him slipped handcuffs around his wrists. His head fell forward, and his shoulders sagged. He averted his head, but Jas could hear quiet sobs.

"You're only taking him home?" asked Jas. "You aren't arresting him?" The kid seemed to be overreacting a little.

"Yep, just taking him back to his mom and dad. Running

away from home isn't a crime." The lieutenant paused and looked at Jas. He was tall and broad-shouldered. His hair was black and his eyes were nearly the same color. The man clearly kept himself in shape. "You want to walk down with us? You're off that quarantined starship, aren't you? I can show you to the hostel. It isn't far, and it's on our way."

"Uh, okay. Thanks."

"I'm Lieutenant Theron," said the man as they walked, "but you can call me Idris. This over-zealous young soldier is Private Trip Cassady."

"Pleased to make your acquaintance, ma'am." The private had a firm grip on young Makey's arm as they went ahead of Jas and the lieutenant. The boy was sniffing and trying to wipe off the snot hanging from his nose with his shoulder.

"Are you the first off your ship?" asked Idris.

"Yes, me and the pilot. But I don't know where he's gone. I'm Jas Harrington. Security officer."

"Security officer? We're in the same line of business, just about. I thought you might be in security from the look of your uniform. Polestar, isn't it?"

"That's right. But my clothes are a little warm for this climate. They're better suited to a starship owned by a company on a fuel-economy drive. I was hoping I could pick up something cooler here. They gave me some paper money, but I don't know how much things cost."

"I know how much you've been given. All the crews they test get the same amount. You should be able to buy a change of clothes with that. There are a few stalls selling clothes here."

They'd arrived at the market, which consisted of only a dozen or so stalls. Three sold clothes, all very rough, simple and similar to what Makey was wearing. Other stalls sold fruit and vegetables and dried beans. One sold simple woven baskets and earthenware bowls and plates.

"I can give you directions to the hostel if you want to stop here and buy clothes," said Idris.

"No, it's okay. I'll make my way back later." She was wondering if Lingiari was waiting for her at the hostel.

"Don't leave it too late," said Idris. "They begin to pack up about half an hour before sunset. No street lights, you see."

Dawn really was the back of beyond.

Private Trip and Makey had drawn a little way ahead of Jas and the lieutenant. She leaned over to speak softly to Idris. "Don't you think it's strange that the boy doesn't want to go home? Before you caught up to him, he was asking for passage on my starship."

Idris grimaced. "I'm sorry to say I don't find it strange at all. Or maybe I should say, not unusual. One thing you've got to understand about the people of this place is that they all belong to a sect. They came to Dawn to live according to their principles. Or more accurately the Global Government heavily persuaded them to come here.

"You could put down Makey's attitude to isolation and a hard life, with nothing more to do than work the family farm day after day. But frankly, the people are so insular and strange sometimes, I wonder what goes on behind closed doors.

"I'd like to help these kids, I really would. But the most I can do is to take them home to their families, where at least they've got food in their stomachs and a place to sleep. It's better than being out on the streets. Believe me, none of them would last long out on their own. There's no safety net here."

"Why doesn't the governor do something?" asked Jas. "Surely that's her job?"

"Huh. *Dawn—a new beginning, a new life for all.* That was the Global Government slogan. Now, how embarrassing would it be for the government if it got out what a miserable hole for misborns Dawn is? The governor keeps up appearances, or she's out of a job."

"Krat." Jas's eyes lingered on the skinny boy walking ahead of her. What a life. She knew only too well what a miserable existence some children led, despite humanity's supposedly great advances. There hadn't been much in the way of reductions in human suffering and cruelty.

"What's the army doing here?" she asked Idris. "There don't seem to be enough people to warrant peace-keeping forces."

"Ah, here we are," he said. stopping. They were outside one of the few two-story buildings in town. It was wide and had two wings stretching back from the road. All the windows were shuttered. "Sorry, I would answer your question, but I have to take this boy home. I'll explain why the army's on Dawn another time, if you like."

"Uh, okay."

The lieutenant smiled, and Jas's stomach tingled. Her gaze went from his even, white teeth to his eyes, which returned the too-long look. "See you another time," she said.

As he moved away with Trip and Makey, her gaze lingered on him for a moment before she went inside the hostel.

She gave the woman behind the counter her accommodation chit and received a simple metal key with a room number on it. She went upstairs and unlocked the door of her room with the key. She felt like she'd traveled back in time and wondered if she would have to light an oil lamp when the sun went down.

Inside, the room was a weird mixture of modern and rustic. She checked out the bed. Metal-framed with a mattress that was the standard mold-to-your-body type, it had clearly arrived on a colony ship. Spread over the mattress were rough sheets and blankets made of a natural thread. The pillow seemed to be stuffed with genuine feathers. The room had no comm, no screens or interfaces, nor any other electronic devices. There was a light strip at least, and from the gentle hum she could hear, the electricity for it came from a generator nearby.

Jas went to the window, pushed the shutters open, and looked out over the low roofs of Dawntown. She wondered where Lingiari was. She should have asked the receptionist which room the pilot was in. Beyond the town, the sun was nearing the hilly horizon. She would have to hurry if she wanted to buy some clothes before the market closed. She was uncomfortably hot and sweaty, and she didn't relish the idea of wearing her uniform for another day.

Returning to the market at a fast pace, Jas managed to catch the owner of a clothing stall as he was taking the last of his items down. He had little to offer that would fit Jas. In the end, she had to settle on some men's trousers that fit her round the hips but ended halfway up her calves, and a baggy tunic. She bought a woven belt to pull in the tunic.

By the time Jas arrived back at the hostel, Dawn's sun had swiftly set, and darkness had fallen like a cloak. She had to navigate the streets with the help of light shining through slatted shutters.

When she found the door of the hostel, she went in and asked the receptionist which room the *Galathea's* pilot was staying in. It turned out Lingiari was her neighbor, but when she knocked on his door, he didn't answer. She tried again. Either Lingiari had gone out or he was sound asleep. If it was the latter, she didn't want to wake him. She would wait until morning.

FOUR

Makey was cutting grass, dragging the cutter over the undulating ground, slicing the plants just above their roots. They called it grass, but Makey knew from reading the forbidden school books that it wasn't like the grass of Earth, and that they only called it so because its growing point was just above the root, the same as its namesake, and not near the shoot-tip like most plants. This meant it could be harvested again and again, as long as the soil sustained it.

"Where were you running to, Makey?" asked Neeve, his sister, as she walked behind the cutter, raking the cut stalks together.

Where Makey was harnessed to the cutter, the straps cut into the welts his father had inflicted with a cane, after the soldiers had brought him home.

"Makey?" Neeve repeated. His sister was five years younger than him, and often annoying, but of all the things he tolerated in his hard life, he minded her the least.

"I don't know. Away. Somewhere away from here."

"Da was so angry when he knew you'd gone, he threw a plate against the wall. Mam and me stayed out of his way."

"I'm sorry."

"It was no matter. I hid in the cellar till I heard him go out to look for you."

Makey grimaced and pulled harder against his harness, feeling the pain was a justified punishment for the trouble he'd caused Mam and his sister. He'd never meant for them to suffer. The extra speed he put on caused the cutter to slip and then jam, stopping him sharply and causing him to stagger.

"There it goes again. Always sticking," Neeve said lightly.

Makey slipped off the harness and knelt to free the cutter. Copper stalks were wound around the rotary blades. Stripped of their outer skins, they oozed red sap. Makey began gingerly picking out the trapped vegetation, but his mind was elsewhere, and before long he'd cut his thumb. Drops of blood flowed out and mixed with the sticky sap.

"Ow," he exclaimed. He sat back on his heels and sucked his thumb.

Neeve dropped her rake and ran to her brother's side. "Have you cut yourself? Can I see?"

"No, it's okay. It'll stop bleeding in a moment."

His sister raised a hand to the sky and said, "Earth Mother, hear me—"

"Stop it, Neeve. I don't want to hear that nonsense. I hear enough of it at home."

Closing her eyes, the girl continued, "Bring healing to my brother. Make him whole and as perfect as you are, I beseech you."

Makey rolled his eyes. He took his thumb out of his mouth. The bleeding was slowing down. A single drop oozed slowly to the surface.

Neeve also looked at his thumb. "You see, Makey? It worked. Earth Mother is making your thumb better."

"No, she isn't. It's getting better by itself."

"No, it's Earth Mother. If I hadn't said the prayer, your thumb wouldn't have stopped bleeding."

"Yes, it would. I know it would, Neeve. I've tried it. When I've been alone, I didn't ask Earth Mother's help, and my cuts got better by themselves."

Neeve shook her head. "That just shows how loved you are, Makey. Someone, somewhere was saying a prayer for you. Others care about you, and they ask Earth Mother for her protection for you, even if you don't."

His conscience twinged. This was Neeve's way of reproaching him for running away and leaving her.

"Neeve, I..." He gestured for her to sit next to him. "When I left home yesterday, I saw a spacewoman in town. She was very tall, and she was wearing a starship uniform. There's a starship above Dawn right now, orbiting the planet. Did you know that?"

Her eyes fixed on her brother's face, Neeve slowly shook her head.

"No, because they didn't tell us, did they? Not Da or Mam, or Teacher Clary. There are lots of things they don't tell us. We see these people from other planets some times, but we're not supposed to talk about them.

"Neeve, I have a secret to tell you, but you mustn't tell Da or Mam, okay?"

"All right," his sister replied doubtfully.

"You know I have to clean the school every night as punishment for asking too many questions in class?"

Neeve nodded, her eyes fixed on her brother.

"I found a cupboard that was locked, and when I broke it open, there were lots of books inside. School books that we never use in class. I've read some of them, and the information in there is different from what Teacher Clary tells us. Nothing in those books says that Earth Mother chose us to come to Dawn as the last step before Heaven. They talk about a group called Green Earthers."

A crease appeared between his sister's brows.

"The books say that Green Earthers believe in Earth Mother," continued Makey, "who bestows health and wellbeing on her followers, providing they live naturally—no artificial chemicals, everything made by hand from natural materials, all food cooked at home from whole ingredients. They believe that nothing bad will happen to you if you follow Earth Mother's rules, and that when you die, you become part of the natural cosmos."

"Makey, what are you talking about? That isn't anything strange, that's the truth."

He sighed. "Is it the truth, or is it just what some people believe? Don't you think that the Green Earthers sound exactly like us and all the other families we know? Only we don't call ourselves Green Earthers anymore because aren't on Earth, we're on Dawn. And we don't have to give ourselves a name because we aren't a separate group; we're the majority here. On Dawn, being a Green Earther just means you're the same as most people.

"It's like our parents brought those books to Dawn to teach us about our group, but then they decided to ignore what had happened in the past and pretend there was only ever one way of thinking about things, that there *is* only one way of thinking about things."

Neeve got to her feet. "Even if there is something in what you read, even if Da and Mam were Green Earthers before they came here, why does it matter? What's wrong with the way we live?" She brushed grass stalks from her knees. "Why aren't you happy, Makey? Why do you want to leave us?" Her voice wobbled as if she were about to cry, and she turned her head away.

A lump rose in Makey's throat as he bent over the cutter once more and pulled free the last of the stalks. "I can't be happy. I've tried. I've tried to do my chores, say my prayers, and be a good son and brother, but it isn't enough. I can't believe this is the best way to live until I've seen the alternatives. I have to find out what else they haven't told us. I want to go to Earth and see other planets."

"But we need you," blurted Neeve. "Who'll cut the grass? Who'll hang it to dry? Who'll help weave it if you go?"

"I don't know, but I can't help it. I have to find things out for myself. I feel like if I stay here any longer, I'm going to die, just the same as if these stalks wound around my throat while I was sleeping and choked me."

Neeve stomped over to her rake, picked it up, and began to violently rake the cut grass. "It's a curse you've brought on yourself, this feeling. It's your own fault. You turned away from the Earth Mother. You don't say your prayers. I know you don't. I never hear you at night, and at the table, you just move your lips without speaking. And now Earth Mother's turned her back on you. That's why you don't want to be here anymore. If you would just start praying again, everything would be okay. You wouldn't want to leave us."

"Neeve, it isn't that, and I don't want to leave you. Not you, anyway. Why don't you come with me? We could escape together, and we could find out the truth for ourselves."

"You'd better start cutting again," replied his sister. "We haven't done much, and Da will be angry." Her face was set, but Makey thought she also looked a little frightened.

"All right." He lifted the harness and slipped it over his head. He'd been the same at Neeve's age. It was only in the last couple of years that Makey had questioned the lifestyle they led and the things his parents had told him. He would have reacted the same as Neeve if anyone had suggested anything different, not so long ago. He didn't know how to convince his sister.

He began to pull the cutter again. In front of him stretched a rolling sea of copper. At that moment, it looked to him like a representation of his life on Dawn. Featureless, monotonous, and unending.

His entire being rebelled against the prospect. He had to leave. He simply had to, though there was nowhere for him to go. He would run away again, tonight, as soon as everyone was asleep. He would head out into the wild and try to make a life for himself there. And if he died, it wouldn't matter. It would be a quicker death than the one he was currently living.

FIVE

Lieutenant Idris Theron led Jas into the army barracks. The sentry checked her ID and gave her a cursory once-over with his eyes as they passed through the gate. Jas wondered what a sight she must look in her poorly made, shapeless pants and tunic, but at least the air could now circulate over her skin and cool her down.

There had been no answer at Lingiari's door that morning, and Jas was beginning to become concerned about the AWOL pilot. She'd asked the woman at the hostel desk if she'd seen him come in the night before, but she hadn't. That didn't mean much, however, because it wasn't necessary to pass the desk to go up to the rooms. It was conceivable that Lingiari was simply catching up on lost sleep after the recent harrowing few days aboard the *Galathea*.

"How was breakfast?" asked Idris Theron.

Jas grimaced. "Interesting."

The lieutenant laughed. "Don't tell me, seaweed soup and crackers? It's the cheapest food available here. And, no, those crackers aren't made from wheatflour."

"Do I want to know what they're made from?"

"Probably not. But if you're still hungry, our army food is a little better tasting…?"

"I wouldn't say no to a second breakfast." Jas's stomach rumbled, and she wasn't sure if it was from hunger or the after-effects of the green, salty soup she had forced into it.

They went into the canteen, where the cook was in the process of closing up the kitchen. Lieutenant Theron's disarming smile worked its magic on the man, and he warmed up some beans and hash browns. Jas's heart skipped a beat when Idris placed a mug of a steaming dark brown liquid in front of her. She leaned forward and inhaled. Her eyes widened. "It isn't…It can't be?"

"It's real coffee. Taste it."

Jas took a sip and closed her eyes as the liquid slipped down her throat. "It's amazing. I haven't drunk real coffee in years. I didn't know life was so comfortable in the military. I'm in the wrong job."

"We need some compensation for working on remote planets at the ends of the galaxy. There are plenty of vacancies, if you're serious."

Shrugging as she took another sip of the delicious liquid, Jas said, "I don't know. I'm not much of a team player. I prefer it with just me and my units."

"Ah, defense units. We have some divisions of them in the army. I've never worked with them close up, though. What are they like?"

"Hmmm…they're kinda like big, dumb, killing machines. Or that's how they seem at first, anyway. Until you're used to them and their little ways, they're pretty scary. But there's something about them…" She paused and put down her cup. "I don't know. I think there's more to units than meets the eye, or more than the manufacturers intended."

"They're part-human, right? Do they seem like it?"

"Not so much as you'd notice at first. Including human neurons in their make-up is only supposed to heighten their intellectual capacity and make them somewhat autonomous, so they'll show initiative in the absence of direct orders, but I think it gives them...a kind of consciousness? Sometimes...you know, this is going to sound crazy, but sometimes I see one of them out of the corner of my eye, and I feel like it's watching me."

Idris' eyebrows rose. "Sounds creepy."

"No, I don't feel it in a menacing way. In fact, it feels comforting, like deep down they're looking out for me." She gave a short laugh. "I'm probably projecting onto them. They say people do that."

"Sorry," said Idris, "that *still* sounds kinda creepy." He looked out the canteen window. "Looks like it won't rain today, for a change. How about I show you around?"

"I'd love that," Jas said, a little too enthusiastically. "I mean, if you have time. Is this your day off?"

"I swapped a shift. We should make an effort to show our visitors a proper welcome."

There was that smile again, and the resultant tingle in Jas's stomach. "Thanks. What do you suggest we do?"

"To be honest, there's only one thing to do around here, and that's buggy riding."

"You mean drive around in those vehicles they have at the shuttle base?"

"That's right. We have a fleet ourselves. We can borrow a couple and drive out of town. Take a look around. I can show you the sights, such as they are. How does that sound?"

"Great."

It certainly was fun taking the buggies out of Dawntown and into the surrounding landscape. The vehicles were perfect for driving over the low hills and soft vegetation. They were very easy to handle. She followed Lieutenant Theron for some way, until the town was out of sight. Then the officer slowed until she drew alongside him, and they drove on side by side, the lieutenant waving and pointing when he wanted to turn right or left. After a little while, he would get her attention only to make faces at her. Jas laughed, and the stress of the last few days began to fall away.

They drove up a long slope. Jas's vehicle slowed down as it struggled to cope with the incline. Then she crested the top, and the view made her draw a breath. She braked and stopped. A brilliant turquoise ocean stretched out on the other side. Idris was already on his way down to it, and Jas pressed the accelerator to follow him. At the ocean's edge, he stopped and got out. Jas drew up alongside. As she opened her door, the deep scent of the water hit her nostrils, and the warm breeze stirred her hair.

Driving around Dawn had been fun, but in truth there'd been little of great interest, once she'd gotten used to the deep copper tinge of the plant foliage. Nothing as specialized as flowers or trees seemed to have evolved yet on the young planet, and there was a monotony to the landscape. But this ocean was something else, and the contrast of the blue water to the native color of the plants made it seem even more vivid.

"It's breathtaking," Jas said.

"Yes," replied Idris. "It certainly is. It's a shame we didn't get here first to claim it."

"What do you mean?"

"Dawn's oceans belong to the Haidiren, except for a few reserves they gave us when the occupation agreement was drawn up. You and I shouldn't really be in this area, near the ocean, but it's okay. No one will see us."

Jas had forgotten that humans were sharing the planet with an alien species. "How come we and the Haidiren are both colonizing this place? I've never heard of that happening before."

"Nope, and for good reason. The minute one side starts to lust after something the other side has, it's the perfect recipe for war, which is the main reason why my division is here. The Haidiren only leave the ocean to mate and reproduce, and even then they never go farther than the beaches. They had inhabited Dawn for decades before we arrived, and we'd established a colony over several years before they knew of our existence.

"Once both sides found out about each other, it was difficult to disband either colony and move out. In truth, I think the Haidiren were too mellow to push it, though it was their right as they were here first. They agreed we could have the land, which they don't use anyway, and a few small sections of ocean, providing we leave them in peace."

"Do they own this spot? Is our being here going to cause a diplomatic incident?"

Idris laughed. "The Haidiren won't tell on us. It's more my superiors who'll have something to say if someone sees us and reports us. But we drove so far out of town, we're alone here, I can guarantee it. There's no one else around for kilometers."

Jas watched the ocean. In all the worlds she'd visited, she didn't think she'd ever seen an expanse of water such a rich and striking color. She let the warm breeze permeate her skin and hair and wondered what the Haidiren looked like. All she knew was that they were aquatic. She didn't think she'd seen a picture of one.

After some time standing in silence with Idris, she noticed that his arm was around her waist. It was a nice feeling.

Six

Lingiari was waiting in the lobby of the hostel when she got back that evening, long after dark, feeling better than she'd felt for a long time. She'd had a wonderful day with Idris, and talking with him about what had happened with the aliens aboard the *Galathea* had eased her conscience a little.

"Where have you been?" she asked the pilot as she came through the door.

"I was gonna ask you the same thing."

"I went to the beach. It was amazing." She was a little breathless after walking back from the army barracks.

"I was looking for you all day," said Lingiari.

"I was looking for you, too, yesterday evening and this morning. What happened to you?"

"Nothing much. I was just looking around the place, then I went to bed early and woke up late. Since then, I've just been hanging about. Looks like you had a better time than me."

"One of the soldiers took me sightseeing. Lieutenant Theron. I'll introduce you. You'll like him."

"Oh, right. Some of the crew arrived while you were gone. It looks like Haggardy's sending them down from the ship and through testing as fast as he can."

"They all passed the screening?"

"It sounds like it. No one remembers anyone arriving who they didn't see again on the other side."

"That's good. I'm waiting to see what happens when Haggardy takes his test. He hasn't arrived yet?"

"No. No sign of him anyway."

"Delaying the inevitable maybe," said Jas.

"Maybe. Have you eaten?"

"Yeah, I ate at the barracks."

"I hope you had something better than what we were served for dinner. Do you want to go out somewhere?"

"Sure," she replied, but when they asked the woman at the hostel desk where they could go, she couldn't suggest anywhere.

"Nowhere at all?" exclaimed Lingiari. "What do people do in the evening around here? Don't you have a vid center or anything like that?"

"Dawntowners stay home with their families, do close work, and pray to the Earth Mother," replied the woman, looking up at the pilot from under heavy eyebrows.

"Sounds a lot of fun," said Lingiari. He turned to Jas. "How about we go for a walk around town? I've been cooped up here all day waiting for you to come back. I need to stretch my legs."

It was dark outside, and Jas was tired from walking the beach and dunes with Idris. She also knew it was hard to navigate the streets without lights, but she said, "Okay, just for a while."

They stepped out into the night. Jas didn't need to have worried about finding their way in the dark, because Dawn's two moons were rising, and the sky was cloudless and shimmering with stars. As she looked up, she felt a familiar chill at seeing configurations that were new to her.

They walked towards the edge of Dawntown. Each street was similar to the next. All of them were deserted, and the night was silent.

"So, what's he like?" asked Lingiari after they'd walked a couple of streets without speaking.

Jas had been so lost in her thoughts, she'd almost forgotten the pilot was there. "Who?"

"This fella you were out with today. The army guy."

"He seems nice. I thought it was kind of him to show me around." Jas wondered at Lingiari's tone, which was tense. Maybe he was stressed about the whole situation. Or maybe he was missing Flux or Navigator Lee.

"You went to the beach? I didn't know there was one close by."

"We drove for kilometers, in those buggy things. Umm...Lingiari..."

But the pilot was distracted. He was peering into the darkness ahead. "Did you see someone cross the street?"

Jas followed his gaze. A dark figure was coming towards them. Skinny and coltish like the fast-growing adolescent he was, she recognized him the moment his face became distinct in the moonlight.

"It's you again," said the kid.

She recalled his name: Makey.

"You must be from the starship too," he said to Lingiari.

"Yeah," replied the pilot. "Do you two know each other?"

"Makey here was asking to join the crew," said Jas before turning to the kid. "Look, even if we had a job for you, which we don't, you're too young. You have to be twenty-one, minimum."

"Aw come on, please," said Makey. "I'll do anything. Anything you say. I have to get out of here. I'll die if I spend another day on this planet."

"Shouldn't you be home with your family, praying or something?" asked Lingiari.

"I don't believe in all that," said Makey. "My parents, my teacher, everyone, they've been lying to us. I found out. I read about many things in books we're not supposed to see. So many things they don't tell us. I've tried to explain to my friends, but no one wants to know. No one will listen. They all want to carry on believing, even when it doesn't make any sense."

Jas bit her lip. "I'm sorry, but there isn't anything we can do. You've got to go home. This isn't the kind of place where you can survive by yourself. You need your family. I know it's hard, but in a few years, when you're older, it'll be easier. If you study, you can get a job on a passing ship, or—"

"I can't study," exclaimed Makey. "Don't you understand what I'm saying? They don't teach us anything. Only about the Earth Mother, and how to farm, and that's it. There are books at school, but they're locked away. They don't give us the chance to do anything different. And whenever starships come, everyone pretends they aren't there. Please help me. You're my only hope."

"That sucks, kid, but—" said Lingiari.

"If you don't help me, I'll head out of town and carry on walking till I die. I can't go home now. Not after running off for the second time." He paused for breath, and his face twisted as if he was trying to stop himself from crying. "My Da'll beat me to death this time."

Jas's eyes widened. "Your father beats you?"

"Yes, if I'm too slow at something or say my prayers wrong. Sometimes he doesn't even have a reason."

Lingiari and Jas exchanged a look. After a moment's silence, Lingiari said, "Come with us."

Back at the hostel, Jas and the pilot sneaked Makey upstairs and into Jas's room. In the light of her single electric strip, the boy lifted his shirt. Both drew in their breath at the sight of his welts and scars. Jas winced at the memory of accompanying Idris and the other soldier as they'd taken the kid home the day before— home to receive his beating.

"I'm sorry," she said. "I didn't know."

"Do you see what I mean now?" asked Makey. "Da says he's the head of the family because that's what's natural, and he has to keep us in order. He ignores my sister, but me, he beats. I've told my teacher, but she just says a father must discipline his children. Will you help me now? If I can't get a job aboard your ship, can you smuggle me to Earth?"

SEVEN

Carl picked up a cracker from the bowl on the breakfast table and pretended to take a bite before slipping it inside his shirt. Four crackers were already secreted there. He wished there was a way to take some of the soup upstairs to Makey, too. The boy was beginning to look thin and pinched after three days hiding in Harrington's room, but the soup was impossible to transport easily, and it would look suspicious if he was seen carrying a mug of the slightly salty, mostly tasteless liquid up to his room. No one in their right mind would ask for seconds unless they were starving.

It had taken the boy's father longer than twenty-four hours to report him missing. Makey had said he was probably waiting for him to make his own way back when he got hungry enough, and he feared the shame Makey's running away for a second time would bring on the family. A man being in control of his brood was important among Dawntown inhabitants, and his Da would lose considerable face.

Along with Harrington, Carl had bought the boy fruit and vegetables from the market and saved him a portion of his meals. But only fresh food was for sale, nothing cooked or processed, and the *Galathea's* crew had been given very little money.

If they hadn't been harboring a runaway, the cash would have been plenty. The hostel provided all meals, and there was little to buy. The amount of food they could give Makey, however, was barely enough to keep the boy going. He was constantly hungry, Carl was sure, though he never complained.

Together, he and Harrington had developed a routine to keep the kid safe. Every night, when the hostel was silent, Carl would go to Harrington's room, then check that the coast was clear. Makey would slip out and down the corridor to the shower, and either Harrington or Carl would linger outside the door to prevent one of the *Galathea's* crew from entering and spotting him.

Every evening, the ranks of shipmates at the dinner table had grown as more and more were processed and stationed on the planet to await their return to the ship. Every morning, those who knew what was going to be served up for breakfast would tease the newcomers with tales of the delicious homegrown, home-cooked meals that Dawn had to offer.

Carl did a mental count of those present. More than three-quarters of the crew had been processed. He wondered what the hostel staff would do with the rest, as all the tables were full. They would probably have to employ a shift system, which would suit Harrington and himself as, currently, they could only attend meals separately, one of them always remaining with Makey upstairs.

Someone was banging a mug on a table. The hubbub faded to a hush, and Carl turned to see who it was. Haggardy. Haggardy had arrived. He must have passed the test. So he wasn't a Shadow after all. Carl took advantage of the crowd's momentary distraction. He grabbed a handful of crackers and stuffed them in his shirt. He now had quite a bulge, so he spread them around and evened them out.

"Good morning, crew," said Haggardy. "I just wanted to say a few words, then I'll let you get back to your breakfast. I'm pleased to report that one hundred and twenty-one crew members have been tested and every single one of them has passed. Today and tomorrow, the remaining crew members will arrive from the *Galathea*. Providing the testing continues without hiccups, I anticipate we will be Earth-bound within three days, and we can all put this episode behind us."

A hand rose. "Permission to speak, sir."

"Go ahead."

"Do you mean to say we're abandoning the mission, and we won't get our bonuses?"

"Continuing the mission is out of the question." A disgruntled murmur rose from the crew. "I'm surprised anyone would think that might be the case. Captain Loba and most of the officers have died, and the *Galathea* has sustained significant damage. It's neither practicable nor safe for us to go on. However, Polestar is always interested to hear from applicants with experience aboard a prospector. You shouldn't have too much trouble finding a new berth."

Just-audible cursing sounded around the room, and cups and cutlery were slammed down. Carl understood the crew's frustration. They'd been only halfway through their mission and had only achieved break-even point for Polestar. A few more resource-rich planets would have made their jobs worthwhile. As it was, everyone had risked their lives and suffered the intense boredom and inconvenience of space travel for the wages sweat shop workers received back on Earth.

Haggardy raised his voice above the griping hum. "I was pleased to hear from the governor of Dawn that you've behaved yourselves so far. I expect your good behavior to continue for the rest of your stay. Let's be the perfect guests, eh?"

The acting master's words had little effect. The angry reaction from the crew continued. Haggardy began to make his way over to Carl, and the pilot's stomach fell. What did the man want with him?

"Lingiari, I'm surprised to see Harrington isn't with you. You two are best friends, after all, aren't you?"

"She ate already. She's up in her room. I'll go get her if you like." Carl swung his legs over the bench he was sitting on and stood up.

"No, no. No need for that. What I have to say is for both of you to hear. I'm sure you'll pass on my message. As you can see, I passed the test. I'm not a Shadow. But I am master of the *Galathea* for our passage back to Earth. I expect you both to accept that and put this nonsense behind us. I have no wish to have defense units trailing me wherever I go.

"When we board ship, you will return to your duties and your normal freedoms. However, should either of you even attempt to question or challenge my authority by word or deed, be assured that you will spend the rest of our voyage in the brig and be tried for mutiny along with Karrev and his cronies when we arrive at our destination. Is that clear?"

"As glass, mate," Carl said. He had a sudden idea. Maybe Haggardy could persuade the governor to look into some of the problems Makey had told him and Harrington about.

"You will address me as—"

"Yeah, whatever. Look, I get it, okay? You're the real Haggardy, but we've got bigger problems right now."

Haggardy's lips thinned to a line at Carl's wisecrack, and his face remained set throughout the pilot's speech.

"This place is kratted. The parents beat their kids and treat them like slaves. They're feeding them a load of BF in school and not teaching them science or maths or anything to do with technology. The poor sods don't have a chance. It's like the kratting Dark Ages around here."

"Hmpf. Have these people broken any local laws or regulations?"

"No, that's the craziest part. There's no law against hitting your kids. They say it's natural. Parents can do what the hell they like."

"Then I'm not sure what you're getting at, Lingiari. What's the problem here?"

"The problem is, no one's doing anything to protect these kids. The governor won't do anything about this stuff, so I was thinking maybe you could—"

"But if, as you say, the parents aren't breaking any laws...?"

"There's more than one kind of law, mate."

"I'm not your *mate*," said Haggardy, his eyes narrowing. "You will refer to me as Acting Master Haggardy. One more instance of insubordination from you, and I'll confine you to your room and garnish your entire mission's wages.

"I'm extremely disappointed to hear that you appear to have been interfering with the running of this colony under its governor. I order you to have nothing further to do with Dawn's inhabitants forthwith. You are to utter no statements that could be construed as critical of its people or its government, nor have any contact with anyone other than crew members of the *Galathea,* except for strictly necessary interactions.

"And you can tell Harrington the same, as no doubt she's also been interfering with local affairs." He raised a finger and pointed at Carl. "I'm warning you, Lingiari, there's to be no offense to our hosts for the rest of our stay, or there will be severe consequences." He left without another word.

Carl went upstairs to give Harrington the bad news. She took it as well as he expected.

"The kratting misborn idiot."

Makey was sitting on Harrington's bed. Carl suspected he slept there while the security officer slept on the floor. The kid hung his head. "No one's going to help me. I told you. I'll have to go out into the wild. I just hope my Da never finds me."

"Makey," said Harrington, "you're going back to that misborn father of yours over my dead body."

"But if your captain won't do anything," said the kid, "how am I going to get away from my Da? If I can't come with you guys, I don't have anywhere else to go."

"We'll find a way, don't you worry," said Carl.

There was a knock at the door. With practiced skill, Makey

got down on the floor and slid under the bed almost before the person finished knocking.

Harrington went to the door. The hostel receptionist was there. She looked from Carl to Harrington. "Someone downstairs for you. Lieutenant Theron, he says his name is." She threw another look between them and left.

A weight settled over Carl's heart at the mention of the soldier's name. But Harrington obviously liked him a lot. He wasn't going to stand in their way.

Eight

Jas met Idris outside the hostel. It was good to see him again, and it was good to get out. She'd spent long hours cooped up with Makey, worried that, if he was left alone, someone would come into her room or he would make a noise and be discovered. If he were taken back to his parents' house, there wouldn't be much anyone could do to help him.

The morning light and the sight of the lieutenant lifted her mood.

"It's good to see you again," said Idris. "Sorry I haven't been round. Since the news about that missing boy came out, we've been searching for him from sunup to sundown."

"I know. I heard about it. It's the kid you took back home the day we met, isn't it?"

"Yeah." Idris frowned. "How'd you know that?"

"I remembered his name. Makey."

"Oh right. Well, we're still searching, but I wondered if you wanted to join us? We're searching a swamp, so it won't be much fun, but...I thought we had a good time the other day..."

"I'd love to come along. Thanks for asking me."

His smile broke through his tired, drawn expression.

———

They traveled in a different direction from the way to the beach. Lieutenant Theron and Jas were accompanied by three soldiers, each in a single vehicle. After traveling for an hour or so, they stopped. Jas didn't see why until she got out. The land before them looked similar to what they'd covered: vegetation of bright copper and other reddish hues, but through the plants before them, patches of water glinted that Jas had failed to spot. If they'd continued on their path, they would have driven right into the swamp.

The soldiers pulled down two boxes that had been stowed on their vehicles' roofs, and as they opened them, the interiors sprung out and began filling with air. In a short time, two dinghies lay next to the water. Oars were slotted together, and coils of rope with rubber-tipped grappling hooks were placed in the boats.

Idris grimaced. "This was a stupid idea. I don't know why I invited you to come help us drag a swamp for a dead body. It's not much of a day out. You can wait here if you'd prefer."

"No, I'd like to help."

The three soldiers got into one dinghy, and Jas and Idris got into the other. The two parties agreed to meet back at a certain time, and they set off in opposite directions. Idris rowed the dinghy out.

"We'll go to the southern edge and work our way back. If the kid did fall in here, he won't be far from shore."

The boat slid through the water easily. Idris avoided the large clumps of plants, and the rest parted smoothly.

"Do you ever come out here to fish?" Jas asked, trying to lighten the mood.

"No fish in these swamps, as far as anyone can tell. There's nothing that you would recognize as fish in the ocean either. There are some *things*, but I'm not sure what they're called. Under the agreement with the Haidiren, we aren't allowed to catch them. All we can harvest from the water on this planet is that seaweed they serve up for breakfast at the hostel."

"Urgh. Don't remind me."

Idris chuckled. "We can eat at the mess hall when we get back. I might even be able to get you some more coffee."

"That'd be great." Jas paused. She wanted to talk to the Lieutenant about Makey, but she wasn't sure how much she should tell him. If he knew that Makey was hiding out in her room, he might feel it was his duty to inform the governor. That would get her into a lot of trouble, and he'd probably feel bad. She didn't want to put him in an awkward position. But if he did know what was happening, maybe he could help.

"Idris, why do you think Makey ran away? He was crying when you took him home. Do you think he was frightened of what would happen to him there?"

"Of course he was. It's not possible to survive out in the wild here. His parents would have been mad that he'd put his life at risk and worried them so much. That's natural."

"Do you think they might have even hit him for it?"

Idris shrugged. "Maybe. Dawntowners are very religious, very strict. But I don't think they would actually hurt him. More like scare him enough to stop him from trying it again. For his own good."

"It didn't work, though, did it? If his father punished him, it didn't stop him from running away again."

"Yeah, well, you got me there."

"What do you think of Dawn, Idris? I mean, what do you think of what the people are trying to achieve here?"

"It's not my business to think anything of it, Jas. I'm just doing my job here. And when I get posted somewhere else, I'll go and do my job there."

"But you must have an opinion. You must have noticed how ignorant the children are. The kind of nonsense they believe in. I mean, do you know what goes on in their schools? What they're being taught?"

Idris stopped rowing and looked strangely at Jas. She clamped her lips and turned to gaze over the water. She'd said too much. How would she know what was taught in the schools unless a certain kid had told her? After a moment, Idris picked up the oars again and continued rowing. They didn't speak again for a few minutes until the boat bumped against a bank. "We're here. Let's start dredging. Do you want to row or throw?"

"I'll take a turn with the oars," Jas said.

They swapped seats, and Jas took the oars from Idris. He sat in the bow and threw a rope, hook first, into the water, which swallowed it. He pulled hand over hand on the rope until the hook appeared at the side of the dinghy, covered in foul-smelling, rust-colored slime. He threw it three or four times more in different directions.

Jas pulled on the oars and maneuvered the boat a little farther along the bank, where Idris threw the rope again.

She regretted her words, which seemed to have killed the good feeling between her and the lieutenant. While waiting for Idris to drag the water, she looked out over the swamp again. Once you got used to the red hues of the vegetation, Dawn wasn't an unattractive place. In every similar waterlogged location she'd been to on Earth, such as in the U.K. and Chile, the strongest repellent didn't deter the ravening insect life. But on Dawn, she hadn't seen a single fly, wasp, mosquito, or other flying annoyance, not even in this swamp.

Complex life had its downsides, and as a young planet, Dawn had none of them.

Then she saw it. Sticking out in the dark, rusty red swamp vegetation, was a patch of green. It stood out so boldly against the copper, she didn't understand why she hadn't seen it before.

She almost dropped the oars. She realized why she hadn't noticed the green thing. It was moving. It was alive, and it had popped into view.

Idris followed her gaze. "Don't move. Stay still, or you'll scare it."

"What is it?" Jas whispered.

"Haidiren. You can talk normally. They can't hear, or if they can, speaking-level noise doesn't bother them. But don't move. They're very sensitive to movement. It'll pick up the movement of the boat in the water, even at this distance."

"I thought they lived out in the ocean."

"They can live anywhere there's water."

"What's it doing?"

"I've only seen them twice before, and each time they were...yes...there it goes."

The green patch in the distance blurred and seemed to shake. It grew larger, and copper patches appeared. Jas realized it was the vegetation behind the creature showing through it. The creature was coming apart. It was breaking into many pieces, and the pieces were spreading out and slipping into the water.

Jas's hand rose to her mouth. In all her years of visiting alien planets and seeing extraterrestrial life forms, she'd never witnessed anything quite like it. One minute the Haidiren was an individual, solid body, and the next, it had dissolved into thousands of parts.

"Is it dying?" asked Jas.

"No, it's reproducing. After fertilization, it breaks into segments, and each segment grows into a new Haidiren. That's what I read somewhere, anyway."

"That's amazing."

"Yeah, it is," agreed Idris, pulling the final length of rope up as the last piece of Haidiren disappeared. "We can go now."

The sight of the Haidiren broke the tension that had formed between Jas and Idris. As she rowed the boat back to their starting place, they chatted and laughed about all the things they'd seen throughout their travels. It turned out they'd visited some of the same planets, and they traded tales of encountering weird and wonderful life forms.

When they got back, the three soldiers were waiting for them.

Their efforts to dredge the swamp had also drawn a blank, of course.

"We had no luck, either," said Jas.

"Yeah, strange that," said Idris in a mildly sarcastic tone.

Jas looked away.

At the army base, she took the opportunity to fill her belly. The food was only average, but compared to everything else Dawntown had to offer, it was delicious. And, true to his word, Idris worked his charm with the kitchen staff and brought her a steaming mug of heaven.

After they'd walked back to the hostel, they said goodbye, then there was an awkward pause. Idris went to kiss her. Jas didn't resist, and she returned the kiss.

Idris was a good kisser, but something had gone wrong somewhere out on the swamp. She wasn't sure what it was, but despite their growing closeness, the spark of her feeling for the lieutenant was no longer burning as bright as it had been.

NINE

It had been easy to evade the humans' tests. Since its creation in a far distant place, the Shadow had lived among the humans, mimicking their ways, until it had been sent with its group to the new world. These new arrivals were not tested. They were the protectors of humans, the fighters, and they were not suspected because they did not come from planets where Shadows had been found.

It had walked the new planet. It had found a place near to the humans' habitation; not so close that the humans quickly noticed, but close enough to bring victims there. It had made the connection, and over time, the trap had grown.

When it was complete, the Shadow selected its first victim. It had needed to act quickly. There was another of its kind in the space vessel orbiting the planet that risked detection if it was forced to submit to the tests.

It had selected a human in authority—a human with control over the others. After she had been replicated, her Shadow would be able to command others to accompany her to the trap. The victim had not gone willingly when she saw where the Shadow was taking her, but it had forced her.

Now, on the other side, in the void, signals entered. Information. Coding of a life form. The human's data flowed in. Chemicals, functions, processes, systems—the tiny messages communicated all they needed to know. What was used to create the human, what was left unused, what waited in the background to be activated.

In the physical world, the human was forced farther in. She would be unable to escape.

In the otherworld, the information that was used to create and maintain her during her brief life—the merest flicker compared to time in the ether—was examined, interpreted, decoded, and finally the blueprint, the map of all that made up the human's physical body, was comprehended.

Next came assimilation.

Everything that made up the human's knowledge, experience, memories, and personality was contained within her physical form. Her nervous system held the information. Capturing the human, disintegrating, assimilating, and interpreting her nerves and brain told all there was to know. The data was complete, and the replication process could begin.

Pushing through into another reality was a great struggle. Worse was becoming separate from the whole. Cut off from the communal mind, the thing forced itself through the barrier. Rivers of fire ran through its new body as it contacted air, temperature, solidity, gravity, and pressure. Its partly formed mouth gaped silently. Skin took color, organs differentiated, and blood permeated newly created capillaries, veins, and arteries. The heart contracted jerkily once, twice, and began to pump.

Senses came online. Nerves transmitted signals about light, sound, touch, balance, position, and smell to the brain. Fired by activity, the brain grew aware. Memories flashed up. Items of knowledge. Feelings. Associations. A lifetime's experience within a few seconds.

The creature breathed. It felt. It knew. It moved. Another Shadow was born.

Time to find more humans.

TEN

Carl was at the window in Harrington's room.

"Jas told me not to open the shutter," said Makey. He was sitting on her bed. None of the windows in Dawntown had glass, and Carl had wondered if it was because it was 'unnatural'. They had wooden shutters made of rows of slats that were angled up to capture sunlight, which meant it was impossible to see out of a window without opening the shutter. Carl had opened it the minute he'd heard Harrington's and the army officer's voices below as they returned from their day out.

His stomach twisted painfully as he saw the two of them kiss. His interest in Harrington, which had once been something quite shallow and physical, had grown over the time they'd spent together fighting the growing menace of the Shadows. He wasn't sure yet what it had grown into. He couldn't put a name to how he felt when he thought about her, but certain situations brought those unnameable feelings strongly to the foreground—situations such as seeing her kiss another man.

"Jas said we mustn't open the shutter," repeated Makey, louder.

Carl closed it and turned his back on the window. *Jas.* Even the kid got to call her Jas. He always called her by her surname, like they were just shipmates, not even friends, and she'd never told him otherwise.

"Is something wrong?" asked Makey.

"No, everything's okay. *Jas* is back. She should be here in a few minutes." Carl sat down and stared, unseeing, at his hands. The few minutes Harrington was taking to say goodbye to the lieutenant seemed to be an awfully long time. Like a child picking at a scab, he imagined what she could be doing that was taking so long.

Finally, the gentle, coded knock sounded at the door. Carl opened it and let the security officer in. Her lips seemed more full and red than usual, and her hair was a little messy.

"Guess what I brought," she said as soon as the door was closed. From a satchel at her side she pulled out some rolls with a pale yellow, creamy filling. "They let me take a bag home from the canteen."

"What are they?" asked Makey as she handed him and Carl a roll each.

"Cheese rolls."

Carl's eyebrows rose. "Real cheese?"

"No, it's cheese spread, but it's pretty good."

Makey was sniffing his roll. "What's cheese? And what's wrong with this cracker? It's too thick, and it's soft."

"It isn't a cracker. It's bread, which is made of flour and yeast. And cheese comes from milk, which comes from cows."

"Urgh," exclaimed Makey. "I remember now. I read about cheese. That's disgusting. Why would anyone want to eat something that came out of an animal's breast?" He handed his roll to Carl, his upper lip twisted in disgust.

"Try it, mate. You might like it." Carl held out the roll to the boy.

Makey folded his arms. "No way. I never heard of anything so revolting in all my life. Except maybe people actually eating dead animals. Can you believe some people did that?"

"Huh, some people still do," said Carl. When the teenager's

arms remained stubbornly folded, he went on, "You know, if you want to travel the galaxy, you're gonna have to get used to eating a lot weirder things than cheese rolls. You won't be able to pick and choose when you're eating aboard a starship. You take what you're given and act grateful for it."

This wasn't strictly true. In Carl's experience, the quality of food aboard prospecting ships wasn't too bad. Eating was one of the few things to break the monotony, and even stingy companies like Polestar recognized the benefits of keeping a crew well-fed. But a little white lie wouldn't hurt. The kid needed to toughen up a bit if, by some miracle, they managed to get him aboard the *Galathea*.

Sighing, the boy held out his hand for the offered roll. He took a tiny bite and grimaced at the taste. Taking a larger bite, he chewed mechanically, a look of extreme suffering on his face. Harrington stifled a snort of laughter, and for a moment Carl forgot what he'd seen her doing with the lieutenant. He began to laugh, too, and soon Makey joined in as he was stuffing the rest of the roll into his mouth, trying to get the ordeal over with quickly and nearly choking in the process.

Someone ran down the corridor outside. Carl put his finger to his lips and mouthed *Shhh* to the other two. They couldn't risk someone hearing a stranger's laugh coming from Jas's room. With a chastened look, Harrington immediately clammed up, and the kid wasn't slow to follow.

In a soft voice, the security officer said, "Sorry, you're right, Lingiari. We can't attract any attention, especially after today."

"Why? What happened?" asked Carl.

"I went with Idris to dredge a swamp, looking for your body," replied Harrington, turning her gaze to Makey. His cheery young face dropped.

Idris, thought Carl.

Harrington shook her head. "I think I said too much. I think he guessed that I know where you are. He might even have concluded you must be here. He isn't stupid, and it isn't like I'd know anywhere else to hide you around here."

"Krat. What did you say?" Carl asked.

"It was innocent enough. I was just talking about the school system here, but how would I know about it? The Dawntowners don't speak to offworlders, and they don't let their children speak to us, in case we corrupt them I suppose, so how would I know about their education? It isn't like they advertize the curriculum."

Makey's face was stricken and pale. "I can't go back home. I can't. My Da'll kill me this time. I know it."

Harrington sat beside him and put a hand on his arm. "I'm not going to let them take you back home. But I realized there's something we haven't thought of. Is there another family you could stay with? A family who'll treat you more kindly?"

The boy shook his head. "My Da's very important. There's no one who'll stand up to him. They wouldn't want to make him feel ashamed of not being able to bring up his own children."

"There's nothing for it, then," said Harrington. "We've got to get you aboard the *Galathea*."

"I dunno how that's going to happen," said Lingiari. "I didn't have time to tell you this morning, but Haggardy's here."

"He passed the test? He isn't a Shadow?"

"He passed the same test as us, so..." He shrugged. "I spoke to him about the situation...just generally. I didn't tell him about Makey. Guess what he said. You know what he's like."

"'We can't interfere.'"

Carl nodded.

"Kratting misborn idiot. You know, I'd almost prefer it if he was a Shadow. At least he'd have an excuse then."

Makey looked from Harrington to Carl. "Isn't there anything you can do to persuade your captain? I know I don't know anything about working on a starship, but I'm strong, I'm a hard worker, and I learn quickly."

"If you weren't a minor, and if it weren't Haggardy we were talking about," said Carl, "you might've had a chance. But—"

"We have to take him, Lingiari," said Harrington. "And you know how to do it."

"I do?"

"You smuggled Flux aboard the *Galathea*, didn't you?"

"Yeah, but, in case you hadn't noticed…" He gestured toward the boy. "He's a little bit bigger."

"Come on, you know about shuttlecraft. Can't you think of *anywhere* we could hide him when we return to the ship?"

Carl frowned. He did know the shuttle model they used on Dawn. He knew it well. Maybe there was a space you could squeeze a skinny kid in. "But it isn't just hiding him on the shuttle, is it? We've got to get him through security at the shuttle base first."

"So let's go to the base and check it out," Harrington said. "Security's my thing."

Despite his hurt feelings about the security officer, Carl's heart warmed. This was what he liked about her—when she had to do something that really mattered, she never gave up.

"Okay. Let's go tomorrow."

Makey clenched his hands into triumphant fists, grinned, and said a quiet, "Yes."

"All right. Goodnight, then," said Carl, and went to leave.

"Wait a minute, Lingiari. Do you think Makey could sleep in your room tonight? This floor's killing my back."

After a pause, Carl replied, "Sure. I'll just check that the coast's clear." He looked into the corridor, trying not to think about why Harrington might really want her room to herself.

Eleven

Jas didn't dare approach Idris for help getting to the shuttle base. He wouldn't take long to guess she was up to something that had to do with Makey, and after their time in the swamp, she wasn't sure how he would react. It seemed like he didn't really care about what was happening on Dawn. He wasn't a bad person, but it was just another job to him.

She and Lingiari returned to the Dawntown parking bay to find the single-seater vehicles they'd used to come into town. Several of them were there, and they were unlocked. It made sense that no one would be worried they might be stolen. The vehicles were programmed to travel only between town and the base, and no one would have any reason to go there unless they were leaving the planet.

Jas and Lingiari had thought up a flimsy excuse for their visit. It wouldn't hold much water, but they couldn't think of anything better, and there was at least a touch of credibility to it. They got into vehicles, and they were soon on their way out of town.

As they approached the base, a shuttle swooped out of the sky, glinting in the sunlight. The shuttle sped like a dart to its destination, slowing quickly as it neared the base. Some more crew members from the *Galathea* were arriving to be tested.

Jas wondered if Karrev and the other prisoners in the brig would come that day. She also wondered how they would test Lee when she couldn't leave her stasis chamber. She hoped the navigator had been okay without her and Lingiari to look out for her.

Most of the crew members had been processed, which meant Jas and Lingiari had only a couple of days at most to figure out how to get Makey off the planet. If they could just get him aboard the ship, they would have few problems hiding him during the trip back to Earth. Once there, things might get a little tricky for him, but illegals arrived all the time, and it was too expensive to send them home. Plus, Makey was a minor. He'd probably spend a year or two in a government home before starting a new life.

Jas's vehicle stopped outside the shuttle base entrance. She got out and went with Lingiari to the door, where two guards stood. They showed the guards their ID. "Is the governor here? Could we speak to her?" As she spoke, prickles ran down Jas's back. Something was wrong.

She looked closely at the guard she was speaking to. He seemed ordinary enough, but something bothered her about him. Without answering her, the other guard spoke into a comm console at the desk. The governor's voice replied, telling him to escort them to her office.

The room and the governor looked the same as they had when Jas had arrived. Nothing *seemed* to have changed, but something had. The security officer and pilot sat down.

"You aren't scheduled to depart today," said Governor Siam. "Is there something I can help you with?"

"We wanted to ask a favor," said Jas. "Lingiari here and I, well, we've been impressed with how smoothly the process of vetting the crew has gone. There hasn't been a single hitch. We were wondering if we could have a look behind the scenes to see how you do things around here. You know I'm chief security officer and Lingiari's the pilot on the *Galathea*? We'd like to see if there's anything we could learn."

The governor frowned. She didn't answer for a moment, and

her eyes became unfocused, then she blinked, as if remembering where she was. "You'd like to look around the base? That won't be a problem. We have nothing to hide here."

She told the guard, who was waiting at the door, to take Jas and Lingiari on a tour. It would have been better if they'd been able to snoop alone, but that was too much to expect.

The place was small. It included a modest shuttle landing pad, lobby, four testing rooms, a holding hall, a waiting room, the governor's office, a meeting room, guardrooms, and a cargo bay for imported goods arriving from Earth and elsewhere. Jas made a mental map of the place: the fastest route to the shuttle, the number of guards, and what weapons they had. She wondered how the guards might be distracted or diverted.

The problem was, the shuttle base was so bare and open. Like Dawntown, the place was minimalist. No screens, nooks, or crannies to sneak a stowaway behind or into, and taking him across the field to the shuttle without being seen would be impossible.

Lingiari spotted the shuttle pilot who had brought them to Dawn, and he went to talk to the woman. She looked upset for some reason, but Lingiari quickly engaged her in a conversation about the shuttle model she flew, clearly refreshing his memory about the interior of the craft.

To Jas's great surprise, the woman suddenly broke off what she was saying and burst into tears, throwing her arms around an astounded Lingiari. At the same moment, a familiar figure burst from one of the testing rooms. It was the man who had tested her. He stumbled out, his hands over his face. "I can't take it anymore. I just can't take it," he muttered.

Then Jas felt it too: overwhelming sadness. It was a feeling of hopelessness and despair, as if she were utterly lost and would never be happy again. She took a deep breath and tried to think through her emotions. This wasn't her. This was coming from something else—something that projected its emotions onto others. She went through the open door of the testing room, and there they were.

The large fungal creatures she'd named Paths had been brought to Dawn for testing. It was inevitable. Jas had found them on the very same planet where the Shadows had put their traps. Of course. They were under suspicion of being Shadows themselves. She was only surprised that the scientists knew how to test these creatures. It meant they knew about them. Even Jas, who had studied hundreds of alien species during her training and since, hadn't known about Paths. She didn't even know what they were really called.

She suspected the testers didn't know Paths as well as they thought they did, judging from the scientist's evacuation of the testing room. She choked back a sob and approached the strange creatures. They seemed to recognize her, because her intense sadness and anxiety reduced and was slowly replaced with relief and happiness.

"It's okay," she said. Did they understand her? If not, maybe they would get the gist of what she was saying. Maybe they could read others' emotions as well as transmit their own. "They've only brought you here to test you. You'll go back up to the ship soon. Then we'll be on our way." As she spoke, an idea occurred to her. The Paths, as she'd noticed when she'd brought them to the *Galathea* were hollow.

Another emotion began to grow in Jas. She felt uneasy and watchful, as if something bad was going to happen, but she didn't know what. The emotion was an echo of how she'd felt in the lobby when they arrived. "You feel it too, do you?" she asked the Paths. "I'm not crazy, then." But she knew she wasn't crazy. Though she had no explanation for her precognition of impending danger, the sense had never failed her.

"What was that about?" asked Lingiari as he joined her, having extricated himself from the sobbing shuttle pilot. "I feel terrible. Oh, I get it. It's those things. You weren't kidding about them, were you." The Paths had been stored in quarantine, far from human contact aboard the *Galathea* after Jas had explained their strange ability. It was Lingiari's first close encounter with them.

"No, I wasn't. They seem to be feeling a bit better now."

"They were upset about being taken from the ship?"

"Yeah, I think so."

A crease formed between Lingiari's eyebrows. "But they're not over it, right? Or...I'm getting that they feel kinda..."

"Scared. They're feeling worried and scared."

"What do they have to be scared about?"

Jas replied, "That's what I'd like to know." But she already had an idea. An idea based on the behavior of the governor. The woman had seemed almost the same, but not quite. That look, that lack of focus—Jas thought she'd seen it before. She'd seen it in the *Galathea's* dead master, Loba, in the geo-phys scientist, Margret, and in the officers who'd been forced into the Shadow traps. Was the governor the same person she'd been when they'd first arrived? Or was she a Shadow?

Twelve

Jas couldn't sleep that night. If the Shadows had invaded Dawn, everyone on the planet was at risk. But she had no proof, and without it, maybe no one would believe her, not even Lingiari. There was certainly no point in telling Haggardy of her suspicions. He wouldn't take any action even if he believed her. If he was interested in anything other than saving his own skin, he would have acted aboard the *Galathea*.

There was also still the chance that he wasn't the real Haggardy. The testing protocols must have failed and allowed Shadows onto the planet, either from the *Galathea* or another ship. If the tests were faulty, they could have let a Shadow Haggardy through, and any other Shadows that had arrived with him.

The governor had seemed normal when they'd arrived, and the Shadows seemed to go for the highest in command as soon as they could. Maybe she'd been the first victim. On the *Galathea,* the second person taken had been Master Loba, and the Shadows' process from that point had been to herd the next lowest in the hierarchy into a trap.

She sat up. A trap. If the Shadows had invaded, there had to be a trap somewhere on Dawn. It would be undeniable evidence.

As the predawn light filtered through the slats in her window shutters, Jas made her plan. She would try to find the Shadow trap. If she found it, she would take Makey and whoever else she could and waste no time getting off the planet.

The kid had slept in Lingiari's room. After breakfast, she brought him some of her crackers and took over from the pilot, who stepped out to stretch his legs. The boy chewed glumly on his poor meal. He was thin and pale from the lack of sunshine and proper food, but his confinement would soon be over, one way or another.

"Makey," said Jas, "have you traveled much outside your parents' land?"

"Yes, we have to," replied the kid. "Every Tenthday, we have to go out alone into the wild areas so we can commune with nature and give thanks to Earth Mother. Well, that's what we're supposed to do. I wander around until it's time to go home. It's Tenthday tomorrow, in fact."

"When you were walking around, did you notice any buildings? Apart from the ones in Dawntown, I mean?"

"No. How could there be buildings out there? Why would anyone make a house in the middle of nowhere?"

"These wouldn't be like a house. They would be shaped like hexagons—six-sided rooms grouped together, making up a building. And they're dark gray and low to the ground. No windows, just a few doors in the same shape, and nothing inside."

"Oh, you mean the Haidiren house," said Makey. "Yeah, a few of the kids have seen that. It's way out of town, next to a river. They must have built it fast, because it wasn't there until recently. I first saw it the Tenthday before last. It looks just like you say." He frowned. "I didn't go inside. We have to keep away from the Haidiren, and they have to keep away from us. It's the law."

"It's lucky that you and the other kids kept your distance. Makey, I don't think that's a Haidiren house. I think it's something much more dangerous."

His eyes widened. "Like what?"

"I'll explain later. But for now I have to go and find it, to check if it's what I think it is. Can you give me directions?"

"Yes, but, I've been thinking about things. Jas, I'm not sure I want to leave Dawn."

"What?"

The kid hung his head. "I keep thinking about my sister and my mam. If I leave, I might never see them again. And they'd be alone with Da. I feel like I should do something to protect them."

"I know that feeling, Makey, and it's understandable that you feel that way. But you're very young. These things aren't your responsibility. It's up to the people of Dawntown to fix problems like your dad's behavior."

"But they won't. I've tried telling people. They don't want to hear me, or they don't care. I don't know what else I can do. But running away doesn't seem right either."

"I'm sorry. I don't have the answer for you. Only you can decide that for yourself. But if you want to come with us, I don't think you should feel bad about it. And I'll do everything I can to help you."

"All right. Thanks, and thanks for everything you've done for me."

Jas smiled. "No problem. Now, can you tell me how to get to that building?"

Makey's knowledge of the surrounding landscape was detailed, due no doubt to his many years of wandering. Jas memorized the instructions he gave. It was in an area of the Dawntown surroundings she'd never been to before, was way out of town, and she needed a fast way to get there. Only one person would be able to help her.

———

Idris smiled, a little coldly, Jas thought, as he came to meet her outside the base.

"It's good to see you," he said. "I came over yesterday morning, but you'd gone out. I thought you might want to join us in the search for that kid again."

"Yeah, sorry, I went to the shuttle base. A little reconnaissance." Maybe he was upset that she hadn't spent one of her last few days on the planet with him, but she couldn't help that.

"The shuttle base?" He looked puzzled, but he didn't take it further. "So...?"

"So I'd like to join you in the search today, but I've got somewhere in mind you might want to look. I have directions."

"You do? I don't see why not. Come on, let's go."

They borrowed two vehicles from the army compound.

Makey's directions were very good. He'd described the landmarks to watch out for accurately, and after a while, they came in sight of a fast river. They left their vehicles and walked north along the bank, where the ground was rocky. The rocks were large and sharp-edged, as if from a landslide that had occurred not very long ago.

"Do you know where we're going?" asked Idris as they scrambled over the boulders.

Jas replied, "I heard there's a building out here."

"A building? What kind of building?"

"Idris, I know it might sound crazy, but if this building is what I think it is, the whole colony is in danger. You'll have to believe what I tell you and help get everyone out."

"Let's see what we find."

The color of the walls of the Shadow trap were nearly the same as the surrounding rock, as if the thing were trying to camouflage itself. Jas almost didn't see it, but it didn't match the irregularity of the natural rock, and its perfectly symmetrical form soon became apparent. She grabbed Idris' arm and pointed the place out to him.

There was no doubt in her mind now. The trap was exactly like the ones on K. 67092d. One or more Shadows had arrived on Dawn, and now their trap was catching the populace and releasing more of its kind into the world. What the Shadows' aim was, she still had no idea, but she didn't need to know.

"That's it, Idris. It's a Shadow trap. They were all over the planet we were on before we came here, and they captured and killed our master and about twenty of our officers. Have you heard of Shadows? That's what they were screening us for at the shuttle base."

The lieutenant began to climb over rocks, heading toward the trap.

"No, don't go in there," exclaimed Jas. "Don't touch it, Idris!"

But the man ignored her. He approached the dark hexagonal entrance. Jas raced to catch up to him. In her hurry, she slipped and gashed her knee on a rock, smashing her elbow at the same time. Painful vibrations ran up her arm and into her shoulder. "Idris, please, listen to me. Please." She got up and clambered over the rocks.

The lieutenant was nearly there. As he lifted a foot to step inside, Jas threw herself at him. She grabbed his thighs, making him fall. He lay face downward in the dirt, half inside the structure's entrance.

"Come on, Idris, get out of there. It's dangerous." She let go of the lieutenant and stood up. He turned over. As Jas met the man's gaze, she gasped. His face was blank. Idris was gone.

He was a Shadow.

She turned to run, but she wasn't fast enough. His hand fastened around her ankle. She fell down, jarring her bloody knee. The Shadow began to drag her toward the trap. Jas's fingers scrabbled to grab a hold of the bare soil. She kicked to free her leg, but the Shadow's grip was like a vice.

Giving a grunt, Jas drove the heel of her other foot into its head. The kick would have knocked out Idris, but it had no effect on the Shadow. Slowly, inexorably, it pulled her inside.

Thirteen

Makey held the shutter open just a crack. It was wide enough for him to see out, but no one outside who happened to be looking up would recognize him. He was alone. Jas had gone out to find that weird building he'd seen by the river. Why it was so important, he didn't know. The spacewoman hadn't said. Carl was downstairs eating lunch. Makey's stomach rumbled. He hoped the pilot would bring him up something to eat soon. He was starving. He'd been hungry ever since he'd run away, but he didn't like to complain.

The pilot had explained that morning that they had to try to smuggle him aboard the shuttle, and what he had to do when he arrived on the ship, so that no one would find him. If he followed their instructions to the letter, Carl had said, he would be able to travel aboard the *Galathea* on its return to Earth. What would happen there, Makey wasn't sure.

Carl had also said something about how he shouldn't tell anyone that he was conceived and born naturally, with no 'modding', and that he should tell people as little as possible about his background, or he might find it hard to get a place at college, or a job. These problems had baffled Makey, though he hadn't said so because he didn't want to seem ignorant. In truth, he was very ignorant, he knew, but that was the least of his problems.

The problem was, Makey still wasn't sure he wanted to go. He hadn't said anything to Carl, but the idea that he was running out on his sister and mother had continued to grow. As well as that, he felt like leaving all the problems of Dawntown behind him wasn't right. There was more than he'd told anyone about—some things that he had only just begun to put together in his mind, or was it that he was finally admitting them to himself? Things like people going missing. People who questioned what was happening on Dawn.

Leaving was cowardly. Jas and Carl didn't quit when things got hard. They'd said it would be difficult to get him onto their ship, but they were going to try anyway. They didn't just give up and walk away, like he was doing.

He watched the people in the street. Most were crew of the *Galathea*, but some were his own people—Dawntowners, going to and from the market or their farms and houses. His heart was heavy as he recognized people that he had grown up around. If he left aboard the starship, he might never see Neeve or Mam again. If he left without letting them know that he was alive, it would break both their hearts. He was sure of that. They had to think he was dead by now.

What had they done to deserve such treatment from him? Nothing at all. Neither his sister nor his mother had shown him anything but loving-kindness all their lives.

Dawntown was busy because it was Tenthday, and after the Celebration, the town would empty as the Dawntowners went into the surrounding landscape to commune with Earth Mother.

Earth Mother was something Makey had never understood. Earth was thousands of light years away, according to the library books. Why would Earth Mother be there on Dawn? Shouldn't she be looking after her own planet? His Da had said that Earth Mother was the guiding spirit for the entire universe. Makey had thought that maybe she should have a different name if that were the case, but he hadn't dared contradict his father. He wondered if there was a Dawn Mother, but he'd never felt her spirit enter him on Tenthday any more than Earth Mother's, as was supposed to happen.

He rubbed his eyes with the heels of his hands. He would not cry. He would not. He was nearly an adult now. He would not blub like a little child at its mother's skirt. But he was behaving like a child. He was running away from his problems instead of fixing them.

A very familiar figure appeared in the street. It was Neeve, going to Celebration Hall. He opened the shutter wide. His decision was made. He would not leave her alone. He didn't care anymore what happened.

"Neeve," he called. "Neeve, I'm up here."

Plenty of people turned and looked toward him, but his sister didn't seem to hear. In another moment, she was gone.

Behind Makey, the door opened.

"Krat, what are you doing, mate?" Carl was back from lunch. He ran across the room to the window and pulled the shutter closed. But he was too late. Dawntowners and the starship crew members in the street were staring up at the window, wide-eyed.

Carl grabbed his shoulders and spun him round. "What are you thinking, kid? We told you to be careful not to let anyone see you."

"I know," replied Makey. "I'm sorry, Carl, but I realized something. I can't go. I can't leave my family. At least not without trying to change things around here. If I run away, everything's going to carry on the same. My mam and sister will think I'm dead, and Neeve's going to grow up just as ignorant as me.

"Everyone's going to continue to recite their Earth Mother prayers when anything goes wrong, and assume that if She doesn't put it right it's because they aren't devout enough. It's wrong, Carl. If they want to believe that, they can, but they can't bring their children up in ignorance. It isn't fair to them. They should be able to choose for themselves."

Carl put his hands on his hips. "You're not wrong. Or at least, I agree with you about educating the kids properly. But what can you do about it? If you go back to your family, from what you've told us, your life'll be in danger. I think it's better if you come with us, or you'll never have another chance to leave."

The footsteps of many people sounded on the stairs, and a loud knocking came from the door. Carl quickly locked it. "Open up," shouted a voice. "We know you've got Makey in there. You've been hiding him."

"I want to talk to them. I want to try to get them to see sense," said Makey.

The knocking sounded again, louder. The doorknob twisted forcefully, and the door rattled in its frame. "Open up. We're taking that boy back to his family." More footsteps sounded on the stairs.

"It's Tenthday," said Makey. "Soon, everyone'll be at Celebration Hall before they go out to pray to Earth Mother. I can talk to them there."

A key was inserted in the lock, forcing the other out. The hostel receptionist must have brought a spare. The door flew open, and several Dawntowners fell into the room in their haste to get to Makey.

He backed into a corner, and Carl stood in front of him, his arms folded across his chest.

"Get out of the way," said a Dawntowner to Carl as he strode up to within a few centimeters of the pilot. "This is none of your business, offworlder."

"The kid just wants to talk," replied Carl. "He wants to go to your Celebration."

"We're taking him back to his family, where he belongs."

"No, he's got a right to be heard," said Carl.

"He's a kid. Get out of the way, or you'll regret it."

The pilot's back was toward Makey, and he looked around the man's shoulder at the angry Dawntowners in dismay. He worried what the Dawntowners might do to Carl.

"You can't take him," said the pilot. "Go and get your governor. She can sort this out."

In answer, a burly Dawntowner swung a fist at Carl, who ducked and struck back, hitting the man in the throat. As he staggered away, two Dawntowners stepped forward to take his place. Carl dodged a punch from one of them, but the other hit him square on the side of his head. The pilot staggered.

Makey couldn't let Carl get hurt on his account. He would have to try to find another way to fix the problems on Dawn. He stepped around the man. "I'll come with you," he said to the Dawntowners. "I'll go home."

"No, Makey," said Carl, shaking his head as if to clear it. "You can't give up."

Turning sad eyes to the man who had sheltered him and become a friend over the last few days, Makey allowed the Dawntown men to grab him and pull him toward the door. "It's all right, Carl. I'm not giving up, but I'll go with them for now."

"Makey, no," shouted Carl.

The Dawntowners formed a huddle around him and led him out of the room and down the hostel stairs. But at the bottom, crew members of the *Galathea* were crowded, drawn by the disturbance. They filled the hallway as they watched Makey and the men making their way down.

Carl's voice sounded from above. He was standing at the banister rail. "Stop those men, shipmates," he called. "That kid's been hiding here because his dad beats him, and they're taking him home for another beating."

The Dawntowners' grips on Makey's arms tightened and they drew closer, crushing him between them.

"Is that right, kid?" asked one of the *Galathea's* crew.

"No," replied a Dawntowner. "We don't beat our kids round here. That's a lie."

"I wanna hear what the boy says," said the crew member who had spoken. The rest of them closed ranks at the bottom of the stairs, forming a mass that was difficult for the Dawntowners to penetrate.

Makey held his breath. He didn't want a fight. He didn't want more people to get hurt. But he was tired of pretending. He exhaled. "It's true."

At his words, the *Galathea* crew pushed up the stairs, forcing the huddled Dawntowners back. The struggle was brief but decisive. Makey found himself quickly extracted and lifted bodily over the shoulders of men and women, away from the people of Dawntown. As they set him down, a man asked, "Where do you want to go, lad?"

"I want to go to Celebration Hall."

He was free, for the moment. What the future held for him would become clear in the next few hours.

Fourteen

Jas let the bloody rock fall from her numb fingers.

It wasn't Idris.

She couldn't take her eyes from the oozing mess that was all that remained of the Shadow's head. His black hair was red, coated in glistening blood. Off-white bone shards poked out, and his brain protruded through his crushed skull. His eyes, framed by their long lashes, stared, unmoving. He looked surprised at this sudden accident; this unanticipated shift from life to death. The lips she'd kissed only the day before last were parted.

As she crouched over the body, Jas reminded herself that it had been him or her. He'd been trying to get her into the Shadow trap, or die in the attempt. She'd had no choice.

It wasn't Idris.

Jas wished that she could cry, but she could not.

She blinked as she returned to an awareness of her surroundings. All was quiet but for the rush of the river. How long had they fought? She didn't know, but the sun didn't seem much farther across the sky than it had when they'd arrived at the river. They might have been fighting for only a few minutes, though it had seemed like ages.

The Shadow who looked like Idris had been stronger than her, and it had assimilated Idris' army training. If it hadn't been for the rock that she had accidentally brushed with her hand, he would probably have won, and right now she would be experiencing the same fate as the unlucky lieutenant.

Had he gone into the structure looking for Makey, not knowing what it was? Or had he been taken there in the way that Margret had taken Loba? Whatever had happened to him, it meant that there was already an unknown number of Shadows on Dawn.

The thought brought her up, shuddering, to a higher level of self-awareness. Pain emanated from her elbow and knee where she'd fallen on the rocks earlier, and it was joined by a severe ache in her shoulder where the Shadow had forced her arm behind her back. She also became aware that her face was wet. She wiped the wetness, and her hand came away covered in blood. Her forehead was cut, and she had a bloody nose. But none of her bones were broken. She'd been worse off after a fight.

Jas stood up unsteadily. Keeping her eyes averted from the prone form at her feet—*It wasn't Idris*—she looked around to get her bearings. She had to follow the river to return to the vehicles. She would take one back to Dawntown, though how she would explain why she'd returned without the lieutenant, she didn't know. Neither did she know how to explain to the Dawntowners what the structure was, or that the soldier she'd killed was actually an alien.

Did they know what Shadows were? She had a feeling the governor had never told them why starship crews sometimes came to the planet, or if she had, she guessed that the locals were so welded to their willful ignorance that they refused to acknowledge the fact of the Shadows' existence.

She began to climb across the rocks, heading toward the river. She didn't take a last look at the structure—*It wasn't....*

There was no doubt in her mind that Dawn was compromised, and every single person on the planet was under suspicion of being a Shadow.

She reached her vehicle quickly, slipped inside, and started it up. On her way back to Dawntown, she tried to figure out what she would say when she arrived, but she couldn't come up with anything. She would just have to play it by ear. She had to urge Haggardy to return the *Galathea's* crew to the starship immediately, and hope that none of them had been taken victim. Dawn's method of vetting for Shadows was obviously flawed. The testers had either failed to spot one among her shipmates, or they'd let one through from another ship, and it had built or triggered the formation of the trap.

Jas pulled up a short distance from the army base and left the vehicle there. She couldn't risk any of the soldiers seeing her and asking why she was alone and injured, or what had happened to Lieutenant Idris Theron. Her throat felt swollen. What had happened to him? She still didn't know exactly what went on inside the structures. Whatever it was, she hoped it had been quick.

She walked into town. The streets were quiet. She thought the Dawntowners must have been out on their nature trek, or whatever it was that Makey had called it. But when she arrived back at the hostel, she was surprised to find that it was also nearly empty. The place had been crowded with most of the crew of the *Galathea* that morning, but only Haggardy was there, with a few of his cronies in the canteen. He was just the man she needed to see.

The former first mate lifted a sardonic eyebrow as she limped toward him.

"Been scrapping again, Harrington? I swear you seek out trouble like a moth seeks oblivion in an open flame. You should be careful. It'll be your downfall one day."

Jas pulled out a chair and sat down heavily. She winced and straightened her injured leg with her hands, easing it under the table. "Shadows are here, Haggardy. You have to get the crew off the planet."

His upper lip curled. "That's ridiculous. We've all been tested. If there's one place in the galaxy there are no Shadows, it's here."

She'd known he would resist, but he would have to act. He would have to do something decisive, even if it would rock the boat and cause his superiors difficulties. The man's attitude made her blood boil, but she wouldn't let her anger master her self-control. Shouting at him would get her nowhere. She rested her elbows on the table and leaned forward. Haggardy leaned perceptibly back. Jas was pleased that her bloody face alarmed him. It might make him easier to persuade.

"Acting Master Haggardy," she began, and the man smiled a little at this unusual display of deference from Jas, "if you want, I can take you, and you, and you," she nodded at the two newly appointed officers sitting on either side of him, "right now, to a Shadow trap. It isn't far from here. About an hour by vehicle. At its entrance lies a body in the form of former Lieutenant Theron, who was stationed at the barracks here."

She swallowed before continuing, "Haggardy, I know your opinion of me isn't high, but do you really think I would kill another human being for no reason whatsoever? Do you really think I would murder someone in cold blood? The Shadow of Lieutenant Theron was determined to drag me into that trap, and he died trying."

Her gaze shifted to the woman and man with Haggardy. She had to trust that, if Haggardy was a Shadow, these two were not. "Do you want me to take you there and prove it to you? The longer we stay on this planet, the greater the risk that someone in the crew will get enticed or forced into the trap, and then that person will come aboard the *Galathea*. If we take him or her to Earth, the Shadows will spread there."

"Why should we take your word for it?" asked the woman.

"Come with me now if you don't believe me. Look, we have

to leave soon anyway. Just bring the time forward. Though I have a feeling that Governor Siam might not be keen to let us go."

"Why? Are you saying the governor's a Shadow too?" the woman asked.

Jas nodded. "On K. 67092d, the first opportunity they had, the Shadows went for the person in command, Loba. Here, that would be the governor." Haggardy's cronies looked troubled, and the old man himself was frowning. She straightened up and looked around the canteen. "Where is everyone?"

"Hmpf, you noticed, finally?" said Haggardy. "Your little interference in local affairs has come to light."

A chill settled on Jas's heart.

"That young friend of yours," continued the acting master, "the Dawntowner you've been hiding from his family, he was discovered."

Jas half rose from her seat. "Where is he?"

"I believe he's gone somewhere they call Celebration Hall. Apparently, he wants to tell the townsfolk his story. Let's hope it's a good one."

Jas was already limping out of the canteen. *Celebration Hall.* She knew it. It was the only three-story building in town. The kid must've made up his mind to stay, but what would his dad do to him? Rubbing the crusted blood from her face, Jas set off in the direction of Celebration Hall.

By the time she got there, the meeting was nearly over.

Fifteen

Makey's footsteps faltered along with his resolve as he made his way to Celebration Hall. Having Carl alongside him helped bolster his confidence a little, but the prospect of confronting Da and speaking out against everything he'd been taught since he was a babe suddenly seemed a lot harder than it had when he'd been hiding in the hostel.

Just a few days' absence from his home, school, and his Da's fields had made his life on Dawn less real to him. His mind had been among the stars and planets for a while, anticipating the exciting adventures he would have when he got aboard the starship with the help of his new friends.

At that moment, as he walked the familiar streets of Dawntown, drawing alarmed glances from latecomers to Celebration Hall prayers, he felt he was still very much on his home planet, and that he would probably never have any other life.

"Buck up," said Carl, who was walking next to him. "Your dad might not come. He might be out looking for you still."

"Oh, he'll be there. Da would never miss prayers. He leads them."

"The father that beats his kids is the prayer leader? Is he the head of your religion around here?"

"Not in name. Earth Mother is the head, if there is one. No one is supposed to tell anyone else what to do, but a lot of Dawntowners look up to Da. He has plenty to say on what is and isn't natural, and that kind of thing. Quite a few of my friends' parents go to him for advice if they aren't sure what they should or shouldn't use, or how the people in their families should behave, or what it's okay to speak to their children about."

"Are you there when your dad's talking with these people?"

"Oh no. Me and Neeve are supposed to be asleep, but our house is small, and Da's voice is loud."

"Sounds like he won't take it well if you criticize his opinions in front of the rest of Dawntown?"

"That he won't."

Carl clapped him on the shoulder. "I'll be there with you, Makey. Say what you've gotta say, then we'll get out of there, right? What's the worst that could happen?"

Makey didn't share the pilot's optimism. He didn't know about the Dawntowners who had gone out to commune with Earth Mother on a Tenthday and had gotten lost, or who supposedly couldn't cope with the tough life and had 'unnaturally' walked out into the sea and drowned. And he didn't know that it was the more outspoken in the community that this had happened to; those who had questioned the Dawntowners' ways. He could hardly breathe when he thought of what he was about to do, but he knew the time for hiding the truth was over.

Celebration Hall was at the end of the street.

Word of Makey's arrival had gone before him. Before he even reached the door to Celebration Hall, Da came striding out. In all his years of witnessing his father's many angry outbursts, he had never seen such fury twist the man's features. Makey stopped, and his legs refused to move another step. Da marched toward him. Makey's head shrank into his shoulders as memories of the beatings he'd received surfaced.

A shadow fell across him. Carl had stepped protectively in front.

"Get out of the way," growled Da. "No one gets between me and mine. Move now, or you'll find out what Dawntowners do to offworlders who don't obey our laws."

"I'm not going anywhere, mate. Not until this kid has a chance to have his say."

"He isn't an adult. He has no right to address the prayer assembly. He can do that when he's eighteen," said Da. "If he makes it to eighteen," he added in a lower tone.

Makey glanced up and caught the black look his father was giving him around the side of the pilot. He remembered the punch Carl had received on his behalf back at the hostel. His resolve began to melt. "Maybe I should go with my da, Carl. I'm sorry I dragged you and Jas into my troubles."

"Good," said Da. "Get over here, Makey. You can apologize to everyone in Celebration Hall for your stupidity, then I'm taking you home."

"Hold on," said Carl, turning to face Makey. He put his hands on his shoulders. "Is this what you want?"

Makey looked into the man's broad, honest features. He couldn't lie to him. "It isn't, but what can I do? You can't help me. It's just the two of us against the rest of them. I'll have to find another way."

"Just us two?" asked Carl. He held out a hand toward Celebration Hall.

Makey had been so focused on the terrifying spectacle of his furious father, he hadn't noticed that scores of the *Galathea's* crew had accompanied them and were lounging against the building's walls. As he gazed at them in surprise, a man gave him a thumbs up. The sight of the men and women from the starship injected him with strength. Like air into the lungs of a drowning man, new resolve flushed through Makey.

He swallowed to stop his voice from quaking, and addressed his father. "I'm going to speak to them, Da. I'm going to speak to the Dawntowners, and there's nothing you can do to stop me."

Carl stepped out of his way. Setting his shoulders, Makey

brushed past his open-mouthed father. He strode into Celebration Hall. His da didn't follow.

Inside, watchers who had been lurking at the windows scrambled to the benches, and the loud hum of outraged opinions quietened. By the time he reached the podium, a tense silence had fallen save for the crying of a tired, hungry baby, which was soon quelled by its mother's breast.

Makey touched the sides of the lectern. It had been brought from Earth, he'd heard, and it was made of a material called wood, which came from plants called trees. Trees grew almost mythically tall, according to what he'd read in the school books. A faint hope stirred in his heart that he might one day see a tree.

He'd never for a second dreamed he would ever stand there. Now that he had his chance, finally, to speak to them all and try to put right some of the things that were wrong, he didn't know what to say.

His gaze roved over the audience's expectant faces. He knew every single person there, either well or by sight. They were all familiar to him. His nervousness fell away. Good or bad, these were his people, and they always would be. That was where he could start.

"I'm one of you," he said. "I've spent all my life on Dawn, working in the fields, going to school, growing up with my family. I've learned and obeyed the rules, said the prayers, communed with Earth Mother. I've done all of it, the same as everyone here. But today I have to tell you that what we're doing isn't right."

He told the audience what it was like being a child on Dawn. He talked about knowing that he was being kept in ignorance, about never being allowed to question anything, about being hungry and cold, about seeing people who he'd loved die without any treatment but prayers. He explained how lost and hopeless he felt because he had no choice in his life; that he was slave to another person's idea of what was right and wrong in the world.

Seventeen years of frustration and unhappiness poured from Makey's heart and mouth. Some of the audience covered their faces and wept. Others frowned. A few got up and stormed out, but most remained in their seats, still and silent, listening. Several seemed to only stare.

Finally, an older man in the audience stood and pointed at Makey accusingly. "That's enough. You sit down and be silent. You've no right to speak to us. What do you know? You never lived on Earth, where half the population is out of their minds on drugs. Have *you* seen first-hand what they did to that planet? The heat and pollution? The destruction?

"What do you know about what your da and the rest of us went through to bring you here? What do *you* know about how we suffered to give you a new and better life? You children are pure. You have the chance to live a natural life, the way you're supposed to. You've no right to criticize things you don't understand. You should be grateful for all we and Earth Mother have done for you."

"Hey," came a voice from the doorway. The lanky form of the pilot lounged there. Jas had arrived, too. "Do you know what his dad does to him?" asked Carl. "Is that the kind of thing your Earth Mother would want?"

"Stay out of this, offworlder," replied the man. "This is none of your business. Go back to your drink and myth."

"When parents beat their kids, I make it my business," said Carl.

"Don't you dare start spreading lies about this boy's father," said the man. "His Da's one of the best of us."

"You sure about that?" asked Carl. "Show them, Makey. Go on."

He didn't want to show them. His father's harsh treatment of him wasn't what this was supposed to be about. Though Da's punishments were bad, there was so much more wrong with how his friends were being raised on Dawn. But the audience was staring. They wanted to know the truth.

Makey quickly turned his back to them and pulled his shirt over his shoulders. The marks of his most recent beating had faded somewhat, but silvery lines marked the evidence of what his father had done to him over the years.

Shocked cries and gasps came from the audience. The baby began crying again, but it was ignored by its mother. The previously silent weeping became audible sobs. Makey pulled down his shirt and faced the audience once more. The older man who had spoken slumped into his seat, his hand over his eyes.

Someone gripped his arm. Carl had come over. "I think you've said enough, mate. That's given them plenty to think about. Look, Harrington's saying Dawntown's in danger. If you want to come aboard the *Galathea*, you've gotta leave with us, now."

But Makey wanted to see his mother and Neeve. He'd spotted them at the back of the room. After explaining to Carl, he made his way over. The audience was breaking up. People were standing and leaving or huddling in groups to talk. A few Dawntowners approached to speak to him, but Makey pushed past them.

When he found his mam and sister still in their seats, he rushed toward them, but his steps slowed. They were looking at him, but they didn't come over to meet him, or even react. Were they angry at him for running away and letting them think he was dead? They didn't seem angry. Their expressions were kind of blank.

"Mam?" Makey squatted at his mother's feet and peered into her face. Something wasn't right. "Neeve?" he said, turning to his sister.

"Makey," said a voice behind him. It was Jas. "Makey, you need to come away."

He stood to face the spacewoman. "No, I've decided. I'm staying here, with my family."

"Yes, you need to come with us," his mam said.

Except... He looked into the woman's eyes. Something made him recoil. He stepped back, bumping into Jas.

"Come with me, Makey, and I'll explain," Jas said.

"No, come with us," said Mam.

"Yes, come with us," said Neeve.

"I...I..."

"Makey, do you trust me?" asked Jas.

"Yes, I do."

"Then come with me now. These aren't your mother and sister."

At Jas's words, the two women rose and grabbed at him. Horror clawing his throat, Makey backed away and fought them off with Jas's help. He forced his way through the crowd and toward the door.

"Dawntowners," shouted Jas as she came with him. "Listen to me. You're all in great danger. Please, listen. There are Shadows among you."

Sixteen

Jas put an arm around Makey's shoulders as they returned quickly to the hostel. The kid had done well, really well. He'd stood up to his abusive father—stood up for what he believed in. But he'd also begun to understand that his mother and sister were dead.

Word from Haggardy had arrived just behind her when she got to Celebration Hall. She'd hardly been able to believe it, but the man had listened to her and ordered an immediate evacuation of the *Galathea's* crew. And not a moment too soon. The presence of Shadows among the audience at Makey's speech meant the situation was already dire.

She'd explained to the Dawntowners the threat that faced them. At her words, Makey's mother and sister had bolted, but she still wasn't sure the town's inhabitants completely believed her. At least they had begun to look questioningly at each other, maybe trying to discern who was a Shadow and who wasn't. At least they hadn't started praying to Earth Mother to solve their problems.

She'd done what she could, but now they had to get back to the ship. And they had to take a certain young man with them.

"You did a great job," she said to Makey.

"No, I didn't. If I'd done a great job, my mam and sister would be going with us."

"I'm sorry for what happened to them."

"You're sure it wasn't them?" the kid asked.

"What do you think? Was that your mother and sister back there?"

Makey looked down and slowly shook his head. "Dawn isn't safe anymore, is it? What are these Shadows?"

Jas sighed. "I don't have time to explain properly, but you're right, Dawntowners are in danger. But that doesn't mean you shouldn't come with us. When we get back to Earth, you can be an advocate for Dawn and convince the Global Government that they need to send out more forces to protect the inhabitants. When the Shadows have been driven out, the government can investigate what's been going on here."

Makey's expression remained troubled.

When they got back to the hostel, all was in turmoil. Men and women were crowding the lobby and stairs, carrying their ship's bags over their shoulders. A full-scale departure was in progress. Upstairs, the doors in the corridors were open, and the remaining crew of the *Galathea* could be seen inside packing their belongings.

They found Haggardy in his room. He'd wrangled himself a large, airy space with a view of the coppery countryside rather than the street. He was folding his spare uniform carefully to put it away in his master's suitcase. The man blinked at the sight of Jas and Lingiari and young Makey.

"Hmpf. If you're here to ask me what I think you want to ask me, the answer is no. Lingiari, I was wondering where you'd got to. You're to report to the shuttle base immediately."

"Hagg...Acting Master Haggardy," said Jas, "this young man's planet is under attack from hostile aliens. He has a right to asylum under Global Government law. You can't...you would be well-advised not to—"

The corner of Haggardy's lip lifted. He stepped close to Jas and peered with mock concern into her eyes. "Are you feeling quite right, Harrington? These recent displays of proper deference and civility are quite out of character for you. Perhaps you've picked up a virus?" He moved back to his case. "Is this the real Harrington? Or are you a Shadow?" He laughed at his own joke before pointing at Lingiari. "You. Shuttle base. Now." He resumed his packing.

"I'm going," replied Lingiari. As he turned to leave, he gave Jas the smallest hint of a wink. He wasn't going anywhere until they figured out a way to get Makey on board the *Galathea*.

Jas remained where she was and folded her arms over her chest.

Haggardy sighed. "Harrington, the entire population is under threat. Are you suggesting we take *all* of them with us? If we can't take them all, who should we take? Which ones? It seems to me that if we're to take anyone it shouldn't be strong, fit Dawn-towners who can fight to protect their colony, like this young man. We should be taking the very old and the very young, the ill and disabled. If you think I'm going to try to explain to the Global Government why I brought him and no one else, you have another think coming."

"Well, you know, that would be a great idea," Jas replied. "Let's take those too."

The acting master paused as he pushed his clothes into his case. "The *Galathea* is a commercial vessel. We are not supposed to interfere in military affairs. Dawn has a fully equipped and staffed military base. We must let them handle it. Our duty is to Polestar's investors. We must return their vessel to Earth along with as many samples of planetary resources as we can take. And that is as far as our responsibilities extend." He snapped his case closed.

"Why am I even explaining this to you? The answer is no. Escort that boy to the street and make ready to leave. The *Galathea* needs her chief security officer." His suitcase in one hand, he went past Jas and into the corridor.

"What the hell are *you* doing still here?" Jas heard Haggardy shout.

"Just going to pack, sir," replied Lingiari, from outside. He'd ignored Haggardy's order and was lingering about.

Jas smiled. Lingiari had a way of not following orders that was far more subtle—and probably far more effective—than hers.

"Get down that shuttle bay immediately," said Haggardy. "It turns out they have two shuttles but only one pilot. We can double the speed of the evacuation with you flying the spare."

Lingiari came in a moment after Haggardy stomped away.

"Did you hear what he said?" asked Lingiari, his eyes sparkling.

"Something about them having two shuttles, and..." Jas laughed as she realized what he meant. Two shuttles, and Lingiari would be flying one. She hugged the pilot and the young man. "Makey, you're coming with us."

Seventeen

Haggardy was right. The *Galathea* did need her security officer. And where Jas was needed right then was on Dawn, protecting her crew. She wouldn't be leaving until she was sure every last one of them was off the planet.

Lingiari and Makey had left for the shuttle base, and the hostel was emptying fast. She doubted Haggardy had taken any measures to ensure that everyone had heard the evacuation order. There could be crew members anywhere in Dawntown.

She had to check the whole place, but walking all the streets would take forever. She remembered the vehicle she'd parked a short distance from the army base. A memory of Idris surfaced, but she forced it away.

Jas jogged through the streets of Dawntown, heading for the vehicle, hoping it was still there. The streets were unusually crowded. Her warning about the Shadows, and Makey's speech and the revelation of his father's abuse had left them disturbed and confused. They were wandering the marketplace and surrounding streets.

The vehicle was exactly where she'd left it, which was unsurprising as it was 'unnatural' and no Dawntowner would have gone near it. Slipping into the seat, she started it up. She would begin her sweep at one end of town and work her way across. It shouldn't take long. Dawntown was barely bigger than a village.

At the town edges, there were few people. The single-story, earth-colored buildings had their doors and shutters closed, and the streets were mostly empty. Jas drew nearer to the town center and saw more pedestrians, but she was confident they were all Dawntowners. She knew the *Galathea's* crew, and they were relatively easy to spot anyway. Few had exchanged their uniforms for the cooler Dawntown clothes. Only a handful had 'gone native' as Jas had. She would need to keep a careful watch for those.

At the marketplace, the crowd had increased since she'd passed through only a short while earlier. As Jas approached in the vehicle, the Dawntowners drew aside with looks of disgust at the machine. She didn't mind. It made it easier to pass through them. But the amount of people meant she couldn't see everyone properly. She stopped and got out for a closer look.

She towered above the Dawntowners. Cupping her hands around her mouth, she called, "Are there any of the *Galathea's* crew here? You must go to the shuttle base immediately. We're evacuating and returning to ship."

The crowd stared, but no one responded.

"Dawntowners, do you know of any *Galathea* crew members who are still in the town?"

A hand rose. "One of yours went off that way," called a man's voice. The hand pointed.

"Thanks," called Jas. She climbed into the vehicle and drove over to the alley the man had indicated. When she got there, it was too narrow for the vehicle, so she got out and continued on foot. A Dawntowner and *Galathea* crew member were heading toward the far end of the alley, hand in hand.

"Hey you," shouted Jas, "we're evacuating. You have to go to the shuttle base, now."

The man stopped and looked over his shoulder at her, but the woman urged him on, tugging at him.

"Come back," called Jas. The man hesitated. Jas began to run over to speak to him face to face. The woman whispered in his ear. He remained where he was, indecisive. Jas got closer, and the woman continued to urge him away. Finally, the man made his choice. With a laugh, he went with the woman and ran away from Jas.

Krat. What was he thinking? Surely he didn't want to stay on Dawn? Why was the woman dragging him away?

Unless...

Jas began to sprint. Running, stumbling, and laughing, the man couldn't match Jas's pace, no matter how much the woman pulled him. The security officer soon caught up with them. The man fell down, giggling and clutching his stomach. He was clearly on a run, indulging in something he'd brought down from the ship. *Misborn.* Had he introduced the Dawntowner to his drug? No, the woman was sober as she stood over him. Her eyes were steel. Her eyes. Then the mask came down.

"Gotta go..." gasped the man, trying to speak through his guffaws, "gotta go out there, for a bit of...y'know...won't be long. I'll make it to the shuttle base. Don't worry."

Jas followed the man's eyes to the undulating landscape at the end of the alley. She couldn't see more than a narrow slice of it, but she knew what was out there. She knew where the woman had been taking him.

"Won't be long," the woman said. "Come on." She grasped the man's hand and tried to pull him to his feet.

"Let go of him," said Jas quietly.

The woman tried to pout, but she did a terrible job, as if the Shadow that had taken her was attempting to act in a way entirely at odds with the dead person's character. "Leave us alone," she said. "This has nothing to do with you."

"Let go of him, or I'll make you," said Jas. "I know what you are."

Something in Jas's face brought the man abruptly back to reality. He slipped his hand from the Shadow's grasp and edged away. As the Shadow and Jas stood looking at each other, unblinking, he stood and straightened his pants.

"I'll...I'll come with you, C.S.O. Harrington," he said.

The words were barely out of the man's mouth before the Shadow was on Jas. She was so fast that she caught Jas by surprise and knocked her flat on her back, leaving her breathless and dazed. Before she could react, the Shadow was on top of her, kneeling on her arms and grasping her throat.

Jas wrenched her body to and fro, trying to throw the Shadow off, but she was remarkably strong. But by twisting her arms, she managed to work them free of the Shadow's weight. It knelt on her chest. Jas, too, fastened her hands around her opponent's neck, and squeezed.

Drawing in a painful breath, she fought against the closing grip on her throat. The Shadow's face was deep purple, and she realized hers must be the same. Black patches appeared before her eyes, blocking her view. The creature's eyes bulged, bloodshot. Gathering the last of her strength before she lost consciousness, Jas forced her grip tighter. Something in the Shadow's throat buckled and collapsed.

Suddenly, Jas could breathe. The Shadow's grip was loosening. The bulging eyes rolled upward, and then it fell to one side, unconscious or dead. Jas lay still as she caught her breath and her sight slowly returned. The sky above was an amazing, beautiful blue.

Her shipmate's face appeared in her view. "Are you all right?"

Jas reached up to her throat. It felt okay, only very sore, and it would no doubt bruise deeply later. "Yes, I'm all right."

"More than can be said for her," he said, scratching his head. "And to think, just a few minutes ago, we were..."

Turning, Jas saw the Shadow, unmoving and lifeless, looking exactly like a woman who had been strangled to death. She turned back and sat up, wondering if she was going to be sick. "I'm sorry," she said to the man, "but she wasn't what she seemed."

"So she was a Shadow?" asked the man. "The testers told us about them. I would never have believed it if I hadn't seen one."

"I'm very sorry," Jas repeated.

"You don't have anything to be sorry for. You saved my life."

"What I mean is, it might have looked like a Dawntowner, but it wasn't. It wasn't..."

"Look," said the man, laying a hand on Jas's shoulder, "don't beat yourself up. It wasn't a Dawntowner. That's clear as day."

Eighteen

Jas put the man in the vehicle she'd left at the entrance to the alley, telling him she would get transportation somewhere else when she'd finished her sweep of the city. She jogged the remaining streets, but found no one else who should have been returning to the *Galathea*. Back at the hostel, she found the place empty except for the receptionist, who scowled at her sourly.

She ran upstairs to her room, threw her things into a bag, and raced down to the street. When she got to the parking bay for the vehicles that went to the shuttle base, there were none there.

Never mind, she thought, she could jog to the base. She could probably do it in less than a couple of hours. She adjusted her bag so that it was as comfortable as she could get it, and set off down the road out of town.

She settled into a fast jog as she left the outskirts of Dawntown behind, not sorry to put the place behind her. Would the Shadow governor of Dawn try to prevent the crew of the *Galathea* from leaving? But no, every so often, up above against the blue sky, silver glints marked the paths of the two shuttles as they flew up and down. The evacuation was going on in earnest.

Maybe Haggardy had had the good sense to keep the reason for their sudden departure secret. If the governor was a Shadow, and if he let on to her that he knew what was happening on Dawn, she would do everything in her power to prevent him from informing the Global Government.

She had no doubt that Lingiari would manage to smuggle Makey aboard the *Galathea*. They'd borrowed a spare uniform from a crew member. In the general confusion, it shouldn't be hard to slip the young man onto a shuttle.

About halfway to the base, Jas began to feel the pace. She was forced to slow down. She'd brought no water, and Dawn's warm, humid atmosphere made it hard to run. She was beginning to notice even the mild inclines of the rolling hills, and she wondered how far she still had to go, hoping it was only the ten or so kilometers she'd estimated. Reassuring herself that she still had plenty of time, she went on.

By the time she'd run another five kilometers, she was jogging barely faster than walking pace. She didn't know the time, but she'd been running for longer than two hours. Long months aboard ship had left her out of shape, despite regular training, and the lack of water was affecting her badly. She was determined to make it to the shuttle base, though, no matter what. She had to.

The first sign she had that she was drawing near was the sound of shooting. In Dawn's silence, the noise was unmistakable. Jas reduced her pace to a slow walk. Who was fighting? The crew of the *Galathea* didn't have any weapons. Was the governor trying to prevent them from leaving? Jas didn't have any weapons either, and her defense units were currently orbiting the planet aboard ship.

The sound of firing grew louder, until finally Jas crested a hill and saw the battle. A mixture of Dawntowners and soldiers—all had to be Shadows—had encircled the base. A shuttle was on the ground, and Jas's shipmates were running to it under fire. Return fire was coming from the buildings. Soldiers were the only people with weapons on Dawn. It seemed that the Shadows and humans had divided into two camps. The Shadows were trying to prevent her shipmates from leaving, and the remaining soldiers were defending them.

And the Shadows lay between her and her only way off the planet.

She watched the battle. The shuttle that was being fired upon took off. Was Lingiari flying it? Her stomach twisted at the thought that while she'd been running, the pilot had been risking his life ferrying the crew to the ship. What she wouldn't give to get a weapon and break the ranks of the Shadows to lend him a hand.

What was she thinking? Of course she could do that. There were armed Shadows right in front of her, and they wouldn't be expecting an attack from the rear. She scanned around for a rock or branch, but neither was to be seen, only the thick, moss-like vegetation. She would have to make do with what she had.

Some quiet scouting found her a lone Shadow. It was a private. He'd gotten himself a nice vantage point overlooking the shuttle base where he could shoot without being easily seen from below. Unfortunately for him, he was easily seen from behind.

A shuttle could be heard flying overhead as Jas made her way toward the man. He was lying flat on his belly, his head peeking over the rise. The soft moss adding extra stealth to her steps, she crept up behind the soldier and swung her bag at his head. The bag was too light and soft to do any real damage, but the moment's distraction it caused him resulted in his weapon in Jas's hands. She pointed it at his face. He was on his back, and she was standing over him, her finger on the trigger.

But as the man stared into her eyes, she froze. It was Trip, the private who had been with Idris the first time they'd met. And she was about to shoot him in the face at point blank range.

Except it wasn't Trip. It was a Shadow, she told herself, and it had been trying to kill her friends. But despite its soulless gaze, she hesitated. Twice, she tried to force her finger to press, and twice she failed. A weird smile began to form on the Shadow's face, and it moved slightly upward. Its movement broke the spell. This time, the Shadow would die.

Excruciating pain seared her side. She'd been shot. She fell to her knees and began to topple to the ground. Another Shadow ran toward her to take the finishing shot. She glimpsed a dark figure approaching.

She waited for the end, but it didn't come. As the Shadow soldier looked upward, its face melted in a flash of laser fire.

The shuttle noise was very loud. Too loud. She raised her eyes to see it was right above her, and Makey was hanging out an open door, a weapon in hand and grinning. As the craft descended, Trip's Shadow took off. The shuttle landed, the heat of its exhaust shimmering the air. Through the open door, she saw Lingiari lean back and say in his Australian drawl,

"Can I give you a lift?"

NINETEEN

The first thing Jas did after boarding the *Galathea* was to find some water. She took Makey with her to the canteen. She was exhausted, but after she'd dealt with her dehydration, she had to find out what was happening aboard the ship.

Lingiari had disappeared, so she went with Makey through the ship's corridors. Disorder reigned. Some of the crew had been injured in the attack of the Shadows as they evacuated, and they were making their way slowly to the medical center. Others were hauling their belongings back to their cabins or hanging around discussing their escape. No one seemed to be telling them what they should do or what would happen next.

There didn't seem much point in hiding Makey. He told her that plenty of the crew had noticed him at the shuttle base, despite his wearing a Polestar uniform. Jas worried that someone would tell Haggardy, and he might order the kid to return to Dawn before they left the planet's orbit. But a funny thing happened as they passed by the *Galathea's* shipmates. They all greeted Jas, but though Makey was plain to see, they acted like he wasn't there. She had a feeling that this selective blindness would continue for the trip back to Earth.

She put the kid in Margret's old cabin and explained to him how the bunk screen worked. She left him staring in open-mouthed wonder at the treasures the ship's database held for a kid starved of information all his life.

The Paths had been brought back before the evacuation, Jas was relieved to discover, and they'd been returned to a remote corner of the *Galathea* where no one would be influenced by their emotional telepathy.

Next stop was the stasis chamber. She'd expected to find Lingiari there, but he wasn't. Only Navigator Lee occupied the room, looking exactly as she had when Jas had last seen her. It hardly seemed possible, considering all that had passed in the few days since she'd left for Dawn.

The navigator appeared overjoyed to hear that she was back, though the stasis' synthetic voice carried no emotional inflections.

"How have you been while we were away?" asked Jas.

"I've been okay. Flux has been keeping me company, though we ran out of conversation after a while. There's only so much you can say about how to catch cockroaches."

Jas laughed. "Talking of Flux, has Lingiari been in to see you yet? I've lost track of him."

"No, Carl hasn't been here. Is he all right?"

"Yeah, I think so," replied Jas, but she began to worry. What had happened to the pilot? She'd barely finished the thought before his lanky figure appeared in the doorway.

"There you are," said Jas. "Where have you been?"

"I had to take the shuttle back to Dawn."

"You what?" she exclaimed. "Why did you do that?"

"It's not our shuttle. I had to return it. I went to pick up their pilot. She flew me up here then took the shuttle back."

"What..?" Jas had no words to finish the sentence. The idea that Lingiari could have been killed while flying back to Dawn was too strong. Memories of the deaths of the last few hours flooded into her mind and began to overwhelm her.

Lee was very interested to hear what had happened on Dawn,

and all about the Shadow invasion. Lingiari filled her in. She wondered aloud how the scientists could test for Shadows, and how one had passed the test and infiltrated the planet.

"Do you think it came from our ship?" she asked.

"Who knows?" answered Lingiari. "I suppose it could've come from another ship that was sent there before us. No one said anything about previous ship's crews they'd tested. But the Shadows seemed to appear not long after we arrived." He turned to Jas, who'd been silent all through the discussion. "What do you think, Harrington?"

Jas couldn't answer. She could only look at the pilot.

"Are you all right?" he asked.

"I killed him."

Lingiari put a hand on her arm. "Who?"

"Idris. I killed Idris."

"You didn't, Jas," said Lingiari. "He was a Shadow."

"I know, but that isn't how it feels."

The pilot didn't answer, but took her in his arms.

"That's their power," said Lee, oblivious to what was happening in the room. "That's the hold they have over us. Nothing's as dangerous as the enemy you can't recognize, except the one you don't want to kill."

Lingiari lifted Jas's chin to look into her eyes. She wanted to cry, but the tears wouldn't come. It helped that she was in Carl's arms.

"If the Shadow that infected Dawn did come from our ship," said Lee, "that means it might have returned with the rest of the crew."

"Prepare to starjump," came a voice over the comm system. It was Haggardy. They were going home.

For the moment, at least, they had escaped.

JAS'S STORY CONTINUES IN …

THE EARTH CHRONICLES

COPYRIGHT

Copyright © 2016 J.J. Green

All rights reserved.
No part of this book may be reproduced in any written,
electronic, recording, or photocopying without written
permission of the publisher or author. The exception would be in
the case of brief quotations embodied in critical articles and
reviews.
This book is a work of fiction. Names, characters, places, and
incidents are products of the author's imagination or are used
fictitiously. Any resemblance to actual events, locales, or persons
living or dead, is entirely coincidental.
First Edition.